D0056640

WHEN THE SKY
FELL ON SPLENDOR

WHEN
THE SKY FELL
ON
SPLENDOR

EMILY HENRY

RAZORBILL

RAZORBILL

An Imprint of Penguin Random House LLC, New York

First published in the United States of America by Razorbill,
an imprint of Penguin Random House LLC, 2019

Copyright © 2019 by Emily Henry

Penguin Random House supports copyright. Copyright fuels creativity, encourages diverse voices, promotes free speech, and creates a vibrant culture. Thank you for buying an authorized edition of this book and for complying with copyright laws by not reproducing, scanning, or distributing any part of it in any form without permission. You are supporting writers and allowing Penguin Random House to continue to publish books for every reader.

RAZORBILL & colophon is a registered trademark
of Penguin Random House LLC.

Visit us online at penguinrandomhouse.com

LIBRARY OF CONGRESS CATALOGING-IN-PUBLICATION DATA IS AVAILABLE
ISBN: 9780451480712

Printed in the United States of America

1 3 5 7 9 10 8 6 4 2

Interior design by Corina Lupp

This is a work of fiction. Names, characters, places, and incidents either are the product of the author's imagination or are used fictitiously, and any resemblance to actual persons, living or dead, businesses, companies, events, or locales is entirely coincidental.

For Jack, Sophia, Jill, Morgan, Nigel, and Nathan,
who saved me back then.

And for my brothers: You're like brothers to me.

ONE

THE NIGHT OF THE crash started like most had that summer: with the six of us, and one mouth-breathing border collie, crammed into Remy's clunky Geo Metro, rumbling down Old Crow Station Lane.

The mist was so thick it swallowed the headlights before they could reach the wall of corn on our right or the woods leaning close on our left, and the moisture was hissing off the asphalt like oil in a pan.

Handsome Remy was driving—he was the only one with a car—and Levi rode shotgun, scribbling notes on the script in his lap.

Side by side, the two of them looked more like an oddball pairing from a John Hughes movie than cousins.

Levi was a six-foot-three online shopping addict and wannabe director with a style aesthetic we'd affectionately dubbed "Technicolor Beach Boy" and a coif of reddish hair. He was also brave enough to own a lot of hats.

Remy, meanwhile, was on the shorter side of average with dark, wavy hair and a slim build he kept outfitted in three (seasonal) variations of a Canadian Tuxedo he'd pieced together from thrift stores, then blown out skateboarding. Because the first colors of fall had sneaked into the leaves, he'd swapped out his basic denim jacket for the one with the wool collar, and as if to spite him, Splendor Township was hotter than it had been all summer.

"What does everyone think of the ghost fart joke?" Levi asked, looking up from the script.

Sofía leaned around me to answer. "I vote we cut it."

"Oh, do you?" Nick teased from the far side of the back seat. "*Do* you vote that, Supreme Court Justice Perez?"

Teasing was Nick's primary love language, but Sofía was an essentially perfect human—beautiful, athletic, next year's likely valedictorian—so the *only* thing we had to tease her about was that when we'd met her in the seventh grade, she'd announced her intention to study law at Boston University.

She rolled her eyes. "*Yes*, Nicholas. That's my vote. Would you care to give yours, or are you part of the forty-three percent of Americans who don't exercise their political voices?"

Nick shrugged and waved one of his thoroughly tattooed hands. "Fine. The joke's garbage." Droog, my family's near-geriatric dog, sat up in Nick's lap and licked his cheek, as if to agree. Then she turned and stuck her head out the window, effectively putting her speckled butt in the center of the car and our conversation.

Levi frowned. "Really? I thought it was solid comedy. Franny? What about you?"

"One of the rare situations where your bottomless fount of optimism doesn't pay off," I said.

Levi adjusted his bright orange porkpie hat and looked to his cousin. "What about you, Handsome Remy?"

"I'd like to go on the record as *still* not a fan of that nickname," Remy said.

The nickname had arisen when a girl in my art class stopped me in the hallway to say, *You're friends with Handsome Remy, right? Could you give him my phone number?*

Every couple of months, someone brought it back into popular use. Usually Nick.

"Maybe you should've thought of that before you grew out those gorgeous dark locks." Nick reached forward and flicked

Remy's wool-lined collar. "You're aware it's nine hundred degrees, right, dude?"

"Are you aware this isn't an ICP concert inside a Hot Topic?" Remy said.

"Ohhhhhhhh," Levi crowed. "Roasted."

"Roasted?" Nick crossed his tattooed arms over the metal band displayed on his black T-shirt, as if to lean into Remy's jab. "Sort of like what this weather's doing to Handsome Remy's flesh under all that wool."

"Lovely, Nicholas," Sofía said, and shuddered.

"When you shudder, something twinges in my spine," I told her.

"Because of the empathic bond of womanhood?" she asked.

"Because your knee is digging into a part of my butt I think is connected to my spine," I said.

"Oh! Sorry!" Sofía tried to make more room for me, but it was no use. She, Arthur, Nick, and I were packed like sardines. I was basically riding on her knees, with my top half hanging out the window where the sticky wind was working to fully tease my already tangled blond hair.

"Take this turn," Arthur said, leaning forward between Remy and Levi. "It's faster."

Despite not knowing how to drive himself, Arthur was pretty confident he knew the fastest way to get anywhere. Of all of us, my brother was the *most* confident about the *most* things, and since he was right about 50 percent of the time, he'd become the de facto leader of our group.

Remy nodded and turned down the narrow road that curved through the forest. The car thunked over a pothole, and Sofía and I winced in unison as my tailbone jolted against her thigh.

Remy's dark eyes flicked toward the rearview mirror, and his dimples surfaced as he grimaced. "Sorry."

Through the dark, the headlights flashed over the green NOW LEAVING SPLENDOR sign, and Nick whooped and thumped the roof of the car, so that the birds inked on his fingers looked like they'd just flown into it. "Yeah, buddy!" he cried, thumping it again. "So long, assholes!"

It was a running joke.

Our township was so small that the NOW ENTERING SPLENDOR sign sprang up on the two-lane road a minute or two before you reached my house, and the NOW LEAVING sign came another five minutes down the road, when the corn dropped away and the dark woods rose to cup the lane like greedy hands.

That the town was called Splendor also seemed like a running joke—one that had long outlived whoever named our plot of dead-brown fields and rangy forest and the single Taco Bell between the high school and the tractor warehouse.

"Don't care if I ever see it again," Arthur agreed, though it took me a few seconds to translate because he had a hand-rolled cigarette tucked between his lips and was using both his hands to try to light it.

Remy tugged on his wool collar and glanced in the rearview mirror. "Could you *not* smoke in my car?"

"No," Arthur mumbled around the cigarette. "I'm addicted, Remy. That's the point."

Levi spun in the passenger seat, training his video camera onto me. "And, Franny, how does it feel to watch your older brother fight the uphill battle of being addicted to novelty cigarettes?"

"I mean, it's terrifying," I said, twisting so my face was smashed against the roof of the car. "One second you're carefree youths, riding bikes and throwing Frisbees, and the next, your brother's under a bridge, wearing fingerless gloves and playing bad Dylan covers just to feed his habit."

"And you, Nicholas Raymond Colasanti Jr.?" Levi turned. "I

understand you're as close with Frances and Arthur Schmidt as a goth can be with anyone?"

Nick's skeletal face scrunched up, and he palmed the camera. "I'm metal, not goth. Now get that thing out of my face, dude." His Southern-skewing accent thickened, like it always did when the camera was on. "I'm doing my pre-shoot meditation!"

"Maybe we should buy ads," Arthur said suddenly, like he was part of an entirely different conversation. He leaned over Nick and flicked his cigarette ash out of the car.

"Ads?" Sofía said. "For . . . ?"

"*The Ordinary!*" Arthur snapped, like it should have been obvious. Like we had all just been sitting in a circle around him, hands extended, absorbing his thoughts.

"We should *totally* do ads," Levi said, immediately excited.

Levi was often immediately excited. His optimism wasn't reserved for bad jokes about flatulence and boldly colored fedoras. It was more wide reaching than that, with a special surplus set aside for *The Ordinary*.

Sofía's brow furrowed. "You want to buy ads for our failing YouTube channel?"

"For our *mockumentary webisodes*," Levi corrected.

"With what money, Spielberg?" Nick said.

"You've got to stay positive," Levi said, and put on a Talking Heads song.

"Ads. Now that's a good idea," Arthur mumbled around his cigarette. As usual he seemed only dimly aware of what was going on with the rest of us. My brother had a kind of laser focus that kept us moving whenever we were working on *The Ordinary*.

Our YouTube mockumentary series was Levi's baby, but when it came to actually filming, he seemed just as content to have us over for movie nights and elaborately themed "parties" (only the six members of *The Ordinary* were ever present, be it for the Quentin Tarantino–themed birthday, the Spielberg birthday, the Wes Anderson birthday, etc.).

When we managed to finish episodes it was usually because they fit nicely with whatever lofty aspiration Arthur was fixated on at the time.

We'd made our "Kite Chasers" episode back when he'd thought he wanted to be an actor (it turned out he was no better at emoting on film than in real life), the "Rock Gods" episode when he decided we should form a band (none of us played instruments), and "The Recluse," our episode about a J. D. Salinger–esque author living in the woods with a bunch of blow-up dolls he believed to be his relatives, when Art was casually toying with the idea of being the next great American novelist (how this was going to prepare him for that career path remains unclear).

What my brother really wanted, I thought, was to be a superhero. But for his last summer before he left for the lone liberal arts college that had accepted him, he'd settled for World's Best Special Effects Creator, and thus the "Ghost Hunters" episode we were on our way to film had been born.

Arthur let out another puff of smoke. "We could get some investors."

Remy smirked at me in the rearview mirror.

We could absolutely not get investors.

Remy pulled onto the narrow bridge that ran over the train tracks, and Nick gasped so loud I hit my head on the car roof twisting to see him.

"Guys," he said, voice low and panicky. He was turned to the window on his side of the back seat, his tattooed fingers braced against the glass. "Did you see that? There was something hanging from the bridge . . ."

I tugged at my nautilus shell necklace, like it was a talisman handcrafted to ward off bridge ghosts.

"Stop it, Nick," Sofía said.

"I swear to Gah," Nick said, laughing. He was always swearing *to Gah*. Allegedly his mom got on him for Using the Lord's Name in Vain, but Nick had a tendency to exaggerate (sometimes called "a lying problem"), and it was possible he felt guilty swearing to the veracity of something he knew was ludicrous. Still, he forged on: "Something's out there!"

"Oh yeah?" I said. I was ninety-nine percent sure he was messing with me, but that last one percent was tightening around my chest. "Like how you swore *to Gah* Katelyn Marsh's mom chased you out an upstairs window onto the roof?"

"Franny, I'm not kidding." Nick slipped deeper into his accent. "There was something—or some*one*—hanging from the bridge."

"I saw it too!" Levi joined in.

Sofía rolled her eyes. "You guys are dicks."

"Yeah, but we're *your* dicks," Nick said.

"Ew," I said.

Nick threw his head back and laughed, and Remy's dimple deepened as he turned off the bridge and sped away from that claustrophobic stretch of wooded road. Levi turned up "Monster Mash," and my anxiety ebbed away.

Everything was right once more, or as right as things got for the six of us.

In a couple of weeks, Arthur would leave for college in Indiana, and Remy would be two hours north at Ohio State. Nick would bump up his hours at Walmart to full-time, and Levi, Sofía, and I would be back in the halls of Splendor High School for our senior year, being occasionally mocked and often ignored.

Things would be different, I knew, but if there were two

subjects I did my best not to think about, they were: a) the past and b) the future.

We turned down Jenkins Lane and followed the gravel road to its dead end. There was nothing but a small electrical substation on one side of the street and the run-down wreck everyone called the Jenkins House on the other, our destination.

Years and weather had stripped the house's whitewashed veneer to a drab gray, and a few small fires started by trespassers had charred the left side of the second floor. The porch had collapsed in the center, brush snaking through the holes, and the black shutters hung askew, like someone had tried to pry them off the house's face, while the blood-red door looked like its center had been smashed to bits by an ax.

Remy cut the engine as a breeze rolled past, rattling the house.

"It's perfect," Levi said brightly, and got out of the car with the camera.

The wind blew a tuft of golden hair into my face, and I pushed it behind my ear, then wiped the sweat from my hairline.

Levi was already shooting B-roll of a loose shutter clapping against the house.

His voice dropped into the nasally, faux-British narrator impression he prized so much: "The travelers arrive to the alleged hotbed of paranormal activity, skeptical and unscathed."

Arthur doled out the equipment we'd brought at the trunk. We didn't have much. *The Ordinary* shoots were casual, the editing afterward practically nonexistent. Within a couple of days, Levi would have slapped tonight's episode online so it could garner our feed's traditional five to seven comments, ranging between "lol some people have too much free time" and "KILL YR SELF."

To be fair, they were right on that first count. The six of us had a *lot* of free time (minus Sofía, who squeezed us in around a full schedule of Achieving Things).

We never talked about it, never said it aloud, but if things were different, if the accident hadn't happened, the six of us wouldn't be here. We wouldn't be the Ordinary; we probably wouldn't even be casual friends.

Arthur and Nick raced up the porch steps, Droog bounding after them. Sofía and Levi were close behind them when Remy fell into step beside me halfway across the dark yard and grinned. "You're not spooked, are you, Fran?"

I looked between him and the crumbling house. The rumor was that the man who'd lived there had murdered an entire birthday party's worth of people.

More likely, the house looked like shit for the same reason the rest of the town did: because we all felt like shit. Half the town lost their jobs when the mill closed down. Foreclosed houses with busted porches and graffitied walls were a dime a dozen here. A birthday party massacre was hardly a prerequisite.

Still, I never would've agreed to come here if it weren't specifically for an episode.

"I'm not thrilled," I finally answered.

Remy flicked on his flashlight, and the beam bounced along the thirsty grass ahead of us. "It's gonna be fine. Ghosts aren't real."

"What about demons?" I said.

"Certainly not."

"Unicorns?"

Remy smirked and shook his head. "What kind of monster doesn't want unicorns to exist, Franny?"

Sofía had stopped on the porch to wait for us, her five feet and eleven inches towering over us even more than usual.

"You absolutely don't have to go in," she reminded me.

"I don't mind," I said, which was mostly true.

Inside, the wallpaper was tattered and peeling. Dust and grime covered the wooden floors, and torn-up books lay scattered across the overturned coffee table, the slashed drapes ruffling with the breeze from the door.

"Look!" Levi lifted his flashlight to a HAPPY BIRTHDAY banner on a red-splattered wall. Droog's ears perked, like Levi had been specifically speaking to her.

Sofía's flashlight lit up her face. "That's not real. Police wouldn't just leave blood all over the wall."

"Care to weigh in, Handsome Remy?" Nick asked. "What would the sheriff do?" He reached for Remy's hair, and Remy swatted his hand away.

"Get your digits out of my mane, Goth Grandpa."

"*Metal* Grandpa," Nick said. He was the oldest of us, a super senior who'd just graduated with Arthur and Remy's class, which put him at nineteenish—though he wouldn't tell us when his birthday was—and he *did* look a bit like a grandpa, with his shaved head and bulgey blue eyes. "Who do I get to be in this episode, Levi?"

"Who do you think you get to be?" Sofía said. "The hillbilly. You're always the hillbilly."

"Give the people what they want," Nick said, and shrugged.

"You're just so good at it!" Levi said.

"I call Nicky Jr.'s wife!" I said, before anyone else could.

Nick gave me a high five that left my whole arm ringing.

He was, technically speaking, the best at improvisation (years of practice making shit up), so I loved partnering with him.

When we'd made "Kite Chasers," he and I had worn matching windbreakers I'd found in a box of Mom's old stuff and spent the whole day chewing gum with our mouths open and gasping,

"Baaaabe! Did ya see that? That's what freedom looks like, babe." It had been one of the best days of my life, until Arthur and I got home and Dad saw me carrying the jackets through the hall.

It wasn't like there'd been a big fight. Dad had just shuffled upstairs with a bottle of beer and the calendar he was always scribbling odd jobs into, leaving us to wonder when we'd see him next.

Since that day, I'd become more cautious. The past had settled over our house like a layer of dust, and I picked my way through our halls careful not to disturb any of it, so Dad and Arthur wouldn't have to remember. I didn't touch the stuff Mom had left behind in the downstairs closet again, and I'd switched the nautilus shell necklace I'd found in my brother Mark's room onto a longer chain so the memory of him could sit over my heart without Dad or Arthur seeing it.

The less we remembered, the happier we all were.

"I say we just do this," Levi said, and turned on his camera, the white light spearing out to catch the sharp angles of Nick's pale face and bulging eyes.

"*I*," Nick hissed, hamming up his accent, "*feel spirits here.* What about you, baby doll?"

Levi swung the camera toward me, its light momentarily blinding me. "Oh, sugar, I feel 'em too."

And then we were off. Sofía became a two-bit medium who only heard the ghosts in the house calling out various Billy Ray Cyrus lyrics, and Arthur became a skeptical scientist who first discovered he was a ghost and then found out he was specifically the ghost of Colonel Sanders, of Kentucky Fried Chicken fame. Remy always had a hard time doing anything but giggling onscreen, which he usually tried to channel as a stoner character who was high, but since none of us except Arthur had ever *been* high, we had no idea how accurate Remy's representation was.

As we moved from room to room, we sank deeper into our

roles, and Arthur killed off his character so he could focus on special effects, running ahead to trigger them as we went.

Upstairs, he set up the fake fire he'd been perfecting all week (three clamp lights covered in orange gel, hooked up to dimmers so that he could make the light leap and dim at random, just like flames), and Levi started up the stairs, backward so he could get footage of us moving in a wide-eyed pack to the second floor through the fake fire.

From there, we made our way into one of the front bedrooms, where the windows faced the electrical substation across the street.

"Um, Remy?" Levi said. "Could you make your face look *less* like you're watching a dozen golden retriever puppies bound toward you? Just one line: 'The spirits are awake.'"

"The . . ." Remy's stony expression twitched. "The spirits . . ."

Droog was getting impatient. She started to pace. Sofía grabbed her collar, but Droog kept whining, straining against her.

Remy settled his face into a serious expression. "The spirits are—"

Droog gave an anxious bark, and Remy's voice dropped off as a gust of wind ripped through the open window, scattering the trash on the floor. Droog's barking amped up, and I threw my free arm in front of my face to block the flurry of dirt and empty Big Gulp cups rolling toward me. With one final bark, Droog broke free and tore from the room.

I looked to Remy for help, but he'd turned to the window, his dark hair ruffling in the wind. Arthur and I exchanged a glance then went to see what he was looking at.

In the light from the electrical plant across the street, we could see Droog running out across the yard, her barks getting lost in the wind. She barreled to the center of the lawn then stopped, spine rigid and tail erect, and I followed her gaze upward.

Silver light was streaking across the black sky, once every handful of seconds.

"Well, gah-damn," Nick mumbled.

"Meteor shower," Sofía shouted as the wind ratcheted up a few notches, sending waves through the grass.

Droog was barking so forcefully now that her front paws kept lunging off the ground. She was raging at the falling stars, or at the sky for dropping them.

Across the street, the low hum coming off the metal towers mounted. The lampposts around the electrical substation brightened, the bulbs glowing white against the black night.

The air buzzed. My hair had gone staticky, strands of blond floating out around me. Arthur's own dark-blond hair lifted in a halo around his head, and his hazel eyes, a mirror of mine, narrowed.

Someone—Nick, maybe—yelped, and I looked back to the window in time to see the row of lights beyond the chain-link fence suddenly spark and go out, blanketing the street in darkness, complete except for our flashlights and the light atop the camera.

The wind stopped. The humming cut out.

Droog stilled in the yard. Everything fell silent except us, our breaths.

All six of us had started leaning toward the window, waiting. Like we expected something to happen. Time went sticky as molasses.

And then, a sudden shriek of metal tore down the length of one of the towers across the street, something exploding into sparking shards.

Then everything went quiet again.

For a beat, we just looked at each other, stunned by the sudden silence.

Arthur broke for the stairs first.

The rest of us took off after him.

When we hit the porch, Droog leapt up and bounded after us across the road.

"Wait—" I shouted as I noticed the yellow DANGER: HIGH VOLTAGE sign on the substation's fence, but Arthur was already halfway up it.

The power surge must've knocked out the charge.

"That's private property!" Sofía warned, but Nick and I were on the fence now, and Remy and Levi were close behind. I heard Sofía groan then start up behind me.

We landed one by one on the far side, and I threw a glance back at Droog, who was whining anxiously. I stuck my finger through and touched her nose. "Stay here," I told her, then chased the others across the dark lot.

"Are falling stars worth anything?" Arthur asked.

"Like money?" Sofía whispered. "They're basically rocks."

Arthur's near-unibrow crinkled. "Why are you whispering?

"Only neighbors this place has are corn and cows," Nick said. "Feel free to shout."

"Besides." Arthur grabbed Remy's shoulder. "We're here with the sheriff's son. What can they do?"

Remy shook Arthur loose. "Ground us."

We crept toward the metal tower where we'd seen the rain of sparks. The top looked like it had been bitten off, the metal twisted and torn like it was nothing but a giant Twizzler chomped in half. The beheaded part was caught between the base of the tower it had come from and the one next to it, forming a twisted bridge between the two structures. The metal groaned as it slid lower along them.

"Look," Sofía whispered.

White sparks were still leaping off the loose piece of the tower, darting out and back in along a set path like a strike of lightning being played, then rewound, then played again.

Arthur led us closer.

The metal shrieked, and we all lurched backward as the broken piece came loose and crashed to the ground.

The light was still there, as if it were growing out of the metal then withering into it. But it wasn't coming off the metal at all. It was coming from the disc-shaped object balanced atop it, the thing that must've hit the tower in the first place.

"What is it?" I breathed as we circled around it.

Levi lifted the camera, shining light on the plate-like object. We hadn't seen the disc from farther back because it was transparent, a little cloudy, like a rounded-out block of ice. The light came from within it, streaking back and forth along the same veins every time.

"It must be heavy to have done this kind of damage," Sofía whispered.

"Do you think it's like . . . part of the comet?" I asked.

Arthur stepped closer. I could already see where this was going. My brother might be the type to obsessively remind me to drink water or take my Mace when I rode my bike to work, but he was *also* the type to try LSD alone and give himself stick-and-poke tattoos during math class.

He did *not* have good impulse control.

"Arthur," I whispered. He ignored me, reaching, slowly, as if in a trance. His fingers spread, the blue-tinted light diffusing between them. *"Art!"* I hissed, lunging to grab his shoulder. *"Don't—"*

He thrust his hand toward the cloudy light.

The last thing I felt was his worn-thin sleeve in my hand.

The last thing I heard was an earth-shattering *CRACK!*

Like the world splitting open. Like my eardrums bursting, my sense of balance and direction coming apart like a piece of fabric being unwound in every direction.

Everything—every sound, smell, taste, and sight—was lost in a blinding white.

And then I was lost in it too.

TWO

FRANNY.

   Frances?
   Franny.
   Fran! Fran!
   Do you hear me—
   Dammit, Franny, just fucking say
   "SOMETHING."

   I tried to blink the light away. My ears were ringing. My head throbbed. The light ebbed back, but not enough. A star-pricked sky should have appeared; night-drenched electrical towers and coils and switches should have resolved around me.

   Instead I found early morning pinks and oranges, streaks of gold filtering through cotton candy clouds.

   Every sign of night was gone.

   "Thank *God*," Arthur gasped. His hands were on my shoulders, gripping so tightly I might be bruised later. My arms were cold. And damp.

   "Are you okay?" Arthur's eyes were ringed in white. His blond hair stuck to his forehead in wet clumps.

   A chorus of dim murmurs drew my gaze to the field behind the substation. Cows. Black-spotted cows packed tight along the fence, fur damp and mist hanging around their baby-pink nostrils. They were agitated, mooing and jostling against one another, and behind them, the rest of the field was empty.

   Every single inhabitant had clustered along the chain link, the sun rising through the pinks and purples at their backs.

16

"Answer me, Franny!" Arthur shook my shoulders.

My eyes traced his right hand. It was burned, a spiderweb of angry red reaching from his fingertips to his forearms. The thing had *burned* him. "Say something!"

"It's morning," I got out.

I was standing in the same spot. The twisted piece of metal still lay on the ground, but the lightning-disc thing had vanished. The electrical towers were still silent, but dozens of birds now sat on the metal beams, fluttering their wings and making throaty *caws* as agitated as the cows' mooing. My body felt like jelly, like my bones and organs had been liquefied and if I moved, I'd lose all semblance of shape.

The others all stood exactly where they'd been a second ago— *not a second ago,* I thought in terror, *hours ago.* Sofía's arms were folded in front of her, her teeth chattering.

Nick shook his head, ran his hands over his bristly hair. "Swear to *Gah*," he said hoarsely. He screamed it a second time as he turned in a circle, eyes bulging as he searched for understanding. "What the hell just happened to us? Where have we been for . . ." He checked his phone. "The past *six* hours?"

"The . . . the comet." Sofía's voice shook. Her dark eyebrows drew together. "The comet must've . . ." She pushed her hair out of her face.

She was wet too. So was Remy. We *all* were, and everything around us.

"Dew," I said. We were covered in dew, as if we'd been standing out here all night.

So why didn't I remember anything?

I clutched my stomach as a cramp shot through it. My mind spun, and I sank my fingers into my knees as something fiery rose through my esophagus. I vomited onto the gravel between my feet.

Another spasm, another cough, but this time there was nothing but the impulse, the hot flash through my skull and an empty retch.

Remy gently touched my back, and a moment later, Arthur patted my shoulder like I was a dog. "You're okay," Remy said. "You're okay. It's all . . . we're okay."

Arthur gave a breathless laugh, like he'd just deboarded a roller coaster, not touched an unidentified falling object and lost six hours of his life.

Nick sank the heels of his hands against his eyes. A sob wrenched out of him. "What happened to us?"

Arthur laughed again.

Levi crouched and picked up the camera. I didn't remember him dropping it. I didn't remember anything. "Battery's dead," he confirmed.

Back by the fence, Droog let out a whimper, and a second later, the sound of police sirens rose in the distance.

"Shit." Remy scrambled to get his phone out, and his brown eyes widened. "The sheriff called twenty-two times."

Sofía tipped her head toward the mounting wailing. "Someone probably saw us here and called it in."

"We . . . we shouldn't be here," Levi said.

Nick laughed coldly. "You think?"

"We never should have climbed that fence," Sofía said. "For so, so many reasons."

Arthur was still scanning the field with flushed, wide-eyed amazement. He broke off when he caught me watching. "Right," he said. "Let's get out of here."

He led the way, and I followed behind the others. The thought of that white light made the nausea twist inside my abdomen again. I pushed the thought back and focused on my tennis shoes.

Just keep moving. Don't think about it. Keep moving.

Something black and feathery appeared in my vision, and I stopped short.

A dead bird, crumpled on the gravel. I looked across the lot and gagged.

Hundreds of them, wings twisted at horrible angles, beaks cracked, blood on the pebbles where they'd hit. Scattered across the dewy substation like some biblical plague.

Sofía gasped, and Nick clutched his stomach, but Arthur stared in wide-eyed fascination. After a beat, he shook his head. "There's no time," he said. "We'll have to come back later."

"Come *back*?" Nick said.

Arthur took off, and we jogged after him. Droog hopped up, eagerly wagging her tail as Sofía reached the fence and started hauling herself up, followed closely by Nick, then Levi, then Remy.

I reached to follow, but a static shock leaped between the fence and me—not a full-on electrical charge, just a spark—and as I recoiled, I saw them:

Dark red scars spiderwebbed up my fingers, reaching halfway up my arm.

Burns, just like Arthur's. The memory of pain and light shot through me so hard I stumbled. Arthur reached out to steady me.

I was trying to keep a lid on my panic, but my voice came out hoarse and high. "What *was* that thing, Arthur?"

He shook his head. The sirens were getting closer.

"Climb, Franny. No one's going to do it for you."

It was something Arthur had said to me five years before, right after the accident. The day we filmed our first episode.

Mark was in the hospital, and by then, we knew he wasn't going to wake up. Between our parents' tearful fights about what to do next—of which there were many—Mom had started to talk about going to stay with her sister in Cleveland.

"He's not even *there*, Rob!" we'd heard her scream the night before. "We have to let him go, or I can't take it here anymore."

"The kids need you, Eileen," Dad had hissed, which had surprised me, because those days, he hardly seemed to realize we were still there.

"How can I be here for *them* when I can't even be here for myself? What about what *I* need?"

Sometimes I thought, *She wishes it was him instead.* Sometimes I thought, *She wishes it had been any of us but Mark.*

The joke was, it felt like it *had* been. Even in his coma, Mark was more real to our parents than Arthur and me. We were ghosts drifting around our house.

We'd faded from existence at home, and in return, home had faded for us. That was probably what had driven us outside that summer, onto bikes and over the fences that circled neighborhood pools, into dark movie theaters through the exits as paying patrons filed out, and across poison-ivy-thick woods.

We spent every waking moment with the living ghosts of Splendor. Remy Nakamura, Levi Lindquist, Sofia Perez, and Nick Colasanti Jr.

At thirteen, Levi was already pushing six feet, with a bleached bowl cut and an obsession with cinema.

He had this idea to make a parody documentary about rock climbers.

Sheriff Nakamura drove us to the park where he used to run, before the accident made it hard for him to walk without pain. The woods there were scrubby and ugly, and as we were winding through them, Nick said, "If this is splendid, I'd rather be ordinary."

Levi launched into the earliest incarnation of his British-documentary-narrator voice. "In a town such as this, brimming with splendor, our six travelers found that to be ordinary was the greater challenge."

Then Nick kicked Levi's butt, and Levi screeched, "NICKY JR.!" in an equally poor imitation of Nick's mom, screaming to him from the window when he ran out to meet us in his driveway.

In the months since we'd become friends, we hadn't seen the inside of Nick's house, and we never saw his mom any closer than that either—she didn't come outside, like, *ever*—but she'd sometimes yell through the glass: *Nicky Jr., your phone!* Or *Nicky Jr., don't you go forgetting your house key!*

"Like it's even possible to get locked out," Nick would sometimes grumble. "Where you gonna be when I get home, Ma? Paris?"

He was allowed to say that sort of thing about her, but we weren't. Our families were off limits, and Nick's especially so—the rest of the town talked about the Colasantis enough.

But the accent—the imitation—he didn't seem to mind that. He happily screeched back at Levi, "You're not my real ma, Ma!" as the two of them raced down the path.

When we finally found the sun-bleached boulders, they were bigger than I'd expected, and stacked on top of one another in a haphazard way.

I was the youngest and smallest of the group, and nursing a fear of heights I'd done my best to hide.

I made it to the top of the first rock, but the second was smoother and higher. The others topped it with a bit of knee-scraping, but my hands started to sweat, and my heart raced, and soon, I was too terrified to move.

"You absolutely don't have to do it, Franny," Sofía said. "If you don't want to, don't let them pressure you."

"You've got this!" Levi assured me.

Nick tried a different approach. "Don't be a baby, Franny!"

"We won't let you get hurt," Remy kept promising.

Levi put his camera down. "Just get halfway. Remy and I will pull you up."

They lay on their stomachs and held their arms out, and I started to pace, and then cry.

I looked to Arthur. I wanted him to tell me it would be okay, or suggest I climb down and wait at the bottom. Instead his brow furrowed; his freckly nose scrunched. His voice came out sharp. "*Climb*, Franny."

I shook my head.

"*Climb*, Franny," Arthur said, more loudly.

I ran my hands through my humidity-frizzed hair.

Please, I thought at him. *Tell me you won't let me get hurt.*

Arthur set his jaw. "No one is going to help you. Don't you get that? *No* one. It *has* to be you."

The tears started sliding down my cheeks, but I took hold of the rock. I stepped into a divot and pushed myself up, once, then again. I moved higher, limbs shaking, tears falling. I was almost there when Arthur's hand caught my arm. With Nick's and Remy's help, he hauled me over the lip and pulled me onto my feet.

My brother gripped the back of my neck and stared into my eyes. His gaze was glassy, but then he blinked and it hardened. There was no softness left for me in him.

Something inside me broke. He was right.

No one was going to help us. We were on our own now.

Arthur pulled me into a rough hug, and I cried into his shoulder for the first and last time that summer. Our friends turned away, busying themselves with whatever they could find.

They knew this was the kind of thing you didn't acknowledge in Splendor. They let me feel my pain alone.

They knew that was what I wanted, because we were the same.

THREE

HALFWAY TO THE CAR, I realized my mistake. I'd spent five years with the same weight resting below my collarbone, and in six hours, I'd nearly forgotten to expect it there.

My hand went to my bare neck. No nautilus shell, no alloy chain.

I'd lost Mark's necklace.

The sirens were wailing closer, and the others were already piling into the car, but I stopped dead.

"Fran!" Remy screamed when he realized I wasn't right behind him.

"My necklace!" I turned, scanning the dew-dusted grass. "I must have dropped it."

"I'm *not* going to jail, Franny," Nick screeched at me. "Get *in*!"

"We'll come back for it," Sofía said.

I jogged across the yard, searching the grass for the smooth spiral of the seashell.

"Come on, Franny," Levi yelled. He was already in the car, Droog's muddy paws balanced on his mauve pants.

"We have to come back anyway," Arthur yelled. "We'll find it then."

"Why do you keep saying that?" Nick demanded. "I'm not coming anywhere *near* this place again."

Sofía smacked his arm. "Of course we'll come back. Franny, just get in!"

Something glinted in the grass off to my left, just inside the range of trees at the muddy edge of the yard. I ran toward it, picked up the bit of metal before I even realized none of us had been over there last night.

My stomach jerked at the object's cold weight. *A bullet.*

A handful more were scattered in the mud, in a spray along a series of boot prints.

My gaze trailed the prints from the woods and across the gravel road, where they vanished only to reappear on the far side and lead up to the fence, though further left than where we'd climbed it.

None of us had gone near these muddy prints.

My pulse spiked. Had someone else been here last night? Could they could tell us what we'd missed, what had happened in those six lost hours?

I scanned the length of the fence for any sign of life, but if anyone *had* seen what happened, they were gone now.

"FRANNY!" Nick screeched over the sirens. "NOW, OR I'M HIJACKING THIS CAR AND LEAVING YOUR GAH-DAMN ASS!"

I tucked the bullet into my pocket and sprinted back to the car.

Remy peeled backward down Jenkins, then dropped back to one mile per hour *under* the speed limit once we were on the cross street. He tossed his phone at Levi. "Text my dad. Tell him we all fell asleep at your house. Hopefully we'll beat him there."

"If someone saw a bunch of teenagers trespassing at an electrical plant and called it in," Levi said, already typing, "the sheriff will respond to that first. I'm sure we're fine!"

Levi, as a rule, was as upbeat as his splashy wardrobe.

"All the more reason we shouldn't be here," Sofía said. She took a deep breath. "We broke the law."

"Will someone tell Handsome Remy to speed up?" Nick yelped. "We're not driving through the main hallway of an old folks' home."

"No," Remy snapped, "but I *am* driving six people and a dog around in a tiny car, after breaking like four laws *and* missing my curfew. I'm not getting pulled over for speeding!"

To me, Sofía's parents *and* Remy's seemed like harsh disciplinarians, but once when I'd said that to Arthur, he'd scrunched his brow and scowled at me. "We used to have rules too, Franny, remember? It's because their parents still give a shit."

I'd done my best to forget that there was a *before*, a time when cussing might earn Mark a mouthful of soap, when riding our bikes home two hours after Mom had told us to be back for dinner would result in a weekend with a list of chores and no video games.

Now we didn't have rules. We also didn't have family dinners.

"Take this next turn, Remy," Arthur said. "It's faster."

Sofía reached around me to roll the window down a couple more inches. A series of purple welts branched across her hand, the same kinds of burns Arthur and I had. Through the back of the headrest, a similar angry pattern spread up the back of Levi's neck.

What had happened to us?

I touched the markings on my hand. They didn't hurt. At least there was that.

I craned my neck to look one last time toward the twisted metal and misty gravel, and the towers gleaming in the early light.

It didn't look malevolent, but something about it made my stomach turn, like my body was remembering what my mind refused to.

The siren faded behind us as we drove in silence. No music, just the whirring of the engine and the mourning doves cooing and Nick drumming out a restless pattern on the foggy window.

"It must've been a piece of the comet," Sofía said finally. "Some kind of . . . trapped energy."

"Right." Nick's accent thickened and his bulgy eyes rolled. "That explains *everything*."

Remy's gaze caught mine in the rearview mirror. His face was pale and drawn. He shook his head, but whatever he was silently communicating, I wasn't getting it.

"Once everyone has breakfast, we'll feel better," Levi said. "I have donuts at my house. I'll make a French press and—"

"Give it a rest, dude," Nick said. "Not every occasion calls for a party at your empty McMansion! We just got, like, brain-melted by space junk, and some of us might not want to go watch *Citizen freakin' Kane*!"

Levi slumped.

"Chill, Grandpa," Remy said sharply. "You don't need to be mean."

"And we didn't get brain-melted by space junk," Sofía said. "There's an explanation for . . . whatever happened."

I thought back to the moment Arthur reached for the disc: the humidity of the night, the chirp of the crickets. And then—even in my memory—the flash of light and resulting pain were so intense I had to close my eyes and bite my hand to keep from screaming.

"Fran?" Remy said, eyes catching mine in the mirror. "Franny? Are you—"

"Just a yawn," I lied. There was no use stoking everyone's worries. Melting down never led to anything good. Besides, the memory was fading, the crushing red pain drawing back.

"Maybe we should go to the hospital," Sofía said.

If there was one place I tried my best to avoid, it was the hospital. Not just because we were already drowning in bills from Mark's five-year stay, but because everything about it brought me back to that horrible summer.

"No hospitals," Arthur said firmly.

"I think . . . I think we just got shocked," I said.

Levi gasped and turned around in his seat. "You did? By that thing?"

"You did too," Nick grumbled. "Back of your neck." Levi reached back, his thick fingers testing the ridge of welts. Beside me, Nick tugged the collar of his T-shirt down to look at his own strange burns, like fingers reaching between his clavicles.

Remy pulled his collar away and glanced between it and the road. "Me too. Stomach."

"*Not* on those washboard skateboarding abs?" Nick grumbled, but his heart wasn't in it.

"I think when it touched me, it got me," Arthur said, "and then I guess it jumped from me to Franny, because she was touching me." His face was flushed and his eyes were bright; he looked like he was hopped up on something.

"And then somehow to the rest of us?" Sofía sounded unconvinced.

"You're the scientist," Nick said. "What was that thing?"

"Passing science class doesn't make me a scientist," Sofía said.

Sofía had never merely *passed* a class.

"I don't know what it was," Arthur buzzed. "But it was something *amazing*."

Remy and I shared a wary look. *Amazing* was one word for it.

We did *not* beat the sheriff to Levi's house. When we got there, he was leaned against the hood of his squad car, his lips pressed into a tight line. Even with all his weight on his good leg, he looked like he might be in pain.

"Guess you guys probably *can't* stay for breakfast then?" Levi said, as if Nick hadn't already punched that idea off the table. Levi's parents traveled so much that he essentially lived alone, and I sometimes got the feeling he was just waiting for the force majeure that would finally fuse the six of us together and eliminate any shred of alone time from his schedule.

Sheriff Nakamura crossed his arms over his beige-clad chest as we climbed out of the Metro, like clowns spilling from a prop car in an old comedy. Droog bounded toward him, wagging excitedly, and my stomach jarred at the trail of missing fur across her back haunch: a purple lightning-shaped scar that looked like it had long since healed.

Her too.

The thought made me dizzy. I shoved it away and focused on Sheriff Nakamura's appraising gaze.

"If you're sleep-driving, son," he said, "you should probably go to a doctor."

Remy grimaced. I looked around, wondering whether anyone was going to explain. Sofía looked like the effort not to spill everything was costing her something precious and irretrievable. After a minute, Sheriff Nakamura sighed and tipped his head toward the Metro. "You go on home, Rem. I'll take the others."

"I can take them," Remy said.

"Oh, no you can't," his father contradicted.

Remy shot me a fierce look that made it clear there was something he needed to tell me but did no good whatsoever in communicating what that might be.

Nick apparently intercepted it. "What are you doing, dude?" he asked. "You look like you're pooping your pants."

"I wasn't doing anything," Remy said, face flushing.

The sheriff's gaze flicked suspiciously between all of us. "You do realize I'm a police officer, right? If you're trying to pass around secrets, don't do it right in front of me. Now, Remy, *go home.* We'll talk about this later."

And that was that. Remy got back into the Metro, throwing me one last worried look, and the rest of us piled into the cruiser.

When we reached Sofia's house, the sheriff put the car in park then turned to survey us. "I'm not going to ask you what you were doing," he said. "I'm just going to hope to God I'm wrong, and that even if I'm not, we can't find any evidence." His eyes went specifically to Nick and Arthur, who were in the back seat with me. "You're good kids. Don't let yourselves get punished like bad adults."

We nodded understanding, but honestly, I had no idea what he was talking about. Even if someone *had* seen us trespassing—the big-footed person with the dropped bullets?—they couldn't possibly think *we'd* destroyed the tower.

How would we have done that? Shot it with a cannon?

Arthur opened his mouth as if to pose the question, but the sheriff held up a hand. "Not a peep, Arthur Schmidt. Remember that anything you say to me can and will be used against you in a court of law, so it's best just not to say anything without your dad here. And possibly a lawyer."

Still, Arthur couldn't resist. Impulse control: not a thing for him. "What are we being accused of, exactly?"

Sheriff Nakamura sighed. "Nothing just yet. So let's keep it that way."

He caught my eyes in the rearview mirror and gave me a strained smile. It was unconvincing, his true emotions far over-shooting his feigned one.

That was something I'd always loved about Remy and his dad, that their feelings were out in the open, honest, even when their words weren't.

Ever since the accident, there'd been an anger in me that never burned quite strong enough to escape. It was stuck in my gut, embers that never died, even as layers of sadness and fear and whatever else got piled over it.

I was angry at the world, for what it had done to us. Angry it would never care. Angry that it would go on like it always had and never acknowledge what had changed.

The voiceless anger had started in the hospital waiting room, my throat aching with all the screams that couldn't find a way out, and that was when I'd looked across the room and seen him.

A boy who couldn't stop screaming. A thrashing boy. Fighting tooth and nail against what was happening, like he could stop it, or at least force the world to bear witness to his pain.

And I'd thought, *You.*

You are like me.

You feel what I feel.

The hospital parking lot was hot, even though it was only May, but the waiting room outside the ER was so cold that all the hair on my body jerked upright.

Voices echoed off the mint-green walls and the televisions playing the local news from the uppermost corners of the room. The ugly pink-and-green chairs along the walls went unused; everyone was standing.

A handful of police officers crowded around the double doors to the ICU, and people were clustered there, arguing with them.

My vision fuzzed as I scanned the mass of people for Mom. *Where'd she go?*

I only realized I'd said it aloud when Arthur answered, "I'm looking, Fran, same as you."

I found her in the corner, pressed up to Dad, sobbing into his chest. His hand was cupped around the back of her head, his mouth murmuring against her forehead.

My stomach felt like it was free-falling through my body.

All I'd wanted on the ride over from school was for Mom to look at me, to reach her hand out, so I'd feel safe, so I'd know that whatever had happened to Mark was fixable.

Watching her fists curl into Dad's shirt, I understood, suddenly, irrevocably, that my mother could do nothing to protect me, or to fix this.

Arthur had wandered off to get answers from a chubby boy in all black with bulging blue eyes, and I was alone.

No one could help me, or even see me.

And then I spotted him: a boy with a mop of shiny dark hair and deep brown eyes, with skinny shoulders and scabby knees that poked out from Dickies shorts. He was arguing with the cops blocking the door.

"Please," the boy said. "Please let me back there, *please*."

One of the cops had him by the shoulders, holding him back. "I know you're worried, buddy. I know you are, but your dad's strong, and there's nothing—"

The boy shook free. "Let me see him! I need to see my dad."

"You need to stay calm. Be brave, okay?"

He started screaming, tearfully swearing, trying to physically move past the cops, but they kept buffeting him back, gently.

Pityingly.

At any other moment, I might've been embarrassed to watch it, wanted to crawl out of my skin at the sight of someone my age kicking at a hospital door, shouting half-formed, swear-laced insults at two adults who were looking at him like he was a toddler hurling a pacifier around.

But I felt it too, everything he was raging against, the way the whole world had become his enemy. I wanted to kick, spit, yank hair, but the thing I wanted to fight was too big and unhurtable.

I wanted to tussle with the dirt, rip the grass out of the earth, smash the hospital windows until someone looked right at me and saw my pain.

One of the officers tried to grab the boy's shoulders, and he tripped backward from her, turned, searching for *something*, someone who could help him, but everyone was wrapped up in their own fear.

I wanted him to know that I saw him. That someone heard him.

When his eyes caught mine, I lifted one hand.

His mouth was ajar, the corners twisted downward, denting his cheek.

Slowly, he lifted his hand. His eyebrows peaked together. They seemed to ask, *You too?*

Two days later, he would walk up to me in that same waiting room and introduce himself as Remy Nakamura, my future best friend (he wouldn't say that part, but I like to think it was implied), and three days after that, Arthur would go out to ride bikes with Nick Colasanti Jr., whose father was killed in the blast.

Dad would drag us along to Nick Sr.'s funeral (Mom would stay at the hospital with Mark), and there we'd see a lanky, dark-haired girl who carried a book in lieu of a purse, though she was polite enough not to read from it until the service was over and she was seated at the dismal potluck's kids' table with the rest of us: me, Arthur, his new friend Nick, my new friend Remy, and Remy's cousin Levi, who was enormous compared to us and, for some reason, wearing a baby blue suit with shoulder pads in it.

When Nick cleared his throat pointedly, the lanky girl set her book down and introduced herself as Sofía Perez, the niece of the steel mill's receptionist and granddaughter of a steel worker.

She had just moved here from New York City, which immediately made her glamorous despite her plain clothes, and she wondered whether we liked our school (we didn't) and whether we played lacrosse (I hadn't even heard of it).

"I tried out for a team once," Nick said, "but then the coach got busted for printing fake money in his basement."

Sofía arched an eyebrow. "That doesn't sound very true."

"I swear to Gah," Nick said, and no one argued.

Sofía turned to me, her dark eyebrows pinching in the middle. "I heard about your brother. That must be so hard."

Arthur bristled beside me, his mood turning the room icy. "What, are you looking for the scoop on the Great Splendor Tragedy like all those leeches taking pictures at the funeral? We don't know what's going to happen, so maybe don't put him in the grave just yet!" Arthur didn't wait for a response, just stood and stormed from the room, leaving behind the chill he'd summoned.

Sofía drew back, teary-eyed. She looked around the table, silently apologizing or maybe searching for an ally, but no one said anything.

She hadn't done anything wrong, not really. Arthur just didn't want to talk about Mark, or our parents, or the way home had started to feel like a sinkhole and the future had turned fuzzy and dark.

He didn't want to talk about how afraid he was, or how much he hurt.

None of us did.

That was the start of our long-term policy regarding the accident—unspoken, but fully understood: Don't say a word.

Five years later, we still didn't talk about it.

Bits of the accident hid in every dark corner of our lives, but dragging them into the light for everyone to see would only hurt worse than leaving them be.

The six of us were destined to be alone, trapped in a grief we weren't willing or able to share, but from then on, at least we were alone together.

FOUR

TURN ON CHANNEL 11 NOW, Levi texted the group. Arthur had been fully invested in googling things like "ice disc" and "magic lightning" and "weird meteorite, lost time" for the last few hours.

He tended to become obsessed with things, especially things he thought could scratch the itch of boredom that came from living in Splendor. One week he'd be hell-bent on becoming a skydiving instructor; the next he'd want to be a tattoo artist, or a pilot, or an actor or a firefighter or a private investigator.

Watching a piece of meteor fall out of the sky was likely to transform his last two weeks here into a quest to become either an astronaut or a geologist.

He sighed as he read Levi's text, then shoved the old laptop we shared aside and turned on the TV.

Sheriff Nakamura appeared onscreen, standing in front of a field. It was almost nine PM, but the footage had been shot during daylight. It was one of those reports they kept running over and over again, a talking head in the corner adding information as the story developed.

"This is absolutely some kind of hoax," Sheriff Nakamura was saying. "There is no natural way for the ground to have become scorched in this intricate pattern without doing damage to the surrounding crops. It's simply not possible. Think of this as graffiti in the extreme."

"What do you have to say about the behavior of the cows?" the news anchor asked. I recognized her as Cheryl Kelly. She'd been the face of the reports about the accident at the steel mill too, though back then she always wore navy blue, whereas now you never spotted her out of her signature red blazer.

The sheriff chuckled and thumbed the front of his hat. "Now, Cheryl, I'm afraid you're going to have to ask a veterinarian, or maybe a bovine scientist, that question."

The screen cut to a different image: a wash of green marred by brown.

Arthur squinted. "What is that?"

The camera panned over the dull brown-green. A series of gray rectangles appeared at the bottom edge of the screen, a thin streak of silver outlining the shapes. Boxy buildings and a fence wrapped around them.

"The substation. On Jenkins," I said. And from the fence along the top edge, brown sprouted outward in a symmetrical pattern. Like a tree's branches, like roots hanging from a plucked wild onion, like the scars up Arthur's and my arms.

The grass was burnt, charred, resembling a hundred streaks of lightning, some of them reaching out through the two acres of corn to the left of the electrical plant.

But there was something else in the grassy field behind the metal structures, something black and white arranged along the charred patterns, mottling the gaps between them into speckled bands.

Cows. They'd moved from their line along the fence that morning and fanned out to graze along the burns.

The screen cut back to Sheriff Nakamura and Cheryl Kelly. My phone rang, interrupting her next question.

"Seeing it?" Levi asked as soon as I accepted the call.

"Uh-huh," I said.

The camera cut once more to the field, and my eyes dipped

to the scars on my arm, trying to determine whether they were, as they seemed to be, identical to the massive pattern burned into the field onscreen.

"You and Arthur need to get over here," Levi said.

"Remy's grounded, remember?" I said. "We have no ride."

"Then ride your bikes."

Arthur shot me a look over his shoulder. "What's he saying?"

"He wants us to ride our bikes over there."

"Not *want*," Levi said. *"Need."*

"Tell him if he's so desperate for company, he can ride *his* bike *here*," Arthur said.

"What's he saying?" Levi asked me.

"He says stop being a lazy asshole," I replied.

"Frances." Levi enunciated slowly: "Go out into your yard, get onto your bike, and pedal your little Schmidt hearts out. You need to see what my video camera caught."

My handlebars shocked me so badly I flung the bike back against the shed where I'd left it leaning.

"What?" Arthur said, climbing astride his own. "Did you see a spider or something?"

I wasn't afraid of spiders, but when I said so, my indignation was lost on him. He was already halfway across the yard.

Arthur never waited for me—he looked back to make sure I was there, and he constantly bugged me about bringing the Mace key chain he'd gotten me for Christmas—but he never waited.

He was morally opposed to slowing himself down, for anyone but especially for me. A few years ago he'd very matter-of-factly told me that the worst thing Mom ever did for me wasn't leaving us, but babying me so much that I couldn't handle it when she did.

It was the only time either of us had said it aloud—*leaving us*—but the fact that Arthur thought I couldn't handle her leaving stung worse than the phrase itself.

I grabbed my bike again, this time careful to touch the rubber handle first, then took off after my brother. The back of my neck prickled, and I fought an impulse to look back. Dad wouldn't be watching us from within the yellow glow of his bedroom window (he never was), and I'd feel stupid for even checking (I always did).

If we *were* being watched, it was probably by *him,* the creepy hermit whose property backed up to ours. He sometimes stood there, late at night, at the barbed wire fence that separated our field from his woods, looking like Frankenstein's monster in his denim bib-alls.

I rode faster.

We turned up the access road to the train tracks, pedaling hard to keep pace as we thundered over the gravel, past the propane tank they used to heat the track switches in the winter and past the giant blue penis Nick had spray-painted on it, then cut through the woods to the back of Levi's neighborhood on the literal far side of the tracks.

He, Sofía, and Remy all lived in the newer part of town—houses built on hills in the late 1950s, with fern-filled solariums and mahogany bookshelves like Sofía's, or home gyms and stainless steel appliances like Remy's. Houses with pools and gardens and forest views, and easy access to both Kroger and Walmart.

Levi lived at the end of a cul-de-sac in a sprawling, mint-colored house, a mid-century quad-level with wide windows, a nearly flat roof, and a lattice carport that jutted out over his parents' twin Volvos. Foliage hemmed it in from all sides, blocking the pool and hot tub from the neighbors' view.

As we glided up the driveway, Levi's head thrust out of the window over the carport. "Finally!"

"Faster than if we'd had to wait for *you* to learn how to ride without training wheels." Arthur dropped his bike in the yard. "Where are the others?"

I kicked my stand loose and followed Arthur to the front steps.

"Nick: work. Sofía: lacrosse," Levi answered before disappearing deeper into the room. "They'll be here later," he shouted. "I called Handsome Remy, but the sheriff answered: He's grounded until further notice. Toss those boxes up, would you? Shouldn't be anything breakable."

He was referring to the three Amazon packages leaned against the front door. "How many of those do you think are porkpie hats?" I whispered to Arthur, who considered seriously before saying, "One."

Whenever Levi's parents were out of town, they left him with a credit card "for emergencies," but they never seemed to question what sort of catastrophe would require their son to order signed movie posters or bulk boxes of sour gummy worms or hats from L.A. specialty stores.

Arthur tossed the packages onto the carport roof, then scrambled up after them instead of just going through the ever-unlocked front door like a normal person.

I would've preferred the latter, but we all treated the flimsy carport roof like a ritual. So I climbed onto the metal awning, flattened myself to the siding, and shuffled over to swing through the window.

Arthur was already standing over Levi's shoulder at his desk, last night's footage pulled up on his computer.

"Where are your parents?" I asked.

"Palm Desert," Levi answered. He was wearing an entirely green outfit, including a hunter-green fedora, which made him look like a burly Robin Hood. "For Sable's second birthday."

Mr. and Mrs. Lindquist were much older than my parents, and both retired, and ever since Levi's (much) older sister started having kids, they'd gone into full grandparent mode, with Levi and his nieces and nephew alike. They were all affection and no rules, and it seemed like they were visiting their grandbabies in California more often than not.

"A *two*-year-old is having a birthday party in Palm Desert?" I said.

"I didn't know there was one of those," Arthur said. "A palm desert, I mean."

"Yeah, like the Springs weren't enough for them," I said. "They had to take the desert too."

"Assholes," Levi agreed. "Come here, Fran. You need to see this video up close." He turned in his chair to face me, the monitor light catching the angry blue bruise on his forehead.

"Levi! What happened to your head?" I asked.

He reached toward the mark. "I was napping and I sleepwalked into a cabinet."

"Huh," Arthur said, peering at the mark like he'd just now noticed it.

He reached out to touch it, and Levi knocked his hand away. "Forget that! You have to see this!" He spun back to face the monitor, and I glanced uneasily at the paused video.

Now that we were so close to it, the idea of seeing what had happened to us—a moment none of us could remember—sent panic through me. I reached for my necklace, and my stomach lurched with the renewed realization that it was gone.

Levi started the footage. "Without further ado, I present to you . . . Some Very Freaky Yet Incredible Crap!"

The camera jaunted up and down, the sounds of Levi's breaths hissing off the speakers. It was dark, except when the beam of light atop the camera managed to catch something. A flash of my shoulders and paint-stained tank top crossed the screen, my hair turning almost white in the light. And there was the side of Remy's face, his neck, his hair. Nick looked over his shoulder, his skin going transparent under the glare so the veins under his eyes looked purple. And then more darkness, Levi breathing fast as he ran between the metal towers.

The camera dropped low, snatching at bits of our legs and shoes, the illuminated gravel blurring past. Levi must've lowered it while he was running. All I could see were his yellow Doc Martens whipping past.

The back of my neck prickled, as if that same electrical charge were in the room now, its static pulling at us like invisible fingers. I edged closer to Arthur and Levi.

I'd been there, seen this in real life, and yet there was a part of me that expected something horrible to leap out. Something we'd missed before.

Something that explained it all.

The movement onscreen stopped. The camera rose, light panning up Arthur's back. Levi's breath came in shuddering gasps.

The hair on my arms stood upright, and I smoothed the back of my head, expecting to find strands dancing in the buzzing air.

But there was no electrical charge in the room. My hair sat in heavy tangles at my shoulders.

Onscreen, the crumpled heap of metal came into view, and then—

My heart skipped as the camera floated closer, homing in on the glassy disc and the streaks of light moving in and out in repetitive patterns, like blood through veins.

"Like our scars," Arthur said, fascinated.

He was right. The light looked just like the marks on our skin, like the burns in the field.

Sofia's whisper came through the speakers now: "It must be heavy to have done this kind of damage."

My own voice answered, the sound of my fear disorienting to me now. "Do you think it's like . . . part of the comet?"

Onscreen, Arthur's red T-shirt, visible in flashes, moved toward the disc.

My voice, the recording of it, sounded foreign in its shock. "Arthur?"

And then, in a flare of blond hair and sun-browned skin, I was lunging toward him. *"ART! Don't—"*

A stark *snap* rang through the speakers, followed by a high-pitched warbling, easily twice as loud as the rest of the audio. The screen went white. "What is that?" I shouted over the warbling screech.

"Sounds like metal," Arthur shouted in reply.

Levi turned the volume down. "It's like . . . *groaning* metal, or something," Arthur repeated.

The metallic warble went on, changing in pitch and volume, and the screen stayed solidly white.

The only thing this video told us about those lost hours was that we'd likely sustained hearing damage during them.

"Why did we just ride two miles in like two-hundred-percent humidity for this, Levi?" I said. "You could have played this horrible sound over the phone!"

"Right!" He pulled up a tool bar. "But I wanted to *show* you something. Look. When the video plays at normal speed, it's white. Just solid white, until the battery died and the video ends. But watch what happens when I slow it way down."

Levi dragged the cursor along the bar at the bottom of the video until the moment before the flash, then tapped a few buttons, and hit Play. Again, that vicious *CRACK* rang out, but the sound that came after was lower, almost like a choir of humming voices.

The white rippled across his computer screen, but instead of a solid blanket of it, this time it flickered. So fast it was almost imperceptible.

Levi looked up at me, eyes alight, then spun to face Arthur. "Now watch." He drew the cursor back and let the scene play out even more slowly.

There was the *CRACK*. The melodic sound like humming voices, or bows being drawn across a hundred quivering violin strings. The flashes of light came slower.

But in those off-moments, when the light retreated, the screen wasn't entirely dark.

I could see myself and Arthur, trembling, shivering like the mugs in our kitchen cabinets when a train rushed past, like we were being electrocuted, seizing, and the whole thing was visible because the light wasn't going out entirely.

Instead it was sucking back inward. Not into the disc—the disc was nowhere in sight now.

No, the light was cycling in and out of something else. A tall, narrow thing that absorbed the light in those jagged streaks and spat them out in every direction only to reabsorb them and repeat.

I stared at the computer, trying to make sense of our impossibly fast convulsions, the sparking eruptions of light, and the shape they leapt from.

"Is that . . ." Arthur trailed off.

In the glow of the computer, Levi's eyes were glassy and his skin looked almost blue.

He jammed the space bar and the video paused, halfway between a flash and a moment of darkness.

Bits of light hung across the screen like frozen confetti. Through the splotches on the right side of the screen, my hand reached toward Arthur's back. Tendrils of light seemed to be sparking off the fabric, crawling up my arm like ants.

And then there was Art, standing with his arm extended toward the disc.

Only the disc was, as I'd thought, gone. And in its place stood a person.

No, not a person. A person-shaped thing, its head and hands and legs all grotesquely elongated. A body made of white light, emanating shards of it in every direction.

I whispered exactly the same thing Arthur had said: "Is that . . ."

Levi nodded. "I think it is. And so do our commenters."

"Commenters?" I parroted. "Mister KillYourself and Mademoiselle RacialSlur have an opinion on what this thing is?"

"Guys," Levi said, pulling up a YouTube Channel—not *The Ordinary*, a different channel named TheFallingSkyIncident, but the video on display was the slowed-down footage Levi had just played. "*Everyone* has an opinion on what this thing is."

"Holy shit," Arthur gasped.

There were nine thousand views already, and the count was rising before our eyes.

"So not only did we meet an alien," Levi said. "We've also gone viral."

I swallowed the fist-sized knot in my throat. "Pretty big day for us."

FIVE

WHAT ELSE COULD IT be? It had fallen out of the sky during a meteor shower. It had hit the earth in a disc and unfurled into a person shape when that disc cracked.

"No way." Sofía was still in her lacrosse shorts and a muddy NYU T-shirt, gnawing on one fingernail. Even so, she managed to be supermodel pretty and smell like a mix of rosewater and tea tree oil. It would've been annoying if she weren't also the most truly kind and sensible person I'd ever met.

Which was why she couldn't accept this.

"What else?" I said. "I mean, the options are basically *that* or superhero."

"Or coincidence," Sofía said. "It's a—a trick of the light. It's a random pattern, and that's just the shape our brains can most easily compare it to."

"It's an alien," Arthur said.

Levi nodded eager agreement.

"It's not," Sofía said.

"We all know where *you* stand, Bill Nye," Nick said. He was wearing the button-up and khakis he worked in, but he'd stuffed the Walmart vest in his back pocket and rolled the sleeves as soon as he arrived, like his tattoos needed to breathe, or maybe we couldn't recognize him without them. "Space light or alien, either way, that thing knocked us out for six hours. Let's just be glad it's gone."

"We don't know that," Levi countered. "The camera died hours before we woke up. We have no idea what happened."

"Exactly." Arthur pounded Levi on the back so hard that he coughed. "Levi's right. We'll have to go back to the field."

Nick's mouth fell open. Sofía closed her eyes and inhaled deeply. They both said, more as a statement than a question, "Why."

For Mark's necklace, I thought futilely.

"For answers," Arthur said. "We witnessed something, and none of us can even remember it. We need to find out what it was. We have to go back."

Nick guffawed, but Levi nodded. "We can get more footage for our new fans on *The Falling Sky Incident*!"

"Horrible name, by the way," Nick sniped.

Sofía dropped her face into her hands and groaned. "You're stoking mania, Levi. You're part of the problem."

"What problem?" he asked, aghast.

"Groupthink!" Sofía said. "Inaccurate assumptions spreading faster and farther than facts!" She looked to me for backup.

I shrugged. "You are so vastly overestimating my understanding of Everything."

She huffed and pushed off the bed. "Okay, setting aside the irresponsibility of sharing that video with impressionable conspiracy theorists, there's the fact that you posted proof we were at the substation that night. Exactly where the sheriff practically begged us to never reveal we went. We broke the law, Levi!"

"I posted this from a new account!" Levi said. "There's nothing here to link this video to *The Ordinary*, or even Splendor!"

"Besides," Arthur jumped in, "don't you think keeping what we saw to ourselves goes against your 'justice for all' thing?"

"That's from the pledge of allegiance, Art!" Sofía said. "Not a diary of my legally trademarked thoughts!"

"Whatever that thing was, the public has the right to know about it, right?" he said. "It's our duty to follow up on this."

He said it with such conviction that I almost believed this had nothing to do with the ways his brain was rapidly calculating how this "duty" could bring him fame or wealth.

Sofía chewed her lip. "If they're really worried about what happened in that field, we should give the sheriff the video. It's the right thing to do."

"And Stanford will be thrilled about your resulting breaking-and-entering charges," Arthur said. "Going to the sheriff would just get us into trouble, *and* we'd lose ownership over this. The whole thing will be swept under the rug."

"I had the same exact thought," I deadpanned. "Harvard will have me out on my butt."

"And my job at the U.N. certainly wouldn't last," Nick added.

Sofía shot me her best *Please be serious* look.

"The comments just keep coming in," Levi said, still scrolling at the computer.

I perched on the edge of the desk and read along with him. There were still plenty of "I hope you REALLY get electrocuted, FKWAD," but there was also enthusiasm.

Alien emojis. UFOs formed from keyboard symbols. "They are here, among us" and various typo-ridden phrases proclaiming the same thing. "This is some real Barney & Betty Hill shit," one person wrote. "Look it up! They saw a strange light on the highway and next thing they know, they black out and wake up thirty-five miles down the road. We are NOT ALONE, PEOPLE!"

"We should turn this into a docuseries!" Levi said. "A real one. We can interview people in town—the sheriff, the owner of the field, maybe someone from Crane Energy. This is a story worth telling."

"Dude," Nick said. "Arthur and Remy have two weeks before they leave for college. Fairly busy time."

"What could be more important than this?" Levi said. "My

parents are gone for eight more days. We can just camp out here, do the whole thing rapid-fire!"

As he twisted in his chair to appeal to the others, I read the top-rated comment: "I want to believe."

Beneath it, the comment with the second highest number of votes read, "FAKE. BAD EDITING."

My eyes caught on a reply to that one.

"It's not fake," a commenter with the handle CitizenOfThe-BlackMailbox wrote. "I saw this, twenty years ago. DELETE THIS IMMEDIATELY AND CONTACT ME: BlackMailboxBill @COTBM.com. THEY ARE WATCHING!!!"

"What do you make of this?" I asked.

"Huh?" Levi spun back, read the comment, and shrugged. "It's the Internet. Best to approach everything with a healthy dose of skepticism."

Sofía crossed her arms. "Something your rabid fan base could learn from you."

"Listen to this," I said, and read the comment aloud.

"We're not contacting him," Arthur said. "We're not contacting *anyone* until we get back to that field and see what we find. This is *our* UFO."

"You're flying way too close to the freaking sun, dude," Nick said. "Talking about *our* UFO."

"Speaking of the *field*." Levi stuffed some gummy worms into his mouth. "What do you think the deal with the cows was? Did you see on TV, how they all lined up on the burns?"

"That part's easy," Nick said. Everyone's attention snapped to him like one of his bulgy eyes had finally popped out of his head and rolled across the floor.

"Not all of us are bovine scientists, Nick," I said. "Explain."

Nick scritched the back of his head, and his fingers lingered, drumming out that restless beat he'd played against the car window earlier that morning. "Magnetic fields."

"Magnetic fields," Levi said in his documentarian voice, adjusting his hat.

Nick scooped up a fallen gummy worm and threw it at him. "Cows eat facing north to south. Or south to north. Either way. People think they sense Earth's magnetism or some crud. Arthur's beloved space critter must've messed that up with its spaceship."

Sofia sighed. "Meteorite. Gas, or energy, trapped in a space rock."

"It wasn't rock," Arthur said. "It was like jelly. Squishy."

"That definitely sounds like space junk," Sofia said.

"Wow, both a bovine scientist and a space-junkologist in the same room," I said.

She shot me another reproachful stare.

Nick rolled his eyes. "No wonder the alien chose us, y'all."

"See, that's the part—well, one of many parts—that doesn't make sense," Sofia said. "If intelligent life were going to reveal itself to mankind, why would it choose six kids in Splendor, Ohio?"

Levi shook his head. "Maybe it crashed. The docuseries will uncover all that."

"Give it up, Levi!" Nick said. "Not all of us have swimming pools full of money and buttloads of free time to bop around town with our fancy cameras and a Nancy Drew notepad. Some of us have jobs! People depending on us to pull our weight."

"We just need to get back to the field," Arthur murmured, as if he were part of an entirely separate conversation.

"Don't use *we*," Nick said. "I never agreed to this little investigation."

Arthur bristled. "Fine, *I'll* know more when *I* get back to the field. Until then, no one say anything about this, to anyone."

Nick scoffed. "No problem. People in this town already got

enough to say about my family without me running around screaming about aliens."

"We need something more definite before we come forward with this." Arthur was still on his own plane of existence. He leapt onto the mattress, then climbed into the hammock hung from the ceiling over it.

"I mean . . . my video's pretty definitive," Levi said, a little put out.

Arthur waved his hand. "It might tickle the whole Conspiracy Rabbit Hole YouTube Crowd, but it looks like a homemade video we put a shoddy aftereffect onto."

"Which . . . is something we regularly do, with consistent online documentation," I pointed out.

"But the video's real!" Levi argued.

"You think the gah-damn FBI are going to investigate this video, find out it's ours, and then scroll through our channel like"— Nick rubbed his chin thoughtfully—"*Damn, Agent Cooper, aren't we lucky these hicks in Asshole, Ohio, had a camera on them the night of this alien encounter?* We make crap like this all the time, Levi. And post it online. No one's going to believe us. I couldn't even get Mrs. Spencer to believe I wasn't the one who spray-painted the dick on the football field."

"Nick," Sofía said. "You *were* the one who spray-painted the dick on the football field."

He threw his arms out to his sides. "But she didn't know that!"

"Apparently, she did." Sofía was the only one of us who seemed bent on slowly guiding Nick to the realization that he had a lying problem. So far she hadn't had any luck.

Nick's lies didn't bother me. They were pretty much always in service of making us laugh, and aside from that, the Colasantis *were* the butt of a lot of jokes (a truck-driver mom who stopped leaving the house after the accident and filled her windows with horrifying antique carousel horses; an older sister who'd started dating one of her teachers two months after graduating), so I didn't blame him for wanting to at least control the ridiculous things people said about him.

But Sofía was a Libra (one who thought astrology was just "something Forever 21 made up to sell nail decals") with a strong sense of justice, and a lie was a lie in her eyes.

"Nick's right," Arthur said. "You can't spend five years avoiding your whole town then expect them to believe you when you tell them something impossible."

Levi frowned. "Or spend five years making *Bigfoot Believers* parodies and then expect your viewers to believe it when you show them the real deal."

"And for that matter," Nick said, "I'm beginning to think my ongoing 'Phallus the Fields of Splendor' project won't help our credibility."

Sofía shook her head. "Phallus the Fields of Splendor."

"That sounds like a thrash metal album." Arthur touched his chin in a way that usually meant he'd had an idea.

"Or a book of really horny poetry," I added.

"It also reminds me of a beloved film," Levi said. "Kevin Costner's brilliant *Field of Dicks*."

"Dude, that bruise on your head looks like a dick," Nick said.

"It looks like Gary Busey," Sofía disagreed. "Since when do you sleepwalk, by the way?"

"Since 9:34 AM today," Levi answered.

"Think that's weird?" Nick said. "When I got home and passed out I dreamed about pianos. Like, exclusively about pianos. Rooms full of them, hallways made of them that ended in little red kids' pianos with German words written in freakin' gold leaf on them. Pianos everywhere."

"We need evidence," Arthur said. He was staring out the window, eyes glinting as his mind spun plans. "We need to make contact."

"Sun," Nick said, holding up a fist. "Your current flight path, Icarus." He took his other hand and slammed it right into his fist, making explosion sounds with his mouth.

"Tomorrow when I get off work," Arthur said, ignoring him, "we'll go to Jenkins Lane and see if we can figure out where that . . . thing went. Or *I* will." He rolled his eyes at Nick.

Levi patted his camera like a puppy. "I'm there."

Sofia sighed. "I'll take a look. But only in a legal capacity, and just for as long as it takes to find the real explanation behind all this."

"I'm not going near that place," Nick said.

Arthur shrugged the sentiment away and fixed his sharp gaze on me. "Fran? You in?"

I didn't like the way all of this somehow kept dredging up the past. I didn't like that it reminded me how mercurial and brutal the universe could be, or that there was no limit on how many random horrors could slash through the same life, and I really, really didn't like the look in Arthur's eyes that told me he wasn't thinking about any of that.

It scared me to see how badly he *wanted* this.

Wanting things was like needing people. It backfired every time.

Soon, he'd lose interest in this, like he'd lost interest in learning to count cards or play the bass guitar or slack line. It would all blow over.

In the meantime, we'd get my necklace back, wander a burnt field, and maybe even generate some ad revenue on our newly viral video.

Then we'd put this all out of our minds, like we did with everything else we couldn't control.

"I'm in."

SIX

BUT WE DIDN'T GO back to the field the next day.

For one thing, there was the violent storm that rolled into town not long after I turned up to work that morning, with angry purple clouds pushing in over the outdoor pool. Within minutes, lightning snapped across the sky toward the soccer fields beyond the water slide, and within half an hour, the YMCA's director called to tell us the forecast wasn't promising and we might as well close the outdoor facility for the day.

So I'd gotten bumped to the front desk, and the guy scheduled there went home sick. I hated working inside on the best of days, and today, there was nothing to do—nothing but a sticky romance novel in the lost and found, which I wasn't brave enough to touch. And even if I'd wanted to continue the unsettling "research" Arthur was pestering us all about in the group texts (I didn't), the storm seemed to be having some kind of adverse effect on both my phone, which kept freezing, and the computer, whose screen started pixelating and shuddering whenever I got too close.

Sofia was working too, but back in the fitness center, so I was left alone in the silent lobby, counting the minutes until Arthur's shift at Walmart and Sofia's and my shifts here ended, and we could finally go put all this behind us, lightning storm or not.

But then, after a segment about a dog who liked to ride the bus played on the muted TV fixed to the lobby ceiling, Cheryl Kelly appeared onscreen in front of the electric fence that guarded the substation on Jenkins Lane.

She was clad in a red windbreaker, and a disembodied hand

floated on the left side of the frame, holding an umbrella over Cheryl's billowing blond hair.

I wondered if someone had told her to swap out the blue she wore while reporting on the steel mill accident for the red she'd been wearing since, or if she'd made the decision herself.

While Remy had his denim and Levi had his loud hats and Nick had his trademark all-black outfit plus an endless supply of neon high-tops, I couldn't imagine committing to one look.

Of course, I couldn't imagine committing to anything. It was best to stay flexible when it came to decisions. You never got what you really wanted anyway. Someday Cheryl Kelly with News 11 would wake up and find a very particular burglar had robbed her of all her red clothing, and she'd have to settle for something teal.

Onscreen, her face was emoting so aggressively I couldn't take the suspense. I left the desk and stood on one of the plastic chairs to turn up the TV's volume.

The TV was old, and as soon as I was eye level with it, it went fuzzy, static pulling monochromatic streaks across the screen. I smacked the side of it, but (shockingly!) that didn't help. I turned up the volume on the off chance I'd be able to hear her through the fuzz (I couldn't!), then hopped off the chair hoping to give it a moment to resolve.

"The plot thickens!" Cheryl Kelly said as she snapped back into red existence. "For those of you just tuning in, I'm standing here outside the step-down transmission substation on Jenkins Lane, where yesterday, we reported about a strange—*and intriguing*—pattern that had appeared in a local farmer's corn crop, as well as his grazing field. While early speculation from the Sheriff's Department focused on the possibility that this was a calculated act of arson, yesterday's investigation has turned up some puzzling—*and startling*—"

"*And startling,*" a voice parroted in breathy falsetto behind me. I spun to find Sofía leaned against the reception desk.

"—new information," Cheryl Kelly finished.

Sofía shook her head. "Why does Cheryl Kelly always sound like she's talking through the first half of an orgasm?"

"Because they cut her off before the second half?" I said.

The segment cut to a wide-angle view of the electrical facility. Yellow caution tape had been wrapped around the fence like a Christmas bow. Several police officers, as well as Crane Energy employees in rain ponchos, stood within the grounds, sharing a conversation we couldn't hear, as Cheryl's narration went on, the screen jumping once more to yesterday's aerial footage of the charred field.

"With the help and cooperation of the property owner, local farmer Garrett St. James, the Sheriff's Department determined that the burns were much deeper than initially thought. Preliminary reports that this was the careful work of pranksters faltered when a dig at the burn site turned up charred soil in the same careful path more than two feet below the surface.

"St. James is now reportedly in talks with a private excavation team. He hopes their assistance will help determine whether this is indeed arson, or if something *beneath* the Earth's surface may have caused the burns through some kind of natural—*though uncommon—*"

"*Though uncommon,*" Sofía breathily gasped.

"—phenomenon!" Cheryl Kelly finished.

The camera cut to a prerecorded interview with Garrett St. James, a mostly bald man with a thin gray swipe of hair backcombed across his shiny forehead, and a gun cradled in his arms like it was a very long baby.

Sofía snorted. "Only in Splendor, Ohio, would someone be

like, *Hey, mind if I bring my gun to this interview?* And then have the news station be like, *Sure, you can make vague threats on our program! No big!*"

"We're gonna get to the bottom of this one way or another and bring him to justice!" St. James was saying, rattling his gun a bit for effect.

I thought about the bullet I'd found, the damp footprints along the Jenkins House. "Do you think he saw anything that night?" I asked.

Sofía shrugged. "Why would he go to all this effort if he'd seen what happened? If he *was* around, he obviously doesn't remember what went down either."

And if he'd seen us lurking around near his property before-hand, he would've turned us in by now. Sofía was right: There was no shortage of hunting guns in Splendor. That bullet could've belonged to my pediatrician as easily as it could have belonged to Garrett St. James.

Sofía turned to me and jutted her chin toward the marks on my hand. "How are you feeling, by the way? Do yours itch or anything?"

I shook my head. "Yours?"

She ran her teeth over her bottom lip. "It's like they're already healed, isn't it?"

"You tell me," I said. "You're the smart one."

She rolled her eyes. "I'm the one who tries."

I had tried once, right after the accident. Getting perfect grades that fall was just one more way I could prove I was okay, take the burden off Mom and Dad. I especially threw myself into my science class, thinking my wannabe-astronaut mother would find some hope in watching me take an interest in the things she'd shared only with Mark.

All I really wanted was to be outside, like I had all summer, running through woods, soaked in sweat, smelling honeysuckle and oleander on the sticky breeze. Instead I'd toiled at the kitchen table for hours on my unnecessarily elaborate model of the solar system, then left it sitting out for upwards of a week, waiting for the moment Mom would notice it.

When she finally did, she didn't say anything, but I watched hurt creep into her eyes. Like it was a trap I'd laid for her. I guess it sort of was.

I pushed too hard.

Three weeks later, she left.

On TV, Cheryl Kelly was standing cozy-close to Sheriff Nakamura again, the disembodied hand splitting the umbrella over both of them.

"Until we can be certain of the cause of this, we are still treating this as a criminal investigation," he confirmed.

"Great," Sofía said over Cheryl's breathy wrap-up. The channel cut to a commercial break, and Sofía eyed me once more. "I guess that pretty much puts the kibosh on today's plans."

I felt simultaneously relieved to have an excuse not to go back to the field and anxious about the necklace, imagining it sitting out there where so many rain boots were stomping around and shovels were stabbing the dirt.

"I guess I'll tell my mom I can go shoe-shopping with her after all," Sofía said, with the enthusiasm most people would muster when talking about a dentist appointment or a Pap smear. "Wanna come?"

When I'd first befriended Sofía, I'd treated visits to her house like field trips to an art museum. Her home was beautiful; her parents were beautiful and warm and funny and loving. They were both ob-gyns, which struck me as *very* sophisticated and meaningful.

Her mother, Dr. Gloria Perez, lived in elegantly casual linen and wool and focused all her use of color and pizzazz on her shoe closet, which I'd regularly begged Sofía to give me tours of.

Sofía didn't care much about shoes, or shopping. She spent half her life in athletic wear and the other half in dark jeans and cheap white T-shirts she bought in multipacks (and looked like a Gap model in), but every few weeks, she and her mom went shoe-shopping.

It was just *their thing*, she explained. I'd gone along a couple of times. The last time, I remembered watching them both dissolve into laugh-tears in the size 9 aisle of Nordstrom Rack when Sofía called a feathery pink heel *something that belongs in Muppets porn*. Later, Dr. Gloria had told us about her childhood in Mexico City and her first boyfriend. She'd told us the way Sofía and I interacted reminded her of her sister, and though a certain melancholy passed over her face, thinking of the sister she'd lost in the accident seemed to make her more happy than sad. She also asked us a zillion questions about the mockumentary and clapped her hands and laughed when we described our plans for upcoming episodes.

I had a great time.

When I got home, I went straight to my room and cried. I hadn't been shopping with them since. In fact, I hadn't even been to Sofía's house again, and once, about a year ago, we'd come close to fighting about it, despite all my greatest efforts to avoid confrontation.

I couldn't explain it: how being around her family—knowing I could never belong—hurt worse than being alone. Instead I'd just blurted out, "We've been spending too much time together." After that, things between us were never the same.

"Fran? Shoes? Yes? No?"

Before I could stumble through an excuse, the desk phone rang. I held up a finger and went to answer. Static filled the line, followed by an ear-piercing squeal. I yanked it away from my ear, wincing, then drew it back as the screech ended. "Splendor Community YMC—"

"Fran!" someone hissed on the other end.

"Remy?" I glanced toward my cell phone on the desk. "Why are you calling me at work?"

"I don't have your number memorized, and this one's online," he said. "Look, I'm on my dad's phone, and I only have a second before he realizes he forgot it and circles back. He's coming to ask you and Arthur questions. You can't tell him anything, okay?"

"About the field?" I said, startled. I thought about St. James, about his gun. "He can't honestly think we had anything—"

"He doesn't," Remy cut me off. "But he can't know you were there. I mean it, Franny. He *cannot* know. I'll explain tonight. Can you meet me at the tracks, midnight?"

It took me several seconds to understand. Despite his Rebel Without a Cause aesthetic, Remy mostly honored his dad's rules, at least when he was already in trouble.

"I have to go," Remy hissed. "Midnight, Fran. Don't tell anyone, okay? I'm serious. Not even Arthur. Not until we talk. And no matter what: You weren't in that field. You were at Levi's, watching *The Shining,* and then we fell asleep."

The line clicked dead, and I stared at the phone, trying to make sense of it all.

"What did Remy want?" Sofía said behind me.

I put the phone down. "Sheriff Nakamura is coming to ask us some questions." I swallowed the knot in my throat. "Remy wants us to lie."

"Like under oath?" Sofía said.

"If it comes to it," I said, "I think so."

Her eyebrow arched, and she studied me with something like suspicion. Or maybe I was imagining it. "And that's all he said?"

There were all kinds of things my friends and I never talked about, dozens of unspoken secrets, not to mention Nick's storytelling. This felt different.

"Pretty much," I said.

Sofia's lips pursed. "Okay," she said finally, and walked away.

Lightning flashed outside the window, and something feathery and black smashed into the door. I flinched and swallowed a scream as I jumped up from behind the desk.

The bird slid down the glass door and dropped lifelessly to the concrete, a thin trail of blood connecting the point where it hit to where it lay dead.

I jumped again as two more hit in quick succession, behind it. I clamped my hand over my chest like my heart was a skittish Chihuahua I could soothe by petting, but it didn't slow and my stomach didn't unknot.

I kept thinking about the mind-bending *CRACK!* and the burst of light that had followed, the way I'd felt like the universe had split down the middle and everything was falling toward the rift, upending the laws of physics and swallowing them whole. In the last second I remembered, I'd lost all concept of up and down, of balance, of my body and its place in space.

I felt fine now, I told myself. *Completely, totally normal.*

But if the birds had been affected this way, what were the odds that we'd been unscathed?

In my head, Cheryl Kelly's breathy voice sang, *The plot thickens!*

SEVEN

AT LEAST THE SHERIFF had come alone.

I would only be lying to one cop, whom I knew, instead of multiple strangers.

The worst part was that Dad happened to be home between jobs, and there wasn't anywhere for four people to comfortably sit in our house.

We had one couch and an off-brand La-Z-Boy in the living room, and the two tiny chairs in our tiny kitchen at the back of the house were covered in mail piles, discarded jackets and bags, leaning stacks of thrift-store *National Geographics* whose photos I'd pined over while standing at the kitchen sink eating breakfast. The surface of the table itself was worse: playing cards and mugs that never made it to the dishwasher, paper towels and junk mail and crumbs that never made it to the trash.

I could tell Dad was embarrassed. Possibly because we never had adults over and he'd just realized how badly we needed to clean. Possibly because he had to sit on the couch between me and Arthur while Sheriff Nakamura perched on the not-La-Z-Boy, looking stern and paternal despite the purple plastic cup of water Dad had offered him, with Droog sitting squarely on his feet.

"I am sorry to just drop in on you folks like this." The sheriff eyed me guiltily. I was dripping wet from the ride home, leaving a full-body print on the couch. I pulled my hands inside my damp sweatshirt pockets to hide the scars.

"No trouble at all." Dad cast an anxious glance between me and Arthur. "I'm just afraid I don't understand what it's all about.

You said there was a fire on Jenkins Lane?" His grimace swiveled between Arthur and me, clearly readying himself for the worst.

The sheriff scooted to the edge of the formidable chair and gave an encouraging smile. "Something like that. You haven't seen it on the news?"

Dad scratched his jaw. "I'm afraid I don't have a lot of time to keep up with that sort of thing these days."

A lie. Sure, Dad was busy, but he was also an insomniac. If you stood in the hallway at just about any given hour of the night, you could hear the soft din of prerecorded baseball games coming from the television in his bedroom. Never sitcoms or action movies or traffic and weather reports. Just baseball games that had already happened. His happy place.

He used to love baseball. Before the accident, he'd played in the church league and everything. Mom didn't know anything about the game, of course. Once, when Mark, Arthur, and I were playing *Mario Kart* in the living room, I'd overheard her pretending to give Dad advice on an upcoming game.

"You see, Rob, what you gotta do is . . ." she'd said from the next room.

"What, Eileen?"

I remembered glancing over my shoulder and seeing him through the kitchen doorway, leaning in close to her, his face dead serious. "Tell me, honey. *How* am I gonna win this game?"

"Well, listen. You've gotta take that ball, and throw it, right into the end zone."

Dad fought a smile. "The end zone is a very important place in baseball."

"Oh, the most important," Mom had agreed, and their laughter had bounced around the yellow-lit wallpaper of the kitchen, a Carole King record softly playing under it all.

I'd hardly cared that they were happy. Back then, it had all seemed very normal, the five of us in that house.

The smell of onions and baking garlic that meant Dad's potato-chip-topped green bean casserole was in the oven.

The spread of Arthur's superhero comics across every surface in the living room.

Mark's mix of art books and science journals stacked neatly on the bottom step so he'd remember to take them to bed with him.

The high-pitched yodel of Mom's laughter filtering into the living room.

"No one's accusing Arthur or Frances," the sheriff said, yanking me out of the memory. "To be frank, Robert, at this point, we're not quite sure what we'd even be accusing anyone of. There's been significant damage to some crops, as well as the little electrical plant down there, not to mention the cows and the birds in the area are a bit agitated by whatever happened, and, well . . . *confused.*" He seemed resistant to saying that last part.

"With all due respect," Arthur said, scooting to the edge of the couch to mirror the sheriff's confident yet casual position. "They're cows. Isn't being confused part of their M.O.?"

The sheriff chuckled, but there was something uneasy underneath it. "Can't argue against that. But the property owner is pretty upset. He's concerned the cows might have been tormented."

Did he see us? I thought again and again, like a skipping record.

"They're beef cows," Arthur said.

I shot him a pleading look he ignored. Lying to the sheriff was one thing. We didn't also need to be assholes.

The sheriff sighed. "Look, under different circumstances, I wouldn't be here, but we're getting a lot of pressure to put a face on all this."

Dad pulled at his flannel collar. "I see."

Arthur cleared his throat. "Sheriff, where do we come into this?"

I'd texted the others to tell them what Remy had said (minus the part about needing to meet me), then ridden straight home and walked into this interrogation.

All I could do was hope Arthur had seen the message, or at least was still committed to keeping *his* UFO under *his* jurisdiction. He was wearing a long-sleeved T-shirt that mostly hid his scars, at least.

"Look." The sheriff thumbed his hat. "I know you all didn't burn Mr. St. James's field, but I *don't* know where you were that night—"

"At Levi's!" I volunteered. "Watching *The Shining.*"

The sheriff held up a hand and continued. "—but from our cursory look at the substation's security footage, the cameras malfunctioned twelve minutes before midnight."

Arthur and I exchanged a look. The possibility of security cameras hadn't occurred to me. I hadn't stopped to wonder why no one had come running out when the disc hit the tower. "Malfunctioned how?" I asked.

"Stuttered and then froze," he said. "To the security guards, it just looked like all was calm. Which is one reason we have to treat this as a criminal case until we know more."

Arthur crossed his arms. "And we're the criminals?"

"Arthur," Dad warned, but the sheriff gave a warm, Remy-esque smile.

"I highly doubt it. But we went ahead and pulled the footage from the new traffic camera. Just to see who all might've been headed that way before the incident."

So St. James *hadn't* seen us.

Splendor's *one* traffic camera, fixed to a two-way stop where three people had died in the last four years, had. Nerves fizzed in my stomach, but Arthur quickly said, "We had to pass through that on our way to Levi's."

The sheriff nodded. "That's exactly what I told St. James. We're following up on every lead, checking for alibis, and for now, we have no reason to doubt yours. But, Arthur, Frances . . . I need you to understand: Whether you actually had anything to do with what happened in that field, if anything turns up to suggest you were there—for example, any of the missing debris—it's going to look bad."

"Missing debris?" Arthur and I said in unison. A wild flare of concern, or maybe something more territorial than that, flashed in my brother's hazel eyes.

Sheriff Nakamura's dark gaze probed us for signs that we were acting, pretending to be shocked by what he'd said. "The top of a tower. Some pieces of transmission lines, a metal coil."

I thought back to yesterday morning. Had any of the wreckage been gone when we woke up? As soon as my mind reached backward, painful white unfurled across it, blocking out the room.

A horrible sound.

White light, everywhere.

Pain in every fiber of my body, cold hardening ice-like in all my cracks, breaking me apart. Force on every side of me, shaking me like gelatin as I hurtle through—

"Why would anyone take that?" Arthur asked.

The white retreated like a tide. I was sitting on the couch, shivering, my fingernails sinking into the cushion and a layer of sweat shining my skin.

No one seemed to notice that I'd just gone to cold, sweaty jelly. That for a moment, I'd left my body.

Oh God. What had happened to us?

My hand went to my throat, searching for something to ground me, but of course the necklace was missing. I stuffed my hands into my hoodie pocket.

"We're not sure," the sheriff answered Arthur. "If someone did in fact cause this, they might have taken it as some kind of trophy. Or someone might've witnessed it and taken pieces as a souvenir. Happens all the time when street signs get knocked over or when stoplights fall during storms."

"Well, we didn't take that junk," Arthur said. "Like Franny said, we were watching *The Shining.*"

The sheriff's lips pressed tight. "The thing is, the debris wasn't taken the night of the incident. It was taken *last* night. The new security cameras malfunctioned, in just the same way, and this morning, the rubble was gone. Which suggests whoever was involved, in whatever capacity, is still in Splendor."

Arthur's brow scrunched as he tried to think through what this meant, or possibly wrestled with frustration that some other trespasser had made it onto the crash site before him.

The silence stretched uncomfortably. Arthur, too deep in his head to bother with this conversation; Dad, possibly too out of touch to remember how to keep one up; Sheriff Nakamura, giving us every chance to fess up without outright asking where we'd been last night.

"Well, I hope you find whoever did it," I said.

You know what did it, a voice warned in my head.

I buried my fingernails into my palms to keep from falling into that fragmented memory of the light.

Sheriff Nakamura smiled faintly. "Well, I should be going. Thank you—Frances, Arthur, Robert." He nodded at each of us in turn. "You've been an enormous help."

We had not.

"Of course, Sheriff," Dad said. "If there's anything else we can do . . ." He trailed off, but honestly, good for him, for managing to fulfill that much of the social contract. "I'll walk you out."

Droog hopped up to follow them. She had no real allegiance to any of us. She'd been Mark's dog, really, ever since he found her by the dumpster behind Burger King with a broken leg. She was content to spend her days following any one of us around, but at night, she still slept on the woven mat at the front door, waiting for her boy to get home.

Dad reappeared a moment later, and I braced for the kind of punishment Arthur and I had avoided for five years straight.

But Dad just looked at us for several seconds, with this open, bewildered expression like we'd been newborns when he left the room and he came back to find us like this.

"You two stay out of trouble, okay?" he said finally.

We nodded, and then he shuffled back upstairs.

When we were sure he was out of earshot, Arthur smacked the pillow next to him. "Obviously the alien took the debris."

"What? Obviously, how?" I asked.

"They'll increase security now." Arthur touched his chin. "It could be days before we can get back into that field."

Good, I thought. No matter how badly I wanted my necklace back, as long as *that thing* was wandering around Jenkins Lane, I wasn't going near it.

Even as I thought it, the white rushed forward over my mind, trying to drag me back.

"It's just a few days," I said. "It will be fine."

What I meant was: *Hopefully you'll have forgotten about it, moved on to something new.*

Hopefully we all would have forgotten about it.

But something about this—the news coverage, Cheryl Kelly's blazer, the visits from police officers—kept pulling me back to what had happened five years ago, trying to hold me captive in memories I thought I'd buried.

EIGHT

THE CAR WAS BARELY stopped before Mom tumbled out of the driver's seat and ran for the hospital's automatic glass doors. It was funny, the things a person remembered to do and those they forgot in crisis. She'd thought to hit the key fob, to lock the Voyager's doors, but she hadn't checked whether we were with her.

Arthur's lanky strides had carried him halfway across the sun-warmed asphalt, but I'd barely managed to get my seat belt off when the van's locks snapped downward.

I hadn't cried when Mom had told us Mark had been in an accident, or on the ride over. But my eyes stung then as I jerked at the handle.

I knew I had to unlock the door to open it—I was twelve, not five—but Mom's shiny curls, her blue cardigan and khaki pants were disappearing through the doors, and I pulled again and again, a jumble of fear and loneliness overtaking any logical thought.

"Don't just leave me!" I hissed as I yanked against the handle. "You can't just *leave* me stuck here."

Arthur had realized I wasn't behind him and doubled back.

"Franny, stop," he said, voice muffled by the tinted glass. "It's locked."

He was annoyed. Some part of my twelve-year-old self understood why he would be, but all I could do for another second was pull at the handle, still crying under my breath, "You can't just *leave* your kid in the car."

"Franny, unlock the car!" Arthur yelled. "I can't do anything to help you! Unlock the freaking car!"

I pushed the lock up, and Arthur threw the door open, then turned and ran.

I jumped out of the van and chased him across the lot, feeling stupid and lonely and angry and scared all at once, feelings caught in my belly like a rock too big to pass through my intestines.

I wasn't thinking about Mark.

All I was thinking was, *She didn't notice I was stuck. She didn't even notice.*

She was a good mom. My parents were good parents. The kind who told you they loved you every time they dropped you off at school or said good night. They took us camping in the summer and bought pumpkins for us to carve in the fall, and they knew our teachers' names and whether we liked them or not, and when I got inside, I was sure she would wrap her arms around me and apologize for leaving me, and I would know that everything was going to be okay.

My bedroom doorknob shocked me on my way out to meet Remy. This was getting ridiculous. In the time since the sheriff left, I'd mildly shocked myself on the teakettle, two light switches, and the spoon I'd eaten cereal with at dinner.

And not when I'd picked it up. I'd just been holding the spoon when suddenly, a pale-blue spark jumped between my skin and the metal.

Whatever else that thing had done to us, it had left me statically charged.

No sooner did I have the thought than the memory rushed painfully over me.

A horrible sound.

No, a terrifying sound, but beautiful. A thousand violins drawn across strings. Sound everywhere. Sound inside me, and the pain it causes. Splitting me open. Too much pushing through me, my body a sieve for the light to pour through and—

I gasped clear of the memory like I'd just come up from water, and collapsed against the door, breathing hard. I reached for the necklace, and my bare throat felt rubbery and foreign to me.

I spread my palm on the door.

Solid, wooden, sticky with humidity. This was real; what had just happened was, at best, a splotchy memory, and more likely, my imagination.

Still, my teeth were chattering, and the pain throbbing through my body was taking its time easing back.

I looked over my shoulder, checking the crease of light around the door to Mark and Arthur's room. I'd waited to sneak out until the last possible minute, with the hope that Arthur would have gone to sleep by now.

But now I was relieved to find the light on.

It reassured me I wasn't alone, that I hadn't actually been pulled out of my house and body, into a blinding white.

You're here and whatever that was, it's over.

I wouldn't think about it again. If Arthur wanted to spend his last two weeks here going all regressive hypnotherapy to recover those few hours, I couldn't stop him, but as soon as I talked to Remy tonight, I planned to be done with all this.

I tiptoed down the stairs, and Droog clambered up from the woven rug, tail thwapping the wall. Silently, I signaled for her to lie back down, but she turned her nose to the door and whined.

I waffled for a minute. If I left her here crying, Arthur might hear and realize I was gone. I grabbed her leash, clipped it on to her, and slipped into the inky night.

As soon as we were outside, Droog started straining against the leash, trying to run back through the field. Usually, she knew better than to tear back there—I wasn't convinced the hermit wouldn't snap her neck and eat the meat off her bones if she got too close to his fence—but tonight she was throwing a fit, crying and pulling desperately.

I dragged her to my bike and carefully grabbed the rubber handle to avoid another shock as I boarded, then looped the leash around my hand. I flicked on the headlight Arthur had attached to the handlebars for my birthday. He was always getting on me for riding without it, just like he did whenever he saw I'd left the Mace key chain at home.

"I paid good money for that!" was his go-to defense for why it made him so angry, but I suspected it had been shoplifted by Nick, who, in addition to lying, might've been a little bit addicted to stealing.

It took only a handful of trips to the mall with him to realize he had a habit of showing up wearing the expensive neon sneakers and black band T-shirt you'd watched him *not buy* the day before. From there, you started to wonder how a part-time Walmart employee—one responsible for keeping his mother fed and housed—could afford to randomly and regularly present his friends with the exact items he'd watched *them* pining over.

Sofia, in particular, responded with visible anxiety whenever Nick gifted her something she'd just been eyeing. But our family's budget was comparable to the Colasantis', and I probably would've felt *more* guilty if Nick had actually spent money on the baby-duck phone case I was now using.

As I pedaled and Droog bounded along beside me, I checked the time on my phone. Two minutes until midnight.

We sped up the access road, and at the top, I hopped off my bike and walked it, Droog and I making our way through the bleached rock to the tracks.

That first summer after the accident, when Remy and I were thirteen and twelve respectively, we'd met here a lot. He wasn't a good sleeper, due to his nightmares, and the sheriff took his phone every night so he wouldn't just stay up playing on it.

But Remy and I had found a way around this: We'd invested his lawn-mowing money in a pair of a five-mile walkie-talkies that could just barely reach between our houses. We'd turn them on every night at eleven, just in case one of us had something to "report," but really, we coordinated meet-ups at the train tracks for no real reason except Remy wanting to avoid his nightmares and me wanting the rush I got from leaving my house without anyone knowing. It made me feel capable and independent, like I could manage the world on my own, without worrying my parents, who were busy with their own troubles.

Tonight, I'd figured Droog and I would have to follow the tracks halfway to Remy's house, but he was right inside the tree line, sitting on the propane tank.

He hopped off it and came toward us, ignoring Droog's excited snuffling, to pull me into a rough hug for a few seconds. The soft scent of grass, sweat, and bonfire hung around his denim jacket, weeks of skateboarding and filming and nights around the fire pit distilled into the smell that would always mean Remy Nakamura to me.

It still caught me off guard whenever he or Levi hugged me. Even before the accident, my family had never been very physically affectionate, but the Lindquist-Nakamura clan were big on hugging hello and goodbye. It took a couple of years of seeing each other multiple times each day for Remy's and Levi's habit to fade. Now their tight embraces were saved for special occasions.

Like seeing each other for the first time after a possible near-death experience.

The white rushes into me, cold and—

"How did the interrogation go?" Remy asked, releasing me. "My dad wouldn't tell me anything."

"It was more weird than anything," I said. "Apparently someone stole the wreckage from the electrical tower. Your dad basically warned us to get rid of it before we get busted."

Remy's brows peaked. "But you didn't take it, right?" Droog nosed his hand, and he began to pet her absently. "Arthur didn't go back for it?"

"He was as surprised as I was to hear it was gone." And twice as intrigued. Ready to follow the missing debris right to the thing from the video. My skin crawled.

Remy's shoulders relaxed. "Good. Your brother needs to stay out of this."

My stomach twisted. Remy didn't know Arthur was absolutely *not* going to stay out of this, because Remy didn't know about the video.

"There's something you need to know. About what happened the other night." Tears sprung into my eyes, not from fear but from the sudden rush of sensation. I jammed my eyes shut.

White light. Voices. Pain that isn't quite pain. It's more like . . . awareness, feeling every fiber of your being existing at once as the cold rushes through it, rattling you.

A gentle touch on my arm brought me barreling back into my body as if I'd been hovering two hundred miles over it and made the journey back in a millisecond. "You remember?" Remy said.

I opened my eyes. His brows were pitched together, his brown eyes narrowed and a worried dimple in his chin. "I'm so glad you remember. God, Franny, I didn't know how I was going to tell you . . ."

I balked. "*You* remember?"

He nodded. "Not all of it, and not all at once, but I think I woke up first—maybe because I was farthest from it. I don't know, but Franny . . ." His voice thickened. "I *saw* what that thing did to you, and I'm—I'm so sorry I couldn't stop it."

"What?" It came out as a whisper. It was hard to hear over the blood rushing through my eardrums, and possibly the crust of the Earth coming apart underfoot. "What it did to me?"

Remy looked stricken. His mouth twisted. His voice was hoarse. "I thought you remembered."

"There's a video," I managed. "Levi got footage before the battery died, and we saw the—the *thing*, made of light, and the way it shocked us. *All of us*," I added, almost defensively.

What it did to you.

Remy's eyes darkened. He turned away from me, gathering himself. I reached for his elbow, and another static shock jolted down my arm.

The white furled across my vision and the not-quite-pain-but-definitely-sensation scorched through my head. As if through glass, I heard Remy swear and jerk away from me, and when the light faded, he was standing a few feet away, breathing hard, gripping his elbow.

His eyes were still fearful and glassy, but somehow unsurprised. "Try to remember, Franny," he begged in that same throaty gravel. "We weren't unconscious, not totally, and if it's all starting to come back to me, it's only a matter of time before the others remember. You need to know what you want to do before that. We need to have a plan."

A knot caught in my throat.

I didn't want to remember.

All I wanted was to forget. If you couldn't control life, you could at least remove yourself from it, never experience its pain too deeply. That was the only way to survive.

But Remy was staring at me, his dark hair fluttering in the breeze, and he was afraid, and I couldn't look away.

"The first blast," he rasped. "When it hit me, it was like . . . like something twice my size was squeezing through me. My whole body wanted to come apart, but that *thing* wouldn't let it."

White light. The afterimage of pain. Cold, invigorating. Like the first crush of the ocean tide on your shins. And all those voices, thousands—no, millions—distilled into something like music, trying to soothe me.

"Relax," they seem to say. "Relax your body."

Remy pushed on through shivers: "On the one hand, it felt like eternity. But on the other, it was over in a second. I couldn't move, or even *think* about moving. It was like I wasn't in my body, or like—the connection between my brain and my body had been unplugged." He ran his hand through his hair. "All I could do was *feel* the light, and if I focused on it, it hurt, but then my mind would start to wander, and there'd be nothing: nothing but white. Like a dream. Or anesthesia, blurring everything out."

My stomach roiled.

Yes, my mind said. *Exactly like that.*

Like those hours had been recorded in our minds in the most jumbled, drunken fashion, and piecing the bits back together would be nearly impossible.

"There's a lot I don't remember until the end." Remy shook his head, trying to choose his next words. "The *being* got fainter with each pulse. Like all that energy that was hitting us was leaching off its body, draining it. But it didn't disappear, Franny. I was conscious enough to see it didn't burn out."

His voice was low and odd. "It started to move. And I promise, Franny, that as soon as I saw where it was going, I woke up." He was talking more quickly now, his words tumbling out, hoarse and wet. "I *promise*, I was trying to get there first, but the blasts kept hitting me, and I couldn't take a single step."

My pulse quickened. The sweat on the back of my neck went cold.

The white light spread out behind my eyes, and nausea rolled through my stomach like laundry caught in a spin cycle.

I knew what he was going to say next.

Maybe I was starting to remember, or maybe my brain had worked out what the worst thing would be—what would scare me to say to Remy more than anything else—and so I knew he was going to say it to *me*.

"It went into you, Franny," Remy choked. "That thing went into you, and that's when it all stopped."

NINE

THE MEMORY FRAGMENTS. THE electric shocks.

The television going staticky?

My phone malfunctioning?

The computer glitching?

I started to pace, like the thing inside me—*THE THING INSIDE ME???*—was a burrito I could walk off. Droog trotted along behind me, crying, agitated.

My stomach twitched. I gasped, bent over by a sudden shot of pain through my ribs. I caught myself against the propane tank, coughing again, dry heaving, like I could vomit the thing up. The ground swayed, and when I looked up, the trees multiplied, drifting apart then back together, hundreds of pendulums swinging in opposite directions.

A numbness spread through me. The woods, the dead grass beyond, my ramshackle brick house spearing the night sky all looked more like a two-dimensional set than an actual place.

This can't be happening, my brain decided, and my body believed it.

I'd felt something similar that day at the hospital, when the doctor had finally come out to the waiting room and pulled us into the hallway where the other families couldn't see.

I hadn't cried, or screamed. Because it couldn't be happening.

And when Mom slumped onto her knees and buried her face in her hands, it should have scared me, shaken me to my core, but that couldn't be happening either.

Remy touched my elbow. "We'll figure it out, Franny. You'll be okay. I won't let you not be."

79

It was so Remy to lie to me like that, to pretend he could protect me. In my mind I heard Arthur giving me the harsh truth: *You need to figure it out. No one else will. You're the only one who will take care of yourself, Franny.*

"We just need some kind of plan," Remy went on. I blinked, trying to make out his face, but the fake world stayed fuzzy and unfocused. "When the others find out, everyone's going to have an opinion, so I need to know, Franny: What do you want to do?"

The others.

Sofía would say I should tell my dad and go to the hospital immediately. Nick would tell me you couldn't trust doctors not to experiment on me, and that meanwhile, all of Splendor would be gossiping about how I thought aliens were trying to communicate with me. Levi would try to convince Remy and Arthur to put off college to focus on the full-length documentary about me for Netflix, and Arthur . . .

Arthur would probably split in half trying to decide whether to buy (or have Nick steal) practical anti-alien gadgets for me or just convince me to help him blow the secrets of Area 51 wide open in spectacular fashion.

As for me, I had no *idea* what to do. I couldn't remember how to breathe. I needed to not think about this.

Arthur's obsession, the sheriff's questions, the missing wreckage (not taken by the alien, not if the alien was in me), and the white light and Cheryl Kelly's red blazer and the video going viral and—

One solid, crystalline thought rose through my mind, like a glowing pin dropped in the middle of an otherwise illegible map.

"The video," I said.

"The video?"

"Levi put it online. It's sort of gone viral."

Remy pulled a face. "Are you kidding? He has to take that down, Fran! What if my dad sees it? Or the St. Jameses, or people from the energy company or—"

"I know," I said. "I'll tell him. But, Remy, someone commented on it and said he'd seen one of those things too. Twenty years ago."

Remy's eyebrows shot up. "Twenty years ago?" Tentative excitement crossed his face. "That's great!"

Great seemed extreme. It was a lead, and not necessarily a good one.

"Twenty years and this guy's still alive," Remy said. "So whatever it did to him, it doesn't sound like it . . . *hurt* him."

He was going to say *killed* and we both knew it. We had no reason to think the thing—if YouTube user CitizenOfTheBlack-Mailbox had even really seen one—hadn't maimed him or made him sick, or even that it *wouldn't* kill him, eventually. We didn't even have a reason to think the thing had entered him, like it had done to me.

But it was a start.

As long as it was real.

"He left an e-mail address," I told Remy. "I'll contact him as soon as I get home."

He nodded. "And what about the others?"

"We don't tell them."

Remy gave me a dubious look.

"Not yet."

Arthur was two weeks out from finally getting out of this town, and already this whole thing was threatening to suck him back in, and Sofía would tell her parents, who would tell *my* dad, who was just about the last person equipped to handle this.

"Just until I figure things out," I said. "I mean, like you said, they might start remembering, but for now there's nothing anyone can do."

Remy grimaced. "You could go to a doctor. You don't need to tell them what happened—just get a physical, and make sure this thing isn't hurting you."

And what if it is? I wanted to say. *You think a dose of penicillin will kill something from another planet?*

But I didn't need to worry Remy more, and I didn't need to think about things I couldn't change, and I didn't need to go to a doctor, for about a million reasons ranging from the fact that we had no insurance and hundreds of thousands of dollars in unpaid bills for Mark's care to the creeping sensation whenever I remembered the comment on Levi's video:

DELETE THIS IMMEDIATELY. THEY ARE WATCHING!

"Fran?" Remy said.

"No doctors yet either."

He studied me for a moment then turned and leaned into the propane tank. I slumped against it too, and Droog sat at our feet, watching shadows dart through the mangy trees that separated the tracks from our field.

We just stood, listening to the conversation of the blissfully untroubled cicadas. They lived, they sang, they died. That was pretty much how it was for us too, so why did it seem so much harder than that?

"You know my problem?" Remy said finally.

"You're tired of being objectified for your beautiful hair?" I said.

Remy set his elbows on the tank and leaned back to smile at me sidelong. "Well, yeah. Just once, I'd like to be objectified for my body. But the other thing is, even though I know better, I just can't stop waiting for things to go back to normal. When I was a kid and my mom died. When the accident happened and my dad got hurt. And now this. It's like I'm always waiting for things to stabilize, but they don't."

I studied him. "You're having them again? The dreams?"

He averted his gaze.

Like all of us, there were things Remy didn't talk about. But that first summer, we'd confided in each other our darkest, most miserable thoughts. We'd sat on these train tracks, though usually farther down, and we'd whispered back and forth, sharing our secrets only once, letting them disappear as soon as they were said, never to be spoken of again.

My mom can't look at me, I told him.

I don't remember my mother's voice, Remy whispered.

My dad doesn't sleep anymore.

Sometimes I wake up screaming. I see the accident. I see the beam fall on my dad's leg.

Once, only once, I whispered, so quietly the words cut in and out: *If it had been me, I don't think she would have left them.*

Every time my dad goes to work, Remy whispered back, *I think he's going to die.*

The nightmares had started when Remy was six, after his mom's aneurysm. Sometimes he dreamt about her ghost. Other times, he dreamt she was alive, and when he remembered she wasn't, her skin withered, leaving behind her skeleton. He dreamt she had fallen off a cliff and was trying to hold on, begging him to save her. He'd wake up screaming, soaked in sweat.

His dad took him to therapy. For a few years, the dreams backed off. Then came the accident.

The sheriff had been doling out speeding tickets and traffic violations at another Splendor two-way-stop-turned-death-trap up the road from the mill when he got the call.

He'd been the first one on the scene, before paramedics and fire trucks.

He'd seen the smoke and the ash and heard the screams, and he hadn't had any backup or even a fire extinguisher.

He'd had nothing, and he'd run into the building. A beam had collapsed on his leg, broke it in three places, and burned his skin badly.

After a year of physical therapy, he could jog, but with horrible pain. Another one of Remy's whispered secrets: the box of prescription painkillers he'd found in the lockbox under the sheriff's bed.

That his dad, who'd once loved a gin martini, had cut out alcohol to counterbalance the damage all those meds would do to his organs.

It was one of the angry embers burning in my gut, that in real life that was what being a hero looked like. That every day, Sheriff Nakamura woke with pain in his leg and an itch behind his teeth and a whole lot of people he'd loved and lost, not to mention a son who screamed himself awake.

That Remy was too brave or selfless to ask his dad to quit, and instead spent his life waiting for the world to try to take something else from him, even while promising his friends the impossible, that he would protect them.

Sometimes the anger was too much. Sometimes I thought that if you peeled back my skin, that would be all that was there: a burning red hate for this world and what it did to people callously, every second, every day.

Remy hadn't mentioned the dreams in easily two years.

The crash was doing the same thing to him that it was doing to me: dredging up everything we'd finally found hidden shelves for.

"Your dad's okay," I said, touching his hand on the tank. "He's safe. This isn't going to hurt him."

Remy scrunched his eyes shut and threaded his fingers through mine. When he opened his eyes again, I could tell how little he'd slept. There were bags under his eyes, and his left eyelid twitched.

"They're different this time," he murmured. "The dreams."

"Different?"

"More . . . *real*, I guess." He shook his head. "I'm even seeing them when I'm awake. Whenever I zone out it's like . . . God, I'm sorry. It's stupid for me to even complain about this."

"Remy." I squeezed his hand. I didn't know how to comfort him. It wasn't something I did, for anyone. I wished I could be more like him, make promises and believe I could keep them.

His dark eyes lifted to mine.

"The stress is messing with all of us," I said. "No one's sleeping well. Levi got this Gary Busey–shaped bruise sleepwalking, and last time I saw Nick, he was practically raving about a tunnel of pianos."

The corner of Remy's mouth ticked into a faint smile. "Normal."

"Exceptionally."

He let out a breath and pushed off the propane tank, releasing my hand. "You're right. I'm sure it's stress, but everything's going to be all right. I need to just chill." He glanced up the tracks. "I should get back. If my dad realizes I'm gone, he'll probably go straight for an arrest this time. You're sure you're okay? I mean, as much as you can be?"

I nodded, perhaps too emphatically. "I'll e-mail that guy and figure this out."

Remy pulled me into another tight hug, and I closed my eyes and sank into it. Who knew the next time I would get to hug him, or anyone? Probably not until Splendor's next natural disaster. I should savor this while I could.

85

"You still have your walkie-talkie?" Remy mumbled into my head. I nodded, and he stepped back. "Let me know what you find out. Actually, just keep me posted in general. I mean it, Fran. Please."

I smiled weakly. "Sure."

"I love you, you know," he said.

My heart leapt.

Arthur and I didn't even say that to each other, but just as with their hugging, Remy and Levi tossed the phrase around like it was free candy in a parade. Often when it landed, it felt more like a grenade than a miniature Snickers.

Explosive, dangerous, overwhelming.

I also craved it, wanted to hear it again as soon as it faded, wished I knew how to pick it apart so I could understand what it meant.

I never knew what to say back. Of course I loved Remy. Sometimes I even wondered if I was *in love* with him, or if there was even a difference. Sometimes I thought he wondered too, but not enough to interfere with his revolving door of short-term relationships with the girls the rest of us never met, except in the school hallways.

Either way, whether I just loved Remy or I love-loved him, opening yourself up like that backfired.

I'd learned from the accident that people, even the ones you love, are temporary.

Case in point: In two weeks, the two people I'd let the deepest into my life would be leaving Splendor.

"You too," I finally said.

Remy smiled and rolled his eyes, gave Droog one last ruffle of the ears. "I know." Then he grabbed his bike and turned back down the tracks.

I wanted to pretend it was any other sticky August night,

that we'd met here for the rush of sneaking out and nothing had happened in that field on Jenkins Lane.

But before I could do that, I had to e-mail CitizenOfThe-BlackMailbox and figure out how to get rid of this . . . this—I couldn't finish the thought; if I did, I'd panic.

I climbed onto my bike and pedaled back to the house, already drafting my e-mail to CitizenOfTheBlackMailbox in my head.

As soon as we hit the clearing, Droog started straining again. I barely managed to make it to the shed without her pulling me off my bike, and as soon as I disembarked, she jerked her leash free and took off full tilt back toward the fence.

Shit.

I flicked the bike's headlight off and ran after her, hissing as quietly yet forcefully as I could, "Droog! Get back here!"

She was old, starting to go blind. I hadn't seen her run like she was *chasing* something in years, and my stomach twisted as I watched her cut through the grass toward the barbed wire fence separating our property from *his.*

Droog was too fast—I wasn't going to catch up to her—but my eyes latched on to the tail end of her blue leash, and I had to act fast.

I dove onto it, stomach smacking the ground, hands grappling for the fraying rope. I hauled her back as I got to my feet, but she kept pulling and crying, desperate to get to whatever she'd seen.

And then I felt the crawling on my neck, that *watched* prickling, and I knew what she was looking at.

Even after all this time, I still responded to the sight of him with needling dread, with hot cheeks and itchy skin.

The hermit stood at the edge of the woods, just inside his fence. He looked exactly how he always did: tall and wide shouldered, scraggly gray hair that tangled around his neck and a night-shrouded face like a skull with weathered, leathery skin stretched tight over it. Even his teeth, long and gapped, unsettled me, and if all that weren't enough, he was wearing his trademark denim overalls, like he was some kind of 1930s ax murderer—a look the most brazen, irreverent kids at Splendor High had been known to replicate for Halloween.

His eyes were the worst part. Cold and dead in a way that made me feel skinned alive as he looked at me through the deepest part of the night.

There was a rumor he only left his house after midnight. There were a *lot* of rumors about him, and having lived an acre from him for the past five years, I could confirm a lot of them.

He *did* only come out after dark, to walk the length of the fence, or rumble off in his too-loud truck down the access road, long after most places in Splendor had closed their doors for the night.

Art loved to flip him off, which made me nervous, given that the man carried a gun at all times and had posted handwritten signs up and down the fence promising he'd use it on trespassers.

That was one of the rumors too: Kids at school, the popular ones especially, had braggy stories about sneaking onto his property and being chased away with gunfire. They whispered about finding human hair in the grass, and dried blood on trees. They said he was a cannibal, that he was supreme priest in a blood cult of one, that he hung dead rabbits on posts to worship the devil or maybe just to scare people off.

And outlandish rumors aside, everyone knew he'd been the one who assaulted Eric Palladin at the Drink Inn and broke his collarbone, even if Eric's family hadn't pressed charges because Eric would've gotten busted for the fake IDs he'd been selling out of his old Volkswagen bus.

The man was a blight no one liked to think of, and even if none of the rumors were true, my blood still would have gone cold at the sight of him there, too close, too dead-eyed.

Because this man, whose name was a curse I'd never spoken aloud, was a murderer.

Wayne Hastings.

The man who'd destroyed this town once, and even now, five years later, haunted it with a hateful vengeance.

The man who'd caused the accident.

He jogged his rifle against his shoulder like some soldier on the front lines, and I dragged Droog backward a few feet, then turned and ran in through the back door as fast as I could, as if I could escape him, as if I could escape everything that had happened since the day he'd ruined my life. I didn't even slow when the doorknob sent a shock through me.

TEN

MOM CAME FOR US at school. Dad was already at the hospital.

Arthur and I sat in the back seat of the Plymouth Voyager, asking questions she couldn't answer.

What happened?

An accident. That's all I know.

Is he hurt?

That's all I know.

We could have asked what two plus two was. We could have asked anything, but Mom had stopped knowing anything, other than that her oldest son had been in an accident.

He hadn't wanted the job at the steel mill. That was what I kept thinking as we sped through the two-way stops on the country roads surrounding the high school, headed out toward a hospital in the suburbs.

I'd bet anything that was what Mom was thinking too: *Mark hadn't wanted the job.*

He'd wanted to take a year off and paint, build up his portfolio to apply to art schools. He needed something good to make up for his terrible grades. He was as spacey as Arthur or Mom, but had neither Arthur's ability to bullshit his way through presentations and essays nor Mom's interest in academia.

He'd inherited her curiosity and her readiness to daydream, and Dad's gentleness and willingness to talk to just about anyone, but his artistic ability was his thing. What people talked about when they talked about Mark.

Mom had begged Dad to let Mark take a gap year, out of

school and without a job. She'd spent four years hearing from his art teachers that he *really had something*, getting pamphlets to expensive art schools sent home with notes that Mom and Dad *should really consider investing in his future*, and sometimes even e-mails from the teachers at those fancy art boarding schools, working artists who'd seen my brother's work in nationwide competitions and wanted to recruit him.

Maybe Mom wanted to make up for what they couldn't afford to give Mark, or maybe she wanted to make up for everything she'd given up herself to raise her family.

She'd been pining for grad school and a NASA job when Mark came along, and so had settled for community college and a research-and-development job at a shampoo factory, and when she told us the story, she made it sound like the world's best trade-off.

But maybe it hadn't been. Maybe she thought that if Mark got to follow his dreams, it would make up for the ones she'd given up.

"Think about it, Robert," she'd begged Dad. "This is his *destiny*. He's already missed out on the camps and the boarding schools and the private lessons. We can at least support him now. We can give him time to focus, to catch up."

"Art school's expensive, Eileen. How's he going to make that dream a reality if he's not willing to do the work?"

Dad knew some guys at the steel mill. Everyone knew some guys at the steel mill. It was almost singlehandedly propping up the Splendor economy.

"Full-time," Dad had said.

"Part-time," Mom had argued.

Mark had stood right there, but he hadn't said anything, just let them wear themselves out. He hated being in the middle of disagreements. Whenever Arthur wouldn't give me a turn at *Mario*

Kart, Mark would just hand his controller over to me and leave the room, much to Arthur's chagrin.

When I was angry, I buried it deep. When Arthur was angry, he'd let it snap out of him like a bear trap. But when Mark was angry, he closed his eyes and thought through it.

While Arthur and I were listening in to Mom and Dad's argument from the staircase, we could see Mark doing just that.

Finally, he opened his eyes and said, "It could be cool. Working at the mill could be cool. It's good pay, and I bet they'd let me take some scrap metal home."

Dad had stared back at him, not understanding what could be cool about taking home scrap metal.

"For sculptures," Mark had explained.

Mom's wide eyes had gone even wider, mirroring Mark's curiosity right back at him. She turned it over. She nodded. "I suppose so."

By then Mark was distracted, staring out the window at something we couldn't see.

He always saw things that Arthur and I didn't. Around that time, he'd been obsessed with Fibonacci spirals, a mathematical concept he'd tried to explain to me for easily two hours.

I was more for climbing trees and tromping through creek beds than studying either one through a microscope and then turning them into paintings, but I loved the way he'd explain something over and over again without any sign of impatience, and I loved watching him look out the window and wondering what magical thing he saw.

Two days after his conversation with Mom and Dad, he'd started the job.

And for nearly a year, life went on pretty much how it always had.

We ate breakfast around the table in the kitchen. We fought over controllers and fell asleep on the floor watching movies with Mom and Dad. Talked about our Halloween costumes too early, and went to church on Easter, and chased Droog around the yard. Looked through Mom's telescope while she explained the Milky Way and the Zeta Reticuli and spiral galaxies, which were, Mark informed us, Fibonacci spirals. Gave up on the exorbitant Halloween costumes and trick-or-treated as ghosts instead, though even *I* was really too old for it.

And most days Mark came home from work tired and too dirty for his taste; Arthur and I came home from school tired and too clean for ours. We spent our weekends stomping through woods and picking ticks off our scalps while he spent his with sketches and blueprints spread across the table, planning what he'd build when his co-worker finished teaching him to weld. Mom and Dad laughed in the kitchen. We argued. We kicked each other. Arthur spat on my face. Droog knocked things off the coffee table and Mom groaned and told her she was a very bad girl, and Mark scratched behind her ears and whispered, *It's okay, Droopy-Baby. We all mess up.* And Mom kissed us good night, and said *I love you* from the hallway just before she turned off the light, and Dad badly sang a few bars of Carole King's "Way Over Yonder."

And if I'd thought about it in those months, I would've guessed life would always go on this way.

You're born. You sing. You die.

Instead, Mom showed up at the school one day in May.

"Was anyone else hurt?" I asked her from the back seat of the Voyager.

She chewed on her thumbnail as she drove. "That's all I know."

My phone kept freezing and glitching and once even shut itself off, but finally, I made it to TheFallingSkyIncident's page.

Only, when I navigated to the video, a notice popped up: a gradient screen with a red frowny face and the message "This video is no longer available due to a copyright claim."

I checked the URL again, but this was the right link.

How could the video be copyrighted? Levi had taken it two nights ago.

The top comment was still *I want to believe,* but right beneath that, the second highest-voted read, *hey DICKWEEDS the videos gone.*

Painstakingly, I scrolled through the glitching column of comments. People who were excited, people who'd linked to their Tumblr posts "proving this is completely edited garbage." Apparently it had something to do with our shadows being incorrectly cast.

I went farther back, scouring for CitizenOfTheBlackMailbox's comment. Within an hour, I'd reached the beginning without finding it. I started scrolling back the other direction, taking my time.

My anxiety was building, and the staticky energy buzzing around me seemed to worsen. The scrolling went slower and slower until I had to sit back from the screen every few seconds to let the comments resolve in front of me.

After two more hours, I had to face it: The comment was gone. And when I searched for the account that left it, that was gone too.

He'd deleted it. Or someone had deleted it for him.

But why would anyone want the video taken down?

I couldn't think about that right now. The important thing was just to e-mail him. I was pretty sure the address had *BlackMailboxBill* or *Bob* in it, and had involved an acronym for *Citizen of the Black Mailbox. BlackMailboxBillBob@COBM.com* or *BlackMailboxBillBob@COTBM.com.*

In the end, I messaged every possible combination I could think of.

That was all I could do tonight.

As soon as I'd had the thought, the lamp beside my bed flickered then went out: another omen, a warning.

Falling through darkness, total, complete. Cold feathering over me, a million fingers of it.

And then, light!

Shrieking past, thick drops like rain swept up a car window on the highway.

Falling is the sensation, but there is no up or down. There's only an object with so much mass its gravity is pulling me.

A great hand, drawing me toward something velvety and dark, a surface still and glassy as water spread out below—ahead of?—me, and when the screaming bits of light hit, they ripple out, flashing, sparking, and when I'm near enough, the total silence, the cotton-eared absence of sound—wavers.

Like thousands of violin strings played all at once.

But in the same way falling has taken on new meaning, so has sound. It is movement, waves that travel through me, invigorating as the cold.

Not painful. Invigorating.

I reach toward the pool, the mass drawing me in, and when my hand stretches out, I am shocked but not scared to realize I have no body.

I am white light, crackling in every direction, and that is what I feel.

My white light falling toward the still pool.

I know it will be warm before I hit, and when I do, I recognize the trillions of sounds humming through me as if they are old friends.

Here to welcome me, calling me by name,

M—

"Whoa there!" The man on the far side of the counter staggered back as I jolted awake, nearly tumbling from my chair in the process. It took me a few seconds of blinking to piece together who and what *I* was, let alone *where* I was.

Sallow overhead lighting. Twin vending machines full of glossy-wrapped cookies and chips. A mounted TV playing a Reese's commercial.

The man on the other side of the counter held his YMCA card out. "Didn't mean to wake you!" He patted the counter. "It's summer. You kids aren't supposed to be tired. Summer's when you should be sleeping in."

I looked between him and the YMCA-emblazoned polo I was wearing. If this random man thought I should be using my summers to sleep in, maybe he'd like to cut me a check. While he was at it, he could handle the minor issue of my alien possession.

I checked his card, handed it back.

He stared at the yellow rubber gloves I was wearing. I'd gotten them out of the supply closet in the hopes they'd impede my electrical charge while I researched light-discs and incessantly checked for a reply from Black Mailbox Bill. It had worked out kind of perfectly: the cheapo rubber composite was strong enough to dull my effect on the phone but weak enough for my electrical charge to still trigger the touch screen. As far as my phone keyboard was concerned, I was basically a normal human again. The gloves had helped; the searches themselves, not so much.

"Thanks, honey," the man finally said, tearing his gaze from the gloves.

"No problem, scout," I said.

He hesitated, visibly confused, then started down the hall. I turned my focus back to the half dozen Wikipedia pages I had open.

Perseids: the late-summer meteor shower of debris from the Comet Swift-Tuttle that orbited the Earth yearly.

Black Mailbox: a (white) mailbox on Nevada State Route 375 that supposedly marked some kind of hotbed of UFO activity.

MUFON (Mutual UFO Network): a UFO-investigating non-profit, one of the biggest in the U.S.

I'd stumbled across plenty of UFO enthusiasts, proclaimed experts, skeptics, and devotees, but I hadn't found a single account of an experience like the one we'd had.

"I'm here at the Crane Energy electrical substation on Jenkins Lane," came a familiar voice, and I looked up to find Cheryl Kelly on TV, in a black blazer and red silk shirt with an enormous bow at the throat. "Where an investigation into the source of some strange burns in the surrounding field has yielded more questions than answers!

"Sources report that though a private crew has excavated upwards of seven feet in some places, officials still have no leads on who—or what—might have caused the burns. And in another new—and *bizarre*—twist, police are now reporting that several pieces of machinery damaged in the initial incident have mysteriously vanished. The Sheriff's Department is asking for anyone with any leads on the missing equipment to please come forward. In the meantime, the search for answers appears to have stalled. I'm Cheryl Kelly, with Channel 11 News."

My phone buzzed with a message, and my heart palpitated as I registered the e-mail alert onscreen.

It took a few seconds to get the message open, and Bill's reply was shorter than I'd hoped for. I made up for that by reading it six times in a row.

> *Hello, friend.*
> *Thank you for getting in touch. You did the right thing. Have you told anyone else what you witnessed? I must advise against*

it. Having been where you are, I hope you'll trust me on this. Take the video down too. If they haven't already seen it, you'll be OK. But if they have or do, you'll need to take extra precautions.

I know what is happening to you, because it all happened to me too: the scars, the energy, the strange images in your head and impulses to do things that are utterly unfamiliar to you— commands, as it were, from the presence you are hosting. There's so much more I should tell you, but this is not the venue. The important thing is, I can help you before it's too late.

I believe you are in Ohio (that is what the networks I am involved in are saying after some sleuthing related to your video; try not to be alarmed, but that IS how simple it would be for the wrong party to find you, and is thus why you MUST COVER YOUR TRACKS).

I am in Nevada. Have checked flights and can arrive in any of the major cities near you by 1 PM. Please let me know what time you can meet. Again, it is ABSOLUTELY ESSENTIAL you tell no one about what you've experienced. NOT EVEN— PERHAPS ESPECIALLY—those you are closest to. All that you share with them will put them in greater danger with those who might wish to find you.

You must DESTROY any evidence you were involved in what that video depicts. If police find so much as a hair of yours near that location, you could be in grave danger.

My intention is not to scare you—you've experienced a beautiful thing, an encounter you will treasure for the rest of your life—but people in our situation have a habit of vanishing without a trace.

I am offering you help at great personal risk, so PLEASE be cautious with what I've told you. Again, share with NO

ONE—not even family—what we've talked about, and waste no time in erasing your tracks.

Stay safe.
Bill

My mouth had gone dry. My throat felt tight. There was no definite proof. This man could still be a conspiracy theorist, someone who wore tinfoil hats and believed the senators were all reptilian shape-shifters.

The scars, the energy, the strange images in your head and impulses to do things that are utterly unfamiliar to you—commands, as it were, from the presence you are hosting.

He knew *exactly* what had been happening to me.

Minus the impulses. I hadn't had any of those.

Yet.

I braced myself against the desk, waiting for the dizziness to pass. The white was tugging at my mind, trying to pull me back, but I sank my fingernails into the gloves, rooting myself in the present.

I flinched at the sudden vibration against the counter and swiped up my phone, expecting to find another e-mail. Instead there was a barrage of incoming texts.

It took me a second to parse out where they were coming from.

I had an individual message with each of the five other Ordinary regulars, along with various group texts. One with just Remy and Sofía. One with just Remy and Levi. One with Nick and Arthur.

That made communicating (while wearing rubber gloves) tricky enough, and then there was the fact that everyone—Nick and Levi especially—was constantly renaming the group messages, making them especially hard to track. The new messages mostly seemed to be coming into a conversation named "Big Old Scientist Brians" that hadn't existed at the start of my shift.

I would've bet money if I went far enough back there'd be an autocorrect typo where someone had been trying to type the word "brain" and wound up with "Brian" instead.

I checked the members of Big Old Scientist Brians. All six of us. The last three messages came from Arthur.

Did you see the Cheryl Kelly report?

Things winding down at Jenkins.

It's time to find the wreckage. Tonight. 8:30 PM, our house.

As I was reading, Sofía's reply came in: *About the wreckage. I have an idea, but we'll need compasses.*

Levi's buzzed in next. *Handsome R's still grounded, but I'll be there. (You guys should sleep over after.)*

And then came Nick's one-word answer to all of it: *No.*

I didn't blame him. I didn't want to go back either.

Levi sent him a bunch of crying faces mixed in with kissy faces.

No, Nick said again.

Fine, Arthur said. *Fran?*

My stomach churned.

I'm in, I typed. I didn't know what I was going to say or do about Black Mailbox Bill's e-mail just yet—I hadn't given him my name or even used my real e-mail account to contact him, and I sure as hell wasn't inviting him to Splendor—but until I figured out whether I could trust him enough to ask more specific questions, I needed to focus on finding that necklace and anything else I might've left behind. Before it was too late.

ELEVEN

"MAGNETISM," SOFÍA SAID.

"Magnetism," Levi repeated eagerly. He was dressed in all yellow and looked like a giant banana.

"Compasses are powered by magnetism," Sofía said. She, Levi, Arthur, and I were standing astride our bikes in a square, front tires pointed in. I'd intentionally put my back to the barbed wire fence at the back of our field.

The sun wouldn't set for another fifteen minutes, so *he* wouldn't be out for hours, but Droog had tried to bolt onto the hermit's property again when I took her out after work, and I'd been paranoid he might appear ever since.

"It's magnetism that makes a compass's needle point to the North Pole," Sofía explained. "Only, *sometimes*, when lightning strikes, it can magnetize the rocks or soil or metal it hits. If any of that light struck the debris, it *might* work the same way. But we'll have to get pretty close to the wreckage before the compass's magnet could respond. Otherwise it'll just pick up the Earth's magnetic field and point north."

"What if it wasn't the same thing as lightning?" I asked.

Sofia frowned. "Maybe it will have the same effect? Or maybe nothing."

"Just keep your eyes open," Arthur said impatiently. "Watch for burns, or anything suspicious, and we'll find the wreckage, whether the compasses work or not."

He pulled the Walmart bag off his handlebars and fished out a compass, handing it to Sofía, who seemed uncertain. "Did Nick . . . *get these* for us?"

"He's trying to pull his weight in his own way," Arthur said, as if we were some kind of military outfit. Sofía took the stolen compass between two fingers, like it was covered in toxic waste, and Arthur went on. "We'll go the long way, through the woods behind the Jenkins House. That way we can make sure there's no one around the power plant or the field before we spread out."

Art handed a compass to Levi, then pulled one out for me. My chest tightened. My mouth went dry.

What if the needle starts to spin now?

What if I'm *magnetized by the thing in me?*

Black Mailbox Bill's warnings sizzled through my mind. I reached out fast, bumping Arthur's arm so hard the compass went flying.

"Jeez!" he yelped.

"Sorry!" I hopped off my bike and discreetly checked the compass before picking it up.

Thank God.

It wasn't spinning. Whatever else that thing had done to me, apparently it hadn't turned me into an outright magnet.

"Be more careful with any evidence you find," Arthur said, and kicked off as I boarded my bike again.

The sun had set by the time we reached the back of the Jenkins House, but I left the headlight off as we edged around the siding.

Temporary floodlights had been erected in a rectangle around the substation's fence, washing the deep blues and greens from the night. A truck was parked on the gravel road, but there was no one in the cab, and the same went for the scuffed yellow Bobcats in the field to the left of the substation.

"No people," Sofía whispered. "But there might be security cameras."

"Stick to the shadows," Arthur commanded. "And if you find anything, don't get too close until the rest of us can join you." He stood on his pedals and cruised down the slight hill, cutting a wide arc around the illuminated portion of road.

"Where should we look first?" Levi asked.

"The point was to split up," Sofía said, and took off in the opposite direction from Arthur.

"Looks like it's just us. Team Franvi. LeFra?"

I was dreading going into the house alone, but I really didn't need an audience for this. "I was going to look around inside," I said. "You should check the woods behind the house."

Levi huffed. "Bunch of lone wolves." He rode into the patch of woods where I'd found the bullets, and I left my bike against the house and headed for the axed front door.

I glanced over my shoulder to be sure the others were out of sight, then took out my flashlight and bushwhacked the darkness back as I scoured the shaggy grass for my necklace.

The pendant was a real nautilus shell. Mark had carefully sawed it open to reveal the many chambers within, arranged in their delicate spiral. He'd coated the whole thing in resin to protect it, then drilled a hole for the chain.

It was the shell that had started his whole obsession. He'd found it on the beach, on a family vacation when I was ten, Arthur was eleven, and Mark was sixteen.

"Do you know why logarithmic spirals matter?" he'd asked us.

We didn't even know what logarithmic spirals were.

"They're everywhere," Mark told us. "In pinecones and sun-flower seedheads and hurricanes—even the way a hawk will approach its prey, if the prey's running in a straight line. It's a spiral where every turn gets bigger by the exact factor it takes to keep the spiral the same shape. It's growing, fast, with each turn, but it's still staying the same. Isn't that amazing?"

"If by *amazing* you mean *boring*," Arthur had said.

Mark had ignored the comment, or maybe he'd been so excited he didn't notice the sand Arthur was flinging at him in an attempt to get him to play some rough-and-tumble game. Mom had looked up from the scientific journal she was reading and laughed. "How could the building blocks of all creation be boring to a child of mine, Arthur?"

Dad had ruffled Arthur's sun-streaked hair. "Add enough math talk to *anything*, and you can take the joy out of it, right, Art?"

"Even the galaxy, the whole Milky Way is a logarithmic spiral," Mark had forged on. "And there are always black holes in the middle of spiral galaxies, but there's a huge city of them at the center of ours! Every one of those black holes came from a dying star—or a cluster of them. As the star loses fuel, it and its temperature change, its internal pressure can no longer resist the star's *own* gravity. The whole star collapses, gets pressed into this *tiny* thing, smaller than an atom, but still with *all* the mass of the giant star. With all that gravitational force now fixed to this *tiny* point."

Something about the description had made me feel vaguely sick. "Stars can collapse?"

I'd looked out across the water, the sand, the whole wild world I loved.

What would happen to all of it, to us, if the sun collapsed? It'd turn into a black hole. It'd suck us into itself and end the world.

"Listen, Franny." Mark turned the shell like it was a Ferris wheel. "All those stars, hundreds or maybe millions, *had* to collapse to make our galaxy what it is."

He lifted the shell to my eye. "It's like this giant manual, telling everything in our universe and beyond how it should work, down to the smallest thing. Isn't that cool? Doesn't that make you feel like you're part of some huge design?"

"Like a huge, boring quilt!" Arthur said.

Mom had sighed; Dad had laughed; Mark had said, "You little butthole!" and thrown a handful of sand at him; and my anxiety about the Inevitable End of All Things had frittered off.

I'd felt, right then, like the universe was in perfect order. Like I was a small part of a huge and meaningful design.

I stepped through the blood-red front door to the Jenkins House, emerging from the memory.

It had been so long since I'd thought about all that. Since I'd thought about Mark, period. Dad still visited him in the hospital every two weeks, and I went along every three visits like clockwork (Art had long since quit), but even when I was there, or when I clutched the necklace for good luck, I didn't think about it.

The accident.

The months after it.

Standing on the balcony outside the master bedroom with Arthur, next to the telescope Mom had once loved, watching her pull away in the Voyager—*just for a few weeks, to clear her head.* Me waving until Arthur snatched my hand and threw it down to my side, snapping, *Don't do that. She's not going to look back, and you'll feel stupid. Don't let her make you feel stupid.*

The pounding that rose from the wall of my brothers' bedroom whenever Dad was out, Arthur's hands barreling into drywall until his knuckles busted open, Mark's old Mucha print hung back up over the holes afterward so no one would ever know he'd put them there.

Sure, I used to feel like I was part of some huge design. That the world, and everything else that existed, was part of one seamless machine.

It was what Mom and Dad had taught us. Dad called the machine's engineer *Holy God* and Mom called it *Good and Miraculous Science*, and as for us kids, we were allowed to call it whatever we wanted as long as our butts were in the folding chairs at Old Crow Christian Fellowship on Sunday mornings, supporting Dad.

Before the accident, Dad having married a "nonbeliever" might've been the biggest scandal Splendor had ever seen. A pastor and a wannabe-astronaut agnostic/atheist.

Most of the church didn't approve, but they liked Dad enough to ignore Mom's absence from prayer meetings and potlucks.

To my brothers and me, there was nothing weird about Mom and Dad's different beliefs, and if it was ever an issue between them before the accident, I didn't know.

Mom could be impulsive and restless like Arthur, insatiably curious like Mark. If you asked her about something she was excited about, she'd trip over the words, trying to get them out fast enough. She told stories out of order, always jumping backward to add bits of information she'd left out, and she was always gasping: when she saw her first lightning bug of the year, when she crossed paths with a rare bird, when she was reading articles in scientific journals, like surprising information had sneaked up on her and jumped out, screaming.

Like both my brothers, she was easily distracted; like Arthur, she was messy, impatient.

When Dad made dinner, the table was set and the serving dishes were loaded by the time the turkey was cooked and the noodles finished boiling, but when Mom cooked, pans caught on fire while she was busy reading about penguin mating habits on her phone.

Together, Mom and Mark formed a kind of feedback loop. She'd tell him about a new purpose just discovered for a specific organ in the human body. He'd tell her about a new artist using fingernail clippings in an interesting way. Tangents abounded.

The only way I knew to break her out of it was to put on Carole

King. Then she'd grab my hands and spin me barefoot through the kitchen, singing, "Way over yonder . . . is a place that I know . . ."

She was still distracted from the task at hand, but in those moments, Mom was mine.

In the rest, she lived in a bubble I couldn't quite permeate, and I sat outside, watching Mark move freely through it from the other side.

"They could shoot off into space and it'd be hours of them waxing poetic about the change in atmosphere before they even realized the ground was gone," Dad used to say.

He was milder, calmer, the type to take a few seconds to think over his words before speaking them, sometimes so long you'd doubt he planned to answer.

Once I'd asked him the question the church busybodies so badly wanted answered. One night on the balcony, while Mom was taking Droog out to pee one last time before bed.

"Doesn't it bother you?" I said. "That she doesn't believe?"

Dad leaned against the wooden railing to stare down at Mom's yellow hair whipping around in the night wind for so long I wasn't sure he'd heard me.

"Everyone's got to have faith in something, Franny," he said finally. "No one knows all the answers to the universe's questions, but I admire anyone who keeps looking up at the stars and asking them questions."

They both believed in the seamless machine.

That a zillion pieces fit together to make something miraculous.

A beautifully ordered universe, where if you talked to the stars, they listened. Where things happened for a reason, be it the design of Holy God or Good and Miraculous Science. Something out there had a handle on this flimsy universe.

When the accident happened, it was like a loose bolt had

slipped off and gotten caught in the universe's cogs. One tiny piece had broken it all. That was what I'd thought.

Now I understood it had never worked to begin with.

Things happened. Random, horrible things no itty-bitty human could protect another itty-bitty human from. The machine was a black hole, a cold, lightless thing.

It did not have nerves or blood-filled veins.

It was not made for itty-bitty, ooey-gooey humans, and it did not care what became of us.

It was a disinterested force, a mass's gravity pulling us toward its center, the point where all things ended.

The only thing you could do was to try not to stare at it as it pulled you closer.

I pushed the thoughts away, buried them in a box with that fierce white light.

I needed to find that fucking necklace and get out of here, forget all this.

My flashlight caught the HAPPY BIRTHDAY banner, the fake blood, the fireplace where Arthur had directed Levi to arrange the fake bones.

I paced back and forth, checking among the glass shards and cigarette butts for the shell, then went upstairs. My stomach tightened as I followed the hall to the bedroom where we'd watched the light fall from the sky.

Focus.

I swept the flashlight across the room.

Nothing.

We hadn't gone into any of the other rooms—the meteor shower had distracted us. Which meant the shell necklace could only be by the fence or *inside* the substation. I turned back into the hall and headed for the stairs.

In the dark room at the end of the hall, something clattered.

Cold dread knifed through my middle. I froze, the flashlight beam shivering on the floor, my lungs pausing mid breath.

My body went rigid and still, but my heart thrummed at hummingbird speed.

The house was horror-film silent. I must have imagined the clatter. I was alone.

Or I'm not.

Or someone was in the room beyond the stairs, holding a chain with a blue-gray nautilus shell on its end.

My skin went cold. Why did I literally never carry the Mace Arthur gave me?

Defiance, an irritating voice answered me. *To prove you don't need his help.*

I didn't. Because I was alone. I'd imagined the sound.

I took another step. The floor creaked. The light in the hallway flickered on and off.

My heart leapt into the tight tunnel of my throat.

Had I imagined *that*?

This house couldn't have electricity, after all these years abandoned. My eardrums pounded with my pulse as I waited, breath held, eyes fixed to the dark floor.

Light flickered once more across the floorboards, and a low hum buzzed directly over my head.

Slowly, I lifted my gaze. The frosted glass dome mounted to the ceiling flickered again, faster, brighter, denting the pitch-black of the hallway. My hair lifted out from my head and my skin prickled, and all was quiet except that intermittent buzz.

And then the sound of movement rose from the room again.

Something was definitely here with me.

Remy was wrong. The thing wasn't *in me.*

Or maybe there were more.

I tightened my grip on the flashlight, like I could bludgeon whatever came running out at me with this half pound of plastic, and slowly, careful not to make a sound, I reached into my pocket for my phone.

The screen fuzzed. The overhead lights flickered faster, as if in response. The thing inside the room moved closer to the doorway, and the light went wild.

I stood there, alone, waiting for it.

TWELVE

ON THREE I WAS going to run.

Through the flashing lights, the buzz of current surging through the house.

I wouldn't look back. I'd get as far away as possible, then call the others, warn them not to go near the house.

Except then Arthur would beeline for it. So maybe not.

One.

More thunking movement. Clumsy, belabored.

Two.

I braced myself.

Three!

I sprinted for the stairs just as the thing came flying out of the room, the lights flaring so bright the hall washed white. Overhead, the bulb exploded, glass shattering, the light winking out.

I screamed and smacked into the wall as a mottle of colorful dots spun across my vision, superimposed over the sudden darkness. I swung the flashlight defensively, and the thin beam of light struck my shrieking attacker and its wild black eyes.

"Raccoon," I gasped, clutching for the missing necklace as the animal barreled back the way it had come, striped tail bobbing.

Just a raccoon.

My heart slowed. I caught my breath, shone the flashlight on the floor, searching for shattered glass.

The frosted glass dome had caught the pieces of the bulb when it exploded.

The bulb.

If the thing in that room hadn't caused that power surge, then what had?

Me? I thought.

The thing in *me?*

The hall rocked. I closed my eyes until the feeling passed. I couldn't think about this right now. I needed to get down to the fence and find the necklace. That was the only thing I had control over.

After that, I'd get more information from Black Mailbox Bill. I'd figure out how to . . . *fix* this.

I went to the top of the stairs and peeked through the doorway the terrified raccoon had darted into.

It was a kid's room, complete with unicorn wallpaper that had been peeled down, words scrawled in red on the blank space left behind. On the far wall stood a baby-blue wooden vanity with a warped mirror, beside a twin bed whose blankets had been thrashed, its pillows bleeding feathers across them and onto the floor.

Through a skinny doorway on the far side of the room, there was a pink-tiled bathroom, and when my flashlight hit the mirror, the words *BLOODY MARY* lit up in red lipstick on the glass.

I turned away, and my flashlight stumbled over a shattered window. Its gauzy drapes were pulled to one side, dancing in the sticky breeze.

That must've been the raccoon's entry point.

I turned back toward the hall, but the flashlight lit on something else, lacquered and cherry red.

Chills slithered down my spine at the sight of the undersize piano.

The gold catch of the light over the brand etched into the top of it: *Schicksal.*

Nick's voice drifted across my mind: *I dreamed about pianos . . .*

hallways made of them that ended in little red kids' pianos with German words written in freakin' gold leaf.

Schicksal could be German, couldn't it?

My skin had started crawling again, but then the obvious occurred to me: Nick must've caught a glimpse of this the night of the crash. His subconscious wrapped it into a dream.

There was nothing creepy about it.

I set my backpack down and took out one of the rubber gloves I'd borrowed from work, slipped it on, then took a picture on my phone and sent it to Nick.

Then I gathered my stuff and headed back downstairs to search the fence line.

Every ounce of optimism I'd started this night with had turned to lead in my stomach. I couldn't possibly make it to where we'd climbed the fence without walking through the light, possibly in the path of a hidden security camera.

Another one of those power surges would come in handy right now.

There's no way you did that.

I felt stupid, but I tried anyway: I stepped up to the edge of the light coming off the temporary fixtures, held my hands out, and thought as hard as I could about the shattering light bulb in the hallway. About energy and electricity and lightning. I even summoned the memory of the white light.

A dark pool ahead of me. Nothing but solid black, and then suddenly, light on every side of me in shimmering streaks of color and—

I opened my eyes. Nothing. I huffed and dropped my hands. Whatever had happened in the Jenkins House, I wasn't its cause.

At the end of Jenkins Lane, a pair of headlights swung onto the gravel, and within seconds I'd placed the shape crawling down the street as a cop car.

Not only was I out of time to search, but if I didn't hide, I'd also ruin any future chance to get back here and find my necklace.

I darted back to the house and crouched against the side of it with my bike as the car slid to a stop. The door popped open, and the sheriff stepped out, rounding the hood of the cruiser.

He touched the radio clipped to his shirt, and his words reached me in bits. ". . . appears to be empty . . . Sure they said the house on Jenkins Lane? It's dark now."

I looked up the side of the house. Someone must've seen the electrical flare when they were driving past and called it in.

". . . I'll take a look," Sheriff Nakamura said. "Go ahead and send another cruiser for backup, but it was probably unrelated . . . just kids getting into trouble . . ."

He started up the yard, and as my heart rate sped, something happened.

A light flashed in the window directly over me.

The sheriff's chin snapped upward, his gaze locking on to where the light flickered.

Shit.

Was I doing this?

At the end of the street, more headlights appeared, and when the sheriff turned toward them, I took my chance: I ran along the side of the house, dragging my bike and trying for a magical mix of speed and quiet that didn't exist.

Any second, he'd spot me, and if he didn't, he'd *hear* me.

I reached the back of the house and dragged my bike behind it.

"Who's there?" I heard.

I climbed on my bike and took off. Branches whipped my face, caught on my clothes. My front tire jerked and stumbled over roots.

Voices called through the dark behind me, and I risked a glance back. Spears of light crisscrossed the night, interrupted by the slim silhouettes of trees.

At least three officers were spreading out behind the house, following me, calling out words I couldn't hear over my own pulpy pulse.

My front tire slammed into something, hard, and jerked sideways, the bike skidding out from under me. I hit the leaf-strewn ground on my side, my breath and a grunt knocked from my body.

The flashlights snapped toward me. I staggered onto my feet, ankle throbbing where it had hit the ground, and the front tire of my bike bent at an ugly angle.

A rocky outcropping, blue-black and easily ten feet high, cut back through the woods in a mossy zigzag disappearing into a forested hill.

If I'd been looking straight ahead, there was no way I'd have collided with the ridge of stone, even in the near-total darkness.

I tried to climb back onto the bike, but it wasn't rideable, and the echoey shouts were moving closer.

I leaned against the boulder and hobbled around it, hauling the bike along with me.

"This way!" someone shouted, and as she did, I spotted it.

An opening in the rock.

It wasn't just a rocky ridge; it was a wide-mouthed cave, its opening hidden under an outcropping about three feet off the ground. From here I couldn't tell how deep the nook was. It might've been more of a hollow than a cave, but it was low and angled away from the house, and if they walked past it, they'd have to stoop to see me.

It was the best option I had.

I dropped onto my knees and backed into the cave, dragging the bike in on its side after me.

It unnerved me, backing into total darkness, not even trying to see through it, but I couldn't risk a flashlight this close to the opening.

I crawled backward and pulled the bike about three feet before the damp, crumbly leaves lining the stone floor gave way to smooth stone and the metal bike frame scraped loudly against it.

Pulling it any farther would just risk drawing attention. I released the handlebar and leaned against the stone wall on my left, its damp, uneven surface soaking through my sweatshirt to kiss my shoulder blade.

I looked toward the entrance, a barely lighter square of black. If the sheriff stood far enough from the cave mouth and shone his light this way, I'd be in full view.

In the stillness, a steady drip echoed from deep within the stone walls.

Which meant the cave went deeper.

There was nothing I could do about the bike, but maybe if I followed the tunnels, I could find another way out of the cave. I could sneak out, report my bike missing, pretend it was stolen—whatever it took to separate myself from what was happening on Jenkins Lane.

I reached up through the darkness, feeling for stone overhead, but my fingers met nothing but cold, wet air. The ceiling was higher back here.

I pushed myself up from the wet ground, slowly straightening my neck until I felt the cold graze of stone. I ducked again, slid my bare hand along the rock on my right as I moved deeper.

One small step, then two, three. I kept moving.

A few yards in, I paused and listened. The drip had grown louder. I took another few steps. The earthy smell of loam and tangy sulfur hit the back of my nose as the wall led me around a sharp right angle, leaving watery grit behind on my fingertips. Now the drip was nearby, ahead on my left, growing into a soft trickle.

I looked back the way I'd come but couldn't make out the entrance. A few more steps around this corner, and it would be safe to get out my flashlight.

It was cold in here, a true bone-cold, and when the slick ground dipped suddenly, I lost my footing.

For the second time in ten minutes, I hit the ground. I managed to bite back a grunt, but the contents of my hoodie pocket went flying, the *zing* of metal and plastic against rock as my compass and flashlight skated down the sloped ground.

For a beat, I lay frozen where I'd fallen, splayed out on my stomach, listening for voices.

But I was deep enough that the sound of the outside world was cut off; I could only hope the reverse was true.

I pushed myself onto all fours and felt over the ground, the glove on my left hand and the bare fingers of my right splashing through shallow puddles as I crawled. I found my flashlight first. The plastic was cracked but the light came on when I flipped the switch, slicing through the black to catch the copper-streaked rock face across from me and the water trickling down it from a crack above. The ceiling lifted even farther here, and I could stand upright with a yard to spare.

As I hoisted myself to my feet, I trailed the light along the miniature waterfall and found my compass halfway between it and me. My ankle stung as I hobbled over to it, steps echoing off the cavern walls, and bent to grab it.

My yellow-gloved hand froze in front of me. The flashlight cast a glare across the compass's face, but it didn't wash it out entirely: A shock of color was visible beneath the light.

The thin red needle.

It was spinning wildly.

My neck prickled.

I drew my hand back but kept the light trained on the compass, and the spinning didn't slow.

The prickling slithered down to my tailbone as I lifted the flashlight, across the glistening floors, into the dark ahead until it hit the back wall of the cave.

The elongated stalactites pointed accusingly down at the twisted metal stacked in front of it. The tower that the disc had lopped off, the massive steely coil, a loop of cables, a stack of metal beams.

I picked up the compass and moved closer.

The needle accelerated into manic spirals.

Something caught under my boot, and I stopped, dropping my light to it. My skin chilled at the sight of the sleek metal cylinder.

I bent and picked the bullet up between gritty fingers.

Something scuffed heavily behind me, and I spun, flashlight extended protectively and bullet clenched in my other fist.

"Is that the same kind you found the morning after the crash?" came a serious, feminine voice.

Dark green eyes, ringed in white. Long brown hair, wet in spots where the ceiling had dripped, and a fire-truck-red flashlight clutched in one hand.

"Sofia," I gasped. "You scared me."

She tipped her chin toward the bullet, and her mouth shrank. "Is it? Do you think whoever dropped that stole the wreckage and hid it here?"

I looked back at the careful arrangement of debris.

Did this mean someone *had* witnessed the whole thing?

Did someone else see what Remy had? The farmer, St. James? Someone else?

Black Mailbox Bill's warning reverberated through me.

People in our situation have a habit of vanishing without a trace . . . waste no time in erasing your tracks.

But what if someone else had *access* to those tracks?

Someone with enough interest in all of this that he or she had hidden the wreckage here?

"Wait." I turned back to Sofía. "How did you know about the bullet?" She'd been by the car when I found that first one, and if she'd seen me pick it up, why hadn't she mentioned it? Then again, I'd been so dazed the last few days I'd forgotten to tell the others about the bullet too.

Sofía's mouth opened and closed a few times. "Franny, I think something—"

The sound of more footsteps and voices cut her off, and moments later Levi and Arthur rounded the bend in the tunnel.

Levi's mouth fell open at the sight of the stockpiled debris.

"Shiiiiiiiit," Arthur said, tracing his flashlight over the steel beams. "Way to go, Franny."

I shook my head. "How'd you find me?"

"Sofía texted us," Levi said.

Sofía gave a one-armed shrug. "I saw you go in, but the sheriff was too close for me to follow you right away. Once he'd turned back, I texted the others."

Arthur's mouth screwed up as he studied my hands. "Why are you wearing one rubber glove?"

"Um." I looked down at the practically glow-in-the-dark yellow.

I couldn't tell him. There was nothing he could do about it anyway, and if Black Mailbox Bill was telling the truth, even knowing could put Arthur—all of them—in more danger than we might already be in.

"I was afraid the metal might shock me." It wasn't totally untrue.

Arthur had already lost interest. He was fixated on the bullet now. "What's that?" He plucked it from my hand and held it aloft.

"It's a bullet," Sofía answered.

I glanced at her. Something was still bothering me—her knowing about the bullet, her showing up in the cave.

She continued: "Franny found one just like it when we woke up after the . . . *you know.*"

Was it possible she already *knew* about the cave? That she wasn't looking for me after all, when she found my bike just inside the entrance?

I was being paranoid.

Wasn't I?

"What does it mean?" Levi asked, wide-eyed, as he took the bullet from Arthur's hand. "Our alien has a gun?"

"It means whoever moved this wasn't an alien at all," Sofía replied. "It was someone who saw the whole thing go down and probably figured he could hawk memorabilia of *a close encounter* for way too much money to UFO-weirdos like your YouTube commenters."

Arthur's brow wrinkled. He shook his head and took the bullet back. "No. Something else is going on here, something bigger. I can feel it."

Sofía shot me a knowing look, like, *Oh, he can feel it, right?*

"Besides," Arthur went on, "Sheriff Nakamura told us that whoever took that wreckage did it during another weird power surge that knocked out the fence and the security cameras."

"See, Sof? That's not something your average eBay salesman can do," Levi said.

But if what had happened in the Jenkins House was any indication, it might've been something *I* could do. Or the thing in me, at least.

Only I hadn't, so who had?

"If our alien is capable of all that," Arthur said, half to himself, "why's it carrying around human ammunition?"

Sofía grabbed the bullet and carried it a couple of yards away from us. She held it with her compass in one hand and shone her flashlight on it with the other. "Look, it's magnetized, just like the other stuff. Maybe whoever—"

"*Whatever*," Levi said, right as Arthur blurted, "Our alien!"

"—put it here wasn't the person who dropped it," she finished. "It's just one more piece of evidence they wanted to sell, or maybe hide."

Her gaze cut toward me with a force that made my throat tighten. Was she accusing me? Or confessing?

Had Sofía hidden this stuff? She didn't have a car, but she regularly borrowed her mom's CRV to get to work and lacrosse. Maybe she'd seen the thing go into me too. Maybe she figured it wouldn't end well for us if that information went public, so she'd decided to clean up anything that linked us to what happened.

But moving the wreckage itself seemed too reckless for Sofía, *and* it wouldn't explain what had caused the blackout at the substation.

Probably Sofía was looking for me to back her up on her perfectly reasonable theory.

"That makes sense," I offered.

She looked to the boys to gauge their reaction. Arthur still had his mouth screwed up. "Levi, you've got your camera, right?"

"Of course!" Levi hurried to get it out of his backpack. "You want to get footage of the debris, or the spinning compass? Maybe we should go back and get footage of us 'discovering it.' I should've been filming for that."

"That doesn't matter," Arthur said. "*Contact* is what matters. We need to figure out where our alien went, and what it wants. We'll set the camera up in a tree outside the cave and see if we can catch it coming or going."

Levi gaped at him. "What if it rains?"

Arthur stared back. "I don't think a little rain would stop an alien from coming back to its hideout."

"No, dude," Levi said. "What if it rains on my camera?"

"Then you'll order another one," Arthur said, impatient.

Levi huffed but seemed to have no argument for that.

"The battery will die," Sofía pointed out.

"Levi just charged it." Arthur pocketed the bullet. "It'll get at least a couple of hours. For now, let's head back to our house. Who knows what brought the sheriff out here or when he might be back."

"Right." Sofía looked toward me. "Who knows?"

THIRTEEN

ON OUR WAY OUT of the cave, I searched Sofía's face for signs she knew about the thing in me, but if she did, she was working hard *not* to acknowledge it.

I wanted to ask her if she was keeping a secret, but among the Ordinary, there was so much we didn't talk about that avoiding touchy subjects was second nature. And aside from that, if I asked her if she knew more about all this than she was letting on, she'd probably ask me the same question right back.

Keeping things from each other was easy; outright lying would be harder.

ABSOLUTELY ESSENTIAL you tell no one about what you've experienced. NOT EVEN—PERHAPS ESPECIALLY—those you are closest to. All that you share with them will put them in greater danger with those who might wish to find you.

But what if Sofía, like Remy, already knew?

And what kind of danger was Bill talking about?

A jolt of dread went through me every time the thought hit me, which happened over and over again while Arthur and Levi were fixing the camera to a tree branch that overlooked the cave. They'd made do with what they had—Levi's bike lock and one of his shoelaces—and they'd wiped the whole contraption down as thoroughly as if it were a bank vault we'd just robbed without gloves

The air felt sticky and unpleasant after the cool of the cave, and with my bike's bent tire, the walk home was miserable. I kept waiting for the sheriff to pull up alongside us and demand to know where we'd been, or for Sofía to announce that she remembered the light-thing going into me.

But we made it to our brick house without any more discussion of the incident, the Jenkins House, or the debris. We propped our bikes against the shed and were headed across the field when a hunched silhouette jumped up from the steps.

"Franny?" Nick called through the dark. In the wash of the moth-encircled porch light, he looked harried and white-faced, even more skull-like than usual.

"Already missing us, huh? I knew it!" Levi cried.

"I knew you'd join the investigation," Arthur said.

Nick marched right past them and bore down on me. "I've been trying to call you for an hour!" His voice was hoarse, edged with panic, and his face was rigid, angry.

"Me?" I looked around at the others, who were as evidently stunned as I was. Nick was like a third brother to me, but he was way closer with Arthur. We rarely *called* each other.

"Yes, you," Nick growled. "What happened? You sent that gahdamn message, then dropped off the face of the planet!"

"What are you talking about?" Arthur said.

"The piano!" Nick snapped.

The *piano*?

The picture I'd sent him. The red kid's piano with the embossed gold lettering. That was what this was about—not the alien inside me, not the secret that had been pressing down on me all day.

"Where'd you see that?" Nick grabbed my arms. The already sharp lines of his face went razor-edged with tension. "I need to see it, Franny." His accent thickened. "Take me to it."

"Chill out," Levi said. "You look like Beetlejuice right now, and it's freaking me out."

Nick shook my shoulders. "Where is it, Fran?"

Arthur shoved him so hard he stumbled back, then reeled toward us, looking like a wounded animal. "Franny, tell m—"

"It's at the Jenkins House!" I snapped, rubbing my arms where his fingers had dug in. "It's nothing to lose your shit over."

The fire faded from Nick's eyes. He jammed his mouth shut and blinked. "It's . . . it's at the Jenkins House?"

"You must have seen it the other night," I said. "That's all."

Nick stared for two complete seconds then let out an embarrassed laugh. He dropped his head, rubbing the back of it. He gave another uneasy laugh. "I'd just about convinced myself it was, like, some kind of message, from . . . you know, your little green friend." He tipped his chin toward Arthur.

"Gray," Arthur said. "It's way more common for people to see *gray* aliens. But ours isn't like that anyway."

Nick gave his head another restless rub. "I really *am* losing it."

Sofía folded her arms over her chest. "Well, I hope you find it fast. Look, we never should have climbed that fence, but we did, and now we have to deal with the consequences. You don't have to believe Arthur's theory, and I certainly don't, but something's going on here, and until Cheryl Kelly's magically orgasming microphone is put back on its shelf and the sheriff's investigation is over, you're as stuck in this mess as the rest of us."

"What are you talking about?" Nick said.

"Orgasming microphone?" Levi asked.

Arthur's brows knit together. "What do you mean, you don't believe my theory?"

Sofía focused on Nick. "Someone else was at Jenkins that night. We don't know who, or what they saw, or what they want. But there's a stockpile of magnetized wreckage in a cave behind the abandoned house. At any moment, someone could connect us to what happened, and we need to have a better explanation than 'we didn't do it!' We need the truth."

The truth. The words rattled through me. If Bill was right, that was something I couldn't let them have.

Nick took a few steps back and lowered himself onto the front steps. "Shit." He shot me a cautious glance, and, misreading my expression, said, "I'm sorry for acting like that, Fran. This thing's really messed with me. I've barely slept since that night. Whenever I close my eyes, I see that damn piano, and when I saw your message—it doesn't make sense, but I felt like if I saw it in real life, maybe it would all be over."

"I think I get it," I admitted. It was how I'd felt about the necklace, like it was the final piece connecting me to something I wanted to forget.

It's not the final piece, though.

There were the bullets, whoever had moved the magnetized debris, the questions from the sheriff, the scars on our skin, the malfunctioning technology and surging light bulbs and the e-mail from Bill about people who'd want to vanish me, and the YouTube video that had been removed for reasons I didn't understand.

There was Arthur determined to make an extraordinary discovery, and Levi determined to find new ways to keep us together, and Sofia determined to find some truth that would justify her momentary lapse of judgment when she'd climbed that fence.

But I'd briefly convinced myself that finding the necklace would end all this, so I understood how Nick could think resolving the mystery of his piano dream could close the box we'd opened.

"So what do we do now?" he said.

"We get a long night's sleep," Arthur said. "We need to be ready to get back to work tomorrow. This is just getting started."

Nick seemed wary, but he let Arthur lead him inside anyway. We all did.

Maybe we were just used to Arthur leading the way. Or maybe Levi, Sofía, and Nick all knew, like I did, that my brother was right.

This was only the beginning.

FOURTEEN

A LITTLE AFTER ELEVEN, I lay awake, listening to the easy rhythm of Sofía's breath in the bed beside me. She slept on her stomach, but whenever she seemed nearly out, she kept twitching awake again, shifting in the bed.

Not yet. I couldn't sneak out to walkie-talkie Remy until she was out. I flipped onto my back and stared at the ceiling.

I used to fall asleep like this every night, gazing at the Milky Way Mark had painted overhead for my eleventh birthday.

I rarely glanced at it these days. Not just because it reminded me of him. That I didn't mind.

But it also reminded me of Mom.

Whenever I looked at it, I pictured her floating through space in an astronaut suit, alone and happy among the stars, happier than she ever was or could be in Splendor, especially now that her one tether to the Great Beyond, the son who understood the awe it struck in her, was lost to her in all the ways that mattered.

Sofía let out a snore. It was time. I turned onto my side, untangling the sweaty sheets from my legs, and slid out of bed.

At my dresser, I stopped and carefully removed the rubber gloves and walkie-talkie, then sneaked out.

I stepped over Droog at the bottom of the stairs, and her tail gave one thump on the mat as her eyes slitted open, but she didn't follow me back to the kitchen.

I moved a stack of mail from the chair onto the table, then sat and turned on the walkie-talkie, tuning it to our usual channel. "Remy?" I whispered after a beat.

A few seconds passed. A crunching sound came over the speaker. "You're okay," Remy said in a rush.

"I am," I agreed, though it didn't feel true.

"Did he e-mail you back?"

"He did."

"Well?" Remy rasped. "What did he say?"

My stomach dipped.

That some mysterious entity is going to kidnap me and anyone who knows what happened.

"Basically he said not to tell anyone, and little else," I said.

"What the hell. What are you supposed to do with that? Why did he even bother e-mailing you back?"

I'd reached out to Remy because I was dying to tell him about what had happened in the Jenkins House, but now that I could hear his voice, now that he wasn't so far away, I couldn't bear to drag him any deeper into this.

I cleared my throat. "I'm going to e-mail him back and try to get more."

Remy was silent for a beat. "Maybe we *should* tell someone. For all we know this guy's a fraud, Fran."

"No," I said quickly. We fell into silence again. Moonlight pooled across the floorboards from the window, and the ceiling fan was still whipping dust through the air, but the air-conditioning unit in the window was silent.

"I'm sorry I can't be there with you," he said.

"It wouldn't make a difference."

"Still," he said.

"Still," I agreed.

The soft static shuffle between our words reminded me he was there, though, on the other end, and even that was a relief.

A floorboard creaked at the front of the house.

"I have to go," I hissed, and turned the walkie-talkie off, slipping it behind a pile of books. I peeled the glove off and tossed it over the sink, then hurried to fill a glass of water.

But whoever was down here didn't intrude, and a second later, I heard the front door squeal open.

"Hello?" I called.

No answer.

I tiptoed down the hall. Droog was standing on the mat, whimpering, her nose pressed to the window beside the door.

I brushed the drapes back and looked out at the shabby yard. A dense fog hovered over it, diffusing the moonlight, wiping everything from sight except the massive, stock-still figure two yards from the front door.

My heart leapt, and fear punched in my stomach before I placed the messy twist of auburn hair and the gentle slope of the figure's shoulders.

Levi, I realized with relief. *Just Levi.*

But what was he doing? There was something eerie about his stiff posture. A breeze rolled toward the house, rippling through the grass and tousling his hair and bright yellow boxers.

He turned on his heel and started walking jerkily, like a mostly naked toy soldier come to life, around the side of the house.

I remembered the shiny purple bruise near his temple. He must be sleepwalking. I doubled back to the coat closet and grabbed a sweatshirt from it, then stuffed my feet into a pair of shoes and ran out the door.

Levi was already out of sight. I wrapped my sweatshirt tighter around me as I circled the house, scanning for him.

A strand of moonlight lanced through the foliage to catch the shocking yellow of his underwear, lighting it up like a neon sign.

He was already across the fence. On Wayne Hastings's property.

I hissed his name, but Levi kept walking, vanishing into the shadow between two trees.

By the time I reached the forest's edge, I'd lost track of him.

I hesitated at the fence.

A six-foot stretch of it had been toppled, laid flat to the ground, but all down the length of it, posts leaned wildly, were uprooted from the mud, and in some cases smashed to bits, the barbed wire strung uselessly across the ground between them.

Had Levi done this?

Had Wayne Hastings *seen* Levi do this?

A breeze gusted fog around me, and the hair on my arms lifted.

I stepped over the fence.

The woods were preternaturally silent. No cricket chirp or cicada song, no owls or foxes or possums skittering through the brush, and the leaves had started to curl, their edges blazing in the fiery tones of autumn.

I broke into a jog, mud and leaf-guts sloshing up my shins as I searched the dark spread of trees for a flash of yellow fabric or wisp of auburn hair.

"*Levi!*" I hissed again. The night swallowed my voice before it could dent the weighty silence. I kept running, calling out to him, until the hermit's A-frame house sprang suddenly into view.

My stomach twisted and dropped, like a drill bit turning through me.

The mucky windows were aglow with amber light, except where the NO TRESPASSING signs and pictures of firearms the hermit had duct-taped to the glass blocked it. All the downstairs windows had deep cracks in them, and one had been boarded up with a square of plywood on which someone had spray-painted MURDERER in a neon yellow that gave Levi's underwear a run for its money.

My stomach lurched at the sight of the word.

Wayne Hastings. The murderer who'd walked free, who'd been cleared of wrongdoing by an internal investigation, but whose every move since the accident had proven he lacked any regret, that he hated all of us.

"Levi?" The whisper barely came out.

I edged around the house, my gaze trained on the windows. A flurry of movement on the roof startled me, and I jerked back as my eyes lifted to it.

The green corrugated metal was barely visible, blotted out by the massive crowd of birds perched there.

Dozens, easily.

Silent, focused, all angled in the same direction, as if they were watching me. My gaze traveled up to the branches overhead, reaching toward the house.

More.

Birds everywhere. Hundreds of them, filling every crook and branch, a near-silent flutter of oily black wings.

All quiet. All watchful.

I thought of the cows at the substation, all lined up along the fence. What had Nick said? That cows grazed according to Earth's electromagnetic field?

Those sharp beaks and beady eyes now all pointed toward me like a hundred accusatory compass needles. I glanced over my shoulder, but there was nothing back there except the shallow valley where the woods dipped.

Something snapped—a branch? The drop of a bullet into a chamber?—on the far side of the house.

A silhouette moving in a stiff, tin-soldier way shambled around the corner of the house.

"Levi!"

I bounded after him, tripping over a pair of padlocked cellar doors that jutted up from a disguise of fog and dead brush.

Of course this creepy man had a creepy cellar behind his creepy house. I wouldn't be surprised if there were trip wires just *waiting* to catch me and Levi in nets.

I fought a shiver and hurried to the front of the house.

Levi stood at the steps, his glassy eyes fixed on the door.

If he heard me crashing through the bramble, he didn't show it. I stepped between him and the door, waving a hand in his face. "Levi? Levi! Are you okay?"

He stared right over my head.

"We have to go." I pushed against his shoulders, but he didn't budge.

"Molly," he mumbled.

Molly? I didn't know any Molly.

I shook my head. "Franny."

Levi pushed past me and took the first step toward the front door.

"Levi!" I hissed, grabbing his elbow.

"*Molly*," he said roughly, and took the next step in a slow, belabored way, like he was moving through maple syrup.

"Save 'em . . ." he grumbled. "*Nottalottatime.*"

My skin went cold. The hair follicles prickled on my thighs and arms.

"You're dreaming," I said. "It's a dream, Levi . . ."

"Mol-ly," Levi mumbled. "It's Mol-ly. Save 'em. I told *youhaveto save 'em.*"

Goose bumps crept over the backs of my arms. "Levi, *come on!*" I tugged on his elbow. He shoved me backward so hard I sprawled out at the base of the steps, a metallic taste flooding my mouth. A yelp tore out of me, loud enough that some of the birds startled.

My pulse sped, my chest tightened, and a cold sweat sprung up on my neck. A hum picked up under my skin, and the lights in the windows began to flicker. A radio burst to life inside the house, the classical music blaring out through the woods, like a call to arms. The rest of the birds exploded like a mushroom cloud from the roof, squawking angrily.

Shit. Now we *really* had to go.

I grabbed the first stick I could find on the ground and hurled it at Levi's back. "Wake *up!*"

He whirled around to face me, mouth open and eyes wide and blinking.

"Franny?"

"Thank God!" I gasped. "You're awake."

The flashing stopped, the music stopped, and in the newfound silence, another sound had picked up behind the house.

Footsteps trudging through fallen leaves, breaking up the silence like a sledgehammer against concrete. The quick gait of someone climbing up from the bottom of the valley that curved around the back of the house, coming to see what the commotion was.

Wayne Hastings was going to find us here, at his front door.

Worse, he was going to think we'd been in his house, flashing his lights, messing with his stereo.

"We have to hide," I said, barely louder than a breath. I clambered to my feet and snatched Levi's hand, nearly pulling him off balance as I darted for the cover of the bush snarled in wild grape and Virginia creeper. We dropped into a crouch behind it, and the bear trap of anxiety around my heart loosened: Wayne Hastings was cresting the ridge, ambling toward his house, but we were out of sight. We were safe. Probably.

And then I saw them, running through the dark, right into the clearing where Wayne was headed.

"What's going *on*?" Levi whispered.

I officially had no idea.

Arthur, Nick, and Sofía were sprinting through the woods, still dressed in pajamas, just as a massive silhouette was moving toward the clearing from the other side, a gun propped against his shoulder.

They stopped short in the shadows when they spotted him, tried to hide behind a thicket of honeysuckle, but it was too late.

Wayne Hastings's rattling voice lashed through the night like a whip.

"What are you doing on my property?"

I'd never heard his voice before. A knot twisted through my throat at the sound of it, and a buzz rose in my skull, as if trying to block it out.

"Whoever's there," he growled, "you're trespassing." He took a step toward them, and the buzz spread through my bloodstream like a million angry wasps. "And I have the right to protect my property."

He dropped his rifle into position, the buzz swelling until I was no longer sure it was inside me, that the electric hum was just within my skull.

The gun faltered, jerked toward the house as the music exploded out of it again, the yellow-gold wash of the windows flaring, intensifying to blinding white so fast the world seemed to disappear before my eyes.

So fast it was like a star had crashed in front of us, cracked like an egg, its runny light gushing out over everything.

The trees, the man, the gun, the house, the others' faces— everything washed out for a millisecond, all sound lost beneath the orchestral blare.

And then the bulbs on the porch sparked, popped, shattered.

Every light in the house flashed in a brief and brilliant explosion, and silence and darkness surged up like jaws to swallow us.

"We have to go!" I grabbed for Levi's hand and took off in a random direction, pulling him along with me through the disorienting dark.

I heard the others more than saw them, barreling through the woods in the same dizzy fervor as Levi and I. My vision adjusted in time to spot the creek ahead, and I snapped out a warning to them as Levi and I leapt across.

Legs pumping, throat burning, I sprinted up the far side.

The man was yelling after us, but his words unraveled beneath the *thunkthunkthunk* of my heart. I released my grip on Levi as he overtook me. Sofía ran past next, followed by Nick. Arthur came even with me next and slapped a hand on my back as he passed, spurring me on.

There was no time—or oxygen—to ask what they'd been doing in the woods; we just ran.

At the top of the hill, we burst from the woods onto the moon-blanched gravel that lined the train tracks.

Loose rock slid out from under our feet as we threw ourselves up the bank. I lost my footing and fell onto all fours, pitching myself back up on the rails themselves. At the bottom of the bank on the far side of the tracks, Sofía and Levi were disappearing into the trees, but Art, Nick, and I wouldn't have time to get down there before the man and his gun caught up.

His shouts were still ricocheting off the trees behind us.

I glanced up the tracks, searching for a better escape route, but the rails stretched out unobstructed for at least two miles. I spun the other way, deeper into Wayne's property.

A couple of yards ahead, the tracks divided, each disappearing into a stone tunnel eaten up by moss and ivy.

"Come on," I whispered, running for the mouth of the nearest one. It was overgrown, foliage hanging low across the entrance so we had to duck to keep from tangling in it as we slipped inside.

The stone walls shut out the moonlight and the shouts, even some of the heat, and when I turned away from the entrance, I could barely see anything.

Nick and Arthur followed, Arthur's Vans shuffling over the worn-soft wood of the tracks and Nick's high-tops faintly scraping along behind them. The overgrowth of grass sprouting up through the tunnel deadened the sounds of our movements, but behind us, the crackle of *new* steps on loose rock sent a shock of adrenaline through me.

I flattened myself to the tunnel wall, holding my breath. Nick and Arthur pressed in close too, like knotting ourselves together would be some kind of defense against a shotgun pellet.

Out in the shadowy blue beyond the tunnel's mouth, the behemoth silhouette stepped onto the tracks and made a slow, counterclockwise turn, scanning for any sign of us.

I willed my heart to stop beating before its deafening pumping could give us away.

Go back, I willed him. *You're not going to shoot us for walking on your grass.*

"Real tired of this," the man let out. He had the voice of a smoker verging on sword-swallower, a scraped-raw tone.

My stomach flipped. My blood felt like it was bubbling, boiling, and my limbs were taut and trembly.

The man stepped closer and my pulse spiked.

He stopped suddenly and looked down at the tracks under his feet.

Beside me, Arthur gasped; Nick approximated a swear.

It wasn't just me shaking. Tremors were racing through the tracks, shivering under our feet.

Outside, the man staggered back, studying the rattling rails.

My spine tingled as the trembling grew and grew, as if any second the world was going to break apart under us.

I lurched against the wall at the sudden shriek of metal. Out on the tracks, the man jumped back from the rails and gaped at them.

The shriek and snap sounded again, and this time, I caught a moonlit glimpse of the switch where the tracks merged.

Two more metallic shrieks came in quick succession as the switch flipped back and forth.

Train warning bells began to blare. Arthur's arms flung out, pressing Nick and me flat to the wall, but he jerked back, releasing me, as a visible spark of light leapt from my skin to his.

He might've said something; I couldn't hear.

The spastic screech of the rusty train switch screamed on one side of us, and the crossing bells raged from the other.

Outside, the man turned an anxious circle, then hurried off, running for the cover of the woods with his head ducked.

As soon as the man was out of sight, Nick bolted from the tunnel, but I didn't move.

There was no train coming.

This time, I knew. This time, I felt it: *I* was doing this.

Me or the thing inside of me.

Art hadn't moved either.

He stared at me through the dark. "Back at the house," he whispered. "Those lights . . ."

I was watching the understanding dawn across his face.

"Arthur . . ." I began, gut twisting.

What could I say?

It's going to be okay?

I'm going to figure it out?

I'm exchanging e-mails with an Internet stranger who says he can help me?

So whatever you do, just don't waste your energy worrying about me?

"I knew it," Arthur whispered.

"You . . . you knew?"

All at once, the life went out of the rails. The buzzing under my skin ceased, like a switch had been flipped. He already knew, and now I didn't have to say it aloud. Didn't have to acknowledge that something was inside of me, filling me with unstable energy and thoughts that weren't mine and—

"I *knew* our alien must've given us something!" Arthur cried. "I *knew* something must have happened to us that night. I wonder— I wonder what else we can do." A slow, glow-in-the-dark smile spread across his mouth. "Franny—Franny, this is amazing! How did we do it? We have to try it again."

Everything inside me collapsed, condensed into something tiny and impossibly heavy.

He didn't understand.

He thought this was the superhero origin story he'd been waiting for. He thought everything was going to be okay, better than okay.

I was a black hole, the force ripping all of them into a place where light and sound couldn't reach them.

My throat ached. "Arthur, there's something I have to tell you."

Sofia stepped into the mouth of the tunnel, Levi and Nick close behind her. "It wasn't us who did that," she said, quickly, like she was ripping a Band-Aid off on my behalf. "It was Franny. Only Franny."

FIFTEEN

THEY STARED.

Scared? Mistrustful? Angry?

Nick stepped back, looking queasy. Levi peered at me sidelong, like he was searching for hidden tentacles, and Arthur's brow hunkered low, his mouth wrinkling.

I was the problem he was trying to solve.

"How do you know?" he asked Sofía, like I wasn't even there.

She sighed. "Because I saw her do it. Every time she uses . . . *the energy*, I see it happen. In my head."

My gaze snapped toward her. "You see what, exactly?"

Sofía folded her arms, and her eyes glinted like emeralds. "Whatever *you* see. Actually, sometimes even when you're *not* using the power, I see what you're seeing. I can't control it much yet. Just . . . one minute, I'm asleep, or at home or practice, and the next—I'm *not*. I'm watching whatever you're seeing play out around me. I saw you pick up that bullet right after the accident, and I saw you talking to Remy the other night at the tracks, and I saw you in the Jenkins House earlier, and then the cave."

How was that possible?

My mind felt like a dandelion blown apart, every thought traveling out in a different direction. I latched on to one: She saw me talking to Remy?

She *knew*, not just that I'd been shocking myself on doors and sending power surges through the wiring in abandoned houses, but possibly—probably—what Remy had told me, and what Black Mailbox Bill had said.

"And you saw me in the woods tonight?" I asked, voice tight.

She looked quickly away from me and nodded at Levi. "I saw what *you* saw, actually," she told him. "It's sort of . . . been happening with *all* of you, and Remy. It's like—I'm tapping into your *channels*, watching your lives like they're TV shows. I guess that's what that thing did to me."

"But . . . but you said you heard her leave . . ." Nick said, disbelieving. "You said it woke you up, and then you saw Levi sleepwalking from the window . . ."

Sofía sighed. "I lied."

"Why didn't you say something sooner?" I demanded.

She studied me with pursed lips, silently communicating something along the lines of *I could ask you the same thing.*

"I wasn't sure," she said. "I thought I was imagining it. Like vivid daydreams. And I figured if you were experiencing something like that, you would tell us. You would tell *me*."

Guilt sank like an anchor in my stomach. It was our non-fight from last year all over again. Sofía inviting me in; me having to shut her out; her unable to understand, with her beautiful house and her beautiful family and their beautiful closets full of shoes.

"Then I saw you going into the cave earlier," she went on. "You know, in my head, and when I found you there, it seemed like proof. But you still didn't say anything."

I had no idea what to say. I could've dealt with her anger, but she just looked hurt. The whole point of keeping things from people was to avoid that look. My body felt too small, shrinking in tight around my heart.

Sofía turned to focus on Arthur. "And then tonight, I knew Levi was outside that creepy little house, even though I'd never seen it before."

For three complete seconds no one spoke. I looked to Sofía,

expecting to find her staring daggers at me. But she wouldn't look at me.

I wanted to tell her this time was different. The last time I'd pulled back on our friendship was to protect myself, but this was to protect *them*.

But from what? If the alien was in *me*, then how had Sofía gotten powers too?

"So . . ." Levi began. "Fran is electrokinetic . . . and Sofía can hack our eyes . . ."

Sofía shrugged. "A bit reductive, but essentially."

"*Awesome*," Arthur murmured, eyes saucer wide.

"Is it, though?" Nick deadpanned.

"Of course it is," Arthur said. "We have to figure out what the rest of us can do!"

"I already know what my ability is." Nick's eyes fixed in the distance as he scratched his head. We all stared at him until he blinked clear of his daze. "The piano!" he said.

"The piano hallway?" Sofía said flatly.

"Yeah . . . like . . . *what*?" Levi said. "Your superpower is being able to dream about pianos?" He added quickly, "No offense, dude. You're great at other stuff."

"No, smartass." Nick smacked the back of Levi's head. "The piano's just some kind of cover. Probably Arthur's *little gray* hid something in it, or some shit, and now he wants me to retrieve it. Probably he left a little code in my brain or something!"

"Can we not say *he* when we're talking about this alleged alien?" Sofía requested.

"Yeah, because saying *alleged alien* three times in a sentence won't get old," Nick fired back.

"We don't know if there *is* an alien," Sofía said, "let alone its gender, or whether it even has one."

"Great point, Sofía," Levi chimed. "We should give the alien a name."

"Not . . . what I was saying," Sofía said.

Arthur tapped his chin. "E.T.? Like the movie."

"There are any number of alien films we could pull from," Levi said. "Let's not go straight for the most obvious."

"Are y'all kidding?" Nick drawled. "Call it Alf, call it Leonard Freakin' Nimoy—this thing is *dangerous* either way!"

"Do you think sleepwalking is my superpower?" Levi's mouth stuttered between hopeful optimism and a frown. "That's anticlimactic."

"Oh yeah?" Nick said. "I'm pretty sure Alf gave me missile codes to activate a piano bomb, wanna trade?"

Tuning everything out like always, Arthur bent to touch the track switch and looked up, eyes lit with excitement. "Still warm. Can you do it again, Franny?"

I shook my head. "I don't—"

"Try," he implored.

Instinctively, I looked to Sofía for support. Her lips were pursed tight, but her eyes were still avoiding me.

It's for the best, a little voice said. *If you'd told her, it would have been too much.* If she really understood what was happening to me, she'd be sitting in the sheriff's office right now, spilling everything.

"Just *try*," Arthur said, impatient.

"You can do it, Fran!" Levi cheered.

The birds tattooed on Nick's fingers seemed to fly across his stubbly jaw as he rubbed it. "Probably should at least try."

I sighed and crouched in front of the switch. I wasn't sure what to do, so for a few seconds, I just stared. When that did nothing, I imagined it snapping sideways, pushed by an invisible force, *by me.*

I tried to summon that charged feeling into the air.

I pictured light crackling off my skin and energy building in my veins until it thrummed and trembled, down through my feet, into the metal rails as it had back in the tunnel.

I could feel all four sets of eyes homed in on me, all four bodies inclining expectantly.

Move, I thought. *Move.*

My mind wandered toward the memory of the white light unspooling across the gravel lot, *into* me. *Move.*

I closed my eyes, and pictured the rail switch flopping like a fish on dry land as that buzz rode through my blood. I could feel the energy, but it was like it was no longer close to the surface, and the tendrils of it I grasped at were evasive, slippery.

MOVE.

My eyes snapped open. Art, Levi, Nick, and Sofía were all still leaning toward me, eyes wide and tense.

The switch was lifeless.

"I can't."

Levi let out a breath, and Arthur pressed his thumb to his chin. "You made it happen back at the hermit's house, and then again when he was closing in on us in the tunnel."

"*And* when you were alone in the Jenkins House." Sofía pursed her lips. "Maybe it's like a defense mechanism? Like adrenaline. Like an energy source that's released when her pulse speeds . . ."

"You're saying she has to be scared?" Arthur asked, and she shrugged.

"Maybe not *has* to be. Being scared or surprised might make her involuntarily release the energy, but there could be a way to voluntarily trigger it."

"Like pee," Nick said. "You can get it scared out of you, but you can also go in the toilet."

"Charming," Sofía said.

"I think she's right," I said. "I can feel it in me, but it's subtle, not like when we were in the tunnel."

"On par with the fainting goat or the dead-playing opossum," Levi narrated, "the Frances Schmidt has been known to respond to threats with displays of electrokinesis."

"Electrokinesis," Sofía pointed out, "does not exist. I'm not even sure that *word* exists."

"Tell that to Electro," Arthur murmured.

"Superhero?" she guessed.

"Villain," I said, and she looked away suddenly. Arthur had never cared for Spider-Man—he was more of a Batman guy—but Mark briefly had, so we were both familiar.

"She has to be scared," Nick mumbled to himself. "We can work with that."

I gave him a shove. "I carry Mace. Think about that before you try to scare the lightning out of me."

"You *own* Mace, Franny," Nick said. "You don't *carry* it."

"She's supposed to." Arthur lit up a cigarette—did he keep hand-rolled cigarettes in his pajama pants now?—and took a long puff. "We'll work at it more tomorrow. I've got a plan."

"Great," Nick called. "So now we just drop the alien hunt you were so amped on for Operation Superhero?"

"We still need answers, something that will keep us *out* of jail if we get linked to those field burns," Sofía said.

Arthur waved, like they were flies buzzing around him. "Figuring out what our extraterrestrial did to us is only going to *help* us figure out what it is, what it wants, and where it went. Trust me."

Levi nodded emphatically. "Right, if it wants something from us, then our abilities are the key to determining that."

My stomach felt like a giant hand was pinching it. Maybe I was coming down with something, or maybe it was simply guilt-induced nausea springing from the secret Sofía had uncovered, and the bigger one I was keeping.

"Y'all need to come back from the Marvel Universe," Nick said. "Franny, Bill Nye, someone be the voice of reason here."

Sofía massaged the bridge of her nose. "I'm actually with Arthur on this. I can't spend the rest of my life popping into your heads. I need to figure out how to undo it, or at least how to control it, and the same goes for Franny. And what about you? Don't you want your . . . *piano nightmares* to stop?"

"Well, you don't need to say it like that," Nick said. "Have you ever tried sleeping with one song on repeat in your head at full volume, nonstop?"

"That's the point, Nick," I said. "We have to figure out how to make this stop."

"And why it's happening in the first place," Levi added. "And document it!"

Arthur turned on his heel and started down the tracks, puffing his cigarette like it was a glass of water he'd found in the desert. "This is going to be amazing," he said, to us or himself. "Absolutely incredible."

I fought another wave of dizzy nausea and fell into step behind him. We all did. We always did, but even so, that didn't mean I wasn't alone in this.

Maybe the shocks we'd sustained at the substation *had* affected all of us in some way—or at least Sofía. Maybe there was alien shrapnel lodged in the others, doing strange and impossible things, but *I* was the one an alien had outright walked into.

When I got home, I was going to write Bill back.

My stomach hitched and gurgled.

First I was probably going to throw up.

* * *

Dear Bill,

Thank you for your reply, but before I can say more, I need proof that you're who you say you are.

Tell me about your "encounter."

How did it all start, and when did it stop?

—F

Dear F,

I've seen three of our Little Friends. My first encounter was in the fall of 1986, during the Orionids. It's a meteor shower, like the one that must have brought your visitor, but this one is the product of Halley's Comet.

I was driving through Texas. At first I didn't think much of it. Shooting stars streaking past on occasion, but that was about it.

Then, suddenly, this light fell from the sky, about a half mile off the road. It didn't move like the meteors—in an arc—it dropped, straight down, brighter than all the lights on the road or anything else.

I thought my mind was playing tricks on me. It was very late, and I'd been driving all day. But as the light was falling, my radio cut out. My engine died. And all the lights down the road blew. Like they'd had some surge of power. The road, my windshield, the desert all went white it was so bright, and then, just as quickly, it went pitch-black. Nearly wrecked my car.

Glass shards landed on the hood, from the blown-out bulbs, and I pulled over just in time to see where the disc hit the earth.

You can guess the rest.

I left my car and walked out to the light. It was crackling in its gel receptacle. When I touched it, the receptacle opened and the being entered me.

So that was how it all started, but as for how it stopped, that's more complicated, and I CANNOT discuss at length in such an insecure way.

What matters is that of the dozen of us I've met since I started my research, I've now lost contact with all but three.

If those responsible for my peers' disappearances locate you, there will be no protecting you. I saw your video had already been removed. That suggests they've seen it. They'll want to keep it quiet.

They'll arrive with a cover story. They will give your family all the answers they want, every reason to trust that they are looking out for you, but trust me: All they want is the being. To them, you are nothing more than a vessel.

I can help you, but we must act fast. Where shall I meet you?
—Bill

Dear Bill,
I understand the need to be careful, but you're a stranger. On the Internet. HOW can you help me?
—F

SIXTEEN

THE NIGHT BEFORE I turned eleven, Mom made red velvet cake. It was terrible. Dense and overbaked, and it had whiskey in the frosting, which Mom insisted shouldn't affect us, but Arthur pretended it had gotten him drunk.

We took it down to the yard, where we sat on a blanket under the stars, making exaggerated "mmmm" noises while we tried to eat it.

"Jeez, Eileen," Dad said. "Where did you ever get the idea to put cream cheese frosting on this meat loaf?"

"Is there garlic in this turd?" Arthur asked.

"Theoretically, I'm good at baking!" Mom cried through laugh-tears. "It's science!"

"See, that's the problem with you science types," Dad teased. "You put too much stock in theory, when you should be putting stock in Marie Callender's."

"Or buying stock," Mark said, "since we're going to keep them in business."

"I think I broke a tooth," I said. "Some birthday!"

Even at 10.9999 years old, I knew how my family played with one another, the rapid-fire sarcasm.

"Oh, honey, I'm sorry." Mom was laughing so hard she could barely get out words and kept having to wipe her eyes. "You're practically Oliver Twist, aren't you?"

Arthur spat his mouthful across the lawn, and Dad chided, "Now, that's not nice, Arthur! What if a poor unsuspecting groundhog wanders across that and tries to eat it!"

Then Mom ordered six lava cakes for delivery from Domino's

and we sat out under the stars, waiting for the weed-infused delivery boy to arrive, and Mark showed us an app he'd downloaded so he could hold his phone up to the night sky and the screen would show him the constellations and cosmic bodies right overhead, with labels and glowing outlines.

It played a beautiful ambient song, slow and swelling, that changed with your movements as if each star had its own variation on the cosmic theme. Soon our giggles died down and we fell into raptured silence. Fresh tears bloomed in Mom's eyes as we studied the sky, and she whispered, "Sometimes I love to feel this small."

"I wish there was a hole in my ceiling," I said. "I wish I could sleep under this every night."

The next morning, on my birthday, I woke to find Mark spreading a drop cloth on my bedroom floor. "Surprise!" he said.

"What," I said.

"I'm giving you a Milky Way," he said.

"What," I said.

"For your ceiling."

Mom came in with muffins then. "Tada!"

Arthur slipped past in the hallway, grabbed one off the plate, and shouted over his shoulder, "Don't worry—I saw her take them out of the package. They're from Sam's Club."

For the rest of the day, the whole family filed in and out of my room, watching Mark's progress. The blues and purples and blacks spread out, the white gaps shrinking into stars and planets.

Despite his artistic talent, Mark tended to dress in worn-out Old Navy jeans and whatever T-shirts he got for Christmas, and that day he wore his BLACK HOLES DON'T SUCK shirt.

He was nothing if not on brand.

Late in the afternoon, Mark took a break to eat leftover pizza with me and Mom, and I asked him, "Why do you like black holes?"

Ever since the day we'd found the nautilus shell at the beach, the thought of them had haunted me. I pictured black holes like toothy mouths, screaming across the universe, swallowing everything in their paths.

Destroying solar systems. Ending worlds.

Massive grim reapers, chasing stars and planets down, forcing them into a place with no sunshine passing through leaves or soft lavender smell on a breeze, no chirping cardinals or voices you knew singing you Carole King, nothing but darkness, loneliness.

They were worse than the unknown: They were the certain Nothing.

Mark's brow crinkled in confusion until he realized I was looking at the white words across his chest. "Oh!" he said. "This doesn't mean, like, *black holes are cool.* That's the joke. People always talk about them like giant vacuums, just sucking everything into them."

"Aren't they?"

"Not really." He shrugged. "Black holes are these massive bodies that suddenly collapsed into one tiny point, right? But they still have the same mass as before, it's just more concentrated, packed into a singularity. And mass sort of creates gravity."

"What's that mean?"

Mom dabbed her mouth with a napkin. "Like with the Earth. It's so massive that if you throw something up into the air, the gravity will pull it back down. Or the sun—it's so huge it pulls on the Earth, and that's why we go around it. With a black hole, there's so much concentrated mass that if something gets too close to it, it falls in. Even light waves can't get out."

"But that *is* scary." I thought about the Milky Way over my bed, its millions of black holes lurking invisibly at its center. I pictured myself falling—if not exactly sucked—into a bottomless black pit.

"Nah." Mark flicked my nose. "It's comforting."

"A giant hole in space?" I said.

"It's not just a hole in space," he said. "It's a hole in *space-time*. The fabric of the universe." He gestured with his pizza slice between us. "Like . . . there's three feet between us right now, and that's the space part, and then there's the time part. If you'd gotten up five minutes before I sat down, then I'd be three feet and five minutes away from you."

"What," I said.

"Time stretches out forward and backward, just like with physical space, and the weird thing about space-time is that really big objects' gravity *bends* it. So time passes differently in different places, based on how strong the gravity is, how much *curvature* the object creates in time-space. Following?"

I was newly eleven. I was not following.

"Say you were in a spaceship," Mark said, "and you dropped someone into a black hole."

My heart sped. My skin went cold. "Why would you do that?"

"You wouldn't. But say you did. You could watch that person falling, and they'd be falling at a normal speed, the speed you'd expect, until they reached the *event horizon*. That's what they call the area surrounding the black hole from which you can no longer escape. That's where the gravity is so strong that you'd have to travel faster than the speed of light to get out of its clutches."

He continued: "So you drop this person, and the gravity pulls on her, and you watch her fall, and like I said, it all seems pretty normal, until she gets close to that event horizon."

"And then what?"

"*Then* she's reached a point where space-time is curved so deeply by the black hole's gravity that time goes wonky. From our point of view, it looks like she's slowing down. Slowing and slowing and slowing, and just before she reaches that point of no return, she *stops*. She freezes, floating just outside the event horizon. We could sit there forever, but we'd never see her *actually* reach the black hole."

"She stops?" I repeated.

"She does and she doesn't," Mark said, obviously delighted. "Out here, in our experience of time, we'd see her stop. But to her, everything seems normal: She keeps falling at the same speed and crosses the horizon. She enters the black hole and she either gets spaghettified—that's when you get pulled into a string of atoms by the pressure of gravity—or she falls right into it and experiences something we can't even begin to imagine! She's both beyond the event horizon, inside the black hole, and she's outside of it!"

"No one can be in two places at once."

"But in a black hole, gravity's so strong that all of *space-time* is infinitely curved," he said. "For all intents and purposes, it's a hole in *space-time*, where the laws of physics break down. Time inside a black hole isn't like time out here. Right?"

"Pretty much," Mom confirmed, smiling. "There's a theory that if you *did* fall into a black hole, that because of the time dilation, you'd see everything that had ever fallen into it or ever *would* fall into it, all at once. All these pieces of our universe's history that we've already lost—every cosmic body we ever *will* lose, and all the events that happened there—all occurring at the same time."

"And then there are wormholes," Mark chimed in. "Tunnels through space and time. If you fell into a black hole, you might travel through it and get spit out by a white hole on the other end. You could see everything that had ever fallen or *will* ever fall through—whole histories of planets and moons and stars, all playing out at once—and then get popped back to some other point in space-time before those things even fell in! Of course, wormholes are still just a theory, but black holes started out as a theory too!"

"Because of amazing math?" Arthur grumbled from the next room, where he was hunched over something at the coffee table.

"Sort of," Mark answered. "The point is, nothing in our universe, even the stuff that's supposedly *deleted* from time and space, is ever really lost. It's just hidden from our sight."

He smiled at me. "There are things about black holes that break all the rules—or *expand them* in a way we don't understand yet. As if the universe wants to exist so badly it makes loopholes in its own rules. I find it comforting, like this is all meant to be somehow, and nothing can take any of it away. Like everything is forever."

Mom smiled at him across the wasteland of greasy paper plates and crumpled napkins. "One of these days, I'm shipping your butt off to space camp, kid."

Arthur jumped up and came into the kitchen carrying a piece of paper and slid it onto the table. "Look," he said. "I drew Batman punching Superman."

"Cool!" I said, but Mom eyed it with a suspicious smile.

"Isn't that the cover on one of your comics?"

"Batman Versus Superman," he said.

"Then you traced it?" Mom asked.

Arthur's face reddened. "No, I drew it."

"Well, you copied it, buddy," Mom said. "Maybe you should try making up your own characters? I'm sure you've got all kinds of ideas in that noggin."

Arthur picked up the drawing and stared at it.

"Can I see?" I reached for it, but he jerked it away.

"You'll get grease all over it."

"I will not!"

"You ruined my controller by playing with it while you were eating popcorn," he said. "You always mess up my stuff, and Mom lets you because you're a small, dumb baby!"

"Arthur!" Mom said. "Apologize to your sister."

Tears and shame rushed to my face. Just then Dad came through the back door, drenched in sweat and smelling like cut grass. He leaned over Arthur's shoulder as he was opening a bottle of beer. "What ya got there, Arto? Did you draw that?" He bent to kiss Mom on the cheek, and she writhed away from his sweaty face. "Mower's out of gas," he said, settling back against the fridge.

"I thought you just filled it," Mom said.

"There must be a leak."

Arthur took his drawing back into the other room, and Mom and Dad fell into their conversation about the lawn mower, and the moment moved on, but I still felt small and incapable and embarrassed.

"Psst!" Mark hissed across the table. When I looked up, he was pulling the nautilus shell out from under his BLACK HOLES DON'T SUCK T-shirt. He'd fixed it to a chain and was wearing it as a necklace.

He tapped the center point of the shell. "Remember, Fran, it's not the size of something that matters in this galaxy. It's the gravity of a thing, how much it pulls on things and where it takes them. You've got gravity out the wazoo."

He dropped the shell and mussed my hair. "Also, I just got pizza grease in your hair."

I awoke to a message I'd been waiting for, but it wasn't the one from Bill.

Ungrounded, Remy wrote. *Meet at WH for breakfast? I have updates.*

Sofia was softly snoring in the bed beside me, but judging from the voices and clinking of dishes rising through the sun-washed floorboards, I could tell the boys were already awake.

I slid out of bed and retrieved the rubber gloves from my

backpack. I'd sneaked down to the kitchen for them last night before I went to empty my wildly unsettled stomach, and then wrote my e-mails to Bill from the bathroom, praying Sofía wouldn't have another spontaneous visitation into my eye sockets.

As it turned out, she *hadn't* heard the conversation with Remy. Her little visitations were limited to sight only, which was great until you were trying to send a discreet e-mail in between puke sessions.

When I got back to the bedroom, though, she wasn't there, and I figured she'd decided to go sleep on the couch. Apparently sharing a bed with someone she couldn't even look at didn't appeal to her.

But here she was, back in bed this morning (our couch was famously uncomfortable), and things were looking better in the light of day. Whatever had upset my stomach—*the crushing weight of this situation, perhaps!*—had passed too.

So do we, I typed back to Remy.

We? he replied.

Sofía sat up groggily in bed, shoving a fistful of dark hair out of her eyes and squinting through the buttery morning light. "Updates?" she said through a yawn. "What updates?"

I stared at her for a minute, then typed back, *Sofía's psychic and Nick's obsessed with pianos. We'll explain everything at breakfast in half an hour.*

"Technically, I think I'm telepathic," she said, reading the message from the far side of the room. "Or something."

She offered a tentative smile, an olive branch, and the relief flooding through me was immediate.

"Get out of my head!" I teased, flinging my rubber glove across the room at her.

"Get out of *my* head!" she squealed back, dodging the glove.

This was how our last fight had gone too; one weird day and then 360-plus more wherein we agreed not to acknowledge the parts of our friendship that could never fit quite right.

"It's bad enough I had to see you poltergeist a house," she deadpanned. "I shouldn't also have to take a front-row seat to your and Handsome Remy's unrequited love!"

"How do you get *unrequited love* out of *that* text message?" I took my other glove off and flung it at her too.

"It's there between the lines," she yelped, lurching onto her knees and hurling the first glove back at me. "The part about Waffle House! Splendor's premier dining establishment! And the puppy dog eyes he gave you during your secret midnight rendezvous!"

"It wasn't a rendezvous!"

It was exactly a rendezvous, but not in the way she was thinking.

Still, she'd touched a nerve, made me feel anxious and *seen* in a way far more uncomfortable than knowing she was able to look through my eyes, and all the pressure points in our relationship gave tiny warning throbs.

But at the same time, we hadn't laughed like this, just the two of us, much in the last year, and there was a pining feeling low in my stomach, like I got when Remy said *I love you*, like I was already missing this moment even as it was happening.

"Are you still mad?" I blurted before I could change my mind.

Sofía's smile faded. "I would've told you," she said. "If it had been me, I would've told you."

"I know," I admitted. But if Sofía suspected about herself what I *knew* about *myself* from Remy, she would've turned herself in to be quarantined and dissected for the greater good.

She was too good, too selfless, to understand someone like me. Meanwhile I'd driven my own mother away by demanding her attention when she was so torn up she could barely get out of bed.

Sofía shook her head. "What did I do to make you not trust me?"

A pit opened into my stomach. I hadn't meant to hurt her. That was the whole point. I'd wanted to be the kind of person who didn't cause the people she loved pain, but somehow, I still managed to poison things.

Sofía had left behind the private school where she could have prepared for her future as a lawyer, she'd left behind her favorite city in the world, her enviable lacrosse team, and a whole host of friends, and she'd been stuck with me: someone who couldn't be the friend she deserved and couldn't really explain why. "You didn't do anything," I said.

Outside, footsteps thundered down the hall, and my bedroom door was flung open.

"Is everything okay?" Arthur asked as he, Nick, and Levi swarmed in. "We heard screams."

"I knew it!" Nick pointed at Sofía, whose hand was still poised to throw the second rubber glove my way. "Girl sleepovers really *are* freakier than boy sleepovers!"

Sofía cleared her throat and pitched the glove at his head. "Put pants on, Grandpa. Remy's ungrounded, and he has 'updates' for us."

"New haircut," Nick guessed.

"New girlfriend," Levi said.

Arthur clapped his hands together. "New superpower!"

"New phone," I said. "Who dis."

"Who indeed," Levi narrated. "The travelers would not see, until they'd tracked down the rare and elusive Handsome Remy for themselves."

SEVENTEEN

"YOU'RE PSYCHIC," REMY SAID.

We were scrunched into a booth, and none of our food had come out yet, but the table was already completely covered in beverages.

Orange juice and water for Remy.

Water and coffee for Sofía, Levi, and me.

Water, chocolate milk, and Mountain Dew for the world's grossest humans, Nick Colasanti Jr. and Arthur Schmidt.

"Actually, it's more like telepathic," Sofía clarified. "Or maybe that's not right. I can't hear your thoughts—before you ask. Actually, I can't hear anything you hear. It's all visual."

Remy blinked at her for a few seconds. "Prove it."

She sighed. "Weren't you listening? I can't do it on command any more than Franny can snap her fingers and start up the stove back there."

Levi twisted in the booth to look over the counter. "Also, that's a gas range, not electric."

"An astrophysicist, a bovine scientist, and a connoisseur of stoves!" I said, trying to drag the conversation away from my ability.

Remy shot me a tense half smile. He didn't love it when I deflected with humor, and with him it was easier not to. Maybe because his emotions rode so close to the surface and that made mine feel more manageable, or maybe because the first moment I'd truly seen him was the low point of both our lives.

I pressed my knee against his, an apology.

He pressed his back, an understanding.

"Just try, dude," Nick urged Sofía. "How many fingers am I holding up under the table?"

"Just your middle one," she said. "Doesn't take a psychic to guess that, Nick."

Remy pulled his gaze from mine and looked to Arthur. "What about you? What's your power?"

"TBD." Arthur fidgeted. "As long as it's better than Nick's, I'll be satisfied."

"Which is . . . ?" Remy prompted.

Nick took a big swig of Mountain Dew and chased it with a swig of chocolate milk. Sofía pretended to gag, which set my stomach back on edge.

"Some piano shit," Nick grumbled, rubbing his head.

"He's convinced the alien gave him nuclear codes in the form of piano chords," Sofía elaborated.

"Just *one* theory," Nick said.

"It's a huge, and possibly ego-driven, assumption that just because Franny and I are both experiencing strange phenomena, your piano dreams have anything to do with what happened that night."

"And what about you?" Remy asked Levi. "Are *you* experiencing anything strange?"

He gave a bearlike shrug then took off his camel-skin fedora and set it on the table. "Maybe the whole sleepwalking thing? It requires more observation."

"Sleepwalking . . . is your superpower?" Remy asked.

"Sleepwalking is my anti-drug," I deadpanned.

"My other car is sleepwalking!" Levi said brightly.

"Sleepwalking: We have the meats," Nick joined in.

We stared at him.

"Did you just use the Arby's slogan for a joke?" Sofía asked.

"And here they thought they'd found the *one* slogan that *couldn't* be made funny," I said.

"Will you all stop it." Remy gripped the sides of his head. "This is serious. Can we quit with *The Ordinary Variety Show* for, like, two seconds?"

I sank in the booth like a scolded kid. Remy's eyes caught mine then flashed away. He cleared his throat. "If this . . . *alien* really is making all this happen, why? I mean, if it's really causing Franny's power surges and Sof's eye-hijacking and Nick's . . ."

"Pianos," Nick said.

". . . sure, and Levi's . . ."

"*Somnambulism*," Sofia offered. "That's the medical term for it."

"Then why?" Remy finished. "And how do we make it stop before we all wind up stapled to tree trunks on Wayne Hastings's property?"

"Obviously, we're going to have to go back to see why it would take us there," Arthur said.

Sofia mouthed, *Oh, obviously.*

"We'll wait until he's not home," Arthur said. "He goes out most nights, for an hour or so."

"And if he doesn't?" I asked.

Arthur shrugged. "We'll give him a reason to."

"Such as?" Sofia was wise to ask; the first image that popped into my head was Arthur dumping gasoline on the hermit's porch and tossing a hand-rolled cigarette onto it.

"I'll think of something," Arthur said. "In the meantime, we've got plenty to do. We need to get the camera back from the cave and see if the alien, or anyone else, came for the debris. We need to take Nick to meet his piano, hone Franny's and Sofia's abilities, and figure out mine and Remy's. The good news is, I have a plan that covers most of that, but the hitch is, we need to go back to the Jenkins House."

Remy ran a hand through his dark hair, then realized what he was doing and slapped it onto the table before anyone could make a crack about it. "This seems like as good a time as any to tell you *my* update," he said quickly. "There's a reason I'm not grounded anymore. Something happened early this morning. There was another big power surge, this time out by the steel mill."

"The steel mill?" I repeated. "There's nothing out there."

Arthur's eyes narrowed. "It makes perfect sense—no one goes out there, ever. It's the perfect place for the alien to hide."

"Yeah, maybe it was," Remy allowed. "But it isn't now. My dad went to check it out this morning, and they'll probably patrol for a couple of days. The good news is, though, they're pretty much convinced there's something wrong with the electrical system that's causing the blackouts *and* caused the burns.

"I guess now that the blame's getting turned back on them, Crane Utilities is pretty much shutting up, paying St. James for the damages to his property, and doing their own review of their systems. My dad thinks they're afraid any more police involvement could turn up some big mistake, and they could get sued, or something. They don't even seem to care about the missing parts anymore."

"So he's just done investigating?" Sofía said, bristling at the thought. "If he suspects a cover-up, he shouldn't give up."

Remy shrugged. "I doubt he'll just let it go, but officially, the investigation's over. I'm sure he'll keep an eye on things, but the security won't be as tight on Jenkins Lane from now on."

Art rubbed his chin. "Perfect. Then Operation Franny starts tonight."

A tremor went through me, and Remy's knee pressed into mine again, this time a promise: *It will be okay.*

"What about my piano?" Nick cried.

"Sure," Arthur said. "That too."

* * *

We headed over just before dark. It was raining, so Remy drove, but we left his car parked on the cross street that ran parallel to Jenkins Lane and made our way through the misty woods to the cave.

"Who's going to get the camera down?" Remy asked.

Arthur clapped him on the shoulder. "Thanks for volunteering."

"Nice try." Remy slipped out from under his grip, and followed me and Sofía toward the cave.

"It's a two-person job," Levi insisted. "I wouldn't want to drop it."

"Why not?" Arthur called, jogging after us. "You'll just order a new one."

"But—"

"Keep your pants on, Levi," Nick said as the rest of us headed for the cave's low mouth. "You don't have to be alone for five seconds: I'm not going in no alien hidey-hole."

He'd been visibly anxious all day, tapping his head and thigh and chin in that obsessive rhythm, and I'd half expected him to back out. Instead he'd been the reason we'd headed over before the sun even set.

"If this piano bomb is gonna kill me," he'd said, "I'd rather just get it over with."

As he and Levi argued about who was going to climb the tree, Arthur dropped into a crouch and crawled into the cave, followed by Sofía, and then me, and finally Remy.

Nick's squawking voice faded along with the soft *taptaptap* of rain and everything else as we followed Sofía's flashlight beam deeper into the cave's antechamber, until finally the ceiling lifted and we could stand.

"Pretty creepy," Remy whispered behind me, his voice echoing as we started down the stone path toward the steady *drip-drip-drip*.

"I wish we'd found this place sooner," Arthur murmured. "Would've made a great hideout."

"For *what*?" Sofía asked.

"For anything," Arthur said.

Ahead, the cave curved in on itself, and as I moved around the bend, I felt a little bit like a piece of food being sucked down an esophagus, passed along by the muscles of an intestine.

Arthur stopped so abruptly he caused a pileup, Sofía plowing into him, me slamming into her, Remy colliding with me.

"What?" Remy asked, stepping out to get a look at the rounded-out hollow where the cave ended, the trickling waterfall that formed a shallow pool in the corner.

Arthur laughed. "It's gone." He patted the stone wall like it was a very good horse. "That means E.T. came back for it! That means the video caught it!"

"Or whoever else might have taken it," Sofía amended. She seemed every bit as optimistic as my brother did that this would prove what she expected it to, though it was no longer clear to me just *what* she thought that might be.

Hope swelled in my chest, a light, shaky feeling like I'd swallowed a bunch of helium.

"We'll know who dropped the bullet," I said. "Whether that was . . . an *alien*, or just a person who saw what happened to us, we'll know."

And once we knew if we had a *human observer*, and who they were, I could figure out what I had to do to make sure our secret was safe, to protect against the people Bill had warned me about.

How I'd convince the person to keep quiet about what had happened was another matter entirely, but I could focus on only one obstacle at a time.

Remy gave me a look that said he understood. We'd told him

earlier that morning about the bullets we'd found both on Jenkins and in the cave, but he and I hadn't managed to have a second alone since breakfast, so we hadn't gotten to talk freely about Black Mailbox Bill's e-mails. And since then, I'd even received another one, though it was just a prompt.

Friend? Bill had written. *Please reply so I know you're all right.*

I hadn't had a chance yet; for one thing, taking my rubber gloves out to type on my phone in the midst of all this might draw attention, and until I knew for sure that the alien wasn't contained to me, I wasn't going to drag them any deeper into this.

For another, every time I looked at my phone, I worried Sofía would mind-meld with me and find out about the e-mails in the worst possible way.

"At least we'll get *some* kind of answer," Remy said, pulling his gaze from mine. "Assuming the video camera actually caught anything."

"It will have," Arthur said confidently, then turned and led the way back out of the cave.

I tried to hang back with Remy, but there was no discreet way for us to talk about Bill or the e-mails or anything else, and when we reached the cave mouth, we shared one last look and crouched to crawl out.

"We'll figure it out," he whispered, and I clung to that promise as if it were one he could actually keep.

The camera battery was, as we'd expected, dead. Levi had brought a fresh one and a backup memory card, but now he wanted to go right back to his house and pore over the footage. The sun was almost down, though, and Arthur was intent on getting back to the Jenkins House for his mysterious Operation Franny.

Plus, every minute Nick put off seeing the piano seemed to bring him closer to the brink of implosion.

So we set off again, hoods up and flashlights off.

We reached the back of the Jenkins House and crept around it silently, but it was like Remy had said: Though caution tape still hung in loose knots along the fence, the wind had ripped it into tattered ribbons, and the temporary lights, Bobcats, and everything else were gone.

Inside the house, we turned our flashlights back on, catching the ghostly patterns of dust kicked up from the floor.

"Stand in a circle," Arthur commanded, taking his place directly in front of the HAPPY BIRTHDAY banner.

Sofía lifted an eyebrow and folded her arms. "Why?"

"Why do you think?" I said. "Because he wants this to be as dramatic as possible."

Arthur lifted one shoulder. "Excuse me for wanting some decorum."

"Where's the piano?" Nick glanced around like he expected it to come barreling into the room with a machine gun.

"First things first," Arthur said. "Now stand in a circle."

Nick seemed put out that Arthur wasn't as interested in exploring his piano lead as he was in *my* new ability, but apparently he was too anxious to look into it by himself, because he sidled up with the others around the overturned coffee table.

"Maybe we should hold hands?" Levi said.

I shook my head. "Or maybe that would turn me into a human electric chair."

"Hands free it is," Sofía said. "Now what?"

Arthur looked at me. "Why don't you just start with the ceiling fan?"

He made it sound so easy, but if I couldn't make the tracks switch on command, I didn't see why this would be different.

Still, the others were watching, hopeful, and Black Mailbox

Bill's warnings kept running through my head. I needed to get a handle on this; to know how to *stop* it from happening, knowing how to *start* it was probably a good step.

I inhaled deeply and focused on the fan and the trio of light bulbs that blossomed from its center.

Was this even something I could control?

For all I knew, the *being* was calling the shots.

Icy dread dripped into my stomach, but I fixed my thoughts on the fan. I imagined it turning. Pictured current crackling through me, leaping toward the wiring hidden behind the drywall.

I dropped my gaze. Levi, Remy, Arthur, Sofía, and Nick were leaning toward me with bated breath. "Could you not stare?" I said. "It's too much pressure."

Arthur nodded. "Let's all turn around."

Still in our arbitrary ceremonial circle, they turned their backs, and I focused on the fan again.

This time, I leaned into the memory of light erupting from the disc. The pain branching across my skull under my scalp, and the humanoid light-face appearing before me for an instant.

But when the memory vanished, the living room was still dark. "I can't do it."

"It's okay," Sofía said. "You don't have to do anything."

"She does," Arthur snapped.

"Arthur," Remy said harshly.

"She's the one it chose to give this to," Arthur said, anger sneaking into his voice. "It could've given it to any of us, but it chose her, and she's going to figure out how to use it." He flashed me a dark look. "Come on. I know what to do."

He broke the circle and marched past the staircase, turning to the kitchen at the back of the house, and we tripped along after him.

He opened the door beside the pantry, revealing the basement stairs, and then held out his hand. "Here. Let me use your flashlight."

"Why?" I asked. "You already have one."

Arthur huffed. "Do you trust me?"

I rolled my eyes. "And they say there's no such thing as a stupid question."

He thrust his hand toward me, and I handed over my flashlight. "Stop being dramatic."

He shone both flashlights down the basement steps, then glanced over his shoulder at the rest of us, gathered there in the kitchen. "Remy, Sof, Nick—I put three boxes in the trunk. Go grab them."

"Are you serious, dude?" Nick said.

"That's half a mile back," Sofía said. "Why didn't you tell us to get them before we left the car?"

"I was hoping we wouldn't need them," Arthur said. "It'll take you ten minutes."

"When did you even put them there?" Remy asked.

"When we stopped by my house and you took twenty minutes to do your business in the bathroom!" Arthur fired back. "Now hurry up—we haven't got all night. And don't open them."

"Why doesn't Levi have to go?" Nick said.

Levi's eyes went wide. He held his hands up in surrender. "I'll go, gladly!"

"No," Arthur said. "You're working the camera."

Sofía shot me a mildly perturbed look, then faced Arthur. "If your mystery boxes will help, then fine, but we're not packhorses, Arthur Schmidt. From now until you leave for school, expect to carry my purse."

He waved a hand. "Just put it on my tab." As the three of them headed toward the back door, Arthur turned to the basement again. "Levi, get your camera ready and wait here. Fran, follow me."

Arthur descended first, dual flashlights cutting tracks down the dusty steps. Three steps from the bottom, a skittering noise rose from the back corner of the basement, and Arthur jerked the lights sideways in time to catch a massive rat disappearing behind a stack of mildewy cardboard boxes.

The air smelled dank and sour, and if there *were* any partial windows, they'd been blacked out. We could see nothing but what the flashlight touched.

As we took the last three steps, I tucked my nose into my jacket and slid my palm along the banister, both relieved to have a guide through the dark and unsettled by the thought that, at any second, my hand could brush something I couldn't see.

I jerked it back to my chest as we reached the bottom step. Arthur's flashlight wandered over the space: cement walls and floors and a labyrinth of cardboard boxes stacked in columns as tall as we were.

"Here." Arthur forged ahead down a seemingly random path through the boxes, and I followed, weaving through, twisting back and forth until I'd lost track of where we were in relation to the stairs.

Arthur stopped and shone the light on the floor just ahead of himself. "Stand there."

I shivered. I was half-soaked from the rain, and it was cold down here, but more than that, it was the dark, the shadows not even flashlight beams could break. "Arthur, what's all this about?"

"Trust me." He jogged the lights on the cement floor where he wanted me to stand.

I sighed and took my position. "Now wh—"

The flashlights winked out.

"Shit," I hissed. "What happened?"

Arthur didn't answer, but I heard a shuffling noise. "Arthur?" I reached through the void for him, and my fingers met cardboard.

I turned, hands extended, feeling for my brother or an opening in the stacks of boxes.

Steps were pounding up the stairs.

"Arthur?!" I half yelped, stumbling forward. "Art, is that you?"

I hit another box and jumped backward, disoriented, lost in the darkness. The angry embers in my stomach flared into something bigger. "Turn the light back—"

My words dropped off at the sound of a door opening, then slamming shut again.

I moved toward the sound, hands still outstretched. "Arthur?"

There was nothing to see. Not even a dappling of moonlight. I reached for my phone, tapped it awake, but the bluish glow barely dented the darkness, and the screen was pixelated, unusable.

"ARTHUR!" I screamed.

My pulse kicked up to full-fledged panic, and my shoulders lifted, as if to protect my neck from whatever could be hiding in the dark as I tried to feel my way back to the stairs. "Arthur, come on!" I choked. "Let me out!"

I jerked backward in surprise and horror as my hands met something stringy and dry. *Hair*, I thought with revulsion, and stumbled sideways.

I swung my phone light toward it even as my stomach clenched, warning me I didn't want to see.

A doll! Just a ceramic doll poking out of the top of a box stacked on top of two more. "Arthur," I shouted, starting across the basement again, hands outstretched halfway. I wanted to find the stairs but only the stairs. *Nothing else, nothing else, nothing else*, I thought.

My fingertips met a smooth wooden surface, and I gasped with relief as I fumbled up it—*the banister!*

I threw myself up the rickety steps and caught the doorknob at the top.

It was locked. "Arthur, *stop* it!" I shouted, shaking the knob.

My heart hammered, and my back tingled like the dark had come alive behind it.

Something rustled on the far side of the basement. *Rats*, I told myself, though really I had no idea. *Just rats!*

But I still couldn't handle having my back exposed. I turned and pressed my back into the door, pounding on it on either side of my hips. "Arthur, stop it *now*!"

He didn't answer. Was he even there? Had he left me?

Was *this* his brilliant plan?

I pounded again, screaming for him, then Levi.

"PLEASE," I begged, turning back to struggle against the knob. "PLEASE."

Glass shattered behind me, and something *scuttled* across the floor at the bottom of the steps, and I whipped around again.

The basement had changed, lightened.

A black garbage bag had been pulled loose from one of the windows, and the resulting trail of light was enough to reveal movement.

Not a rat.

Something much bigger, hurrying through the shadows toward me.

A scream tore out of me. The lights overhead stuttered.

Oh my god.

There actually *was* someone in here.

I threw my body against the door, screaming. The lights strobed.

There was someone in here with me, a figure cutting toward me through the dark.

I slid down against the door, curled against it, fists pounding.

There was screaming on the other side of the door now too—Sofia and Nick—they were trying to get the door open, screaming my name.

But they weren't the only ones. Someone else was screaming it much closer.

On the stairs below me.

The lights surged brighter, so bright I couldn't see. Not just the overhead light, but whatever light lay beyond the now exposed window—the substation maybe, or the porch lights, or something else.

And then my eyes adjusted and I saw him bounding up the stairs toward me.

The figure who'd torn through the window covering. The other person calling my name.

"What?!" Remy shouted, wide-eyed, as he thundered toward me. "What is it, Fran? What happened? I heard you from—"

"Remy?" It was just Remy?

My heart felt like it was dropping back into my rib cage. The lights went out. The door behind me opened, and I fell backward, sprawling out across the filthy linoleum floor of the kitchen.

EIGHTEEN

LEVI, NICK, AND ARTHUR stared down at me, splayed out on the linoleum in a daze. Sofía ran over and crouched beside me. "What the *hell* were you thinking?" she screamed at Arthur.

Remy jogged up the stairs and knelt on my other side as Sofía helped me up to sitting.

"What happened?" he asked. "We were behind the house when we heard you screaming."

"*They* happened," Sofía raged. "When Nick and I got in here, they were holding the door shut while she screamed bloody murder!"

Levi tried to hide by sinking into himself, but his height wouldn't allow it. "We thought you needed to be scared, Franny, and—"

"You mean *he* did." Nick rounded on Arthur. "This is what it's come to? You almost gave us heart attacks! Handsome Remy broke a gah-damn window to get into that basement! We thought something was killing her!"

He shoved Arthur, but Art barely seemed to notice. He was staring at me, breathless and flushed in the sober light of Sofía's LED lantern. "It worked. I knew it would work."

"I can't believe you," I spat, staggering to my feet.

He blinked, coming back down to earth. As his eyes met mine, his victorious expression faded into guilt, which quickly dissolved into a mask of cool indifference. "Yes you can."

"Fine!" I shouted. "I can, and it makes me sick. How could you do that to me?" Now I shoved him, as hard as I could.

He stumbled into the kitchen countertop but quickly regained his balance and advanced on me. "I did that *for* you, and you know it! You have a gift, and you need to know how to use it, Franny!"

"Why?" I demanded, heart thudding viciously. "Because that's what you would do? Because you can't stand being normal? You'd scare your sister to death just to feel like you've got a starring role in a comic?"

Arthur's eyes hardened and he stepped forward, forcing me back. "You said you trusted me. You knew what that meant."

The anger dimmed just a little, crumbling back into the secret knot it usually lived in. Some part of me *had* known. I'd seen his shiny plan glinting behind his eyes and been complicit, because I wanted to understand and control this.

"You didn't have to take things that far," I said weakly. "Were there even mysterious boxes back at the car?"

Arthur cracked his knuckles. Hair sticking up in wild tufts, he looked every bit an evil mastermind. "Not as such."

I faced Levi, who once again shrank like a Newfoundland who'd peed on the carpet.

"We never would've left you alone," he said guiltily. "We just needed you to *think* you were. We wouldn't have let anything happen to you."

"She could have gotten seriously hurt and you wouldn't have even known," Sofia said. "She could have fallen down those stairs!"

Arthur's lips tightened. "I didn't think of that." He turned toward me. "Franny, I'm sorry I scared you."

Nick slow-clapped. "So he *does* know the words."

"There's a reason we tried standing in a circle, sending prayers up to a ceiling fan first," Arthur said. "I knew this wouldn't be fun, but I also had a feeling it would work."

"And it did." My hands were still trembling and my voice came out thin and broken, but my body was abuzz.

Energy crackled along the life lines on my palms.

I looked past Arthur to the light over the kitchen sink.

It was different this time.

I knew what it was I was looking for in myself, as if I'd found a new muscle—a *slew* of them—that I hadn't known before. They were—the closest word I could find—sore, distressed from exertion, but that made it easier to locate and engage them again.

I felt them spiraling down my center: at the crown of my head, in my throat, and under my sternum, all the way down to my crotch, and when I focused on them, it was like they could reach outside my body.

The more I focused, the farther I felt them extending. Though I saw nothing, I felt when they reached the bulb over the sink, and a second later, soft, golden light swelled to life from it.

"Holy—" Nick whispered, and the others turned to the sink, going silent, as if any noise would break my concentration, and it might have.

From the bulb, I pushed onward and felt the energy extending both left and right, branching out to travel through the underside of the cabinets on the wall.

The light fixtures set into them lit up one by one as I felt the energy reach them. When they were all lit, they pulsed faintly, light rising along with an audible buzz.

That's me! I thought of the sound. I felt it inside my body, *and* I heard it with my ears, and I knew the two things were the same.

I was hearing myself, my energy, pass through something else. The others were silent, holding their breath.

I held my focus on each of the connections I'd formed and moved slowly around the corner, back toward the living room, seeing how far behind me the trails of energy could stretch.

The others stuck close to me, moving in a silent pack. Tentatively,

I reached out for more: lit up the lamp on the floor beside the coffee table, the overhead lights, a box fan propped against the wall. I felt myself stretching thinner, starting to shake, but I could take it further.

I turned to the stairs for the second floor, and the not-quite muscles in me pulled tighter as the energy reached up.

If I'd had a marker, I could've traced the wiring hidden within the ceiling. I could *feel* the hidden veins of the house like they were an extension of me. The light over the carpeted steps eased on, and I started climbing, taking the buzzing energy all the way to the second-floor hallway.

The farther I spread myself, the more I felt the strain. I was shaking from it, like I was holding a metal bar over my head while someone added more weights. It was a new kind of pain I didn't have the vocabulary to describe, like there was an invisible layer to the human body that usually lay sleeping around us, an inactive shell.

That didn't make it any less real.

I sucked air through my teeth as the *weight* built, the light unfurling into the bedroom where the piano sat as we slowly edged into it.

I couldn't hold it much longer. I needed to release my grip, little by little; dropping it all at once seemed as risky as if it had actually been a dumbbell.

I closed my eyes and pictured the kitchen below us, traced the outreached energy all the way to its farthest point until it was like I was holding that bulb over the kitchen sink in my hand.

I released my grip, and the feeling of the energy drawing back was a relief. I checked the other bulbs, loosened my hold on them, the pressure lifting, the hum lessening as the not-muscles retracted into me.

At the bottom of the stairs, the living room went dark, and then the stairs, and then the hallway where we stood, and the bedroom right in front of us, my eyes splotching as they adjusted.

"Oh my God," Sofía whispered. "It's real."

Nick laughed uneasily. "My Gah, indeed."

A shiver passed through me as I met Remy's dark, worried gaze. It was real, and it was really inside me.

"Think about everything we can do with this," Arthur whispered.

"Everything *Franny* can do with this," Sofía said.

"We could make money off this," Nick said.

Levi had his camera out, trained on me. "Not to mention, be *famous.*"

"It's bigger than all that," Arthur said. "We're going down in history. People are going to remember our names. We're doing something important."

"We still need to keep this to ourselves until we understand more," Remy said tensely, looking away from me.

I understood his anxiety, but I didn't want to think about it. I wanted to bask for a second, to pretend this was as exciting as the others seemed to think it was, without worrying about what the thing in me might *do*, or any of Bill's warnings, or *anything* else.

"We're going to have bank vaults we can dive into," Nick said.

"We're going to win awards," Levi said.

"Only if we *actually* figure out what's going on here," Sofía said.

"This is like . . . like power," Arthur went on. "Like purpose." He lit up a cigarette in the house. "After everything that's happened to us, it's like . . . we're finally *getting* something. We finally *are* something, that matters. An alien *chose* us, for something important."

The six of us looked at one another for a long, laden moment. Goose bumps had sprung up beneath my damp clothes, but the knot of anxiety that had been building in my chest all week loosened a bit.

Maybe he was right.

We had the video from the cave, and soon we'd know who'd dropped those bullets. We'd have proof that they'd taken the debris, so we'd have leverage to make sure our secret was safe (if we even needed it). We were figuring out what had happened to us and how to control it. The investigation was winding down.

I couldn't remember the last time I'd actively thought, *Things are going to be okay.*

But it honestly, truly looked like they might be.

"Nick," Sofía said, nodding through the doorway to the little red piano against the wall.

Nick drifted forward, and we hemmed in after him. He ran a hand along the dusty top of the piano.

I hadn't noticed last time that chunks of it had been gouged out, that every bit of surface that hadn't been carved or chipped had been graffitied in Sharpie. "It's the same one from your dreams?" I whispered.

His fingers played on a massive chip in the corner. "This was there," he said, brow furrowed. "But the rest of it wasn't."

"It looks like a regular piano," Levi mused. "Except . . . you know, small."

"Definitely doesn't look like a secret spaceship or anything," Remy agreed.

"Well, he hasn't played it yet," Arthur said, without a hint of irony. Levi even nodded. After everything else we'd seen, why *shouldn't* this be something spectacular, some alien secret?

Nick slid onto the undersized bench, examining the keys wordlessly as his fingers trailed over them too lightly to make sound.

"It's kind of sad," Sofía said, walking a half circle around it. "It's so small. It's like—hard not to think of it like an abused puppy."

"Nicky Jr.," Arthur pressed. "We don't have long . . . someone could have seen the lights again."

Nick depressed one of the keys, and it brayed gracelessly.

"Yikes," Levi said.

Nick pressed another key with his pinky. In the dim light, the blurry bird tattoos on his fingers blended into the words scribbled over the ivory keys. He tapped the highest key, then went down the line playing all the rest in quick succession. Every once in a while, a saggy, deflated noise rang out, but for the most part they sounded okay.

Levi poked a key too. Without looking up, Nick swatted his hand away.

Remy snorted. "Now you know how the rest of us feel when you pet us, dude."

Nick set both hands on the piano, slowly, carefully.

No one moved; we held our breath.

Nick played a note—or was it a chord? It required at least three keys and it rang out low and calm, the slightest bit dissonant but not at all ugly. His hands moved position and he played another, and then his fingers began to move more quickly, skating across the keys with ease, pulling notes from them expertly, apart from the occasional *honk* of the more severely out-of-tune keys.

The smile slid off Sofía's face, morphing into an awed O.

"What the . . ." Remy breathed.

Levi lifted his camera and hit Record.

It wasn't proficient . . . it was *enchanting*. Nick's hands danced over the keys. The song was *felt*, tender and melancholy and haunting. His eyes closed, his brows knit together, and his lips pressed tight. As the song sped, it became hard to tell where his fingers ended and the keys began, he and the piano fading into each other.

As far as I knew, the closest Nick had come to playing an instrument was three weeks with a trumpet in seventh-grade band class. He swore he'd quit because the teacher hated him, which I'd always assumed meant he'd taken advantage of the opportunity to make a lot of well-timed fart noises until finally, he'd been asked to drop the class.

Maybe this should have been less shocking than what I'd done, but to me, it wasn't. This thing Nick was doing was entirely foreign. It was from outside himself.

It was a gift.

The song ended.

Nick opened his eyes and drew his hands back from the keys. The whole room seemed to draw its first breath in minutes.

And then something thudded heavily to the floor behind me.

All of us spun toward the sound.

Remy was on the ground, his eyes rolling, his back arched and limbs contorted in odd, sharp angles.

A low, horrible sound gurgled from his throat. The others were running toward him.

Nick screaming Remy's name.

Sofía calling out for someone to dial 911.

Arthur shouting that we *couldn't*, we were trespassing.

Levi screaming that it didn't matter.

But I was frozen in place, all my floaty optimism turning into ice inside my chest as my best friend lay writhing on the floor.

"What's happening?" Levi shouted through tears, trying to hold Remy down.

"He's having some kind of seizure!" Sofía said.

"The song!" Nick yelped. "The song did it!"

"Don't be stupid," Arthur snapped.

The pressure inside me was building, and I wasn't strong enough to hold it in. The lights shivered overhead and the hum rose until everything in the room was quivering.

And then, all at once, the tension left Remy's body. He slumped to the floor. His pupils reappeared, and he blinked sleepily up at all of them gathered over him. Recognition filtered into his gaze and he shifted, started to push himself up.

The lights went out and an inhuman sound scraped out of me as my relief hit like a wave. My knees buckled, bringing me down beside Remy's legs, a strangled sob spearing through me.

I thought he was going to die.

"It's okay," Levi said, touching both my shoulder and Remy's elbow with the same anxious pressure. "It's okay. It's all over now, whatever it was, and everything's fine."

"We need to get him to the hospital," Sofia said.

Remy shook his head. His dark eyes were wide and his mouth had a grim set to it. "I know what caused it." He looked at me. "I thought they were just dreams, but they weren't. I think . . . I think I just saw the future, and if I did, everything most definitely isn't fine."

He staggered to his feet. "We need to get out of here, before anyone turns up."

NINETEEN

"IT WAS THAT FREAKING song," Nick said as we were running past the cave, back toward the car. "I'm telling you."

The rain had picked up, and thunder was booming overhead as we sprinted through the forest. With any luck, anyone who might've seen the light show at the Jenkins House would've mistaken it for lightning.

Either way, I doubted it would be safe to go back there again.

"So it *was* like a nuclear code!" Levi said. "It unlocked Handsome Remy's brain!"

"It didn't unlock my brain," Remy said. "I've been having these dreams ever since we found the disc, but they were shorter, little pieces."

"What about the seizure?" Sofia asked. "Has *that* been happening?"

"I—don't know," Remy said.

"How can you not know?!" Levi demanded.

"I don't know!" he shouted back. "There were a couple of other times I woke up on the floor or the couch, but I didn't remember what had happened—I felt like I'd just drifted off and had the dream. I don't *remember* having a seizure."

"But you remember what you saw?" Arthur yelled over another thunderclap.

We'd just made it to the edge of the woods, legs drenched in mud, heads sopping wet, and Remy stopped halfway between the trees and the car, his hair plastered to his face with rain. "I thought they were dreams." He looked haunted, shaken. "Get in the car. I'll tell you everything."

We moved toward it, but I stopped short at the sight of something white and rectangular tucked into the windshield wipers.

"You guys!" I shouted. "What's that?"

Arthur came to the hood of the car to see. "Religious tract? Who cares?"

But when I reached for the soggy fold of paper, something small and solid slid out of it and nestled into the bottom corner of the windshield.

"Is that a rock?" Arthur asked.

My teeth had started to chatter. It wasn't a rock.

Remy came to stand beside me as I reached for the small, blue-gray circle and the long chain attached to it.

An uncanny tingling oozed down my spine as I lifted the nautilus shell. Its smooth, resin-covered surface felt at once familiar and foreign in my palm, and revulsion rose through my stomach as I turned it over.

How did it wind up here?

"Your necklace?" Remy murmured.

I dropped it into my pocket and pried the soggy paper open.

It was so wet the blue-ink words had blown apart into smoky Rorschach blots, but I could still make out the two words scrawled there, oversized and jagged.

I KNOW.

"What is this?" Arthur asked, brow furrowed.

I shook my head. I couldn't speak. My throat felt like it was collapsing.

"Just get in the car," Remy said calmly, quietly, so the others wouldn't hear, but they were still standing at the car doors, watching us. "We'll figure this out. It will be okay."

He was lying again, pretending we had any real control over whether everything ended up all right or not.

Sofía's gaze dropped to the note, and her lips pursed. "Whoever dropped the bullets must've written that. They must've been following us."

Every beat of my pulse seemed to shake the whole world. My mouth had gone dry, and there was a ringing in my ears.

Someone knew what had happened to us, and Remy was having seizures and visions, and everything was coming apart.

"We need to go," Remy said, touching my arm. "We'll figure this out later. Please."

But I stayed rooted to my spot. "What did you see?" I asked him.

Levi, Arthur, Nick, and Sofía all floated out into a semicircle around us. Their gazes traveled between the note (*threat?*) and Remy. The muscle in his jaw leapt.

"The end," he said. "I think I saw the end of the world."

TWENTY

"IT WAS SPLENDOR," HE said. "I saw your house."

Arthur pushed forward. "Our house?" Thunder boomed, and the raindrops sliding down his freckled face shivered. "You saw our *house*? In a vision, from the alien?"

"Not just your house," he said. "I saw Levi's too, and the old movie theater, and the steel mill." He shook his head. "The whole town was being destroyed. The roof was ripped off Wayne Hastings's house. Its whole top floor was destroyed, and so was yours. Beams, hubcaps, pieces of refrigerators were everywhere. There was . . . this *thing*. This big metal thing. A machine, I guess. I think it was causing it. Like maybe it was a weapon."

He tipped his chin toward Nick. "Like you talked about with the piano, except . . . something *huge*, and made of steel."

Sofía sank onto the hood of the car, her face paling, and creases etched between Arthur's eyebrows.

He took a step, rubbing his chin. "The E.T. must want us to stop it. That's got to be what all this is about. It's given us some kind of—*coded* information, and Franny's ability because it . . . it wants us to save Earth."

Remy gave me a dark look.

I wondered if he was also thinking about Bill's e-mail:

Impulses to do things that are utterly unfamiliar to you—commands, as it were, from the presence you are hosting.

I swallowed a knot. "Or maybe it wants us to destroy the planet."

Arthur shook his head. "That's not it. That's not what's going on."

"Of course it is," Nick said, voice uncharacteristically restrained. "Think about it, Arthur. Remy's got the overview, and Levi's wandering around at night, probably doing that thing's dirty work, and Franny's probably like . . . a freaking battery."

"And what about you?" Arthur poked Nick's chest. "And Sofía? You're playing the piano like an angel, and Sof's able to watch over us from anywhere! Those are gifts, Nick!"

Nick scoffed. "For all we know, I'm just here to operate some alien control panel, and as for Sofía—she could be your precious E.T.'s security feed, keeping track of our progress! That thing didn't come here for us! It came here for steel, and we're the poor saps who happened to cross its path and get roped into this! Fifty bucks says when we watch that video from the cave"—he whirled around to point at Levi—"it's *him* lugging those beams out of there."

The blood drained from Levi's face.

"He wouldn't have had time," I argued, though I wasn't sure. "I heard him leave the house."

I clutched the shell in my hand, but it was no comfort.

Someone *knew* what happened to us, and if they'd told anyone . . .

Another crackle of thunder shook the puddle-heavy asphalt, the hood of the Metro, the misty woods behind us.

Maybe it was for the best if someone found us, someone took us away before we could do . . .

Whatever that thing wants us to do.

The whole world seemed to kaleidoscope in front of me.

I felt sick again. Actually, the nausea had been building for some time, along with a sharp, cramping pain down my center. I leaned into the car, trying to hide the jolt ripping through my spine.

"This has gone far enough," Sofía said. "We have to tell someone!"

"*No*," Remy snapped. "Not yet. That's a last resort, only."

"Well, we've officially reached the land of last resorts!" Nick said. "Haven't you been listening? We're possessed by an evil alien!"

Possessed.

The word sent shock waves through me. Was I? Possessed? And what about the others? Micro-possessed? Tainted by alien shrapnel, as if it had whittled itself down to a size that could fit inside me, and stored the final slivers in them?

Was that why Sofía could see through our eyes?

Because that *thing* was in *all of us*, in some capacity?

Levi looked as queasy as I felt. He rocked between his feet, swaying like a redwood considering just packing it in as a tornado spun toward it.

"You want me to prove you're wrong?" Arthur said sharply. "Let's go watch the video."

"Fine!" Nick stormed to the car's back door. Arthur stomped around to climb in on the opposite side, and Sofía sighed and followed. Levi still hadn't moved. His bottom lip was trembling, from cold or fear.

"We don't know anything," I told him.

I'd meant it to sound comforting; it didn't.

"The video will help," I added.

Remy bumped his elbow. "We'll get answers," he said for the second time that night. "This is good."

"Sure," Levi said. "Answers."

The problem with answers was you almost never got the ones you wanted.

Sometimes it was better to float through that liminal space that came before you found the truth. If I could go back to the hospital waiting room, and stand there, alone, inside those sliding glass doors, and exist forever in a world where I still might hear that Mark was okay, I would.

But I couldn't.

We got in the car and drove to Levi's house in silence. When we arrived, no one climbed the lattice; we filed through the door and went straight to his bedroom.

Mr. and Mrs. Lindquist were still out of town, and the house had fallen into disarray, the lowest point it reached between their bimonthly housekeeper visits. Usually, we would've teased Levi about the paisley socks left on the floor, the mustard-yellow trousers discarded over the sofa arm, and the novelty soda bottles resting on the bathroom sink.

Tonight we were silent.

It only took a minute to get the video pulled up. The process of dragging the cursor back and forth in search of any significant movement took longer.

"Slower!" Arthur commanded whenever he thought Levi might've zipped over something, whereas Nick impatiently growled, "Faster!" every few seconds.

"Wait!" Sofía finally cried. "What was that? Go back."

Levi dragged the cursor back a centimeter.

"Farther."

He pulled it back until a dark blur swam onto the screen.

"It's too dark," Arthur said.

"It looks like this was taken underwater during a lunar eclipse," I agreed.

Nick prodded the screen. "That's obviously Levi. Look at those huge shoulders!"

"That person's wearing a shirt," Sofía said. "When we found Levi, he was a square inch of neon fabric away from butt naked."

"He might've stripped afterward," Nick said.

"That's what I went to bed in," Levi said. "You were there, dude!"

"You might've gotten sleep-dressed beforehand, then stripped afterward."

Levi screenshotted the figure across several frames, then opened some photo-editing software and began playing with the brightness and contrast.

"Look." He pointed to something on the figure's shoulder. "Long hair. I think it's a woman."

Nick and Arthur leaned in, scrutinizing the blur that might or might not have been long, glinting hair.

"I don't know . . ." Nick began.

"What's that?" I pointed at a little dark rectangle on the figure's chest a couple of inches below the clavicle. There was a hint of the same shadowy shape on the other side.

"Weird metal nipples?" Levi asked.

"I think they're hooks," Sofía said. "She's wearing a jumpsuit."

"No," I said. "It's overalls."

Nick made a face. "Who wears overalls? St. James? The farmer who owns all the land that got burnt?"

Not in his interview he hadn't, but I could think of someone who did.

I watched the realization dawning across Arthur's freckled brow just as it was hitting me.

The person who'd witnessed the incident, the person who'd stolen the material and left the creepy *I KNOW* note, who was at the center of this, just like he was at the center of everything that happened five years ago.

I squeezed the nautilus shell necklace in my pocket to keep the sudden dizziness from tipping me over

His name tasted like poison. "Wayne Hastings."

TWENTY-ONE

IT WAS A DANGEROUS job. Everyone knew that. But the accident shouldn't have happened. The crane that broke had been scheduled for maintenance the day before.

That was what all the papers would say, all the talking heads in the weeks following the accident endlessly pulling at the same strings, trying to find more-concrete answers in the knotted center.

The employee responsible for the maintenance had called off work that morning, for the rest of the week. The team had been short-staffed, so they'd put off the repairs.

For one day. Sixteen hours. Like fate's evil twin had been doing the scheduling that week.

It shouldn't have been enough time for anything to go wrong. It was like those expiration dates they put on milk: a lie for the sake of caution.

Deadlines for maintenance came long before maintenance was necessary.

But then someone—not the man originally scheduled to do the maintenance, but someone who'd had to take his place—had climbed onto the forklift to work on the crane.

The crane's hook block had fallen off midservice.

Hook block.

There was a phrase I hadn't known five years ago but now would never forget. I'd googled it. I could picture a hook block easier than I could picture Mark's conscious face.

The investigation was a series of guesses; everything was too burnt, too melted to say for sure.

But they guessed that the hook block had come loose. They guessed it had hit the pot full of hot metal sitting beneath the crane. They guessed the sudden force had tipped the pot, and when the liquid iron hit the damp sand surrounding, it had triggered the explosion.

Journalists wondered whether it was possible someone could have loosened the hook block beforehand.

Some even speculated about the employee who'd called off suddenly. *How could you know you were going to be sick for a week?* they wondered. They shared vague quotes from private sources implying the employee *might have been disgruntled*, that he *rarely spoke or interacted with co-workers*, that he was *strange and jumpy*.

There were petitions, hashtags, online groups, all demanding answers, demanding further investigation.

But there was no evidence, and the news anchors were careful to never say his name.

It didn't matter.

Wayne Hastings was in the air, thicker than the ash that fell on Splendor for days after the explosion.

The name was whispered and screamed, repeated a thousand times in the school hallways and the aisles of Kroger and the hospital waiting room.

Wayne Hastings.

Oh my God.

Wayne Hastings dropped the bullets. He left the note. He took the debris. He knew about the disc.

Was he going to turn us in, or was he *one of us*?

"What if he has something?" I gasped. "What if the alien gave *him* something, like it did to all of us?"

"Well, not *all* of us," Arthur bit out. "*I* still have *no* sign of a gift, whatsoever!" A little dent divided his unibrow. "*I'm* the one who poked it," he growled, "and you all get the powers!"

"Want to trade places?" I snapped. "You can have them."

Arthur's eyes darkened. "You think that's possible?"

"Franny," Sofia said. "What are you saying?"

"What if he's building it?" I said. "The thing from Remy's vision—the machine, or weapon or . . . *whatever.*"

"Oh my God." She pulled her phone out and started typing.

Arthur shook his head. "We're missing something. Something important. The E.T. isn't here to hurt us. It chose us!"

"What are you doing?" Levi asked Sofia.

"What do you think? I'm calling the police!"

"No!" Remy snatched her phone.

"We have to tell someone!" she said. "For all we know, he's building some kind of superbomb!"

My stomach tightened. I felt the hum quickening in me, the pressure building, the energy jittering under my skin. "She's right," I said. "This is all getting too dangerous. People could get hurt."

"And if we announce what happened to you—to all of us," Remy said, "*we* will get hurt. We'll end up in test tubes." He picked up his car keys off Levi's desk and turned, appealing to the others. "We don't have to tell anyone about the disc. All we need to do is take Wayne out of the picture."

"And how do we do that?" Arthur asked, apparently enlivened by the thought that his self-imposed destiny could remain intact.

"We go to the station," Remy said. "We show my dad the video of Wayne at the cave, and we lie through our teeth about everything else."

Sofia grimaced. "We can't lie to the police!"

"Remy says the world's ending, and that's your concern?" Nick said.

"It's a start," I said. There was no part of me that believed it would be enough. But it was a start. "We get Wayne taken out, and he can't finish whatever he's building. Or maybe the police will find it—disarm it."

"I'm in," Levi said.

Nick rolled his eyes. "Fine. But if this doesn't work, we turn ourselves in."

"Seconded," Sofía said.

"Fine," Arthur said bitterly, for once outvoted. "Maybe that *is* what it wants. To stop him. I guess it doesn't matter how we do that."

The Splendor Sheriff's Department was a squat brown building at the edge of town and looked more suited to be the gift shop at a shoddy state park than the headquarters of a police force.

The sign was vaguely and inexplicably western, like a prop from a cowboy movie, but once we got inside, it was as quiet and sleepy as any small office. Wood laminate lined one wall, and the blinds were slatted open, the elongated ceiling fluorescents casting glares across the deep blue panes and washing out the already washed-out blue-gray industrial carpet.

When we came in, dripping, the officer at the front desk took her feet off the desk one at a time and rolled forward in her chair. "Remy?" she said, squinting at him, like she couldn't be sure in this very, very offensive lighting. "You look like you've been swimming in that storm out there!"

At the sound of his son's name, Sheriff Nakamura's head popped out of the glass-walled office at the back of the station. He quickly tried to hide his own concern. "Is everything all right?"

Remy nodded. "Can we talk to you for a second?"

The Nakamura men studied each other for a moment. The corners of the sheriff's mouth creased. He looked like he was bracing himself to discover we'd dumped several bodies in a nearby river.

"Come on back," he said finally, lifting his coffee mug.

We filed past the three other officers. One was laughing on his desk phone, and another had a game of solitaire up. "Slow night?" Remy asked.

"You could say that." The sheriff closed the office door behind us. "There was another surge down at the substation, but they called to let us know they didn't need assistance."

"Did you go anyway?" Remy guessed.

The sheriff arched an eyebrow. "I drove past. Didn't see anything suspect." He leaned against his desk and folded his arms. "Now why don't you all tell me why you're here?"

Arthur crossed his arms, a grumpy mirror of the sheriff.

"Wayne Hastings took the debris," Remy blurted. "We have video evidence."

The sheriff's eyebrows lifted. He set his mug on the desk. "You have video of Wayne Hastings *stealing* debris?"

Remy shifted. "Well, no. We found the debris in this cave . . . behind the Jenkins House. So we set up a camera, and we caught him taking the debris out of it."

The sheriff dropped his chin. "And you didn't think to tell me when you *found* the debris?"

Remy frowned. "No?"

His father sighed. "But you see the debris on this video?"

"Not exactly," Levi answered, handing over the flash drive he'd put the copy onto. "It's really bad quality, and it cuts him off right here." He poked the center of his chest. "But you can see his creepy overalls and that he's carrying something. Probably. And the stuff was gone after that!"

"Well, the problem here is we've got no proof that the materials ever *were* there."

"I'll testify," Sofia said.

"Look, you all," he said. "Even if we had solid proof Wayne took that stuff out of some cave, that doesn't mean he stole it."

"Search his house," I said. "It's there. It's got to be."

"I can't do that without grounds," he said. "And even if Wayne Hastings *did* steal a bunch of twisted metal crap from them —which, as I said, I have a hard time believing—I doubt Crane Energy wants to press charges at this point. They've got bigger fish to fry."

My heart started to race as the possibility of resolving this shrank before my eyes. "He's dangerous," I said. "You don't know what he's using the parts for—you don't know what he's capable of."

The sheriff's expression softened. "I know you kids have every reason in the world to hate Wayne Hastings," he said gently. "But I want you to leave him alone. He gets enough harassment. The man's harmless."

"You don't know that!" I screamed, smacking his desk and surprising myself as much as anyone else.

The sheriff's stunned expression held for a beat before it resolved into something stern. "Frances, I know—"

"You're not even going to listen to us?" Remy cut across him.

"Remy, of course I'm listening. I'll always listen, but—"

"But you won't actually do anything," Remy said. "You'll run into a burning building for Joe Ass Shmo from two streets over, but when *I* need something from you, I'm just on my own."

"Remy." The sheriff reached for Remy's arm, but he shook him off, and Sheriff Nakamura's face twisted. "You're *not* on your own. You'll never be on your own."

Remy laughed. "Really? Because my mom's dead, and you're a police officer who's not following up on a dangerous person."

Right then, he was the secret Remy who'd whispered his fears to me and then pretended they vanished on the breeze, and the way his father was staring at him made me think the sheriff had never seen *this* Remy at all.

Didn't he know what his son's nightmares were about?

Didn't he know his son *hated* that he was a cop?

"I'll go to Wayne's house tomorrow," the sheriff said. He gave a tiny shake of his head. "I'll ask him if knows anything about the wreckage or the power surges, but I can't barge into his house without a warrant, and I can't get one of those without evidence."

For a prolonged moment, Remy and his dad faced off. "Do you understand?" the sheriff finally asked, quiet, gentle.

"Yeah," Remy said, and jerked the office door open. "Got it loud and clear."

He was already out the door when his father's face crumpled.

After a few seconds, the rest of us awkwardly shuffled toward the door, and Levi cleared his throat. "Good to see you, Uncle Reo."

The sheriff's dark eyes shifted over each of us. "You kids be careful, okay?"

By the time we made it to the parking lot, Remy was in the Metro, idling at the curb.

"What now?" Nick asked as we piled in. "We try the FBI? Do they have an alien hotline?"

"We get better evidence," Remy said. "We find whatever Wayne is building and get pictures."

"Exactly," Arthur said, confident and optimistic once more. "The alien wants us to destroy what Wayne's building, to prevent global catastrophe. That's why Levi sleepwalked to his house. That's what our purpose is—*to save the world!*"

I wanted to scream at him to stop. I didn't know how, after everything, he could believe in purpose, in great commissions that fell from the sky.

If people had purposes, then why was Mark comatose in a hospital bed? Who decided to cut Nick's dad down in the prime of his life, to give Nick's mom a grief so big and terrifying she couldn't get herself to leave the house ever since? To put her in a situation where she could no longer work, and her nineteen-year-old son was responsible for keeping a roof over their heads and fancy-ass stolen sneakers on their feet?

Who or what took Remy's mom from him, robbed his dad of his health and comfort? Stole Sofía's aunt and grandfather, and with them, Sofía's perfect future?

Maybe there were people who had purposes, but we weren't them.

Not people in Splendor. At least not the Ordinary.

It wasn't our purpose to save the world, but I wanted to anyway. Or at least to save the five people smashed into the car with me, who'd already lost too much.

My destiny. Whether that meant burning Wayne Hastings's house to the ground or turning myself in, somehow I'd save them.

"He has a cellar," I said. "He keeps it padlocked and covered with branches. If he's hiding something, it's there."

"Oh God," Sofía said, rubbing her head. "We're going to break into it, aren't we?"

"I am," I said. "It's up to you what you do."

"Good thinking, Fran," Arthur said. "The cellar. I should've thought of it."

Sofía took a deep breath. "If we don't find what we need, we *have* to call in the big guns."

"Like tomorrow," Nick said.

"Agreed," Levi said.

Remy's eyes met mine in the rearview mirror. I nodded, despite the anxiety piercing through me. "Tomorrow."

This was our last chance.

TWENTY-TWO

WE DECIDED WE COULDN'T all go.

Most nights Wayne Hastings drove off in his old Ford truck in the dead of night for an hour or so, and if he was gone when we got there, we'd have free rein to search, so long as we had a lookout who could warn us when he was returning.

"And if we get there and he's home," Sofía added, "we'll want to be ready to follow him if he takes off. Wherever he's going, there could be more evidence."

"You can take my car," Remy said. "I'm going to the cellar." I was surprised Sofía seemed poised to argue that she *also* wanted to be a part of our crime spree, but Remy said quickly, "You're the only person I trust to drive my car. Please."

"Wow," Nick said. "Rude."

"But you have to respect his honesty!" Levi said.

And so when we got to our house on Old Crow Station Lane, Sofía, Levi, and Nick stayed in the Metro to stake out the end of Wayne Hastings's driveway, while Remy, Art, and I got out to search his property.

"We should take Droog," Arthur said as we headed across the field. "She hasn't gotten out much since all of this started."

"Are you kidding?" I said. "If he catches us, he'll shoot her without hesitation. No way. I'll take her out to pee before we go, but I'm not bringing her with."

"He won't actually shoot us," Remy said, following us inside. Droog popped up from where she'd been sleeping on the rug inside the door, her tail thunking the wall. "Right?"

"Are you asking me to *guess*?" Arthur replied.

From upstairs, the dreary murmur of baseball commentary was leaking from the master bedroom.

Dad was already asleep, or nearly there. Good. That was good. The last thing he needed was to find out about all this.

"You live next to the guy," Remy said.

"Yeah, and do everything I can to pretend he doesn't exist." Arthur clipped the leash onto Droog's collar and then handed it to me.

"Is he really nocturnal?" Remy asked. "I mean, if this doesn't work out tonight, we can go back in the morning."

"I work," I said. "So does Arthur."

"And Nick," Arthur said. "Not that *he's* been much help."

As soon as we were out the door, Droog pulled me around the house to where she could see the woods. Usually, we just let her out and she did her business unsupervised, but all week she'd been like this. "See?" Arthur said. "She wants to go on our mission."

"Too bad." I yanked her back. "This is basically the one thing on the planet I'm responsible for, and I'm not letting her get skinned and hung on a tree with a pentagram carved into it."

"What's that?" Remy said, and bent to brush the fur on Droog's haunch to one side, revealing the purple web of scars. "She got hit too?"

I nodded. Somehow, she managed to keep straining as she crouched and peed, her nose sniffing wildly in the direction of Wayne Hastings's forest.

Remy shook his head. "Do you think she has an impulse too? Like Levi's sleepwalking? That the . . . *alien*"—it was clearly a challenge for him to even use the word—"put something in her too?"

Arthur scoffed. "Right, now even the *dog* is getting a superpower. Of course."

"Dude," Remy said. "Will you stop acting like this *isn't* the worst thing to happen to any of us?"

"Maybe for you," Arthur said coldly. He jerked the leash from my hand and pulled Droog back to the house. "Get the bolt cutters from the shed, Fran."

Remy made a pained expression as his eyes flicked toward me. "I didn't mean to . . . I just meant that this isn't *a gift.*"

"I know," I said, opening the shed.

I'd been feeling nauseated and crampy ever since we left the Jenkins House, and now as I scanned the crowded shelves for the bolt cutters, a searing pain shot from my skull down to my tailbone, knocking me off balance.

"Franny?" Remy stepped in close, and I grabbed his arm to steady myself as dizziness and pain pummeled me. The white unfurled across my vision, and for a second, I was falling through darkness again, light screaming past me. "What's happening? Are you all right?"

I blinked it back, and Remy's dimpled face pieced itself together in front of me. "I'm fine."

The corners of his mouth twisted down. "You're not," he whispered.

"I will be."

"Promise me," he said.

Tears sprang into my eyes.

"Please?"

I tore my gaze from him and grabbed the bolt cutters. "Come on. Arthur's waiting."

We met him at the fence. The overturned posts had been righted since we were last here, but Arthur pried one loose and tossed it on the ground. I handed him the bolt cutters then stepped over the barbed wire, back into the perma-hush of Wayne Hastings's woods.

The three of us communicated in nods and waves. We kept our flashlights off until absolutely necessary, which meant we could barely see one another.

My phone buzzed in my pocket, and Arthur gave a sharp, reproving look as I slid it out of my jacket. The screen glitched for a second before I could see the message preview onscreen.

Another e-mail from Bill: *FRIEND! You REALLY MUST CONTACT* . . .

"The others?" Remy whispered. "About Wayne?"

His name sent an icy drip down my spine. I shook my head and slipped my phone back into my pocket. We were almost there.

We'd come a roundabout way, up through the valley behind the house to his back door.

The windows were dark, a good sign.

We crept to the house and split up: Arthur edged around the left side, and Remy and I hurried, bent, around the right, glancing up the side of the house for signs of life in the dark windows.

We came around front, and from the far corner, Arthur nodded the all clear on his side. Remy touched my arm, then pointed toward the truck parked on the gravel driveway.

He's here? he seemed to ask.

Arthur propped the bolt cutters on his shoulder like Wayne Hastings's gun and marched in place, then drew a circle in the air with his finger.

What the hell is he doing? Remy's expression seemed to ask now.

Walking. The. Grounds, I tried to mouth back, but by then, he was distracted, staring with a repulsed expression toward the roof. In my peripheral sight, Arthur's gaze juddered up too.

I was startled anew by the eerily still birds gathered on the green roof, all angled in the same direction, their focus fixed off the back right corner of the house, the same as they'd been the other night.

Only this time, I wasn't standing there.

The birds hadn't been pointed toward me at all.

I thought about the weird behavior of the cows in the field behind the substation. What had Nick said? That usually, they grazed north to south, along the Earth's electromagnetic field, but the blast must've disrupted that.

Birds used that same field to navigate, didn't they?

Could they have been confused, like the cows and the compasses had been?

I hurried back the way we'd come, and Remy ran alongside me. Arthur met us behind the house and tried to silently ask us what we were thinking, but I was on a mission. We trekked past the cellar doors to the edge of the valley.

The branches overhead were even thicker with birds here.

In a panel of moonlight, I stopped suddenly, grabbing for Remy's hand before he could go any further.

The soft *pfft pfft pfft* of the falling rain seemed to fade away, leaving only the rush of my own pulse in my eardrums as I studied the dirt and brush under my feet.

Dead. Blackened. Charred.

A thin burnt streak snaking out through the mud in an intricate, vein-like pattern.

"The burns couldn't have reached all the way from Jenkins," Remy whispered. "That's miles away, and we would have seen them in your yard."

He was right, but that didn't change that there *were* burn marks here. We followed them down the hill, through a tunnel of black: feathers in branches all around us, and the charred dirt underfoot.

Arthur produced his compass from his jacket and angled it under the moonlight so we could see the needle spinning. We took off down the hillside along the trail.

My phone buzzed.

Another e-mail from Bill.

It had only been fifteen minutes since the last one.

I glanced at the preview: *THE U.S. GOVT WILL TAKE YOU. IT WILL BE ALL TOO EASY IF* . . .

I jammed the phone back into my pocket and ignored the crawling of my skin. I couldn't deal with him right now. One thing at a time.

Mossy branches lay scattered across the ground, splintered at the ends like snapped bones where the energy must have hit them. We stepped over them and followed the streak toward a small clearing, where four other jagged burn marks met it, like points of a star.

My skin heated and itched as I stepped into the center and slowly turned, staring at the thousands of watchful black eyes, heads that cocked and twisted curiously at the sight of us.

And worse, at the birds I now realized lay along the burn marks in lifeless lumps, just as they had back at the substation. There were feathers scattered across the forest floor, black and brown and gray and red, like a plague.

Remy swallowed. "I wonder if the blast confused their sense of direction so much that they dove."

"I knew it," Arthur hissed. "He's *not* one of us. There's a *second* alien! An *evil* alien, that we have to stop!"

My stomach roiled. It wasn't just the birds or the prospect of a second alien, though those weren't helping. I took a few dizzy steps before I caught a tree and retched into the mud. Remy was beside me in a second. "You're sick," he said. "We should get you home."

I shook my head and righted myself. "I feel better now."

Remy shook his head angrily. "We should be closer to figuring this out by now. Can't Bill do *anything*?"

I glanced at Arthur to see if he'd heard, but he was snapping pictures of the burns with his phone. As the flash went off, another painful spasm went through my esophagus, and I hunched over, vomiting.

Remy swept my hair back with one hand and drew light circles on my back with the other until the sickness had passed. I spat into the mud to get the taste out of my mouth, then straightened.

"We need to take you to a doctor," Remy whispered. "We won't tell them about . . . We'll just see what they can do."

I shook my head

"Something's wrong, Franny."

"I'm handling it," I lied.

I clutched at the tree trunk, waiting for the next jolt of pain twisting through my gut to let up.

Cold wind. Light falling all around me, being pulled into the center by an insurmountable force and the sound moving through me, everything, all at once, happening again and again—

Focus on the tree, I told myself, but it wasn't working. I was lost in that dark place.

Something pressed against my hand. *Hold on to me*, came a voice through the darkness.

"Hold on to me, Franny," Remy said again, and I opened my eyes and stared at my hand, still on the trunk but knotted tightly into his.

The creases of my raw pink knuckles, the light blue chips left on my nails from when Sofía brought polish to work for us last week digging into his hand, the red scars twining all the way from the tips of my fingers down my wrist and up to my—

The scars. They started halfway up my hand. There weren't any on my fingers at all. I stepped back from Remy, pushing my sleeve up, and found the jagged ridges faded a half inch below my elbow, where they used to end.

"My scars," I said. "Look. My scars. They shrank." I thrust my arm out in front of Remy, and Arthur shone his phone toward us as he trudged over.

Remy's mouth screwed up. "Are you sure?" He lifted his T-shirt around his stomach. "Mine too," he said. "It's like a third of the size it used to be." In fact, it was little more than a wine-colored V-shape under the right side of his ribs.

Arthur turned his arm over under the light, illuminating the intricate pattern of purply-red. "Mine's the exact same."

"What do you think this all means?" Remy asked.

Arthur looked back to the burnt mud. "Like I said, we've definitely got *two* aliens in Splendor."

"Not that," I said. "The shrinking scars."

His brow furrowed. "No idea. I'm more concerned with saving the world."

His phone chirped just then and mine buzzed in my pocket and Remy's must have too, because he took his out as well.

It was from Nick: *Creep on the move! Following!*

Another e-mail popped up from Bill, blocking out Nick's text. *Frances*, it read, *Only I can help you. DO NOT TRUST THE . . .*

My heart gave one sharp pulse.

Frances.

Frances?

When had I told him my name was Frances?

I wouldn't have done that.

I couldn't.

I didn't.

My blood went cold.

"Earth to Franny!" Arthur was saying, waving the back of his hand in front of my face so I could see the stick-and-poke letters spelling out BUTT on his knuckles. "We don't have much time— *come on!*"

He was right. Now was our chance. Probably our only one. We bounded up the hill and beelined toward the cellar.

Remy and I tore the brush aside, and Arthur stepped in with the bolt cutters at the ready. He crouched and fitted them onto the loop of the padlock.

"Wait," Remy said, and we both froze and looked at him. "After this, we're officially criminals. I mean, not fence-hopping delinquents. We're talking felony-ing our way into someone's cellar."

"Yeah?" Arthur said.

"That's all," Remy said. "I just wanted to commemorate the loss of our innocence. As you were."

Arthur cracked a smile, and an exhausted, fairly sick laugh rocked through me. "Farewell, indeed."

Arthur put pressure on the bolt cutters, and the padlock snapped, dropping with a clatter against the wooden doors.

Remy reached forward to open it, but I brushed his hand aside. "Let me," I said. "That way, if we get arrested for this, we can tell your dad we coerced you."

He smiled faintly. "Who would buy that?"

"You won't be the one who opened the door."

"So?"

I shook my head, trying to explain. "You're the one who has stuff to lose here. College and a career, and all that. When this is all over, you need to be able to get out of here, Remy. You have to leave before this town sucks out your soul, which means maintaining *some* level of plausible deniability. You're the one with the future."

"Stop it, okay?" Remy said sharply. "You have a future. And wherever it is, I'm in it. I'm not leaving *you*."

Arthur squinted between us. "What the hell are you two even talking about? Just open the door!"

So Remy reached out and opened that last door, the one we couldn't close again.

Maybe we couldn't close any of them, right from the very beginning.

When Mark was painting the Milky Way on my ceiling for my birthday, he told me something: Black holes were like punctures in the fabric of space-time. If you dove into one, you'd cross its horizon at the same moment as everything else its gravity had ever pulled there.

You'd see it all, every single bit of time and energy and material the black hole had ever experienced, its entire life flattened. No order, no causality, just a bunch of shit.

Everything, all at once.

That was what the accident had done to Splendor. As soon as we'd crossed that event horizon, we'd been doomed to everything our shit-town's gravity could pull into itself.

Remy opened the door, and Arthur led the way down the rickety stairs, and I followed.

It had always been like this. Every time we'd opened a door, it had been this door. Every time we'd followed him down, it had been this set of stairs.

Now we would finally see where we'd been going.

TWENTY-THREE

EVEN OUR FOOTSTEPS SEEMED to whisper as we descended, making no more noise than the faintest scuff of rubber on concrete.

We felt our way down the stairs. Remy's flashlight clicked on, swinging back and forth like a light saber until it caught on the metal racks that lined the right and back walls of the room. On the left, rusted metal hooks held tools aloft: axes, snow shovels—*guns*. Lots of them.

An immense, wood- and foam-dusted worktable occupied the center of the room.

Something metallic clinked and rattled as Remy's flashlight caught on it: a single bulb and chain mounted in the ceiling beside the worktable. Arthur tugged it, and sallow light unfurled like a blanket across the table. There was an industrial-strength lamp clamped to the edge, and some kind of saw mounted on the other side. The surface was sprinkled with both wood and metal shavings.

"He's building something, all right," Arthur said.

My spine crawled. "Or he already built it."

Remy picked up a twisted piece of steel, six inches long. "Maybe there are blueprints."

There was a leather-bound folder on a shelf beneath the tabletop, and he stooped to grab it. Arthur set the bolt cutters down and walked along the racks, examining the mix of extension cords and dusty soup cans, oversized water bottles and small generators, fans, lanterns, blankets.

"Maybe he thinks he can survive whatever that *thing* does,

down here," Arthur said. "Maybe he thinks if he builds this thing, they'll let him live."

He stopped and ran his fingers over a toolbox. "If we could just find *our* alien, this would be so much simpler." He turned back to us. "Where could it have gone?"

Another cramp went through my center. I stepped back and gripped the edge of the metal rack on either side of my legs.

"No idea." Remy's eyes darted to mine then back to the leather folder in his hands.

I closed my eyes and gritted my teeth, fighting the white trying to overcome me.

"Fran?" Cast in stark light and shadow, Remy looked like a woodcut of himself. He lifted an oversized sheaf of paper and held it toward me.

Arthur perked up with interest. He grabbed it before I could, and his expression transformed.

As far as I knew, my brother wasn't afraid of anything, except maybe dying in a particularly boring way. But his body had gone rigid, and the tan leached out from under his freckles.

"Are there more of these?" he said huskily.

Remy's mouth juddered, but no sound came out. He'd gone as pale as Arthur, who pushed him aside and started flipping through the stack of papers on the table.

"What is it?" I asked, stumbling forward.

Schematics?

A journal about his time with the alien, or a confession that he'd loosened the hook block at the steel mill?

A *Why I Did It* letter?

Arthur tried to block my way as I came forward, and that was when I knew it must be something worse. Something horrifying, something I'd never unsee.

My phone buzzed, and I heard Arthur's chirp—Remy's had probably gone off too—but neither of them reacted. They were quickly sifting through the papers, spreading them out across the tabletop in a mania, all while Arthur kept his back to me, all while he tried to block me out.

I pushed past him. This time, I knew, I couldn't afford to look away.

At first I was so stunned by the light, careful lead sketch that a bubble of relief rose through my chest. It was just a drawing. A portrait.

Then I pieced together the thick wavy hair, the unruly eyebrows and speckled cheeks and bony shoulders.

It was me.

The phones chirped, buzzed, soundlessly vibrated, and we ignored them.

My throat felt like it had collapsed. I couldn't speak. Blood rushed past my eardrums, and a forceful buzz went through me. The lights overhead stuttered, but I was too dazed to reel back the energy pouring off me.

Art and Remy were both flipping furiously through the papers, the images in them blinking in and out of view beneath the flashing light.

Me.

Me.

Me.

Droog.

My *parents*, I realized. Mom twice more, then Dad, then Droog and me. A drawing of Arthur, before his tattoos, before he'd cut the bowl-like mop of blond hair off. Another of me. There were dozens, easily. Drawings of me perched on the propane tank, minus the mustachioed penis. Sketches of Mom looking through the telescope she used to keep on the balcony outside her and Dad's room. Dad lying on his back on a blanket in the grass, and Droog jumping over him.

Our phones went off again, ignored.

"Oh my God," I gasped as my eyes fell onto a blur of lead I hadn't noticed in the corner of the drawing in my hand. I checked the one beneath it and beneath that. Two letters scrawled on every page. Initials.

M.S.

Mark Schmidt.

My skin erupted in goose bumps. "He took these from our house," I whispered, and then, the much worse realization: "He's been *in* our house."

Why?

What did he want? To figure out what the thing in the disc had told us? To hurt us?

Remy's phone started ringing. "*Shit*," he choked. "All these texts—we have to go. He's on his way back!" He answered the call, and on the other end, I heard Nick spring into rapid-fire talking.

I spread the drawings across the table with shaking hands.

"Take pictures," I told Arthur. "We need to get proof."

He was staring at the table in a daze, fear torquing his features. The buzz in me was worsening, the lights still strobing, and reaching for my own phone would be useless.

"Art, *now*! We have to go!"

He shook his head. "We can't leave these here. He can't *have* them, Franny! They're *Mark's*, and they're—they're our *family*!"

"Arthur, unless the sheriff finds them here, we have nothing!"

"He'll think we planted them anyway!" Arthur cried. "He's more suspicious of *us* than he is of this asshole!"

"Then we'll find some other way to lead him down here," I promised. "Just take the freaking photos, Arthur!"

Remy hung up the call midword and held up his phone, snapping a few pictures. Then he pulled the chain to turn the light off, but it did nothing. My emotions were out of control, and so were my surges of power. In the flashing light, I thrust the pages back into the folder, all except the lone drawing of Arthur, which he grabbed from my hand.

There was no time to argue, and even if there had been, I was momentarily distracted by the sight of my own arm.

The scars had shrunk again; I was almost sure.

Whatever. It didn't matter right now.

I stuffed the folder back on the shelf under the table, and we fled.

At the top of the steps, I grabbed the broken padlock as Remy and Arthur pushed the doors closed—it was extremely unlikely a man with something to hide wouldn't notice the missing lock, or that his stuff had been disturbed, but there was nothing else we could do.

The rain had stopped, but everything was drenched and muddy as we sprinted through the woods, away from the gravel driveway and the sounds of tires crackling up it. We ran down through the valley, then curved back toward our house, and when we reached our property, the others were *just* pulling up.

We ran up, and they jumped out and met us partway, and everyone started talking at once.

"Wait!" I half shouted over the din as I latched on to something Sofía had said. "The *steel mill?*"

"What about it?" Arthur said.

"That's where he went," Nick explained. "First to a cemetery, then to the steel mill."

"Is he building the weapon out there?" Remy asked.

"We don't think so," Levi said.

213

"We couldn't follow him into the cemetery without making it too obvious, and we couldn't get all that close at the mill either," Sofía said, "but it looked like he was loading more metal into his truck. Like stripping the wire and pipes from the building."

"I don't understand," Arthur said.

"It was bound to happen to you eventually," Nick said.

"There was no sign of the materials in his cellar," Arthur said. "If he's not building it at the mill either, where do you think he's doing it?"

"In his house?" Sofía said. "Somewhere in the woods?"

"Did you find *anything* we can use?" Nick asked. "A jar of human teeth or something?"

Remy flashed me a dark look. "You could say that."

Arthur held out the picture on his phone, and the others stared at it.

"Dozens of those," I clarified. "Well, not that, exactly. But drawings of our family."

"He's been *drawing* you?" Levi said, wide-eyed.

"Not quite," I said.

"They're Mark's," Arthur explained. "He stole them."

My gut twisted as I thought back to what the sheriff had said when he'd questioned us about the substation. "It might be some kind of trophy. Maybe he's got stuff from *everyone* who was hurt in the accident."

"If this dude's got serial killer trophies in his basement, it's officially time to stop calling it *an accident* and call the police," Nick said. "Again."

"We need to get them out here before he moves anything," Arthur agreed.

Remy looked to me, and I nodded. He took out his phone and paced the length of the car as he dialed. "He's not picking up."

"We'll have to go back to the station," I said.

"By the time we get there and the sheriff gets back *here*, the stuff could be gone!" Arthur cried.

Remy thrust his phone toward Levi as he climbed back into the car. "Put that on speaker, and don't stop dialing until he answers."

For what felt like the millionth time that night, we squeezed back into the Metro and took off, but we'd barely reached the haunted bridge when the incessant ringing over Remy's loudspeaker cut out, replaced by a clamor of voices. "Hello?" Sheriff Nakamura said over the wash of sound.

"Where are you?" Remy asked. "What's all that noise?"

"I'm at the station." There was a harried edge to his voice. "I know we need to talk, Rem, but right now's not a good time. Things have suddenly . . . picked up here."

Remy's jaw worked anxiously. "Is it about Wayne Hastings?"

"What? No, it's . . ." A few seconds passed, and then the drone of the busy station went silent as a door clicked closed. "Are you injured? Are you safe?"

"Injured? No," Remy said.

A knocking sound came over the line. "Hold on a second."

The murmuring voices crept back in and the sheriff said, "Tell Agent Rothstadt I'll be right out." As soon as the background noise vanished again, the sheriff sighed. "Sorry about that, bud. We got a late-night visit from the FBI."

"The FBI?" Remy said.

My heart thudded. Remy's eyes met mine in the rearview mirror.

"Yeah, it turns out those burns in the field were caused by a piece of a satellite," the sheriff said.

Piece of satellite, Arthur mouthed, clearly offended by the very notion. I tried to smile at him, to communicate *Yeah, ridiculous*, but I'd just gone so dizzy the car was capsizing before my eyes.

The FBI.

The FBI was *here.* Were they the ones who'd taken the video down? Did they know it was us in it? Did they care?

"We don't know much else yet, but there are concerns about radiation," the sheriff was saying. "They've got military here setting up a temporary facility and everything, so I don't want you kids going anywhere near Jenkins Lane, got it?"

Remy stared hard into my eyes via the rearview mirror.

"Rem?" the sheriff prompted.

He pulled over onto the shoulder abruptly and put the car in park. "Got it."

"What did you need?" the sheriff asked. "Everything okay?"

Remy's mouth opened and closed. Bits of Bill's frantic e-mails were carouseling through my mind, and the others must have been able to hear my heart racing guiltily, fearfully.

I should have told them.

I might be the one hosting the alien, but we were all in that video. If I'd told them what Remy knew, one of them would have talked sense into me. I would've turned myself in before it came to this.

Before it came to them.

"Remy?" the sheriff pressed.

Nick's eyes bulged as if to say, *Dude! Go on!* and Arthur spun his finger, like *Get to the point*, and Levi and Sofía both leaned in, urging Remy onward.

Just then, headlights hit the rearview mirror, and a black SUV appeared on the curved bridge behind us. The long black car slid past, sleek and inky, followed immediately by another, and then another. A fourth, a fifth.

Remy was watching them with a tensed jaw. My mouth had gone dry as sandpaper; the buzz revved through me, jostling, eager, as fear coiled through my body, but I released my grip on those non-muscles, and it dispersed in my body again.

The ground shivered as the sixth and final Suburban skimmed past, and in its wake, a solid-white semitruck appeared, brakes spitting and hissing as it jerked through the corkscrew of the road.

"Are you there?" the sheriff asked.

Remy cleared his throat. "Shoot. I just blanked."

"What?" Nick demanded from the far side of the back seat.

"I'll call you back, Dad," Remy said, and hung up.

"Dude," Levi said gently. "What's the deal?"

The semitruck rumbled past, and another one sloughed out of the blue-green foliage, followed by a third.

There was something nightmarish and impossible about it, like I was watching the woods lay eggs, long and shining in the moonlight.

"Why didn't you say anything?" Sofía demanded.

"The FBI is here," Remy said.

"So what? They're busy with the satellite crash! We need to get Wayne behind bars, Remy."

"*Not* a satellite," Arthur growled.

"Not the point!" Nick said. "The man who ruined our lives and stockpiled your brother's stolen drawings is building a weapon for aliens, and Remy's having visions about the world ending! I personally am *thrilled* the FBI's here!"

The shadowy fold of the woods delivered a fourth and final semitruck.

So many trucks.

So many voices at the police station.

So many people here, all searching for us.

For the thing in me.

The power trapped under my skin was too much. The memory of light searing across my mind was too much. Their arguing was too much.

"It was supposed to be our discovery," Arthur was saying. "Now they're going to take over the whole thing."

"So what?" Sofía said. "The world will still be saved!"

"Those trucks were *in* my vision," Remy said, spinning in his seat to face us. "This doesn't change anything! The FBI isn't here to save the world."

My own body felt claustrophobic, and I couldn't get a good breath.

"Then what are they here for?" Nick demanded.

I threw open the back door and tumbled out onto the shoulder, gasping for oxygen. I bent over and pressed my hands against my knees as I struggled to inhale.

Two more SUVS were roaring past behind the trucks, bumping up behind them like security guards.

"Franny?" Sofía said, jumping out of the car and trailing me to the evergreen trees. "Franny, are you okay?"

I turned back to her, staring through the heady clumps of mist drifting through the headlights.

I tried to speak, but no sound came out. I shook my head. Remy opened his door and stood, his silhouette peering over the car at me as Sofía took two slow steps, murmuring, "It's making you sick, isn't it?"

I blinked at her.

"I know it is," she said shakily. "All night you've seemed like you were about to collapse. . . . Using that power is *hurting* you."

It should've been obvious, but it honestly hadn't occurred to me before then.

Every time a burst of the power receded from my body, pain and nausea raced in to take its place.

Every time I tapped into the energy, the pain got a little worse.

"Whatever's going on," she said, voice wet and rattling, "please just *tell* me. For *once*, just tell me."

Tears flooded my eyes. I felt suddenly small, helpless. The others had gotten out of the car too and were watching, waiting for an explanation for my outburst.

The last thing I wanted to do was tell them, but it was time.

I could end this for all of us, if I was just honest.

"Remy's right," I rasped. "The FBI isn't here to save the world."

"We don't really know what they're here for," he cut in. "But whatever it is—"

"They're here for me," I said. "For the thing inside me."

TWENTY-FOUR

"IT WENT INTO ME," I said. "I didn't remember at first either, but . . ."

Remy turned away, shaking his head angrily, but it was never his job to protect me, and I shouldn't have let him try.

My heart pounded as I went on. "But at the end, right before we came to . . . the thing walked into me. That's how it disappeared, when it all stopped. It entered me."

There was a beat of silence.

Levi's mouth dipped open. "What. The."

Nick's eyes bulged. "I swear to Gah."

Arthur went white-faced, and Sofía stepped back, like she'd been pushed.

"That's what you've been keeping from us?" she said.

I glanced at Remy. He'd walked into the middle of the road, his hands folded behind his head like he was stretching his neck.

I took a deep breath. "There's more." I held my phone out to Arthur, but he made no move to take it. He was stunned into uncommon silence and stillness. "I e-mailed that guy. Black Mailbox Bill, who said he'd seen one of the discs? Look what he said."

Arthur stared at the phone like it was a living rabbit I'd just pulled from Levi's fedora. Sofía took the phone instead, and Nick and Levi crowded around her, reading over her shoulder.

"Okay, now we *really* need to tell someone," Levi said. "We've got to blow this thing wide open."

Remy spun back. "And this is why we didn't tell you."

Levi looked gobsmacked. "You knew too?" he asked, right as Arthur sprung back to life, saying to me, "You told *him* and not *me*?"

"I was handling it," I explained.

"Obviously not," Arthur argued.

"I was *trying* to," I said. "I thought if Bill could tell me what had happened to *him*, then—"

"Then you could just leave me in the dark?" Arthur demanded. "You trusted a total stranger over me, Franny!"

"Oh, come on, Arthur," Remy said, stalking back toward us. "You might not have known the thing was in her, but you knew it had done something to her, and all you cared about was getting enough groundbreaking footage to land your own Wikipedia page."

"That's not fair," Levi said. "We were all affected—we didn't know she was any different!"

"She's shooting lightning out of her fingertips!" Nick said. "Not that it matters, because as soon as you realized that thing had affected any of us, you should have given a rat's ass what that might have meant! But *you* weren't affected, Art, so of course it was all fun and games! Of course it was all just trying to find the next thing that could fucking turn you into someone, so you can finally out-shine your brother, no matter *what* or *who* it's costing!"

"Thank you!" Remy said, caught up in the moment, but I was staring at Arthur, watching the expression melt off his face like he'd been slapped.

"Stop it," Sofia said quietly, but Nick was rounding on me and Remy now.

"And as for you two, I don't know why, but I expected better! You knew what kind of danger you were putting us all in, and you said nothing! Didn't even warn us that every second we stayed in this shit-show, we were risking being—being *disappeared* by the gah-damn U.S. government! I'm so freaking tired of all your lies and secrets, and that goes for all of you!"

"Are you *kidding*?" Arthur laughed harshly.

"Stop," Sofía hissed. "This isn't helping anything."

"You're a shoplifting addict who never even lets us past his front door," Arthur cried at Nick. "We don't even know your birthday! Every story you tell is about nine percent factual, Nick! You lie more than you tell the truth, and we all pretend not to notice, so that you can continue in your delusion that you're just a normal guy with a normal life, and not a teen caretaker for a stay-at-home hoarder!"

After five years, the laws of our private universe had been violated, and now the fabric of us was set to come apart.

The Ordinary was teetering, ready to shatter in a way that it could never be put back together.

"You're damn right!" Nick shouted. "I take care of my mom! And if something happens to me, that's it! She's got no one else. She'll die under a box of used batteries she's saving in case she ever gets around to recharging them, and no one will think to check on her for weeks!

"You think you and Franny have it *so hard* trying to get your parents' attention, but guess what, man: Assuming an alien doesn't kill you or the FBI doesn't cart you off, you're leaving in a week. You're getting out, and you don't even have to feel bad about that, while I'm here getting shit-talked for life. I might as well have just stayed in twelfth grade for five more years! That's as close to a life as I'm getting, staying in this dump, but there's nothing I can do about it, because someone needs me here.

"Sorry *your* life matters so little that all you can do is fill up the void with bullshit schemes and—and Amazon packages and toys and freaking slumber parties"—he waved a hand toward Levi, who went red-faced and staggered back—"just so you don't have to be alone with yourself for thirty seconds, but some of us have people counting on us and actually have to *work* for our money!"

"Nicholas!" Sofía shouted. "That's enough!"

"Oh please!" Nick said. "Don't go all *defender of the weak* on me—turn yourselves in to the FBI or don't, but leave me out of it. I'm done, like I should've been from the beginning. I'm done."

The ground felt like water under my feet. Actually, my whole body felt like water, like my skin was as thin as a balloon and any second, everything in me might come rushing out.

"Of course you are," Arthur said. "Just walk away from the most important thing that's ever happened to you."

"Wake up!" Nick said. "We're nothing kids from a nothing town. You think we were chosen? We were in the wrong place at the wrong time."

"The right place!" Arthur slammed a hand against the car. "We might be nothing kids from a nothing town, but that's not enough for me, and I know it's not enough for you either! Aren't you tired of being the leftovers? I *know* we're the kids they don't look at. We're like—shadows burned onto the ground by the accident. Maybe this thing chose us because we're survivors, or maybe it's that we were just the only pathetic option it had, but we're the ones with the gifts! We have a chance to matter!"

Nick shook his head and took a few steps back. "I'm done." He turned and stalked down the road through the blaze of Remy's headlights, and the energy was still building in me, crackling inside my skull until I couldn't think straight, couldn't parse out the accusations and demands hurtling back and forth around me as everyone broke out at once, shouting over one another.

"How could you keep this from me? I'm your cousin!" Levi was saying. "Why do you always choose *her* over me?"

"Because Nick's right! Everything's just a game for you, Levi! We're just more of your accessories!"

"How would you know? We never even talk anymore! You spend half your time with girls I never even meet and the rest whispering with Franny like I'm not even here!"

"Please, stop!" Sofía pleaded. "We need to figure out what to do next."

The whole world was coming apart.

The island we had built for ourselves. The place where none of the ugly shit was supposed to be able to intrude, where the ash from the accident wouldn't fall and the things we feared were never said.

My whole world was coming apart, and I had caused it.

By telling them the truth. By needing them when they could barely withstand the pressure that was already on them.

It was my parents' fight in the kitchen all over again. It was Mom crying behind closed doors, begging Dad to understand. It was the Voyager pulling away from our driveway, two weeks after Wayne Hastings moved in behind us, Arthur's fists whaling against drywall.

It was my model of the solar system on the table, Mom's windbreakers in my arms the day we filmed "Kite Chasers."

"I'm done," I said, barely louder than a whisper, but under the cousins' arguing no one heard.

I took a deep, painful breath. "Take me to the station," I shouted. "I'll tell them it's in me."

The arguing stopped. Remy, Levi, Arthur, and Sofía all looked at me

"I'll show them," I said, trying to sound more confident than I felt. "And I'll tell them about the visions. I'll just say *I* had them."

The four of them blinked at me. I was a stranger, speaking an unfamiliar language. I was a living ghost, standing in their periphery as their problems and fears took center stage.

"What are you talking about?" Arthur said.

"I have to turn myself in. It's the best way, probably the only way out of this."

I expected Remy to lie, to say that we weren't out of options yet, that we hadn't reached our last resort.

I expected Arthur to argue we couldn't just turn everything over to the FBI, that *we* were the ones destined to save the world.

I expected Levi to insist the world deserved the truth and we needed to stick together indefinitely to deliver it.

And I expected Sofía to admit I was right: that turning me in was the only reasonable course of action we could follow, given Remy's visions of world-ending peril and the total collapse of our plans to prevent those visions from unfolding.

Instead, she looked right at me, heat flaming in her cheeks and sparking in her eyes. "No."

"No?" A humorless laugh went through me. "What do you mean, *no*?"

"I mean *no*." She took a deep breath. "It's time for you to accept that you're not in this alone and to stop acting like we're just some people from your math class who misspell your name when we sign your yearbook. Nick was right. We all lie and keep secrets, and act like we're doing one another some big favor by not talking about what's happened to us in the last five years, but we're *not*, and I'm sick of it. You didn't even tell me about this Black Mailbox guy even after you *knew* I'd started seeing through your eyes and could bust you."

I opened my mouth to explain, but she cut me off: "And that's okay. I forgive you. I know it's hard for you to trust people."

My eyes prickled. An uneasiness jostled in my stomach. I started to argue, but she forged on.

"I *know* you think I'm going to let you down, and I probably should've given up on this friendship a long time ago, but I can't, because I know you too well—even the parts you try not to share—and I love you.

"If we're going to survive this, we need to stop lying to each other and keeping secrets. I'll start: It sucks loving someone who doesn't want to be loved, who won't let you care about them—who doesn't even want you to notice or care when they're hurting."

Tears brimmed in my eyes, the knot in my chest dangerously loosening, threatening to let my body come apart. I didn't understand where all this was coming from—what she was saying, what I was feeling. I didn't understand why I kept picturing the hospital parking lot or why this conversation felt like it was cutting into me, deeper and deeper. *"Sofía."*

"No," she said again, sharply. "Admit it: You didn't tell us that *thing* went into you because you were afraid we'd fail you. You're always afraid we won't choose you, so you don't even give us a chance to. But of course I would. Of course we do. You're my family, Fran."

"It doesn't matter now," I choked out. "There's nothing you can do. Turning myself in is the only answer."

Levi shook his head. "No."

I looked to Remy for support, but he shook his head too. "You already know, Fran. I'd trade this whole stupid town for you."

"That's morally indefensible," Sofía said. "But same."

I was trembling, barely keeping a lid on the buzz running through me. "What if it's not the whole town?" I managed. "What if it's the world?"

"Either way," Levi said, "we're going to save it."

"We'll find a way," Remy agreed. "We'll get through this together."

I looked to Arthur. He hadn't moved or spoken. His hazel eyes were narrowed and his mouth pressed closed. There was something uncomfortable, maybe even perplexed, in his expression, and he looked away quickly, running his forearm up his hairline to catch the sweat beading there. He cleared his throat, but his voice still came out thick, sort of overcome. "Thanks," he said quietly, his eyes darting low across the others. "Thanks for watching out for Fran."

Sofía rolled her eyes. "Just to be clear, Franny's my favorite, but I would have the same opinion if it were *you* with an alien parasite, Arthur."

"Same," Remy agreed.

"I don't play favorites," Levi mused. "But I would lie to the FBI for any of you, and for Nick."

"Either way . . ." Arthur didn't look at them, didn't look at me. He took a few more seconds to gather himself, nodding. "Thanks."

I tried to say it too, but I couldn't. I turned away, trying to discreetly wipe tears off my cheeks. I felt arms come around me and smelled Sofía's rosewater as she tucked my head under her chin, the itch of the power slowing in my veins. "You're my sister," she said.

I closed my eyes tight and nodded into her shoulder until I'd gotten control over myself. I pulled back finally, sniffling, and looked at the ground. "What about Bill? Do I e-mail him back?"

For once, Levi, Arthur, Remy, and Sofía were in complete agreement.

"No way."

"Absolutely not."

"*Hell* no."

"What are you thinking? He's some guy on the Internet, Franny!"

TWENTY-FIVE

WE AGREED THAT LIFE had to appear to go on as usual, to not draw attention, and so I'd come to work, but now, with ten minutes until 6:30, when my shift ended, I couldn't help but pace behind the desk.

I checked the group message again. Someone had renamed it "THE FIRST RULE OF FIGHT CLUB," but there had been no new messages since Remy's noon update—that he was still waiting at home for his dad to show up so he could show him our evidence against Wayne—and Sofía's two PM text that she was leaving lacrosse practice and to keep her posted.

As long as the FBI was around, we'd have to lie low, but the sooner we led them to Wayne, we hoped, the sooner they'd be gone. Rather than risk going back to the station, Remy had taken Levi, Art, Sofía, and me back to our house, where the Doctors Perez already thought we were sleeping over, and then Remy had gone home to ambush his dad with what we'd found in Wayne's cellar.

Only, as of noon, the sheriff still hadn't made it home for so much as a change of socks.

Still, it had been more than six hours since then, and Remy hadn't replied to either of my *Any news?* texts, which seemed strange. Black Mailbox Bill seemed to have finally gotten the hint and stopped e-mailing me too, and while I knew the others thought it was for the best, the silence was deafening.

For all I knew, by ignoring him, we'd lost our one chance out of this.

Or maybe he'd only stopped e-mailing because he *had* to.

Because someone had finally found him.

The bells rang over the glass doors as my replacement, Grace, showed up for the evening shift. She waved and pointed to the locker rooms without removing her earbuds, indicating that she needed to change, and I gathered my stuff and came out from behind the desk.

The windows were washed in an eerie gray-green, and though the rain had let up, fog hung in its place. The repulsive humidity from outside had sneaked its way into the building, frizzing my hair and coating my skin in a sticky layer of sweat.

To be fair, I'd been sticky since I got here—I was fairly sure that barely sleeping last night had left me with a low-grade fever. Just as I'd finally started to drift off around three, I'd heard a commotion in the front yard and looked out my window to find Arthur cursing up a storm as he fixed my broken bike wheel. And then at five, I'd awoken again, this time to the sound of Levi sleep-tripping through the hallway, and I'd had to run downstairs and forcefully shake him awake before he could march outside again.

"Stop him," he'd been grumbling, sending prickles out over and under my skin. *"Youavetostop hmmmm."*

Sofía had heard the commotion and come to help. "Wake up, Levi!" she'd kept saying. "It's Fran and Sofía. You're dreaming."

But just like the other night, that had set him off in a new direction, grumbling something like *It is Molly* or maybe, Sofía had pointed out, *Moll-E.*

"As in Wall-E?" I'd said, laughing.

"I don't know! Maybe it's some kind of alien naming convention!"

For a very brief time this afternoon, I'd renamed the group text "The Alien Formerly Known as Moll-E," and she'd sent a quick mid-practice text saying, *You Schmidts! Unhappy when I'm a skeptic; unhappy when I try to embrace this ridiculously absurd situation we've wandered into.*

She had a point. Hosting the consciousness of an alien named Moll-E was no more unlikely than hosting an alien consciousness, period. And Molly *had* turned out to be a convenient shorthand for "extraterrestrial being" in the group text.

A blur of red caught my eye from the TV, and I jerked my gloved hand out of my sweatshirt pocket, lunging for the remote to unmute Cheryl Kelly as she appeared.

When I recognized the huge blue facade behind her, my stomach dropped.

"I'm here outside the Splendor Township Walmart . . ." she began, and my eyes went instinctively to my phone, checking for messages from Arthur or Nick I already knew weren't there.

". . . where Crane Energy officials are investigating another in this week's long series of blackouts. While the power has since been returned, a fourteen-minute loss of electricity in the early hours of this morning led to a shoplifting frenzy, whose cost for the store may have totaled several thousand dollars, including—*disturbingly*— a three-hundred-dollar gun safe, four propane tanks, and several high-end power tools. While the blackout appears to have affected the entire block, Walmart was the only business that was, in fact, open at the time of power loss. Police are advising nearby business owners to check inventory for signs of theft anyway."

The scene cut to a prerecorded interview with a large-toothed "Walmart shopper," and I dialed Arthur as quickly as I could.

The call went straight to voice mail, and I hung up, steeling myself to call Nick. It rang endlessly, but he didn't answer.

I typed into the group message: *Saw the CK report! What's going on there???*

The truth was, I could guess.

There was only one other person, besides me and Molly the Benevolent Alien, who might be able to cause a blackout.

And that stuff he stole. Propane tanks, a gun safe, who knew what else.

And what did it mean that he'd left his house this morning? He *never* left his house in the morning.

It means he's hurrying, I realized.

It meant we were nearly out of time, and meanwhile the FBI had probably been circling Arthur and Nick all day.

My gut clenched. I texted the group again: *Remy, you NEED to send your dad to Wayne's NOW if you haven't.*

As soon as Grace reappeared in uniform at the end of the hall, I hurried to clock out and ran into the humid parking lot, almost smacking into the blue Cadillac idling outside the doors. I waved an apology and headed for my bike.

I thought about going straight to Walmart to check on Arthur and Nick, but according to the report, the power was back on now, and the last thing we needed was for me to make a spectacle with another blackout.

If we were careful, this could work out for us. We could nudge the police toward Wayne Hastings; they could find the stolen material, which would tip off the FBI that he'd been there during the blackout; and when they came to investigate, they'd find the burns.

But if they found *those* burns, they'd know there were multiple crashes, and I doubted taking *one* alien host would satisfy them when they had proof two might be walking around Splendor.

I'd figure that out later. The point was, we couldn't let Remy's vision come true.

I turned my bike toward home and pedaled up the slope of the parking lot toward the street. Through the fog, the headlights of the idling Cadillac caught the corner of my eye again. It had pulled forward, making its way toward the driveway. I set my feet on the asphalt, waiting to let the car pass me, but it stopped, the driver waving for me to pass.

I kicked off again and crossed the street, fast, before some car could barrel through the fog at full speed, and turned left along the grassy shoulder.

Thunder rumbled in the distance, and the energy in me jumped, crackling in response.

My gaze swept across the intersection as I turned onto Old Crow Station Lane and dipped into the ditch alongside it, mud spitting up against my ankles as I pedaled. I ducked my head as a car sped past, kicking rainwater into my hair. I tugged my hood up as it slowed onto the tree-lined shoulder ahead of me.

The blue Cadillac's lights went off.

Blue Cadillac.

It probably wasn't the same car. And if it was, it wasn't following me. It was a coincidence.

I rode farther off the road as I approached. The passenger window was rolled down, a bundle of folders and papers resting in the seat, but I couldn't see the driver.

I held my breath as I rode past, and a moment later, the car pulled onto the road again and sped away.

See? I thought. *Nothing.*

I flinched, nearly crashing into an old oak, as my phone vibrated in my sweatshirt pocket. I regained my balance and fished it out with my gloved hand just as I was clearing the copse of trees.

My eyes darted between where my house had come into view ahead and my phone screen.

I tapped the call on and lifted the phone to my ear. "Levi?"

"*Finally,*" he gasped on the other end. "Why isn't anyone answering their phones?"

"They're at work," I said. "Or at least Arthur is, and Nick's just ignoring us, I'm pretty sure. No idea about Remy or Sof."

"Where are you?" Levi interrupted.

"Almost home."

"Don't," Levi said.

"Don't *what*?"

"Don't go home," Levi said. "They're at my house, Franny."

"The others are? What's going on—"

"No," Levi hissed. "The freaking *FBI*. They're at my house. They're taking like—they're taking *everything*. They have a search warrant."

I almost dropped the phone as I looked back toward my drive-way. Two black Suburbans were parked in it, right behind Dad's truck.

"Hello?" Levi said. "Franny?"

My voice came out shaky. "Everything?"

"They're loading up boxes of my stuff. My cameras, my computer, all of it."

"Where's the video?" I asked. "From that night?"

"I've got the memory card," he said, "but there's a copy saved on my computer. Look, the sheriff's here too. He told me not to say anything just yet. They're taking me in for questioning—"

"Questioning?" I bit out. "What could they possibly pretend to *question* you about? You didn't do anything!"

"I know," Levi said. "The sheriff's pretty mad. I guess they already picked up Remy early this morning when the sheriff wasn't home, and they still haven't released him."

Remy.

They'd had him all morning. That was why he hadn't replied.

"I'm sure he's okay," Levi said, anticipating my fears. "They can only hold him so long, and I doubt he's said a single word. He knows his rights. Anyway, I'm trying to get ahold of my parents, but they're, like, in a dead zone, and—" Levi dropped off. I caught the faint murmur of Remy's dad talking in the background.

"Levi?" I said, then more urgently, "Levi!"

"I have to go," he said. "I'll call you as soon as I can. Don't go home, Franny."

The line clicked dead.

I was even with my driveway now. I thought I saw the drapes move in the front window. My whole body was shaking.

I kept pedaling. I didn't know where I was going. Not Levi's house or Remy's. I couldn't risk going to Sofía's or Nick's either. I could head to Walmart, but that was five miles in the opposite direction, and they were probably under observation now too.

The panic was building, and as it did the headlights of passing cars were flickering in and out.

Shit. I focused all my energy on pedaling, on getting as far from my house as I could, typing out a message into our group chat as I went: *DON'T GO HOME.*

What were they doing at my house?

What were they telling Dad they were doing at my house?

What excuse had they given Sheriff Nakamura for digging through his nephew's stuff?

For taking his son?

I lurched back onto the asphalt in time to pass under the stone bridge that held up the train tracks, and the car passing through in the opposite direction slammed on its horn at the sight of me.

I turned my handlebars so hard I nearly fell off my bike as I shot out of the tunnel and onto the cross street beyond. I jerked the bike right again as the left handlebar clipped the rearview mirror of a car waiting at the stop sign there. Fog slipped down my throat as I swore and lost control, careening furiously into the marshy bank off the road.

The gray world cycloned around me as I flew clear of the bike and tumbled through the soggy end-of-summer grass.

I was vaguely aware of the car turning around, to check on me, maybe, or more likely to scream at me for hitting their mirror. I staggered to my feet, left ankle stinging where it had caught most of my weight, the same one I'd rolled the other night, and swung my legs back over the bike, kicking off hard.

There was no time to look back.

I needed to get somewhere safe. Somewhere isolated, where no one would think to look for me.

The cord of energy running through me shivered, like a metal coil charged to the brim.

I hadn't realized I was already heading there.

To the mill.

I chanced a look over my shoulder, to see if the car I'd clipped was still following me. It was, but the driver was taking it easy, cruising along the rain-slicked road at the approximate pace of an eighty-year-old who'd given himself forty minutes to make it to bingo night at Ray's Sports Bar & Grill.

He was crawling along like he had no intention of catching up, leaving plenty of space between us.

Between me and his powder-blue Cadillac.

But when I looked back at him, he sped up.

TWENTY-SIX

THE CADILLAC'S OLD ENGINE whined, and the windshield wipers made rubbery squeaks in time with my racing heart.

Pedaling through the marshy grass was slow going, but moving up onto the road wasn't an option.

One swift jerk of the wheel and he could be in front of me, cut me off.

My lungs burned. Condensation slipped into them with every anxious breath. There was no one else around. No foot traffic on these country roads. No other cars.

Ahead on the left, another road dead-ended into this one. I'd have to ride in front of the Cadillac to turn onto it, but if I managed it, I could cut into the wooded gap on the road's far side and lose him.

I concentrated on my stinging thigh muscles rather than the crunchy pain shooting through my ankle. Overhead, something popped and shattered—a streetlight, raining glass down on the Cadillac's hood.

The driver hit the brakes, the wheels skidding sideways along the slick road then whipping back in the other direction as he corrected his mistake.

It was enough. I shot clear of the hood of the Cadillac for a second, two seconds, three seconds, and ramped back up onto the road, straight toward the tilted sign for Galbraith Road and the pine trees beyond it.

The Cadillac's tires shrieked as the driver hit the gas again. I stood, giving full weight to my pedals as I forced the bike forward in furious pumps. I hit the edge of the road, thunking into the mud beyond with another painful spurt up my leg.

The headlights flashed across the trees ahead of me, and the car's brakes squealed as the driver made a sudden turn, and then the engine's hum rose to a roar as it sped off.

I didn't look back. I didn't stop to catch my breath or check my phone.

The trees thinned out until I was smack in the middle of the dead mill yard, the rust-edged towers and ragged block buildings stabbing the gray sky.

I'd be safe here. No one would find me. I could call the others, and—

And what then?

My mind slogged through murky thoughts and half plans. All I could do here was hide and wait.

I slid off my bike and stumbled toward the nearest supply warehouse, foisting most of my weight onto my handlebars as I stumbled over the train tracks that had once brought raw materials from West Virginia and Kentucky and taken the steel made here to just about everywhere else.

Mom had drawn a diagram of the mill in crayon on a paper place mat at the Macaroni Grill once, her eyes lighting up like she was telling a particularly juicy fairy tale.

It's extraordinary, really, she'd said. *People have been using iron to make tools for practically all of human history, since long before we knew how much of it there was in the Earth's core.*

It had fallen from the sky, she'd explained, eyes going wide and glossy. *Meteorites. Rock from space that changed all of human history. Isn't that extraordinary, how a rock from space could change the course of the world?*

Her eyes had flicked to Dad, who'd given a little smirk and a nod. *It's extraordinary*, he'd agreed. I was probably no older than seven, but even then I'd seen through his words: *You're extraordinary.*

The tracks were hardly overgrown, devoid of rubble and trash—trains probably passed through here still, though without any reason to stop.

Ahead, fog clustered around the towering, twenty-story blast furnace like the ghost of the ashy carbon dioxide that used to spit out from it. Drizzle bounced off the metal incline ramp that led up to its mouth. One of the skip cars still sat a third of the way up the metal-webbed tunnel, permanently paused, probably still holding its fuel or ore, while the other cars were visible at the bottom.

It was hard not to imagine that rusty little box holding its breath, waiting to see the outcome of the chaos that had left it stranded, suspended six stories over the ground.

It looked sad, the way the toys you didn't really like did.

At least it wasn't the kind of thing kids lined up to shoot with BB guns, like the Jenkins House.

Even after five years, the mill still felt like a kind of holy ground, a gravestone over something you felt in your bones you shouldn't disturb.

What little graffiti had been dashed across the rusty metal and gray brick was limited to prayers and bittersweet platitudes. Across the doors of the building was written in bright violet, RIP NICK. I'LL MISS YOUR BIG BALD HEAD, BROTHER.

My gut twisted like a wrung-out rag. There could've been any number of Nicks working at the mill that day, but Nick Colasanti Sr. was the first to come to mind. Was he bald? In the few pictures I'd seen, he was always wearing a mesh-backed hat. When I tried to picture him, I just saw Nick in the hat.

If the accident had happened a few years later, it *could've* been him—Nick Jr. or any of us. Not Remy—he'd been college bound since first grade, even if all he really wanted was to skateboard, and not Sofía, who'd been planning to be a lawyer ever since the pre-accident summer she'd spent binge-watching *Law and Order: SVU* with her grandma on a visit to Splendor.

But Arthur, Nick, Levi, me. It could've just as easily been any of us.

There was a padlock on the door, but it had been clipped. Apparently not *everyone* avoided this place.

My skin crawled. Wayne Hastings hadn't.

Any other time, that would've scared me off, but any other time, I wouldn't have come here in the first place.

As I stumbled inside, the ground beneath my feet was soft, with the give of moss or thick carpet, and yet clouds of soot and dust kicked up around me. Another tremor dropped through me, a sounding line that couldn't find the bottom of my stomach.

I'd been in here exactly once. Mom had asked Arthur and me to drop off Mark's lunch when he'd forgotten it. The place was blurry in my memory, a messy amalgam of what the place that nearly killed my brother *would* have looked like, not what it *did* look like.

What it *did* look like was somehow worse.

I had expected the black: the ash coating everything, the rubble where the explosion had begun; the metal oxidized and flaking from where the roof had been blown clear, leaving millions of dollars of equipment exposed, just like the skip car.

The white was what surprised me. The gallons or tons of foam or powder that had been sprayed over everything.

If someone had led you, blindfolded, to this room, you might for a moment think you were looking at mounds of snow. Or heaps of chewed-up newspaper, piled for the ultimate papier-mâché project. The softness of the ground made sense now.

I was walking on that last moment, when firemen wandered through this place, eyes stinging, hearts pounding, hoping—*against all evidence*—there were more survivors, people trapped under rubble near the fringes of the room, with no more than minor burns.

I doubled over, gagging. My eyes stung from smoke that wasn't there, from chemical-laced smells I couldn't place.

I didn't know how praying worked, or if it did, but I prayed right then for something that had already happened.

I prayed Mark had had his back turned. I prayed he hadn't seen the rush of hot metal coming toward him. Maybe he'd even been staring out the window at the field beyond, tracing Fibonacci curves in wildflowers, counting spirals in a dandelion, doing any of the things I pictured my brother doing, when I could conjure up anything but that steadily beeping hospital room.

Purpose. Meaning, connection. That was what he'd found in those things, in drawing them. I hoped that had been what he'd seen in those moments, even if it was a mirage, rippling through the heat waves sent across the room.

It was possible: He'd been almost to the door, heading out for a lunch break, when it happened. They'd found him caught under a metal pipe that had been thrown by the blast, but the burns on his feet and legs and hands weren't so bad they wouldn't be usable if he woke up.

How usable, though? Would he ever draw again?

I backed up to the door as a desperate, helpless scream worked its way out of my chest.

Anger, anger, so much anger. And here I was, as alone as I'd felt for five years. Finally safe to let it out.

Spit flew from my mouth, mixed with the piles of *everything* around me. I doubled over and screamed again, until I felt that jittery energy flowing out of me in every direction. Until a— probably the last surviving—light bulb surged bright and snapped apart, raining glass into the desert of ash. Until the red-painted fire bells on the wall began to scream with me.

The flame winked out as quickly as it had come on, leaving me empty, achy, gasping for breath. I swiped the back of my hand up my mouth, drying it, wiped at my tear-streaked face with my fingertips.

The damp hair on the back of my neck began to prickle then, just a second of warning.

"Quite the show," said a man's voice behind me. "That must make *you* Frances."

I spun toward him. He was standing in front of the door, dressed in a bucket hat and iron-crisp Members Only jacket three shades lighter than his mocha-khaki pants. The man was easily seventy years old, white-haired and starting to stoop. He shuffled toward me, his hands raised in appeasement. "No need to be alarmed."

I took a step back, and fear as big and hard as a jawbreaker caught in my throat.

"In fact, it's essential you remain calm." He was a heavy breather, the kind who gave a damp exhale between every couple of words, his lips smacking audibly as they parted to let in new oxygen. "Our bodies aren't meant to channel the energy in that way. If you keep up like that, it's going to make you very sick, young lady."

I glanced between him and the door. His thin lips twisted into a smile, and he touched his chest. His hand was so papery his veins were visible as blue rivers beneath his skin, except where the sun had left dark spots. "It's me."

I recognized him, but not because I knew him: because he'd been following me in the blue Cadillac.

He patted his chest once more, and the movement revealed a shiny, black rectangle tucked under the jacket at his hip.

Gun, my mind registered, and it was like I could taste the bullets in the back corners of my mouth, between my molars, even down in my stomach. Cold and tart metal all through my body. My heart rate skyrocketed, and I took another step back, trying not to react to the sharp pain in my ankle.

He took another step forward, and his white eyebrows, thin and widely spread, lifted in surprise. "*Bill.* Black Mailbox *Bill*, Frances. I'm here to help."

My throat loosened, just a little. *Black Mailbox Bill* wasn't much more comforting than *me*. Either way, a stranger had tracked me down, flown across the country, and cornered me in an abandoned steel mill.

"What are you doing here?" My voice came out hoarse, and I fought to control it. "How do you know my name?"

"Now calm down," he said. "You can trust old Bill."

I disagreed. You couldn't trust anyone who referred to himself as old Bill. My eyes flicked to the outline of the gun inside his jacket.

"Ah, this?" he said lightly. "This isn't for *you*. This is in case—" He reached for it, and all at once the machinery hummed to life, the fire bells roaring against the wall. Bill jerked his hand away and held both hands up again, like I was the one with the gun and I had it pointed at him.

The current running through me dropped off, and the room fell silent in response. Bill gave a tense smile and dropped his hands to his sides. "I was just going to say, this is for *protection*."

"Protection," I repeated.

Bill gave a somehow smug nod. "From anyone who tries to get his hands on either one of us, Frances. I'm sure you understand what a risk it is, my coming up here."

"How did you find me?" I demanded.

"I've got a lot of help with the MUFON community, and

once we'd placed the location from your video, it just took a little digging. You kids really *should* be more careful how you use your social media."

"Lesson learned," I said.

Bill chuckled. "Now, how about this, Frances? I'll set my gun down, and you can take a load off that bruised ankle for a minute while we chat. But only for a minute. If *I* could figure out to look for you here, others won't be far behind. We've got to get you somewhere safe."

"Like where?"

Bill's watery blue eyes crinkled. He smacked his lips. "Don't you worry about that."

"Oh, I'm worried, Bill," I said. "Put the gun down."

Something surprising flared into his eyes, and his leathery face went rigid for a beat. Then it relaxed and he slipped the pistol from its elastic holster.

He held it up, hand shaking a bit, then bent at a snail's pace and set it on the ground near his feet.

I considered having him kick it over to me, like people did in cop shows and movies, but we weren't in a dark school or an underground facility with polished cement floors. We were standing in inches of soot and ash, and I doubted much less than a professional punt would get the gun anywhere near me.

"You—you said MUFON helped you find me," I said. The *Mutual UFO Network*. I'd read about them when I was digging through Wikipedia, trying to make sense of what had happened to us. MUFON was the largest, and oldest, collective of armchair UFOlogists in the world.

"Not in any official capacity," Bill answered. "But the community's expansive, and members are willing to help. This trip is—so to speak—off the books."

That same smile flicked across his broad lips, which were dried and cracking but very pink. "I had an analyst friend take a look at your footage. That was where all this started. He confirmed what I already knew—that it was real."

Bill took another small step. This time I didn't move. My ankle *was* bruised, and it was swelling too.

"You have a couple of enthusiasts right here in town. Did you know that? A Mr. Doug Rosenbaum?"

I started. "Principal Rosenbaum?"

Bill nodded. "He was the first to give us an ID of Levi Lindquist. He had some ideas of who the girl could be."

"There were two girls." Maybe I shouldn't have said it, brought Sofía into it, but I was unnerved. I didn't want him to be too sure of everything he'd figured out so far.

But he only nodded calmly. "Sofía Perez."

The pulse traveled out from me like a mushroom cloud, a sudden singular thrum of energy all throughout the building, every piece of machinery still connected to wire, and worse, the lone blast from the bells.

Bill winced and plugged his fingers in his ears, swaying briefly on his feet. "Not so good for my vertigo," he said when the sound had stopped. His tone was light, but that something in his eyes had sharpened, darkened. "I was less concerned about Sofía. I needed to find the host."

The sterility of the word sent another shiver through me.

Bill took another step, and this time I couldn't stop myself from jerking back, my ankle screaming in response. "I remember how it felt," he said quietly. "All that power, all that light."

With his last step forward, I became aware of how tall he was. Not as tall as Levi, but easily as tall as Sofía.

The wrinkles around his eyes tightened, fine lines spreading out like cracks in glass. "The *glory*." His face relaxed once more, the fiery thing in his eyes replaced by the watery twinkle that had been there before. "You feel it, don't you, Frances?"

I shook my head. "I know it's in me. I don't know why, or what it wants, or *how* it's doing this."

"What it wants? Now, that's going to take some time and cooperation to figure out. But as for *how* it's doing this, well, the science is heavy on the pseudo, but as far as I can tell, the beings are made of an energy akin, if not quite identical, to electricity."

He huffed through a few more humid breaths and licked his lips. "If these—these *remarkable* beings were to move freely through the Earth—well, they'd blaze right out."

"You said they were electricity," I said. "Not fire."

"Right." Bill wetted his lips again. "Right you are, Frances. But we're not talking light switches and copper wire. No, these things are much more . . . volatile. Like lightning. I've interviewed eleven people with encounters like ours, and from that research, I believe the gel—the meteorite debris the creatures land in—is some sort of protective conductor, something that allows them to exist in our physical and seeable world indefinitely. Maybe even a magnetic field, stoking the electric current, you see?"

I'd gotten such a bad grade in physics class that I couldn't even be sure this was the sort of thing you'd *learn* in physics class.

Bill went on. "But when that structure's compromised, the beings start to lose their form. They've got one of two options: Light up like a dying star, expel all that energy in an electrical storm until there's nothing left of them, at least not any place that we can see. Or they can attach to a host. Use a body as a conductor."

He took another step. "Now, here's the thing, Frances."

His expression was friendly, and the gun was still on the ground, but I stepped backward anyway.

"Our bodies? They're not the same thing as the disc you found. Every pass of the current through you costs something."

He took another step. "At this rate—setting off alarms and powering up furnaces—you're liable to burn right through the energy in you, and kill yourself doing it."

My gaze dropped to the scars on my arm. "Ah," he said. "Exactly! You understand! As you expel the power, the markers of it on your skin will fade."

"Why didn't you tell me that to begin with?" I said. I thought of Remy, shut into an interrogation room with an FBI agent. How many times had he had his vision? Had his scars disappeared yet? "If I'd known that," I went on, "I could have burned through it by now!"

Bill shuffled toward me, and I took another half step back.

"If there's no alien in me, then the people you say are after me—they wouldn't have any use for me."

Bill's mouth went slack. Another step through ash for him. Another anxious half step back for me. "And you would do that?" he said in a low voice. "Pity. You're just like all the others."

"The others?" I said.

"The others," he hissed. "Everyone who's ever squandered this precious gift! You'd be okay dumping the being right out of you without ever knowing why it came!"

I tried to step back again, but my shoulders met metal. I'd backed into the forklift, caught between it and Black Mailbox Bill.

"You'd give up all that it shows you. The keys to the very universe! Things no other man on Earth has seen."

His white eyebrows twitched. He was too close now. I could smell the heady punch of his aftershave, that fake ocean breeze, and see the sagging pores on his nose and cheeks.

Bill harrumphed. His glittering eyes swept skyward, his hand arcing up to mirror the path. "What's *out there. Who's* out there.

Everything the being has seen and felt—eons' worth of information that has been hidden from us since the birth of the universe, and—*and* proof!"

"Proof?" My voice was small, smothered by the layer of ash and rubble coating everything.

"Of *them*." The words hissed out of him like air from a teakettle. His eyes bulged in their sockets, all the manic energy of Nick but none of the warmth. "Of where they come from. Of what lies beyond the limits of our human understanding and the technology we have to advance it."

He took another step, trembling. "When you close your eyes, you see it, don't you?" he whispered, wispy brows knitting together as his gaze darkened with focus. "All that light, and that *sound*—the sound you *can feel*. The voices—zillions of them, whole civilizations that came before us, and maybe even those that come after us! All drawn into that same timeless place. You still can *feel* that, can't you? You haven't wasted too much yet, have you, Frances?"

"I need to go," I said, heart thudding as he pressed in tighter.

"That feeling of—of *utter* connection. There's nothing else like that. *Nothing*, and believe me, I've looked. There isn't a drug or a piece of art or a temple on this earth with a feeling like that, that *bliss*. No amount of money can buy your way back to that pool of light and all those voices and—" His words caught in his throat. He seemed suddenly sick, his skin sheened with sweat, his legs wobbly as he took another step. "*All* that light."

"I really need to go," I said again. "My brother will be wondering where I am."

Outside, thunder rumbled, and the darkness in Bill's eyes cleared. His mouth softened, and he blinked rapidly, like he was caught off guard to see me standing there. "Yes, yes, of course. And he won't be the only one. We can discuss this more at the safe house."

"Safe house?"

I wasn't going anywhere with Bill. Not with shaky, half-desperate Bill, whose voice went hoarse with awe when he talked about the creature in me.

He adjusted his footing. "Frances, do you know what will happen if they find you?"

He waited just long enough to make me wonder whether the question was rhetorical, then went on. "It won't matter whether you've got any of the extraterrestrial left in you or not. They'll want to test it. They'll tell your folks they're taking you in for questioning—oh no, not for something *you've* done, but for something they'll say you witnessed. Something you were exposed to, maybe. They'll say they need to run some tests, see whether your *immune system's* been compromised, courtesy of some Russian satellite that fell out of the sky, or some such nonsense."

The word *satellite* sent a dizzy wave through me.

"You'll say you feel fine," Bill said. "But they'll frighten your folks enough to get them to sign some waivers, and next thing you know you're in quarantine. And as they're running some tests you'll realize—hey, I'm *not* feeling so well after all. You'll think they might have been telling the truth. When your parents come in to see you, they'll notice you're not looking swell. You won't be able to hide it, what with all the drugs they'll be pumping into your system. Your illness will progress quickly. One night, your parents will be at your side, through a protective layer of plastic, of course, and the next morning, they'll get a knock on the door letting them know their little girl didn't make it.

"Tragic, I know," Bill said. "But hardly the worst part. The worst part is the body—contaminated, highly toxic! It cannot, safely, be released. Your folks might be ticked, sure. Might even go so far as to call a lawyer friend, but things will be settled quietly in the end, with a check and a nondisclosure agreement. Now." Bill's eyes brightened and his eyebrows lifted. "Will they *actually* kill you? I can't say. The accounts I have of this are from *our* end of things, Frances, the little guy, not the suits. I don't know what happens at that point.

"Maybe they keep you in a lead box and feed you on a tray pushed under the door until they're good and finished. Maybe when they realize there's no trace of your little friend left in you, they toss you into another round of *unrelated* experiments, the kind that's supposed to be illegal. The point is, you'll be more than dead to your friends and family. You'll be erased." He smacked his lips, beleaguered breaths grating out of him. "That's what will happen to you, Frances. If you don't come with me somewhere safe right now."

He knew about the satellite. He knew they were saying the field was contaminated.

And staying here wouldn't keep me safe. If he could find me, they could too. Maybe he was right.

"I'll just . . ." I cleared my throat. "I'll just let my brother know—"

Bill shook his head. "They'll be monitoring your friends' and family's calls. They're tracking your phone too. We've got to discard it and get out of here. They're likely on their way right now."

My mind whirred, cycling through my options. Bill was a stranger, a strange stranger, but he was right about the phone—if TV and movies were any indication, a person with resources could use it to find me.

Still, I wasn't going to get in a car with him. At least not alone.

"I have to get ahold of my brother." I sidestepped him, but Bill moved into my path, his hand held up, fingers splayed.

"I can't let you do that, Frances."

"Then it's lucky you can't stop me." I sidestepped again, but he was already in front of me, hands buried in the pockets of his Members Only jacket.

"Frances, be reasonable. This is what's best for everyone—you, your brother, your friends, the being."

"*Me* be reasonable?" I said. "I'm a teenage girl, and you're the old man who came across the country to corner me in an abandoned mill. If you want to help me, then let me get out of here before anyone else turns up."

I ignored the pain searing through my ankle and pushed past him. He snatched at my elbow and caught a fistful of sweatshirt.

I tried to yank my arm back, but his other hand shot out and knotted into my hair, pain shrieking across my scalp as he dragged me toward him. I tried to scream, but one of his arms had already snaked around my throat, his papery palm flattening across my mouth and his elbow pushing in on my windpipe so hard it made me cough.

Stars popped behind my eyes, and my eardrums gave a red-hot throb at the sudden noise of the fire bells.

I grappled at Bill's arm, but his grip only tightened as his other hand reached for something in his pocket. *Another gun*, I thought with a burst of fear that sent a rumble of current through the warehouse.

I clawed more viciously at his arm, and he jabbed the heel of his foot down hard on my ankle, making red explode behind my eyes.

What had I done? What had I done, staying here with him, when no one knew where I was?

He'd freed the thing in his pocket, and in my peripheral vision I watched him whip the white rag out, then bring it toward my mouth.

I could barely breathe as it was, and then the damp rag was being plastered over my nose and lips, his palm cupped over it. I couldn't breathe at all. Couldn't breathe, couldn't smell or taste whatever was on the rag, but I had an idea of what it must be.

"Don't worry," he coughed. "The energy won't be wasted. Just like when the gel receptacle was destroyed, the being will leap to the nearest body when its current host dies."

A quiver ran down my center as I thrashed against him. The room seemed to pulse around me, shrinking as it went. The corners of the room fuzzed and dimmed until all I could focus on was the block in my throat and the buzz building in my middle.

I tried to concentrate, but panic sent my mind and gaze zigzagging uselessly. They hit the clock over the front doors, still quietly ticking out time five years after anyone was left to watch it.

Tick. Tick. Tick.

How long had it been since I'd breathed? My limbs felt heavy and clumsy. But still, that buzz was there, zealous, eager. *Use me*, it seemed to say.

The forklift, I thought. If I could power up the forklift—it was already angled right toward us.

But even as the buzz was building, the world was getting foggier. My legs were turning into jelly and my lungs were stuttering.

In the movies, this always looked so quick. Painless.

A chloroform-soaked rag swept over the mouth. Eyes rolling back, knees dipping. An unconscious body caught by people in black uniforms.

For me it was five minutes of clock hands ticking. Five minutes of fighting for breath. Of lungs burning, imploding and feeling like I was going to die before the world started disappearing, blotting out bit by bit.

The ground turned soft as warmed butter under my feet.

And then a red face punctuated by curling white eyebrows was over me, a voice melting out of it, slowing impossibly.

"I *am* sorry, Frances," Black Mailbox Bill said. "If I didn't do this, it just would've been someone else. Isn't it better this way? Isn't it better that someone who *really understands* gets the gift? Someone who will appreciate it."

And then the dark closed in.

TWENTY-SEVEN

A SHARP *BANG*. THE thunder of footsteps scuffing over cement. The sudden intake of breath and a feminine grunt as something whistled through the air, cut off by a meaty *thump*. The crackle of a storm, and then the feel of rain, splatting against my face.

The pain in my ankle being transmitted to a spot behind my eye that *thwump-thwump-thwumped* with every pulse of my heart.

My brain felt like alphabet soup spun through a food processor. Fragments of words, images.

That grunt again, a voice I recognized. And then a sickly, humid huff of breath against a clean-shaven upper lip.

Another roll of thunder.

It came back to me. Poured into my mind as quickly as it had rushed out. I'd been drugged.

The girl's voice let out a scream, and my eyes snapped open. The burnt ceiling was gone, replaced by dark gray clouds swirling overhead, lighting up. Pebbles, not ash under my hands. And the sound—feet scuttling through gravel.

She screamed again.

I sat up with another jolt of pain.

The powder-blue Cadillac was parked in front of me, trunk open and waiting. My legs were dirty, scraped. I'd been dragged.

Behind the Cadillac, a silver Honda CRV had parked at a mad diagonal, headlights piercing through the rain, engine still humming and driver's side door hanging ajar.

I recognized the lanyards hanging from the rearview mirror.

Christ Hospital, where Sofía's mom worked.

Sofía.

I tried to jump to my feet and collapsed with a shriek against the bumper. My ankle was swollen, bruised green.

Back between the noses of the two cars, I could still hear the chaotic scuttle of feet, the grunt and huff of two people locked in a struggle. *Sofía*, my mind repeated.

I heard that sound again, something singing through the air, smacking something hard and meaty.

I clawed my way along the side of the car toward the noise, pausing at the sight of my backpack open on the ground there.

My phone. He would've taken it already, probably stomped it into pieces. My heart sank into my stomach. I couldn't call for help. We could make a run for it, but he had a gun.

We could hide, but who knew how long it would be until he gave up, until someone thought to look for us here? Someone other than the people who had Remy locked in an interrogation room and lackeys carrying boxes out of Levi's house.

Sofía and Bill scuttled into view, backlit by the headlights.

Bill had his arm around her throat, the same as he'd done to me, that rag smothering her face. Sofía was swinging her lacrosse stick, trying to hit him over her shoulder but having no luck.

I shoved myself off the car and barreled toward them. I hit Bill from the side and took him down on the hood of the CRV, and Sofía went skidding through the gravel.

Bill rolled quickly over on the hood beside me, his belly pinning me to the car as he worked at the gun caught in its elastic holster. He swore, his mouth twisting open so that spit glistened in its corners and his spearmint-tinged breath hit my face in a hot rush.

"Sofía!" I screamed, trying to push him off me. My arms were pinned against my chest, where I had no leverage.

Bill let out a satisfied sigh as the gun finally came loose.

"Sofía!" I screamed again, eyes and throat burning. The energy was building in me, shivering to a peak.

Sofía was crawling through the grass after her lacrosse stick. She grabbed it and leapt to her feet, but Bill rolled over, throwing an arm out to hold me behind him against the hood as he raised his gun on Sofía instead.

The energy plumped out, pushing against the constraints of my body, like a sponge filled too fully, too fast, with nowhere to empty.

Sofía froze, her dark hair plastered to her face in rain-soaked clumps and her lacrosse stick hovering over her shoulder.

"Get in," Bill panted at her, jerking the pistol toward the Cadillac's trunk. Sofía's eyes darted to it, then fixed back on me. Her stance widened.

"Drop it," Bill said, "and get *in*." He lifted the gun higher, training it on her forehead.

A burst of energy rippled out through me, overflowing, breaking out of me.

He flinched as the Cadillac roared to life. The headlights flashed on, staring us down from one side while the CRV's glared at us from the other.

Bill adjusted his papery grip on the gun but kept it trained on Sofía. "Now, Frances, you're only making things worse." His thumb massaged the trigger. "Don't cause a scene."

The lights all down the train tracks behind us were winking on, piercing through the gray-green storm. A massive shriek tore through the rainfall as the rusted skip cars suddenly lurched to life, riding up the conveyor belt toward the blast furnace.

Bill swore but didn't move. His car alarm had tripped, the CRV's too, triggering a strobe effect on the headlights. He spun in place, looking toward the access road he'd taken to get here.

I took my chance: I ran toward the Cadillac, and Sofía dove behind its trunk as Bill's gaze snapped back and the first bullet went off.

I threw the driver's side door open and hurtled inside, jerking the car into gear and slamming the gas.

Bill's eyes went wide in the fluorescent white of the lights as I shot toward him. His hands lifted at his sides and his mouth dropped open in an ellipse as I sped toward him. I could hear Sofía screaming, running alongside the car. "No! Fran, no!"

She darted out in front of me, hands waving frantically, and I hit the brakes as hard as I could, spinning the wheel to miss her.

Lights shattered and popped all down the tracks, and I jumped out of the car the second it screeched to a stop.

Bill was screaming, bent in half with his hands cupped over his eyes. Sofía was holding something small and pink up defensively in front of her as she bent to scoop his discarded gun off the ground.

She looked at me, blood dripping down her cupid's bow, breathing hard. I froze, staring back at her, shaking from fear and confusion and fatigue and pain.

I had almost died.

I had almost killed someone.

The machinery had all fallen silent and still.

Bill wasn't screaming anymore, but he'd dropped onto his knees, rubbing fiercely at his eyes.

"Are you okay?" Sofía asked me, voice ragged and breathless.

I nodded once, despite the trembling, despite the weakness and the dark specks dancing at the corners of my vision.

I almost died.

Almost killed someone.

My abdomen felt like it was splintering, poison sloshing in my stomach from the aftereffects of the power.

I tried to speak. No sound came out. I swallowed and tried again. "How'd you do that?" I barely whispered.

"Mace," she rasped, shaking the pink canister in her hand. "You should really consider getting some."

She gave a tired, shaky smile. It was a delicate thing, like a newborn bird or a piece of spun glass still wrapped in the tissue paper. Genuine, but breakable.

My teeth were chattering; so were hers. "How'd you know I was here?"

Sofía's smile faded. "Molly."

"The drug or the alien?" I said.

She threw her arms around me, and I hugged her back, shivering. "You're here," I wheezed.

"Always," she murmured.

In the distance, sirens were wailing. We pulled apart and turned to watch the cop car hurtling up the road. "Did you call the police?" I asked.

She shook her head, watching the car's serpentine path toward us. "I texted the others. Maybe someone panicked."

I took a shallow, unsatisfying breath. "Tell me it's going to be okay."

Sofía stared at me for a beat, then threaded her hand through mine. "I promise I'll be there with you, even if it's not."

I looked at Bill, kneeling in the dirt, scrubbing at his eyes.

"At least I didn't kill a man," I said.

"At least he didn't kill you," she said.

The cop car came to a stop, siren falling silent though the lights kept spinning and other sirens were ringing out in the distance.

Both front doors popped open, and before Sheriff Nakamura had so much as gotten out of the car, someone else leapt from the passenger seat and flew through the rain to us, his burgundy rain jacket flapping in the wind.

"I've been calling you for twenty minutes!" Levi said, catching both of us in a painful hug. He drew back, and his gaze wandered to Bill. "That's him? That's Albert Kingston?"

"That's Bill," I stuttered. "Black Mailbox Bill."

Levi nodded. "That's his real name, Albert Kingston."

"How do you—" Sofía began.

"His wife contacted the sheriff when he was taking me down to the station," Levi said. "She found the messages on their home computer and was worried. I guess Albert's been into this stuff as long as she's known him, but the last couple of years he's been obsessed, always talking about finding a way to re-create his *encounter*, wanting to 'feel the light' one more time before he dies. He told her he was on a business trip in San Antonio, and when she saw the e-mails . . ."

Levi shook his head, wiped water from his thick reddish lashes. "She found others, messages to another guy who found a disc in Nashville. He's been missing since two days after Albert's last e-mail with him. When I got Sofía's text that she saw you at the mill with some guy, I just . . . I didn't know what else to do. I'm sorry, Fran."

Everything left in my roiling stomach felt like it had turned to cold, dead weight as his confirmation sank in.

Two more cop cars came wailing around the bend, windshield wipers ticking madly, and behind them, a sleek Suburban with windows so black they looked like matte paint.

Sheriff Nakamura was moving toward Bill now, with his gun trained on him.

"You did the right thing," Sofía murmured to Levi.

"You had no other choice," I agreed. But everything Black Mailbox Bill had said would happen to me crashed to the forefront of my mind like a tidal wave. "Just remember. It was a fake video. Some UFO zealot tracked us down because of a *fake* video. Just stick to the story."

Sheriff Nakamura had Bill on the ground on his stomach, the sides of his open Members Only jacket splayed out like wings and his arms twisted behind his back to be handcuffed. The sheriff was reciting the Miranda rights, but his eyes were on the blast furnace.

No, not on the blast furnace. On the two skip cars parked partway up the incline, one closer to the top of the tower than it had been an hour ago, the other visible when it hadn't been for years.

Sheriff Nakamura's eyebrows pinched together, and his mouth stopped moving as he studied the building.

I gripped the nautilus shell and focused on that, clearing my mounting anxiety before I could send the skip cars shooting off the ramp into the sky, right before the eyes of the blazer-clad woman stepping out of the black SUV, followed by the man in fatigues who'd been driving.

I could see the badge clipped to her jacket from here, along with the razor-sharp smile she offered as she surveyed us through the fog.

Sheriff Nakamura dragged Black Mailbox Bill to his feet, his eyes still puffy and red, and as the sheriff led him past us toward the cruiser, Bill/Albert looked between me and the FBI agent approaching in low, sensible heels.

"It will be worse this way, Frances," he croaked over his shoulder. The sheriff gave him a sharp pull "Trust me. It will be so much worse."

TWENTY-EIGHT

HER NAME WAS AGENT Rothstadt, and she had a sharklike smile that must have helped earn her this job.

"You're not in any trouble" were the first words she said to us through that smile. Her blond hair was styled in soft curls. Her suit was navy, and her small hoop earrings were silver, matched to the crucifix around her pale neck. "We just have some questions for you regarding a piece of satellite debris whose crash we believe you witnessed."

She'd forgotten to hold the smile in place, but she flashed it again, a bookend for her words.

Smile—frightening statement—smile.

"Your parents have already been contacted," she added. "They'll be meeting us at our compound."

By then, Sheriff Nakamura had gotten Black Mailbox Albert into the back of his squad car and hurried over to join us. "You mean *station*," he said.

Smile. "No, unfortunately we've determined that this matter will have to be handled at the temporary facility we've set up for the length of our investigation." *Smile.*

"Well, we've got our own investigation on our hands," the sheriff said. "We need to get the kids' statements about a murder suspect. In fact, we'll be needing to get a statement from my son down at the station as well."

Smile. "As soon as we've finished with him, and the others, we'll bring them straight to you." *Smile.*

"These kids have just endured something terrible," the sheriff said.

Smile. "And this is a matter of safety. We have to verify there's been no . . . contamination. It shouldn't take long." *Smile.*

The smile hadn't worked on him, and she could tell. "I understand you're concerned about your nephew, but the sooner we handle this, the sooner he and your son and the others will be able to get back to their lives."

He'd squared his shoulders, gone rigid like he was caught halfway between fight and flight.

Even now, wedged into the Suburban's leathery back seat between Sofía and Levi, I didn't know the answer.

If I tried to burn out the energy now, what would happen? Would being useless to them help or hurt me? And what about the others?

Was staying calm and playing dumb our way out of this? Or were we climbing into their cage?

Maybe there was no way out, whether we fought or not.

And Remy. What about Remy? He was already in their custody. . . .

I closed my eyes and focused on calming the skitter of my heart and the tautly humming cord of energy through me.

It was so stuffy in the car it was hard to get oxygen.

Breathe. Stay calm and don't think about anything.

One popping light bulb and I'd lose plausible deniability about Molly the Alien.

I'd risk all our lives.

They'd taken Levi's and Sofía's phones (*Smile.* "Just a precaution," *Smile.*) as soon as we were in the car, out of the sheriff's sight. We had no idea where the others were.

The thought of my brother—being taken, alone, out of Walmart and shoved into the back of a car by armed guards—sparked hot across my mind, and I pushed it away as fast as I could.

I couldn't panic, and panicking was all my muscles, heart, and brain seemed bent on doing.

What about Remy?

Don't think don't think don't think.

Had they really told our dad to come to the compound? Would he even come if they had?

Don't think don't think don't think.

Fear spiraled through my stomach, twining around the cord of electrical charge like the stripes on a barbershop pole. I changed my mantra.

Remy will be okay. Arthur will be okay. We will be okay.

I opened my eyes. In the front passenger seat, Agent Rothstadt hurried to smile. It reminded me of something.

It reminded me of Black Mailbox Bill.

It reminded me of hunger.

We'd stopped at a railway crossing. The SUV ahead of us had made it across, but we'd just missed our chance—the automatic gate began to lower, blocking the road from the tracks.

Rothstadt straightened in her seat, facing the fog rolling up from the tracks over the quickly darkening windshield. She dropped the smile immediately, an actor exiting the stage to hide in the wings. She sighed, checking her watch.

Sofía caught my eyes. If she was trying to communicate something, I wasn't getting it.

The train had reached us, chugging past in screaming bursts, the road trembling, the car rocking.

Sofía mouthed something: *Wait.*

For what, I didn't know, but she clearly knew *something* was coming.

The passing train blotted out most of the moonlight, sending it through only in blips between cars.

In the flickering blue light, with his eyebrows peaked, Levi looked toward us. Something had changed in the car, an energy all three of us felt. The buzz through me felt like the plucked string of a harp, only instead of slowing, the vibration was speeding up.

My heartbeat followed. *Stay calm,* I told myself. *Wait.*

The last car of the train whipped past. Its metallic groans, the shriek and chug and breathy whistling, faded. The red lights stopped flashing. The gate lifted.

The camouflage-donning driver didn't move. Rothstadt looked at him. We all did.

But he was staring at the manila envelope resting on the dashboard. It was shivering, *tap-tap-tapping* against the plastic as it rumbled. The train was gone but the whole car was still shaking.

"What's that?" Rothstadt asked.

The driver shook his head. Rothstadt turned in her seat. *Smile.* "Almost there." *Smile.*

She nodded toward the tracks. The guard seemed unsure, but he put the car in drive and rolled over the uneven surface with a *th-thunk.* The fog washed over the car in waves, thick, strangling blankets.

We *th-thunked* back onto the road. The guard huffed, flashed his brights into the writhing wall of white. "What the . . . ?" he said under his breath. Rothstadt checked her watch.

Sofia's eyes stayed on the rattling manila envelope.

We were crawling along the road now. The fog was too thick to see the pavement, or the grazing pastures that rolled along our left, the cornfield and electrical towers up ahead.

The car was really shaking now, the envelope buzzing against the dash. In profile, Rothstadt's lips pressed tight, wrinkling so they looked like a wound stitched together. Her blue eyes were wide and glassy.

The car was silent except for the slow squeak of the wipers against the misty windshield and the feverish tapping of paper on plastic.

The vibration grew until all of us were shaking, until the trees on the right side of the road, visible in breaks in the fog, were dancing, leaves glinting like silver dollars as they fluttered toward then away from the streetlamps.

The vibration had a sound now, not like the train whooshing past. A rumble like earth-bound thunder.

"Stop the car," Rothstadt said.

The guard already had, but he put the SUV in park. In the rearview mirror, I could make out the Suburban that had been following us, and it stopped as well.

"Stay with the witnesses." Rothstadt swung the door open and climbed out, shoes clicking as she walked along the headlights' trail. She paused, staring into the foggy night, her blazer taut on her lifted shoulders, her hand resting at the gun on her hip. She turned back, hand cupped over her eyes to block the light as she stared through the front window. She shrugged, and her voice reached us dimly: "Nothing."

But still the ground was vibrating like a massage chair, and the envelope was jittering on the dashboard.

THWACK. The car bounced as something thumped against the roof.

Levi and I jumped in our seats, but Sofia stayed still, calm. The driver swore under his breath, hand going toward his own gun as he eyed the sunroof suspiciously.

Rothstadt was still standing in the middle of the road, blanched by the car's headlights. She had her gun drawn, but her eyebrows were knit together in confusion as her gaze wandered from one side of the road to the other.

"FBI," she called out. "Come out slowly, with your hands up!"

Her hand slid into her pocket and withdrew a phone. Gun still poised in her right hand, she lifted the phone to her ear with her left.

THWACK. The car jogged again. Then twice more as two black objects careened into the hood of the car.

Levi's hand slapped to his mouth, stifling a yelp. The guard undid his seat belt and scrambled out of the car to get a better look as the three of us leaned forward to see what had struck us.

Birds. Two more hit in quick succession, beak first, blood spurting toward the windshield.

The other soldiers, the ones from the second car, were moving tentatively around us on either side, trying to see what the holdup was. Rothstadt was striding back toward the car, calling out to them, but the rumbling was too loud to hear.

The fog broke apart as they came barreling toward us, a moving sea of black and white and brown.

Cows, *hundreds* of cows breaking through the mist with wide, wild eyes and hoarse screams of panic, hooves pounding the asphalt, shaking it, as they stampeded toward us.

Rothstadt and the others dove out of the way as the crush of cows hit the front of the car like a wave, breaking around it, surging past on either side, their noise drowning out the shouted commands of Rothstadt and the others.

"You knew?" Levi crowed enthusiastically. "You knew we were about to get ambushed by *cows*?"

"I'll explain later," Sofia said. The car rocked violently as the cows converged around it, mooing and groaning against it on all sides.

Hooves pounded and slid against the hood as two cows tried to pitch themselves onto it. Gaping mouths and wild eyes pressed in against the windows, thick tongues drawing patterns of slime on the glass as the animals pounded against the car. The herd hit the left side of the car so hard the tires lifted off the road, and all three of us screamed as they slammed back down, just in time for the right-side tires to catapult off.

Snatches of shouts broke through the chaos. Camouflage was visible in flashes as the soldiers tried to push through to reach us.

Sofía gripped my arm and shouted over the noise, "Are you ready?"

"Ready for—" My voice wrenched into a scream as another slam against the left propelled the car over, glass shattering on impact, raining down on us from the uptilted left side of the car. Hanging hard against my seat belt, I threw my arms over my head as glass fell on us like confetti and cows pushed in around the window.

Still suspended in his seat belt, Levi jerked back from them, bracing his legs against the driver's seat headrest to push himself deeper into the car.

"We have to go," Sofía hissed. "Now." She unclipped her seat belt and crashed to what was now the floor, the shattered right window flush against the asphalt. I followed suit, dropping beside her. Levi was still hanging, dodging the wild-eyed cows like some reverse version of whack-a-mole.

Sofía reached across me and undid Levi's seat belt. He dropped like a sandbag against my forearms, crushing me to the car door-turned-floor. We were all smushed together painfully, but Sofía climbed clear, toward the upturned window.

"They'll crush us!" Levi said.

"Or we'll get shot!" I added.

Sofía looked back over her shoulder, her face dark in the foggy night. "Can you trust me? Just once, I need you to."

We wouldn't always have each other. No one could have a guarantee like that. But so far, Sofia had come through for us—for *me*—every single time we needed someone.

Every time I needed *them*.

"Of course we trust you," I answered for both of us.

Sofia nodded. "On the count of three, Franny's going to take out the lights. As soon as that happens, we run. Follow me, okay? Unless they're too close—then go wherever you can and hide. I'll come back for you. I'll find you. You don't need to contact me."

She waited a moment for me and Levi to nod, then she did too. She turned toward the shattered window, bracing her feet against the seat, cupping her hands against the fragmented edge of the window. "One." She jogged herself, like she was warming her muscles for the jump.

A gunshot snapped through the cool night, but the cows didn't disperse; they just became more agitated, frantically kicking at the car.

"Two," Sofia said.

I closed my eyes, felt the hot thrumming cord through my center, the series of not-quite-muscles I'd found that night locked in the Jenkins House basement. I flexed them, felt the energy jittering as it surfaced, eager to be unleashed. I adjusted my crouch, getting my weight over my feet so I could spring out as soon as Sofia had cleared the car.

I focused on my heartbeat, on Sofia's and Levi's breathing. White unfurled across my mind, and when it faded, I saw the velvety darkness, felt the cold air batting against me, the glittery streaks rushing past on every side, singing as they went. The still pool waiting to swallow the light.

I finally understood what Bill had meant: what a shame it

would be to lose this. How lonely my own body might feel when the being sharing it with me left, taking with it whole worlds I'd never know.

The power built. I could hear it singing through me.

The shouts and moos, the gunfire and crinkle of grass, and the distant barking of some farm dog all faded into a rush like tinnitus beneath the voice.

Soft, warm, massive.

Pushing against my confines and then—

"Three!"

—breaking out.

The console, the headlights, the streetlamps, the radios, and cell phones, the lamps on yellow laminate tables in kitchens blocks away, the low-slung wires dancing through the rolling fields on silver towers.

I felt myself—*or Molly?*—touch them all, felt them light up under contact. My eyes snapped open on all-encompassing light, light so bright no images came through it.

And just as my eyes began to adjust on Sofía's tennis shoes scrambling out of the car, everything went black again.

A haze of colored pixels exploded across my eyes, afterimage burning on my retinas, but I didn't wait for it to clear. I hoisted myself upward, palms meeting rubber, metal, and glass.

Shoulders hitting fur and muscle. Wet tongue on my cheek, breathy snort on my neck as I scrambled, unseeing, into the night. My ankle raged as I dropped beside the car, collapsing on the street.

I rolled sideways as fast as I could, slamming into hooves that danced near my head. I pushed myself off the ground, batted back and forth by the sea of bodies as my eyes adjusted to the velvety night, latching on to fragments of moon-streaked fog.

I tried to run but my footing was unsure, my legs unsteady.

It wasn't just the darkness or my ankle, or that every shambling step I took brought me into another haunch or snout or tail.

My whole body ached. Pain seared behind my eyes, and nausea wriggled through my abdomen like it was looking for an exit. The cord of energy in me felt strong, like it was close to the surface and my body couldn't handle it.

Bent in half, I shoved off the side of a cow and stumbled forward through the pitch-black street.

I couldn't see the soldiers or Agent Rothstadt. I couldn't see anything but flashes of fur, shimmers of starlight fluttering across pale branches.

Where was Sofía?

Where was Levi?

A spasm of pain rocked me off balance again, sent me doubling over just to catch my breath.

What was happening to me?

I reached out—grabbed for anything—and caught a tree trunk, pushing myself upright, turning in a circle as I searched for the glint of the overturned car. The current of cow bodies had carried me farther than I'd realized. I was a yard into the woods on the far side of the street from the field. The road itself was still in chaos, soldiers and cows crashing into one another, blocking each other's way. Three cows peeled off from the writhing mass and thundered toward me.

I dragged myself along branches, gritting my teeth to keep from screaming in pain as I ran. I glanced over my shoulder. The cows were closing in on me, the white rings around their eyes suddenly visible as they hit a patch of moonlight.

They were scared, I realized. Not running *at* me but running *from* something.

Two veered left around a thick spruce and the third cut to

the right, revealing the thing bounding after them, leading them toward me.

Long white fur turned silver by the moonlight, ears wicked back, and tail juddering anxiously side to side.

Droog?

A bark snapped out of her as she came toward me. I expected her to come to me, but she barked again as she ran past, leaving me to stare, confused, after her.

I couldn't get my bearings, couldn't understand anything really, except that she'd been herding the cows that had rushed our car.

I jumped as someone grabbed my shoulder from behind, spun toward the panting person in a panic. "Sofía!"

"Follow her," she got out between breaths, hitting my back between the shoulder blades to get me moving.

"Where's Levi?" I asked as we took off again.

A crash in the woods to our right answered. His silhouette waved an arm over his head as he jogged alongside us. "*Let's go,*" Sofía warned.

We followed the flash of speckled white through the brush.

"Where are we going?" I hissed.

The corners of Sofía's mouth twisted into a grimace. She either didn't know or wouldn't say.

I didn't ask again. Every time I told myself not to think about the pain, it seemed to double, and when I started to stumble, Levi grabbed my elbow and hauled me back up, tugging me along. There were voices behind us. Flashlight beams. The whip of chopper blades picked up at our backs.

Wherever Droog was leading us, it had to be close—she'd started to double back to check on our progress, bounding back out of sight for a minute at a time then circling us, drawing us nearer to the destination, herding us.

Muffled voices called out through the woods as we moved, and to our left, the trees thinned and splashes of shocking light caught on something white and glossy in the distance. It stretched out indefinitely alongside us, and as a breeze rolled through, rustling the woods, the white thing rippled.

"That must be the compound," Levi whispered, tipping his head toward it.

It was something like a massive white tent, I realized, with hallways tunneling off in different directions, nearly as big as our high school. I stopped short and stared through the dark trees, finally piecing everything together.

Halfway between us and the massive tent, there was a strip of gravel road, lined with semitrucks, blazing white under the glare of the floodlights mounted on tall structures every few yards along the tent, washing the already muted colors from the camouflage-print fatigues of the figures moving around in the street.

A taste like hot metal rushed over my tongue.

Droog had led us right back to Jenkins Lane, to the makeshift compound we'd been trying to escape.

Wind tore through the forest, making the branches whip and snap. Light sliced from the sky, and a deafening *fwooop—fwooop—fwooop* thrummed all around us.

Levi's and Sofia's hair flapped viciously in the wind as all three of us lifted our gazes to the angry sky.

A black helicopter cut across it, suspended by the furious snap of its blades.

The noise amped up as two more appeared, lights scouring the woods and field beyond.

A wave of panic raced through me, hot and electric.

Every light in the field—around and inside the tent, shining down from the helicopters, the trucks' headlights—surged in response, went blindingly white for an instant then cut out just as fast as the power overcame the wiring.

The world plunged into darkness. The whirring overhead slowed. The wind pattern changed as something massive dropped like a cartoon anvil toward the field. Voices called out in every direction.

"FRANNY!" Levi grabbed my arm, and yelped as a spark jumped between us.

The sound—the sight of him stumbling back—snapped me out of it. The power coursing through me hit a wall, and my fragmented senses clicked back into place seconds before the helicopters would have smashed headlong into the tent and anyone inside of it.

The lights flickered back on. The blades spun to life, and the choppers jerked upward out of their nosedives.

Beside me, Levi was pulling his own hair and gasping to catch his breath like *we'd* been the ones to very nearly die.

"Oh my God," I wheezed. "Oh my God, I'm sorry. I almost . . ."

Sofía touched my arm. "But you didn't." She nodded toward the blur of white and fur zigzagging ahead of us through the backyard of the Jenkins House. "We have to go."

My feet finally unfroze, and we went back to running, chasing a border collie through the woods, but the block of ice in my chest didn't thaw.

TWENTY-NINE

"WHERE ARE WE GOING?" Levi repeated my question as we ran.

"Sof?" I prompted through gritted teeth. The pain in my ankle returned with renewed fervor, competing with the dizziness and nausea that kept bending me over.

Sofía shook her head. "I knew someone was coming for us—I could see them leading the cows, but I figured it'd be Arthur or Nick or something. Now it makes sense why my viewpoint was so low . . ."

"*That's* how you knew what was happening?" Levi asked, voice cracking. "You were reading Droog's mind? Like you read ours?"

"I guess . . . I mean, she must've been affected by Molly too. It's the only—" She jumped out of the way as Droog circled back at top speed, then went on. "The biggest part of the consciousness might be in Franny, but obviously there are bits in all of us, and I guess I can access anyone—or dog—that might be housing some of that."

"Well, at least we're getting the mechanics of this down," Levi said, determined to be optimistic despite the choppers circling overhead.

"So we don't know what we're doing, or where we're going?" I asked.

"I figured she knew what she was doing!" Sofía cried.

"My *dog*? Sofía! There's being open-minded, and then there's—" This time, *I* jumped out of the way as Droog wound another circle around us. My gaze followed her trail through the trees, but she made a sharp turn before she reached the Jenkins House and bounded toward a copse of trees halfway between us and the decrepit back door, on which block letters sprayed in yellow paint read *murderer*.

"I know she's a dog!" Sofía said. "But we're just humans, and that doesn't stop you from giving the streetlights of Splendor electroshock therapy! Droog just led a stampede to break us out! I thought she had a plan."

Droog came to an abrupt stop in front of the cave, pitching her front paws onto the ledge over its mouth.

"Shh!" Levi waved a hand toward the pinprick of light visible beneath the lip of the cave. The light turned off before our eyes.

"There's someone in there," I whispered.

Droog pushed off the rock and sprinted another circle around us, trying to draw us in toward it. Sofía crept forward, and when Levi reached for her elbow, she shook him off and kept going. I wasn't sure why we were bothering to move so stealthily.

Whoever was in there had clearly heard our approach—why else would they have turned off the light?

Sofía caught my eye and tipped her chin toward a pile of brush just behind the thicket of trees. Something was hidden under the tangle of fallen branches and dead leaves. I moved closer.

Bikes?

I leaned toward the bramble, peering through the darkness at the battered blue Schwinn underneath. I recognized it. It belonged to—

"Nick?" Sofía said, surprised.

"Franny?" a boy's voice called from inside.

"Wait, Arthur?" Levi called back.

Droog's tail wiggled, and she let out a cough of a bark in greeting.

"Did I just hear Droog?" Nick called, and with her tail wagging and nails clacking, Droog crouched and darted into the darkness.

"What is this, some kind of demented tribute to 'Who's on First'?" I said.

There was a shuffling from within as we approached, bent low, and finally a lantern went on inside, casting Nick's and Arthur's faces in a golden glow. Relief throbbed through me at the sight of them.

A part of me, I realized, had been braced to never see either of them—but especially Nick—again.

Something came over me, and I dropped onto my knees and threw my arms around Nick under the low overhang of the cave entrance. He blinked his surprise at me for a few seconds before hugging me back. "Well, nice to see you too."

"What are you guys doing here?" I asked, pulling back.

"Especially *you*," Levi murmured, kneeling awkwardly beside me so we were on the same level. "I thought you were 'done.'"

Nick grimaced. "I thought I was too. I went home last night, and I slept like a baby for the first time all week, and this morning, I was sure I'd made the right decision, getting out while I could."

"Wow, great story," Sofia deadpanned, still standing, and crossed her arms. "Glad you found your bliss."

"And *then*," Nick twanged, "I went to work. And there was a power surge and a blackout, and I knew it must mean Wayne was there. That he was up to something. I told myself it didn't involve me. And then the texts just kept coming in. About Remy waiting for his dad to come home, and from Franny, warning us not to go home, and Sofia having her vision of Franny at the mill.

"And every message that came in, I told myself it wasn't my problem. My family is my only problem, my responsibility. But then Levi sent us the message about that Black Mailbox Bill guy, and how his wife was worried he might've come after Franny, and I looked across the store and watched Arthur just walk out. Just leave work, and it hit me."

"That you were a giant selfish idiot?" Sofía said.

Nick rubbed his scalp. "That I would've chosen y'all too. If I were an alien who wanted to save the planet Earth, and I could only have five people—and one dog—I would've picked you. Because no matter what we don't say, I know you all. You'd walk away, in the middle of anything, if one of us needed you. I guess what I'm saying is, you're my family too, and I'm sorry."

Levi shifted between his knees and cleared his throat. "I meant *literally*, how did you end up here, in this cave, but I guess that's all good to hear too."

Nick and Arthur exchanged a look. "That question's a little trickier," Arthur said. "And a long story. What about you guys? How'd you find us?"

"Ditto to Arthur's answer," Levi said.

Overhead, the steady beat of helicopter blades was sweeping back this way.

"Let's get into the cave," Sofía said, "where they can't see that light."

We crawled inside then got to our feet and made our way to the waterfall in the back hollow, but as we were going, my ankle screamed and another blow of vertigo hit me hard, knocking the world off balance.

The shadowy cave slanted, the ground rising up beside me like a wall, and my cheek, my ribs and side slammed into it.

Sofía yelped my name and hurried to where I'd fallen, and even she was rocking like a pendulum in front of me. Her voice was warbling. The world was in flux in front of me.

Levi, Nick, Arthur, and even Droog crowded around me too.

"Stay with us, Franny," Nick was saying. "We're here, so just stay with us."

Remy, I thought. *What about Remy?* We needed to get Remy.

I started to push myself up, but Sofía eased my shoulders back against the wall as she leveled her gaze on me. "It really is making you sick," she said. "Whenever you use the power?"

Art looked at me hard and clicked on the flashlight in his hand to better appraise me.

"Maybe," I said, then after another moment, let the truth out. "Yes."

"Shit," Nick said.

"What do we do?" Levi asked. "How do we fix it?"

"We don't." My heart palpitated. "At least not right now. We need to worry about Remy."

Art jerked his chin over his shoulder. "Did you see that giant plastic bag over the substation? We think that's where he is."

Levi nodded. "That's where Agent Rothstadt was taking us before we escaped."

"Agent Rothstadt?" Nick said.

"Escaped?" Arthur said.

"We were rescued, actually," Sofía said. "By your dog."

I took a deep breath before launching into the whole story as quickly as I could.

"So we *can* use it up," Arthur said when I'd finished. "That's why your scars have been shrinking?"

"Oh," Sofía said. "Okay, we're not going to latch too tightly on to the part where we almost died?"

"According to Bill—Albert—every use of our abilities should let off some of the energy in us," I answered Arthur. "If we can get rid of it, Agent Rothstadt and the others might not have any use for us. But the problem is Remy. We don't know if he's got any power left, if they've seen his scar or not."

Arthur was studying the purple ridges on his arm as he clenched and unclenched his fist. "What about me? How am I supposed to get rid of my scars when Molly totally stiffed me?"

"Look, dude," Sofía said. "If I could give you Ordinary-Vision in 3D, I would gladly trade you."

"I'd give you mine too. You totally deserve it," Levi said without a trace of irony.

"Thank you." Arthur shot a resentful look at Droog, who wagged excitedly.

"Did Droog bring you here too?" I asked.

Arthur's eyes flicked to Nick, and they held a silent counsel.

"What is it?" I asked.

"Seriously," Levi said. "For all we know Remy's strapped to a metal table right now, so please hurry and just say it."

"We weren't trying to come here," Arthur said. "The stampede pushed us this way. We were trying to get to the quarantine tent."

"We knew they had Remy," Nick said. "And when the group text went silent after Levi sent those messages about that Black Mailbox guy, we thought either they'd gotten the rest of you or *he* had. And if that was the case, we didn't have the resources to get you back, *or* to stop Wayne. Turning ourselves in seemed like the best option."

Turning themselves in?

After everything that had happened last night? When Arthur and the others had stopped me from doing the same thing and ending this before Remy or anyone else got hurt?

"And then what?" I snapped, surprised by my own anger. The cord in me went taut, ready, eager. "Then all of this—*everything* we put ourselves through this week would've been for nothing!"

"You would've been safe," Arthur growled.

"For how long? How long *does* a human dissection take, Arthur?"

"Longer than a bullet to the brain!" he said. "You heard what the sheriff said about your bud Black Mailbox Bill! He was planning to murder you. He had every nook and cranny of our lives mapped out—he knew exactly how to play you! You're lucky it wasn't over in seconds, Franny! At least if we'd turned ourselves over—found you—you would've had a little longer!"

"So what?" I screamed. "I would've been dead *and* you would've been dead."

"You think I care?" Arthur screamed back. "You think I'd want to be here alone?"

His words hung in the air. My eyes stung, and my throat felt like a paper finger-trap pulling tight, shutting out all the air.

Arthur stared back at me. I imagined my expression must look just like his: crumpled, broken.

Nick cleared his throat. "Look, y'all, what matters is we're all together, and we're safe. Now we need to get back to the plan."

Arthur's eyes scrunched closed, and he massaged the bridge of his nose. "The plan was to lie low. In what world is *that* plan salvageable at this point?"

Seeing him like this—watching him give up—sent a searing pain through me.

The hyperventilating, blood-rushing, ears-ringing feeling of knowing you've just lost your grip on your life, that it's drifted away from you.

I looked away from him to keep the emotion from exploding out of me in lightning streaks.

"Fine," Nick said. "We need a new plan: We get Remy, go stop Wayne from blowing up Splendor with his Super Machine, burn through our energy to get rid of our scars, then turn Wayne over to the FBI and pin the whole thing on him."

Levi's eyebrows pitched up as he turned toward me. "You can get us into the compound, right?" His gaze dropped to the shrunken scars, just barely visible below my sleeve. "You've got enough of the power left to take out their electricity one more time?"

"Absolutely not," Sofía said. "Look what that energy's doing to her. She can barely sit up. It's probably giving her some kind of radiation poisoning or something!"

"I've got enough," I said.

Sofía pressed a palm to her forehead, rolling circles against it. "Franny . . ."

"I've got enough to cut their power," I repeated. "I've got nothing to stop bullets."

Levi gave a half-formed shrug. "They won't fire on us. They need us."

"There's a lot of them," Arthur said. "Even without electricity, we won't be able to get through *all* of them."

"So we need a distraction," Nick said. "Get them busy before we make our move."

"The only thing that's going to get *those* soldiers out of *that* compound," I said, "is me."

"And if your electrical blast is on the other side of town," Sofía added, "then it's *not* here, cutting the compound's power."

"So we've got to Ferris Bueller them," Levi said.

"Say what now?" Nick said.

"Oh, come on. You guys have seen *Ferris Bueller's Day Off*. John Hughes at his best? Matthew Broderick has an epic day skipping school?"

"If you have a point, you should make it before Nick pulls your underwear over your head," I warned.

"He sets up a fake Ferris to trick his parents. A complicated system of pulleys and recordings and a Ferris dummy, so that when his parents come in, they think he's in bed sick, like he told them he would be."

"Levi, I love your zeal," I said. "Truly, it's inspiring. But I suspect a Franny doll won't fool Agent Rothstadt."

Arthur snapped his fingers and pointed at Levi. "We need a fake light show. We need to make a *blackout.*"

"There's no way," Sofía said. "Unless someone in this cave has access to five hundred vacuum cleaners and the world's longest power strip—"

"I do," Nick said.

At first I thought he was joking, and Sofía's and Arthur's matching expressions of irritation suggested they did too.

But Nick wasn't smiling. "My mom, you know. She keeps stuff." He cleared his throat. "Like Arthur mentioned last night."

"She's a hoarder," Levi volunteered.

"Thinks we need to be prepared for the apocalypse," Nick said. "The point is, a few months back, you could barely move. It was disgusting. Cat hair all over everything. Cat *turds* you couldn't get to because they were shoved so far back between towers of L.L.Bean catalogues and jumper cables and generators—mostly broken or expired junk she buys on eBay. So I started cleaning it out when she was sleeping. Only I couldn't really get rid of anything in case she noticed it was gone. So Remy loaned me his car, and I put it all in storage."

"He let *you* drive his car?" Levi said. "Am I the only one who hasn't?"

"If you've got a storage unit, I guarantee the FBI already has someone sorting through it," Sofía said.

"Then it's a good thing I didn't put it in a storage unit, Sherlock."

THIRTY

WITH REMY'S CAR, IT would've taken seven minutes to get to the derelict-but-still-functioning movie theater across from Walmart. As it was, skirting through the shadows on bruised ankles and empty bellies, it took an hour and a half.

The CINEMA sign glowed an ugly orange, mismatched to the shade that ran in a thick stripe down the otherwise Barbie-skin-colored building, and the pockmarked asphalt was slick with oily puddles that rippled when the sticky wind blew over them.

"Back when Ma was an owner/operator, she worked out a deal with the guy who owns this theater to park her truck here when she was home. He made the mistake of telling her she could keep it here as long as she wanted, when he sent his condolences," Nick explained as he led us to the semi parked in the back row of the lot.

"It was supposed to be a temporary break, a bereavement leave of absence." Nick leapt onto the tailgate and fumbled with the padlock. "Only her bereavement wasn't temporary, so the break wasn't either."

He tossed the lock onto the asphalt and slid the door up, ducking into the shadows. Arthur and Sofía followed, but even though my pain and nausea had let up enough that I could hide them, I was far from jumping into truck trailers and hauling equipment around.

I stayed with Droog and Levi to keep watch as the others sorted through the mess packed into the truck.

On the way over, Nick had explained the way his mom's collecting had started as a sort of doomsday preparation. She filled their cellar with first aid kits and water jugs, soup cans and batteries.

She didn't want to go back to work until she could be sure Nick and his sister, Clarissa, would have everything they'd possibly need at home.

It had gone on for months: researching, visiting thrift shops and big-box stores for supplies. "The more she prepared, the less safe she felt," Nick had said.

And then there was her husband's stuff. All she had left of him: the receipts and styrofoam cups in his car, the torn work shirts he'd stuffed in a bag to patch or donate. His favorite old movies, the collectible bobbleheads he had believed would make them rich someday.

She'd asked Nick to handle selling the truck. Instead, he'd gotten a job and secretly kept paying the lease. He was planning to drive it someday. He'd keep taking care of her, bring her everything she needed, but he'd have a bed in a dark, empty truck cab to climb into at night. He'd have windows that weren't blocked by stacks of coupon books and newspapers and postcards from local political candidates from the past five years.

He'd be able to leave Splendor without leaving her.

"Feel that?" Levi said, voice cracking anxiously.

I blinked clear of my daze. His eyes were on the sky. The twenty-four-hour glow emanating from the CINEMA sign mixed with the moonlight beyond the swirling black clouds to cast the night sky in an eerie gray-green.

A wave of warm wind hit me, wheezing and whistling, rattling the metal door of the trailer. The throaty *rip-rip-rip* of helicopter blades sliced through the quiet.

"They must be doing another sweep," Levi said. He grabbed Droog, and we climbed into the claustrophobically packed trailer as quickly as we could. Arthur looked up from the tangle of Christmas lights he was wrapping around his arm.

"The helicopters are looking again," I said. "They're all the way out here."

Arthur looped an extension cord around his neck like a scarf. "Then we'd better hurry and give them a show. Levi, grab what you can. As soon as the sound stops we've got to move."

Levi and Sofía took a load of stuff across the street to Walmart, while Nick, Arthur, and I worked furiously in the movie theater parking lot, starting with the Christmas lights. Fifty-eight strands, plugged back to back, zigzagging through the lot with the final plug ending near an outlet we'd found behind the hedges on the side of the building. We'd hooked one power strip into it, and then plugged six more power strips into *that* and a few more into each of those. The plan was to plug the lights, and everything else we'd brought, into the power strips, then turn them on all at once.

We moved as fast as we could, working up a lather of sweat as we jogged between the trailer and the outlets, lining up vacuums and coffee makers and TVs in the mulch surrounding the hedges. Droog trotted back and forth, watching or herding or a little of both.

If I thought about our stupidly vague plan too long, I wouldn't be able to ignore how stupid and vague it was. Instead, my mind would wander to Remy—where he was, what they might be doing to him—and then my chest would buzz and ache, and my anger would grow in me, and—

I hacked the thought off and jumped up onto the truck bed, feeling through the dark until I found an old metal fan with dust caught in its blades, alongside a radio. I grabbed both and hurried back to the hedges just as Nick and Arthur were setting down a microwave.

"Seriously?" Arthur said, wiping sweat from his top lip. "Your mom hasn't missed her microwave?"

"Didn't you know?" Nick hunched over his knees as he caught his breath. "Microwaves cause cancer, or syphilis or something. Plus she's got four others. Think she plans to weaponize them if Earth's last stand turns out to be zombies."

Arthur straightened, dusting his hands off on his jeans, and coughed out a laugh. He shook his head and laughed again, louder this time. Nick started to laugh too, and for some reason, in my complete and utter exhaustion, my days' worth of fear, the sound was contagious. I started to laugh too, tears squeezing out of my eyes.

"Zombies," Arthur barely got out. "If only it had been fucking zombies, we'd be ready."

Nick giggled and scratched at his jaw. "Ma didn't think of aliens."

A guffaw burst from Arthur, and he leaned against the side of the building, chin bobbing at his clavicle as he cackled.

It was the fatigue, but it didn't matter. I couldn't have made it stop if I wanted to. The laughter bubbled through me, breaking any last vestige of control I had over myself. My legs felt like jelly. My hands felt like jelly.

I slumped against the wall beside Arthur, who reached down and gripped the top of my head like it was an armrest as a giddy shriek rose out of him.

Nick squatted, one tattooed hand palm-down on the asphalt to keep his balance, as he laughed.

Gradually, the mania settled. The three of us fell silent, staring at one another.

"I love you guys," Nick said after a minute.

It caught me off guard. He had never said it.

My throat felt tight as I opened my mouth a couple of times. Finally I got it out. "I love you too."

Arthur put his palm over his eyes, and his shoulders hitched. I thought maybe he'd started laughing again, but he wasn't making any sound, and soon, I realized he was crying. For once, I didn't pretend not to notice.

Nick and I stood and circled up around him, wrapped our arms around each other, around him. We were all afraid, and there was nothing any of us could say to change that.

Overhead, the clouds had thickened, black, writhing masses that billowed in the wind, diffusing the moonlight into a soft, slippery thing.

Across the road, Levi waved his arms, signaling he and Sofía were ready.

It was time.

We pulled apart. Nick climbed into the truck and started it up, then patted the seat to call Droog up. She perched on his lap, front paws propped on the open window, and Arthur and I got into position at the hedges while Sofía and Levi did the same on the far side of the street, all four of us waiting for Nick's signal.

We crouched, waiting, eyes locked on Nick in the truck's cab.

It all came down to this.

"I do," Arthur said, without looking up from the plugs. "Love you."

"I know."

Arthur smiled faintly. "You're like a brother to me, Franny."

I rolled my eyes and shoved him, tried to hide the spasm of pain that passed through me, but Arthur didn't miss the hiss of air between my teeth. His smile faded and he faced Nick again. "Let's save the world."

The semitruck's horn blew once, quick and severe.

A beat of silence and then a second blast. I lifted my hands, fingers spread, ready to go.

Nick hit the horn a third time, held it down so that it blared out like a siren across the lot, and we flew into action, stabbing the prongs of the three master power strips, each completely loaded with six *more* power strips, into the outlet.

The sea of light unfurled.

The calm night filled with sound, began to roar, with fans and vacuums and KitchenAid mixers, ten-foot-tall pumpkin inflatables and antique neon bar signs and static-filled TVs, old boom boxes with cassette tapes still in them and hair dryers and clippers, and alarm clocks and electric knives like the one Mom used to insist on—badly—carving our Thanksgiving turkey with.

So much power, but it wasn't enough.

Soon the helicopters would be back. They'd see us here. Actually catch us—and then there was Remy, what must already be happening to him with every minute that passed—

We'd lose whatever tiny edge we imagined we had.

The quiver of energy began in my chest, rising to meet my anxiety, offering itself to me. *Here*, it seemed to say. *I have what you need.*

I closed my eyes.

I had to be careful. In control. I couldn't lose it all or there'd be no way to get Remy out. Just a little bit. A *tiny* bit.

The energy in me was buzzing, thundering, a tremor all through my veins. I felt it curl down the lengths of my arms, extend through my fingertips like rapidly growing claws.

A tiny bit, I told myself as I released it. *Just the smallest—*

Darkness, whole, absolute.

Silence. As if I were trapped beneath tons of water.

A voice broke through it. *"—DID SHE—"*

The darkness shuddered, cracked.

Flickering light passed overhead. Color, almost. Dim, gray. Vibration beneath, around. Warmth and another voice. "—*on. Wake*—"

The darkness reared up, crashed over everything. Nothing but solid black. Nothing, I was nothing. Bodiless, floating like a—

It pulled back and I saw dark clouds were swirling ahead, on the far side of glass. Rain splattering. Windshield wipers squealing.

Nothing. There was nothing. A feeling cooler and darker than sleep.

"—ODDAMMIT, FRANNY, WAKE U—"

Absolute darkness. Aloneness.

Pain flaring through me. Metal in my mouth. Water in my throat. My eyes flew open as I coughed. Hands passed over my back, pushing me up to sitting.

Hands patting my shoulders roughly as I coughed, the tangy, thick liquid spilling out of my mouth and into my lap. My body ached. I tried to stretch but my feet met resistance. *Window*, I thought dimly.

Dark fields and telephone poles whipping past below my shoes. Wherever I was, I was moving. To my left were two shadowed bodies, kneeling. Two shadowed faces.

Moonlight hit them in ripples, lighting them up in ghostly blue. Arthur and Sofía.

"You shouldn't have done that." Arthur's voice came out scratchy, like he'd been screaming. I tried to stand, but Sofía's hands pressed me back down by the shoulders. I was vibrating. Everything was vibrating.

Another voice came from over Sofía's shoulder. "We thought you were *dead*," Nick said, and threw a look over his shoulder.

Finally the pieces came together. I was lying on the mattress in the cab of the semi, just behind the seats, where Nick and Levi were sitting. Droog curled up on the floor between them. Thin strands of rain rushed up the windshield as we sped down Old Crow Station Lane, and wind batted at the sides of the truck with so much force that Nick had to keep jerking the wheel to the right to keep from wandering into the other lane.

"You shouldn't have done that," Arthur said again.

He was right; I felt like Nick had driven the truck over me, then backed it up to do it again.

Sofía laid her cheek in my lap and wound her arms around my waist. I wrapped my arms around her, giving an approximation of a hug, and when my hands came away, dark prints stayed behind on her white T-shirt.

Blood. That was what I'd coughed up. I could taste it now. I cleared my throat. "Did it work?"

Nick laughed in the front seat. "Oh, it worked."

I crawled toward the window, peering out at the houses flying past. Dark. Every window, every porch light. But then again, it was the middle of the night. Later than the middle of the night, possibly. I glanced toward the dashboard clock.

"4:22," I read aloud.

"Yeah, sorry," Levi said softly. "We tried to get you up in time for 4:20, but—" He winced as Nick's hand flew out and smacked the back of his head.

"It's out," Arthur confirmed. "Everything's out from Walmart to here, and maybe farther."

I pushed my sweatshirt sleeve up, searching for the web of scars. "No," I choked out. *No, no, no, no.*

Gone. It was gone. My head spun. I pitched sideways and Sofía caught me, pushing me upright. I hunched over my knees and gripped the sides of my face in my hands. "No," I managed. Tears mixed with the blood in my throat. I wanted to hit something, to throw sparks in every direction, but I couldn't.

My arm was smooth and blemishless, my body was wrecked, and whatever part of Molly I'd had was gone.

It was all gone.

Arthur shook my arm. "It'll be okay."

"It's gone," I gasped. "It's gone and—"

I shook my head and Arthur grabbed my face. "Stop it, Franny. You're not in this alone, okay? You don't have to figure this out by yourself."

"Remy—"

"We'll get Remy," Arthur promised.

"I won't be able to do anything," I said.

"We'll get Remy," Arthur said.

"Of course we will," Levi said.

"Damn straight," Nick said.

"Look." Sofia pointed to the window on our left. A black SUV whipped past, followed by another, and another, and another. Light poured onto the windshield, turning the raindrops to diamonds as a parade of helicopters flew over us.

They were heading toward the source of the blackout, toward our Ferris Bueller dummy.

The engine growled as Nick pressed the gas pedal to the floor.

THIRTY-ONE

THE CAMP WAS IN turmoil. Voices and uniforms passing back and forth, flashlights snapping on but doing little to crack the darkness that had engulfed the field.

The final blast of my energy had done the job: The blackout had reached all the way to here.

We pulled off the road alongside the corn just before Jenkins Lane, and for a beat, sat in silence, preparing for the stupidly impossible and impossibly stupid thing we were about to do.

Levi opened his door first, and Droog dove out, disappearing into the corn before I could grab her.

My stomach bottomed out. How would the soldiers react if they saw her running through the dark at them?

Sofía touched my shoulder. "I can see her. I think she's leading us. Or Molly's leading us through her." She blinked, eyes clearing, and headed toward the trail of broken cornstalks that zigzagged ahead through the field, where Droog had gone. "Come on."

We left the passenger door ajar as we siphoned into the field, following the herky-jerk path all the way to the back of the plasticky tent.

We crouched in the corn, a few yards away, trying to see if and how she'd gotten inside.

A vicious gust of wind picked up a tattered strip of the tent material, slapping it against the tent's side. "There," I whispered, pointing at the distressed dip in the dirt just below the tear. She'd dug her way in.

The question was how long until a circling guard spotted the hole. Even if we managed to scramble in after her, how were we going to keep from being caught in there?

"Should you try to find Remy?" I whispered to Sofia.

She was staring up toward the roof of the tent, at three vaguely triangular shadows that appeared to be mounted there. "I think I have a better idea."

Wings lifted, fluttering from the center shadow's sides. Blackbirds, I realized.

"They must've been here that night," she whispered. "I can see from them, which means I can keep watch, at least on the exterior guards."

"And what about everyone inside?" I asked.

"One problem at a time," she said.

"More like one hundred," Levi said.

"Who's going in?" Nick asked.

Arthur balked. "All of us."

"How's that for discreet?" Nick hissed. "Four kids, a dog, and the jolly red giant." He jerked a thumb at Levi, whose bearlike silhouette bristled.

"Well, *I'm* going in," he said. "Remy's my cousin. He'd go for me."

"You're twice Remy's size," Nick said. "You'll be lucky if the tent doesn't get caught on your head and turn this whole thing into a Marmaduke comic."

"I'm going—" Levi began.

"No way," Nick argued.

Art shushed them. "Give it up, Nick. He's going—you and I will keep watch out here, make a distraction if we need to. Now give Levi your pocketknife."

Levi held up his hands and whisper-yelped, "I'm not going to stab anyone!"

Art rolled his eyes. "It's not for stabbing. That border-collie-sized hole in the tent isn't going to cut it for you." Nick slapped the knife into Levi's hand, and Arthur's sharp gaze wandered across us. "Everyone clear on the plan?"

"That there basically isn't one?" I said. "Got it."

"All right then." Arthur stuck his hand into the center of the little circle we'd formed. Nick followed suit, then Levi, then I did, and finally Sofía put her hand on the top of the stack. "*Team Molly*, as quietly as possible, on three," Arthur said.

We pumped our hands three times, and breathed the words as one: "Team Molly."

Still crouched, Sofía and I turned toward the tent, each taking a deep breath. She closed her eyes, concentrating, finding her bird's-eye view. No sooner had she settled into it than she released a gasp.

Her eyes snapped open, and she snatched at my hand.

"*Now!*" she whispered, and took off, dragging me toward the tent, Levi bounding after us with the knife. Sofía reached the structure first, throwing back the torn piece of tarpaulin—or whatever it was—and shoving me in. My eyes pinballed, searching, as I dove through on all fours and found myself in a small, stuffy room.

Empty, I thought with relief, then lurched forward as fast as I could at the sensation of Levi's face colliding with my butt. He was caught at the shoulders, Sofía stabbing through the material in hasty swipes around him. I reached out to try to tear more open but withdrew my hand just as fast as the knife swiped toward it.

A panel fell away and Levi was through, Sofía scrambling in after him. I faced the inner wall, a clear plastic panel with a zipper running through it to form a door. There was a small metal table lined with paper on my right, and on my left stood a jar-topped cart, full of swabs and cotton balls and medical tools.

It was an exam room.

Outside, the storm was picking up. A gust of wind tore down the side of the tent, rattling it, slapping the torn flap against the side. The whole structure stretched upward, shivering, then relaxed again, plunging the dark tent into silence as the wind let up.

"What now?" Levi whispered. Sofía gave a shake of her head and closed her eyes, a crease drawing between her brows as she concentrated. My eyes went instinctively toward her elbow. The scar had shrunk again, shriveled up like dehydrated roots. There was no more than a half inch left.

What happens if we get to him? I thought. *What if we get in but can't get out?*

Sofía's arm flew out and grabbed a fistful of my sweatshirt, keeping me still and low to the ground seconds before voices drifted toward us, muffled by the plastic.

My throat clenched. Pain pulsed behind my eye and throbbed in my bad ankle as two figures, blurred by the material, appeared in the hallway outside the exam room.

They moved past at a steady clip. When they'd disappeared, Sofía's grip loosened and she moved forward, whispering, "We have to get to the center."

Levi and I followed, bent like cartoon bank robbers. I pressed my face to the plasticky wall, trying to see down the hallway as Sofía unzipped the door and beckoned me and Levi through with a tip of her head.

The wall on our right was obscured, a nearly opaque white, but two more empty exam rooms were visible through the plastic sheeting on the left, metal tables and tool carts barely visible in the darkness.

The hallway dead-ended, jerking to the right at a ninety-degree angle, but Sofía stopped us just shy of the corner, waiting and listening.

Another trill of wind hit the top of the tent, punching the

material down so loudly I bit my tongue to stop from shouting in surprise.

I looked up, peering through the darkness to watch another breathy *smack* hit the material, followed by two more. I pulled my focus back to the tent, instead of the storm brewing beyond.

Sofía peered around the plasticky corner, then took off running again, her steps crinkling in the post-wind silence against the squishy material lining the ground.

As Levi and I jolted after her, a pulse of pain went through my ankle, so severe that my knees buckled. Levi caught my arm, hauling me upright on a diagonal without slowing.

Halfway down the back hallway, Sofía stopped abruptly, and when I froze, I heard the soft *squish-squish-squish* of even footsteps coming from the tunnel that bisected the one we were in.

Sofía turned and pointed frantically back the way we'd come, shoving us along.

We sprinted back, spinning clumsily around the corner. Sofía grabbed a handful of my hood and stopped me from going any farther. Through the dark, I could see her pantomiming listening, cupping one hand around her ear.

The steps were getting quieter, until they were altogether gone. I studied Sofía, trying to communicate, *WHAT THE HELL NOW*. She nodded and turned back, and then we were off again down the back hall.

We paused at the intersection to listen, but the wind was pummeling the compound walls like massive fists. It was impossible to hear anything over it.

A sudden cramp in my abdomen doubled me over, and the shift in my weight made my ankle feel like it was cracking in half. I stuck out a hand to brace myself against the tent, but the whole wall was bucking now, waving and billowing.

It's going to come apart, I thought dizzily. *The storm's too much.*

Levi pulled my arm around his neck, balancing me against his side.

I shouldn't have come with them. I was slowing them down. I wanted to tell him to go on, but I couldn't do anything except grit my teeth through each new spasm and burst of pain.

Sofía leaned around the bend, checking that the coast was clear, then shot a look over her shoulder that was somewhere between ecstatic and terrified.

"This is it!" she whispered. "Droog came this way!"

She turned the corner and ran, Levi and I stumbling through a three-legged race after her.

The walls and zipped-shut doors on either side of us were opaque, but Sofía knew where she was going now. She stopped at the third door on the left and bent, pressing her ear to the wall.

Outside, the tornado-watch siren started to wail.

Even if Remy had been in there screaming our names, we might not have heard him.

Sofía stepped back from the door, appraising it.

There were no tears or scratches in the door panel. If Droog *had* made it in there, she'd done it without ripping through it.

More likely someone had found her. If she was lucky, maybe they would've just tossed her out, chalked it up to more strange animal behavior like the cow stampede or the suicidal birds.

But what would stop them from hurting her?

The world swayed. I could still taste globs of blood trapped around my molars, and the back of my skull throbbed where I must've hit the cement when I passed out in the theater parking lot. The inside of my body felt like hot, burbling poison, and the outside felt brittle. Levi pulled hard at my arm, keeping me on my feet as I sagged.

We'd made it this far, but this one last moment—this was going to be what sent the whole thing crumbling down.

Sofía blew out a breath and closed her eyes, concentrating. Trying to find Remy or Droog, or maybe just checking the bird's-eye view from outside, I wasn't sure.

When her eyes snapped open, there was a look of shock on her face. She glanced toward the inside of her arm.

There was no sign of the raised ridge running along her skin. She shook her head. *Gone.*

Her power was gone, just like mine.

THIRTY-TWO

THE SIREN WAS STILL screaming, punctuated by shouts from within and outside the tent, indiscernible in the chaos. Soon they'd be swarming us, and we had no extra line of defense. No electrokinesis, no telepathy, no Remy, and no time.

My stomach spasmed. There was nothing else to do: I pried myself free of Levi, stumbled forward, and reached for the zipper.

Before my fingers ever got there, it started to move.

Someone was coming out.

The top of the flap curled open, like paper running from a flame, and the face behind it wasn't Remy's.

The soldier stared at me for a beat, stunned into stillness, and in that second, I saw the tatters of the wall behind him, whipping in the wind.

The room was empty—no Remy, no Droog, but signs that they'd been there!

That they'd ripped through the other side and gotten out!

In the next instant, as my eyes flew back to the soldier's, he recovered.

He shouted something and reached toward his waist.

The last thing I saw was his fingers making contact with the gun, and then the world seemed to rip apart.

The walls billowed inward. The roof lifted, buoyed by wind, and all down the hallway the stakes leapt out of the ground just in time for the ceiling to be thrown back downward.

The fabric hit me on all sides, knocking me down with its speed as it tangled around me, the wind pummeling against my back. I fought against the material, pulling it away from my face to get a good breath. The wind was so loud I could no longer hear the siren.

I pushed myself up onto all fours and stuck my arm up, tenting the material over me as I screamed for Levi and Sofía. I couldn't hear the sound of my own voice over the wind.

And then, just as quickly, the fabric rebounded upward, just long enough for me to spot Levi on his stomach ahead of me, one arm bent protectively around the back of Sofía's head. The fabric flapped down again, slapping me in waves as I army-crawled toward them.

"WE HAVE TO GET OUT OF HERE," I tried to yell.

Sofía understood enough to yell back, "YOU THINK?"

Another gust flattened the tent again, cutting me off from them. Cutting me off from air and moonlight. This time, when I fought against it, it was useless. The wind was too strong; the material was too heavy, wound too tightly around me. I couldn't get any oxygen. My arm muscles burned, and my intestines felt like they were being wound up with a roll of barbed wire.

It was like I was drowning.

I could fight or I could relax and slip into it, let the darkness swallow me.

Some instinct in my brain clicked into place, and I lost control over myself, went limp. My mind felt light, like a balloon lifting out of my body.

Even so, another part of me was screaming in the distance: *I CAN'T BREATHE I CAN'T BREATHE I CAN'T—*

Light pierced the fabric two feet to my left, and cool air blustered in. A hole!

Something had just torn a hole in the fabric. And then another, first a sharp puncture and then a slice as a knife drew a wide swipe in it. *Nick's knife.*

The dim outline of hands snatched at the rippling fabric, tearing the hole wider until I could see the figure crouched on the other side. Levi reached out for me and pulled me through. The fabric caught around my hips, and I kicked against it until I freed myself the rest of the way, then lurched onto my feet between my friends.

The tent was two-thirds flattened, metal posts jabbing out of the fabric at odd, broken angles, and tattered bits waving like defeated flags. A person-shaped blob fought against the fabric three feet away from me—the soldier who'd nearly grabbed me—and all around the camp, others were rushing to help, silhouettes sprinting toward the collapsed structure, pulling people out.

But halfway across the ravaged cornfield, one other person was standing totally still. One other person and a dog.

Dark hair that fell to a wool-lined denim collar, turned up against his neck.

My ankle, my stomach, my head—all the pain in my body vanished under the wave of relief that hit me.

I hadn't realized I'd started running until Remy did too, Droog jogging along beside him.

We collided in a hug, his hands clutching the back of my head, running over my hair roughly, my face burying into his neck. My body shuddered, unable to cry anymore, as the wind battered us. Morning couldn't be too far off, but it was still too dark to see much of him. I could smell him though, breathe in the bonfire smoke that always clung to his jacket and the sweet-grassy smell his skin and clothes picked up after skateboarding.

Thank you, I thought. *Thank you thank you thank you.*

He pulled back enough to kiss the side of my face, and I knotted my fingers into his jacket. Levi and Sofía reached us, slamming into us like a basketball team at the final buzzer. Levi's arms roped around us, squeezing so tightly it was hard to breathe.

The relief was short-lived. The sight of Droog cutting a trail through the field, galloping toward the truck, reminded me where we were.

Across the field, the soldiers were realizing Remy was missing, shouting as they dug through the still-writhing tent. The corn had taken a beating in the wind, stalks broken and blown over in every direction. It offered about as good a hiding place as a camo jacket.

"THERE!" I heard someone yell. The four of us leapt apart, as two soldiers came running toward us.

It had to be the stupidest thing we could have done in that situation, but it wasn't the stupidest thing we'd done that night: We turned and ran.

The field was alive, dancing in the storm, grazing my skin like a hundred tiny knives as I swam through it. The wind bolstered me sideways, backward, and every step I took gave my leg muscles a feeling like being shredded—but I could see the truck in the distance, the door hanging open.

Arthur standing outside it, beckoning us on with a blown-out cigarette still hanging from his mouth. Levi reached him first, practically dove from the edge of the field into the truck, and Sofía bounded in after him, followed by Droog. Ahead of me, Remy burst from the corn next and reached the door, throwing a look back to check my progress.

I was still a good six yards off, fighting the pain in my abdomen, pushing my legs and swollen ankle hard as they could go.

Arthur was still waving me on. Remy was still watching my too-slow progress from the truck's doorway.

His eyes went wide, his mouth dropping open, and I knew there must be someone right behind me now.

I was only a few yards away now. Almost there.

Remy took one step toward me, but Arthur grabbed the wool

of his collar and jerked him back, screaming something I couldn't hear as he shoved Remy toward the waiting semitruck, where Levi grabbed him.

Remy was screaming, but Levi wouldn't let go of him, and Arthur was coming toward me.

My legs were numb, thudding uselessly into the wind. The world had been dark already, but now it seemed to shrink around me as my grip on consciousness slipped.

No. I had to keep running.

With the wind resistance and my fatigue, it felt like I was sprinting through Jell-O. Rushing into an ocean that kept pushing me back.

Arthur was yelling my name now, running full tilt to me, his wiry arms pumping at his sides, his cigarette falling, forgotten, from his mouth.

He was close enough that I could see the fear in his face.

Bright, unhindered horror. I couldn't help it. I looked over my shoulder, expecting dozens of soldiers, dozens of guns.

But there was no one in the corn behind me.

Only dark clouds, congealing over the field: angry, gray things that rushed like a river, spiraling. A funnel was beginning to form, stretching down toward the ground not far behind me.

The siren was still blaring. My heart palpitated as shreds of fabric, metal shafts, paper and plastic debris skated across the ground, lifting and dropping as drafts of air caught at them.

A metal pole slingshotted toward me, and blood spurted into my mouth as my teeth caught my tongue again.

It was an instantaneous thought. Wordless, more like a feeling really, but had it known language, or had time to be translated into English, it would've been something like *END.*

Something grabbed hold of me and jerked me sideways, and the metal pole spun past, smashing into the side of the truck trailer. I spun to face Arthur. His bushy eyebrows were high up his forehead, and his mouth was taut.

I tried to say his name, but no sound came out. I couldn't feel any part of my body. My legs were giving out. He clutched me to him and screamed into my ear, "I GOT YOU, FRAN."

And then we were moving, my feet barely kicking as he pulled me along to the open door. I couldn't make my legs work, but Remy and Nick were reaching down and Arthur was boosting me up, and then without any climbing, I was inside.

THIRTY-THREE

REMY PULLED ME ONTO the cot in the back with the others, and Nick hit the gas so hard the passenger door flung shut, and I fell across Remy and Levi both. Lightning struck somewhere to our left, and the thunder cracked out within a second of it.

"Where are we going?" Remy asked as he pulled me over to sit between him and Sofía. "I mean, what are we doing? Fleeing the country?"

A look passed between Arthur and Nick.

"Guys?" Remy pressed. "There is a plan, right? You didn't just steal me from—from the U.S. Armed Forces and the FBI without a plan. . . ."

"People can't be stolen," Levi said. "We either abducted or rescued you."

"And that," Remy said, "will depend somewhat on where you're taking me."

Nick spun the wheel suddenly down the curvy, wooded road that connected to Old Crow Station just under the train tracks. The tail end of the truck skidded one way through the rain then back the other as Nick corrected. "The plan is to save the world. Everything beyond that is somewhat up in the air right now."

"Okay," Remy said. "Then how do we save the world?"

Tree branches were tearing loose ahead of us, flinging themselves across the road. Either a train was passing over the tracks now or the tornado was making a comparable sound.

Sofía made a face. "That's somewhat up in the air right now too."

"TBD," Arthur confirmed.

"And the tornado is certainly a complication!" Levi added just as a spruce branch struck the metal guardrail on our left.

"Your scars." I reached for the hem of Remy's shirt. "Are they gone?"

He peeled the fabric off his stomach

Relief gushed through me as I let out a breath. "Gone," I told Nick and Arthur, who were craning their necks to see even as Nick was maneuvering the semi over the bridge.

"I don't understand—how did they just go away?"

"They're linked to the energy," Sofía explained. "Physical markers. As for how we know: long story."

"That guy you and Franny were secretly e-mailing turned out to be a murderous psychopath who tried to kidnap Fran and in so doing revealed some more information about how this alien parasite operates," Levi said. "So not *that* long a story."

Remy's gaze wrenched toward mine, and his dimple appeared along with an angry twist to his mouth. "Bill tried to kidnap you?"

Nick punched the brakes and turned the wheel sharply, spinning us onto Old Crow Station, and I stifled a scream as the back of the trailer slammed into something we hadn't managed to clear, then scraped along it.

Remy was still waiting for an answer, brow dented.

"I'm fine," I promised. "Sofía saved me."

He grabbed for my hand and squeezed it, as he studied me for a few seconds, and then he let go. He caught the sides of my face in his hands and kissed me. It was warm and rough and short and right in front of everyone, which made it embarrassing and wonderful and weird and completely normal. It was perfect, even if it didn't last very long, and even if it never happened again.

"What in the Sam Hill?" Nick cried from the driver seat. My

cheeks were on fire, but Remy looked totally unembarrassed and calm and Remyish.

"*Obviously*," Sofia said. "What good do those huge eyes even do you, Nick?"

"About time!" Levi held up both his palms to us. "Up top, Fremy."

"Please, no," I said.

"What, do you prefer 'Renny'?"

"Absolutely not," Remy said.

Arthur had been watching the whole display. "Weird," he said, brow furrowed, then turned back in his seat, disinterested by the whole thing.

Sofia cleared her throat. "Anyway, I'm officially out of power. What about you, Levi? Have you checked your scars since last night?"

He twisted on the cot so she could pull his shirt collar down his back. "Gone," she confirmed.

"That just leaves Arthur and me." Nick steered us onto the access road that ran to Wayne's cabin in the woods.

It was almost morning now, but the sky had gone darker than it was an hour ago as the funnel cloud in the distance behind us pulled everything into it.

As we drove past our house, the shed door blew open and smacked the side of the building. Shingles were ripping loose from our roof, and grocery bags and plastic bottles picked up by the wind down the road were flying through the sky.

Dad's truck wasn't in our driveway.

Where was he? At a job? On his way home?

We rumbled into the woods, curled up the drive, but stopped before we reached the cabin.

"What's the goal?" Remy shouted as we jumped out of the truck and into the wind. "To find the machine or find Wayne?"

"We need both," I said.

The machine to save the world.

The man to save ourselves.

As for how we'd get rid of Arthur's scars before Agent Rothstadt and the others showed up, I still had no ideas. Fleeing the country was looking better.

"In this storm, he'll be down in the cellar!" Arthur said.

"But the machine's not!" I screamed over the tornado siren.

"The storm's too dangerous—we'll get it after! Come on!" Arthur led the way, wielding a random pipe he must've found in the truck like a baseball bat.

The padlock on the cellar hadn't been replaced, and Arthur threw one green door open, pinning it back against the wind as we raced down the steps with nothing to protect us but our sheer number.

All we had to do was subdue him and keep him there until the others showed up.

But the light wasn't on, and in the jade glow coming from above, the cellar appeared to be empty. Nick reached the pull chain and tugged, but the power was out here too.

"He's not down—" I turned toward the stairs, and my words dropped off.

Arthur was still standing at the top, looking down at us. With one hand, he held the metal pipe, and with the other, he clutched the cellar door.

"What are you doing?" I asked. "Get down here!"

His eyes were sharply focused on me, and his wide mouth was tensed.

For a second, as I watched his matted blond hair cycloning around his freckled face, everything seemed to go silent. Arthur's mouth opened. He shook his head, and then his voice cut through, calm and quiet and sure: "Like a brother, Franny."

I lunged for the stairs. "No!"

Arthur was already closing the cellar door, shutting me off from him and whatever he was about to do.

I flung myself up the steps and slammed my palms against the door just as it dropped into place, cloaking us in perfect darkness. The door jogged an inch, but no more, and I heard the metal pipe scraping along the surface on the far side, as Arthur slid it through the handles to lock us in.

"What's he doing?!" Nick shrieked.

I couldn't answer through my tears, through my fists pounding uselessly against the wood as I screamed his name.

"There were lanterns," Remy said somwhere in the dark behind me. "I saw them the other day." There was a rustling along the metal shelves and then a click, a flood of fluorescent light just as Sofía raced up the steps. She thrust her shoulder against the door while I kept pounding on it, but it didn't budge.

She looked at me, wide-eyed, confused. "Did he lock us in?"

"Why would he do that?" Levi asked.

I couldn't answer. The door was rattling on its hinges. The storm was deafening. I pictured Arthur being swept up by a gust and slammed into a tree.

Shot by Wayne Hastings.

Forced into the back of a black SUV by Agent Rothstadt.

Taken somewhere I'd never see him again.

Maybe his plan was to do all three.

He still has scars.

A wordless scream tore through me. I pounded harder against the door.

Not him. Not him too. Mom may have never belonged to me, but Arthur was mine. Even when he held me back, even when he rode out ahead, he was mine.

"Fran, you're bleeding," Remy said. I shook him off and ran back down the stairs, Nick jumping out of the way as I beelined for the wall of tools.

I pulled an ax down and headed back for the stairs.

"There's a tornado out there, Franny!" Levi said.

"My *brother's* out there," I screamed.

Because no matter what he was willing to say to get me to climb, Arthur had always been my safety net.

He'd always been there, waiting in case I fell, and I knew he couldn't always be, that life made no promises. But right now, in this moment, I still had him, and he still had *me*.

"My brother's out there," I repeated, "and I'm going to get him."

"The worktable." Sofía jogged back down to the wall of tools. "Anyone who wants to stay should barricade themselves in with it when we're gone."

I looked at her as she hauled a sledgehammer down from a hook on the wall. She shrugged at me. "Your brother can't get *all* the credit for saving the world."

"I wasn't saying I'm not going, by the way," Levi said. "Just establishing the stakes!"

"And *I* just wanted you to stop breaking your hand bones," Remy said seriously.

Nick pulled a shovel off the wall. "I came back for a reason, y'all. I'm with you till the end. I swear to God."

"See?" Levi said. "Nick just used the Lord's name, and you *know* he's not doing that in vain."

"No way in heck," Nick said. "Ma's probably got me bugged."

Even Droog gave an anxious wag of the tail, like she understood and agreed.

My instinct was still to tell them to stay, that I didn't need them, but that wouldn't work any more than Arthur shutting us into the cellar had.

They were mine too, and I was theirs.

I turned back to the doors and swung the ax into the wood. Beside me, Sofía slammed the sledgehammer into the other door. Nick's shovel speared through the space between us, cracking the place where the doors met, and together we swung, pounded, and smashed the door apart enough that I could reach through the hole and knock the metal pipe out of the handles.

Remy shoved the doors open, and we scrambled out with our tools still in hand, makeshift weapons.

The forest was in chaos: massive branches blowing across the ground, trash and bits of wood and shingles everywhere, wind so strong we couldn't run straight, and an electrical charge in the air that I knew wasn't coming from me.

My legs felt weak and my ankle was on fire, but I promised myself this was the home stretch as I broke into a sprint. Lights flickered in every one of the cabin's windows, and the front door was open, clapping the side of the house.

I stopped just inside, grip tightening on the ax, and surveyed the first floor. All the windows were open, everything within gusting around. The bookshelves along the wall were half-empty, their contents spread across the blue floral couch and the bulky coffee table and the floor.

The five of us stood for a beat, scanning the mess in the flashing lights of every bulb and lamp in the house as Droog trotted forward, sniffing madly. "Spread out," I said. "Be as fast as you can."

We veined out through the house with great effort as the gusts fought to push us off course. I pulled myself up the staircase by the rickety banister, and on a step near the top, a flash of red caught my eye. A four-by-six photograph, pinned against the step by the force of the wind.

I glanced over the banister into the room below with new understanding. The books spread across every surface, pages whipping wildly, were photo albums, *all* of them.

I reached for the picture in front of me, and my stomach tightened. *Everything* in me tightened, though now there was no energy bound up in me.

In the photograph, a tow-headed girl with bushy, over-sprayed bangs sat at a cherry-red piano, fingers braced against the keys, her smiling face turned over her shoulder toward the camera, but not so much that you couldn't read the hot-pink Puffy Paint bubble letters arcing across the back of her black T-shirt:

MOLLY.

My ears started to ring. My heart felt more like a thrumming engine than a beating thing, resting between pulpy pulses.

Molly.

Not an alien at all.

A human.

THIRTY-FOUR

A PERSON.

The little girl who'd lived in the Jenkins House.

Who'd owned that red piano.

A person, a person, a person.

My heart thundered.

What did it mean?

Why did he have this girl's picture? Was it stolen, like the drawings?

Trophies? I thought, followed by *ARTHUR!*

I stuffed the picture in my pocket and ran up the steps, rivulets of pain tracing up my ankle. Through the flickering light, I spotted Arthur's bony frame just inside the first doorway. I choked out a wordless sound of relief as I ran to him, but he didn't react to me.

I froze just inside the room, feeling like I'd missed the top step, when I saw why.

There were only two things in the room: a piano on the right wall and the massive hunk of metal in the middle, easily fifteen feet wide and five feet tall, a mess of twisted, melted, welded metal.

Right there in the middle of the floor, on the tarp where it must have been built—it never would have fit through the door, and it was so heavy the floor bowed a bit under its weight.

A Fibonacci spiral.

I felt like the fabric of the universe was coming apart around me, like all this would float away and I'd be suspended in endless darkness.

"It's just like the one he was planning to build," Arthur murmured under the terrible noise of the storm.

In my mind's eye, I saw Mark bent over the table in the kitchen, late afternoon light spearing through the windows over the sink, catching in his hair and dappling his shoulders as he worked and sketched out the blueprint.

He was getting scrap metal from the mill.

A co-worker was teaching him how to weld.

"No." I shook my head. "It's not Mark's. It's a weapon. It's—"

"Empty," Arthur rasped. "Nothing but a spiraling tunnel. I crawled all the way to the center."

My ears and throat and stomach suddenly felt like they were full of cotton. I swayed in the doorway, unsure whether it was the wind or my own imbalance making the world rock.

It had to be a weapon.

It had to be.

It had to.

"Just a stupid fucking sculpture," Arthur said. "Just Mark's sculpture."

I moved deeper into the room, touched the dense exterior of the spiral. The way all its parts had been chopped up and redistributed gave it the look and feel of a fossil, something ancient, rough edges and sediment preserved for centuries but still solid enough you could push it off a short cliff and it might hold together through the fall.

Tears rushed into my eyes as I followed the spiral back to its end, the three-foot-high opening of the tunnel that twisted into the center of the sculpture.

I looked out the window, wiping my eyes. The woods below looked like they were raving, boughs lifted high and seizing low, snapping and flying and stabbing where they hit.

"It doesn't do anything?" I croaked, turning to Arthur. "Why would he do this? Just to torture us?"

Not a weapon. Just some kind of sick game.

There was no weapon.

There was no alien.

There was no greater purpose.

We'd been wrong about everything, except that Wayne Hastings was dangerous.

Molly. A person. What had he done to Molly?

We'd misread everything, probably imagined half of it. We'd been exposed to something, maybe even an actual satellite, that night, and our subconsciousnesses had gone wild, filling in all the blanks, pulling bits of what we'd seen at the Jenkins House apart and teasing them into a full-blown story.

Arthur's mouth hung open as he tried to find words. "I thought . . . This is really it, isn't it? We're not heroes. We're not chosen. We're just . . . us, like we've always been."

The desolation in his voice and face was unbearable.

I couldn't push down the feeling anymore that I'd disappointed him, that his whole life had been one disappointment after the next, just like Mom's, and all the love I had for him could never make a dent in his pain.

I'd tried not needing him.

I'd tried letting him and the others help.

I'd tried being there so he could lean on me.

I opened my mouth—*to say what?* That we needed to go? Arthur knew that. He knew we were standing up here, risking our lives for nothing, and it struck me deep in my belly that I could drag him downstairs again with me, shut him up safe in the cellar with the others. But I could do nothing to make him want this life we had.

A downed power line snapped against the window, and the flickering lights finally went out, leaving us only with the sky's eerie green light.

I turned away from him. "Arthur . . . we have to—"

His strangled cry cut me off.

I spun back as a dark figure slipped through the doorway and slammed Arthur backward into the wall. The two silhouettes tumbled to the ground, and as Arthur tried to scuttle away, the man snaked an arm around his throat, hauling him back while his other hand kept its grip on his hunting gun.

"What are you doing in my house, boy?" the man roared, his arm tightening so there was no way for Arthur to answer.

He shook Arthur again, his voice slurring out of him along with a sweet, grainy scent.

I braced the ax over my shoulder and ran around the massive spiral, but the man clumsily lifted the rifle barrel in my direction, and Arthur coughed something resembling my name.

"Drop it," the man said. "Now."

The ax handle slid clear of my hand and clattered to the floor. The man's gun dipped and leveled as he surveyed me through the dark. "Vandalism wasn't enough anymore?" he said in a low, furious voice. "Spray-painting my goddamn walls and knocking over my fence starting to bore you? You kids think you're some fuckin' angels of vengeance?"

Wind upended the lamp on the piano, sent it smashing into the wall then spinning across the floor. The man's grip must have loosened, because Arthur snatched the gun and tumbled clear of him on the floor.

"You think I need *you* to remember what happened?" the man growled, lunging after him. "Every day here is a penance."

I spun, searching for the ax. It had blown—*a blade, blowing around a room*—under the curve of the spiral, the handle just barely protruding. I clambered after it, snatched it, and stood as Arthur scuttled back toward the window, shakily holding the gun.

Downstairs, someone was shouting, calling our names, but that didn't stop the man. He crawled toward us.

I braced the ax against my shoulder like a baseball bat as Arthur pushed himself up against the wall beside me.

Wayne Hastings labored to his feet and lurched toward us, a disconcerting sob racking his huge form. "And that hasn't been enough? You won't even let me *die* in peace?"

Die?

The sickly green light from the window poured around Arthur's silhouette, catching the edges of the man's weather-beaten face as he took one more shambling step forward.

And then the light hit him, full force, and if the gun was loaded, we must have been very lucky, because when Arthur dropped it, no bullet snapped out.

"You," Arthur said.

His voice was all wrong.

Light, high-pitched.

It wasn't angry. It wasn't thick with the hate that was filling me up at the sight of Wayne Hastings and his rain-drenched tangle of gray hair, his flannel sleeves and rain-speckled denim overalls.

The expression on the man's horrible, leathery face melted into stark confusion.

The moment held us captive, three flies caught in amber, and maybe this spell wouldn't break for hundreds of years until scientists found us frozen beside this behemoth Fibonacci spiral.

But then something cracked overhead, a new strand of light unspooling through the ceiling as part of the roof tore away.

Wayne's cold, dead eyes ricocheted up to it, then back to us.

"You need to get out of here," he said, a voice as papery as the skin of a garlic clove.

Arthur took a dazed step, and my grip tightened on the ax handle. "I know you."

Wayne's mouth twisted hideously. "Everyone knows me."

"I *know* you," Arthur said again. "Your face. I know it. I keep feeling like—you're her father. How is it possible you're her *father*?"

I shifted between my feet. "What are you talking about?"

Was he having some kind of breakdown?

There were steps pounding up the stairs now.

Arthur's gaze flashed toward me. "Molly. He's Molly's father."

"What?"

"I recognize him. It's not memories, exactly, or visions. I just . . . It's a feeling. I recognize him. I know how she feels about him. I feel it." He looked toward the scar on his hand, and my eyes followed.

It was happening so slowly that at first I thought I was imagining it, but after another second, I was sure: The wine-colored scars were retracting.

I didn't understand. If Molly wasn't an alien, if she was a person, then none of the rest of this stuff—our so-called *powers*—could be real.

But the veinlike welts were retreating, and Arthur was *feeling* something.

When I looked back to Wayne, what little pinkness he'd had in his cheeks had drained. He was staring at Arthur. "You . . . you knew Molly?"

"It's her," Arthur said to me. "His *daughter* is the consciousness."

My rib cage felt like a trapdoor yanked open, my heart plummeting into my stomach.

Right then, the others burst into the room, Droog at their heels, tools-turned-weapons raised. Nick ran right toward Wayne, shovel wound up for a swing, and Remy was right behind him with a butcher knife.

Arthur threw himself between them and Wayne as the old man tripped back in surprise. "It's not a weapon!" Arthur screamed. "He's not building a weapon for an alien!"

"That's exactly what I saw in my vision!" Remy gestured toward the spiral. "That's it!"

"But it's not a weapon," Arthur insisted, and as if in agreement, Droog ran right toward the man and sat on his feet, crying faintly.

Levi seemed unsure. So did the others, and I was with them.

Maybe Molly hadn't been an alien. Maybe she'd been a person, and he was her father, but that didn't account for the stolen drawings, the creepy bunker, the march along the barbed wire fence with his gun. And if we *had* been infected with bits of her consciousness, she was still gone, still *warning* us about this man.

"He's still a killer!" I said. "He still killed Nick's dad, and hurt Mark—he still killed Molly!"

A strangled gasp escaped Wayne. "Kill . . . Molly?"

"No," Arthur said, shaking his head. "Put the weapons down. I'll explain."

"What is there to explain?" Nick cried. "This man is dangerous!"

"Nick." There was a spark in Arthur's eye. "The song." He jerked Wayne's hijacked rifle toward the piano. "Play the song."

Nick stonewalled him. It was so like Art, to make demands with no explanation.

For all we knew, the tornado was headed right this way, and even it wasn't, Rothstadt was.

But it was also like Arthur to put the pieces of something together, to have a master plan.

"Trust me," Arthur said. "It's what you have to do. It's the last piece."

Nick stared at him for a long moment, but no one spoke and Arthur didn't back down. Finally, Nick handed the shovel he'd been holding to Levi, and gave Art, Wayne, and the spiral a wide berth as he made his way to the piano.

His fingers floated onto the keys so lightly they didn't make a sound. After a moment of just feeling them, he sat on the bench, and his joints curled and stretched to the end of the ivory keys.

His shoulders relaxed, melting into a new shape in the last beat of silence before his hands sank, coaxing sound from the instrument.

A note rang out, quivering until it faded entirely before he played another, and then he fell into a slow, tender rhythm.

We stood in an anxious clump around the spiral, Wayne backed into the corner with a stricken look, like not even he could believe how stupid this was, and Droog curled up against him. I thought dogs were supposed to be good judges of character, but she was nuzzling into him, pushing at his hand with her snout.

We needed to get down to the cellar, I kept thinking. It was all I could focus on at first.

But then, as before, the song did something to me. It was just so familiar, so haunting and tragic and preternatural.

Arthur had to be right; it had to mean something.

We fell into a kind of daze, and Wayne backed into the wall, pale as a ghost. As Nick sank into the melody, my chest felt full and my throat tightened.

The song was more than happy or sad or scared; it was everything, all at once, a full lifetime of events and the feelings that went with them collapsed into notes.

I pulled out the picture of Molly at the piano.

I closed my eyes as the sound pushed through me and the

memory of that star-swept black spread over me, the choir of voices singing out from the streaks of light as they dove toward the warm darkness below.

This song. This, I thought, had been what was emanating off the body of light I could just barely remember from Molly's consciousness. This song was the sound of her, screaming across the sky. It held her whole life between notes, untranslatable to words.

I held my breath as Nick approached the final note, and I knew he must be thinking that when that sound finished its quivering, faded into the hum and roar of the storm, the last spark of her would go with it from us, and from the world we lived in.

We would no longer be connected, to one another, to her. We'd say goodbye to the glory and mystery and connection that Black Mailbox Bill/Albert had craved at any cost, and we would just be us: the six of us again. The Ordinary.

Nick relaxed into the final chord and it hung there, like I'd known it would, and I wasn't afraid for the moment it would end, but I was sad, because I would miss it.

I closed my eyes, wanting the sound to overtake my other senses, to become a smell and a feeling—maybe a temperature and a humidity, the feeling of the air itself—and a taste and a color.

It stretched out, thick as honey waiting to drop, and behind my eyelids, I saw white light rushing past.

Somewhere, far from here, I felt myself hurtling through the starry black, and I heard voices singing the word, and I felt the chill beating against me, and I waited.

The sound was there, there, there, there, and then, at last, it was not.

Slowly, I released my breath. The world had gone quiet. Perhaps the storm had moved on.

I opened my eyes.

Wayne was crumpled in the corner, his massive hands covering his face as silent sobs heaved through him. Arthur knelt and touched his back.

Wayne looked at my brother; my brother looked at Wayne. "I wrote that for her," Wayne wheezed. "Some of it, but not all. It was her song. It sounded like her."

"She loves you," Arthur said.

"She did," Wayne said. "She's gone."

"Yes," Arthur said.

In profile, my brother looked more like a child than he had even when we were kids: that eager swoop of his nose, the furry jut of his eyebrows and sun-dappled freckly skin, the way his wide mouth opened in a breathless circle. "She's not here anymore, but wherever she is, she loves you.

"She came to us," Arthur said. "I don't understand how, but she did. She fell out of the sky, and she left pieces of herself in all of us, and when I saw you—I could feel it right away, what she'd given to me . . . I know everything you mean to her, and everything she wants for you. I don't have the memories, but I have the feelings." There were tears in Arthur's eyes now. "I know you were always there. You never let her down."

Wayne's features pinched as he looked down to the scar on Arthur's forearm, which had shrunk to little more than a purple blot between his thumb and forefinger.

Wayne shifted back from him and reached for the hem of his own sleeve. He pushed the flannel to his elbow, revealing an intricate pattern of scars that extended beyond where we could see. He reached for the other sleeve and pushed that up too, and we stared as he undid the topmost button of his shirt and pulled it down enough for us to see the tail end of more purple scars, like octopus appendages clinging to his skin.

"It was worse," Wayne murmured. "In the beginning. It's been shrinking some every day since it happened, since I found it." The eyes I'd always thought of as cold and dead turned to me. They were dark but full of life, so much pain and hope that I shifted under their weight.

I saw what I'd missed before. The hollowed-out cheeks, the dark circles, the pale sheen of his skin. Wayne wasn't a monster; he was sick, in pain.

Like I had been every time the power coursed through me.

He reached into his pocket and pulled out a piece of paper, folded into a smooth square. He held it out to Arthur, and Droog licked affectionately at the man's wrist.

"I'd never drawn a day in my life," Wayne said. "And then, a couple of weeks ago, I was out in the woods. Kids kept knocking down my fence, but there was nothing I could do without involving the police. So I took to walking the perimeter. That's what I was doing when I saw it fall, this disc, filled with light. And when I touched it, something strange happened. Something . . . extraordinary. It was nighttime when I found it, and then I blinked and it was dusk."

Arthur took the paper and began gingerly unfolding it.

"You were out almost twenty-four hours?" Levi asked.

"He got a whole consciousness," Sofía said. "Each of us, we only got a sixth. Not to mention whatever stray bits hit the cows and the birds, and Droog."

Arthur had the paper unfolded now. His shoulders hitched and his eyes scrunched tight, his hand covering his face as a silent wave of tears hit him.

"Arthur?" I whispered.

He shook his head, unable to speak, and blinked against the tears streaming down his cheeks as he held the paper out to me.

I moved forward in a trance to take it from him, and a sound died in my throat.

I clutched my necklace, but I was unmoored anyway as I stared at the drawing. Understanding crashed over me, but I was too scared to accept it. The pain would tear me in half if I was wrong.

The sketch was of me and Arthur, like the ones in the cellar. Much younger, mid-jump, hovering over my bed, the Milky Way painting half-visible across my ceiling.

"I couldn't stop drawing them," Wayne said. "I didn't know what it meant. I knew who you kids were, but not why it was happening. I thought maybe it was guilt, about the accident. That it was driving me out of my mind. Or maybe I had some tumor pressing just right on my brain."

I was barely hearing it, barely aware of Sofía and Levi and Remy and Nick crowding around me to see the drawing.

I stared at the initials scrawled in the corner.

M.S.

The drawings in the cellar weren't stolen. Wayne had done them, the same way he'd built the spiral, the same way Nick had played the song.

With someone else's memory.

I looked toward the sculpture, the massive Fibonacci spiral, proof the universe was in order, that some things might change size but they never lost their true shape.

That things could be hidden but never truly erased.

He was here. Some part of him, a passenger in Wayne Hastings.

"Mark," I said.

THIRTY-FIVE

TEARS SLID DOWN MY cheeks, hitting the lead on the page, diffusing it, but I didn't look away. I didn't want to stop seeing it, to stop feeling both my brothers here with me.

"We found the others in your cellar," Arthur said thickly. "There must have been dozens of everyone else, even Droog. But there was only one of me."

"It was something about the eyes," Wayne said. "I must've tried hundreds of times. I tried for days, but I couldn't capture it."

Arthur closed his eyes and buried his face in the crook of his elbow.

"I started to think it meant something," Wayne wheezed, from physical pain or emotion. "That I was supposed to protect you or something, so I followed you one night, and you went to my old house. Where we lived when Molly was alive."

"You *lived* in the Jenkins House?" Remy said.

Wayne nodded. "It was too much after I lost her. All the memories. The death threats and graffiti. I couldn't blame anyone, but I wanted to be left alone. So I moved back here. I hadn't been to that house until the night you found that disc, and I didn't stay long then either. But the next day, I heard there'd been some kind of incident there. And it didn't take me long to realize the same thing had happened to you that had happened to me. I didn't know what to do, whether it was really dangerous, or what it meant. I didn't know how to reach out to you, after everything that had happened. I tried to put it out of my mind. I focused on—on this instead."

He gestured toward the sculpture. "I didn't know what it was,

324

only that it mattered. Before I found the disc, I'd spent five years wanting to die. I wanted to forget what happened five years ago, but I couldn't. This was the first thing that had mattered in a long time, but when I finished it . . . I just wanted it all to be over. I heard the tornado sirens, and I thought maybe it could finally be. I could stay up here and wait."

"It was really an accident then?" Remy said.

"Why weren't you there?" Nick demanded.

Wayne's forehead creased as he studied Nick's expression. "You had someone there . . . at the mill, the day of the accident."

Nick shifted minutely between his feet. "My dad."

"Nick Colasanti," Wayne said. "You look like him."

Nick's shoulder jerked like he was trying to bat away a fly without using his hands. "Why weren't you there?" The wind was picking up again, rising to a fever pitch, and Nick had to shout to be heard over it.

Wayne's brow wavered. His voice cracked on her name. "Molly." It took him a moment to say anything else. "She was a sleepwalker, real bad. Would do things like turn on the oven and try to climb the ladder to her tree house. My wife and I, we started keeping locks on everything, but if she knew where the keys were, sometimes she'd just take them off anyway.

"We even turned her doorknob around so we could lock it from the hallway at night, keep her inside. She had her own bathroom, though." He paused, eyes scrunching shut. "My wife woke up to the sound of the tub running." His voice rose as he forced out more. "When we got there, she was lying in the tub, still in her pajamas. But we thought we got there in time. She coughed up the water. She woke up, and we were so happy. So relieved. But a few days later, Molly was sick, burning up. She had a fever of 103."

He let out a gusty breath, drew another in. "I called in to work sick. Took Molly to the hospital. But it didn't matter. We lost her anyway. We lost her. And then six months later . . . my wife was gone too. Cancer."

No one spoke for at least a minute as Wayne gathered himself in the renewed vengeance of the storm. Nick was staring at the floor. Levi stood beside him, a hand clamped on his back.

"It's not like I think two bad things cancel each other out," Wayne said. "People always say they don't want anyone to feel bad for them, but is it so bad to want that? Is it so evil to want anyone on this earth to love, or even like, you, enough to care that—that"—he clamped his hand hard over his heart, and his voice came out threadbare—"you hurt too.

"I never felt like I deserved forgiveness, and I knew no one would ever love me like my kid did. I just wanted anyone to know me well enough to know how sorry I'd always be. It's selfish, but I wanted someone to know I'd lost her."

Nick's wiry arms crossed. He stared down at the crown of scraggly hair bent in front of him. "What did the song mean?"

Wayne lifted his face and blinked against the tears clouding his eyes. "I wrote it when she was born. Was as close as I could get to explaining how she made me feel."

Nick's lips pressed together as he considered. "Then I do know you," he said. "I know you pretty damn well, Wayne."

Art touched the last blot of his scar. "And I love you."

"And I forgive you," Remy said.

My throat felt tight, a physical resistance to saying the words I needed to get out. The tears kept spreading out across the drawing I was holding with a death grip. "I don't believe there's a reason all those bad things happened," I whispered, forcing my gaze up to Wayne. "The accident, or your daughter's death. Sometimes shit just happens. Horrible, cosmic-level shit.

"But maybe sometimes things *do* happen for a reason too. In the gaps between all that. Like maybe the world tries to repair itself, to heal or just, like, adapt. What happened wasn't your fault. A million different things had to go just wrong for that accident to happen, and I don't have a good reason it worked that way. But a million different things had to happen just right for us to be here right now too. For me to be standing next to this"—my voice broke—"piece of Mark. For us to have him back for even one minute. And that's . . ." I searched for a word that would capture it, that even stood a chance at gesturing toward the enormity of it all.

"Extraordinary," Arthur whispered.

All around the room, chins dipped in solemn agreement.

"Do you think there are others?" Nick asked, turning his eyes to the ceiling as if he could see the stars far above the green-glowing sky. "Out *there*? Or maybe even others that crashed here."

I knew what he was thinking, knew that it must hurt for him and Sofía and Remy and Levi to be in this room without the people they'd lost.

"Yes," I said.

Wayne's eyes glazed; he was half listening at most. "She went to Jenkins. She went right home."

The wind screeched through the house, and the walls bowed outward, like an inflating balloon. Overhead, a beam snapped, and a collective scream went up around the room as it speared the floor beside the spiral.

The door ripped off the hinges and flew past Levi, clipping his side before smashing up against the hole in the roof then dropping back down.

"Get out of here!" Wayne screamed just as half the roof peeled back like aluminum foil.

Outside, the woods looked like a shag rug beneath a high-powered vacuum. A shovel flew past the window, followed by a sheet of red-painted wood that might've been a wall from our shed.

"IT'S HAPPENING," Remy screamed. "THIS MUST BE WHAT I SAW."

His words played through my mind.

The roof was ripped off Wayne Hastings's house. Its whole top floor was destroyed, and so was yours. Beams, hubcaps, pieces of refrigerators were everywhere.

"WE HAVE TO—"

I screamed and jumped backward as another beam sprang down to stab the floor in front of the doorway.

And then the walls were bowing again, the rest of the metal roof ripping away.

The piano went skidding across the floor, and I felt myself lift an inch off the ground as a gust batted at me.

Oh my God.

It was a tornado. All along what Remy had seen was this tornado, and we were right in it.

But *how*? *How* had Molly known about something that hadn't happened, period, let alone when she was alive?

Someone grabbed my arm hard. Wayne, towering over me. "GET IN," he screamed, dragging me toward the spiral. "HURRY!"

Nick was crawling in, followed by Sofía. Remy was trying to usher Levi in next, but he shook his head and pushed Remy through instead, screaming, "TOO BIG. I'LL HAVE TO DO THE OUTER RING." He shoved Droog in next as Arthur crawled to the other side of the tunnel mouth, and Wayne pushed me, bent in half, through the wind.

It grabbed hold of me, started to buoy me up, but Wayne's grip was firm, and then Arthur's and Levi's hands were reaching out and I stretched out my arms to them, and they caught me.

My brother's fingers locked on to mine, and he pulled me into the metal with him.

We crawled as far in as we could, as fast as we could, packing ourselves into the tiny, dark space, and then Levi was wedging in behind us, and finally, Wayne turned sideways to form a wall against the mouth of the tunnel.

Art ducked his head and wrapped his arms around me, burying his face into my back. I reached out through the dark for the others' hands, recognizing their individual grips on either side of me, Droog's soft fur.

A vibration passed through the spiral as something heavy fell across its top, and then something else, which skidded over it with a deafening screech.

"IT'LL BE OKAY," Wayne screamed. "YOU KIDS ARE GOING. TO BE. OKAY."

The words turned in my chest like a skeleton key, unlocking something I'd managed to keep secret from myself, even while Remy and I whispered our fears back and forth on the moonlit train tracks. Wayne had sloughed all the mud and leaves I'd spent five years packing onto it away, and now my insides felt watery, loose.

You kids.

Kids.

Was that what we were?

Not ghosts. Not too much, too needy, too in the way, too selfish, not too afraid.

Just kids. Kids, pretending to be okay in a world that wasn't.

I shut my eyes tight and tears squeezed out of them as I gripped my friends a little harder, as they gripped me a little harder.

I smelled Sofía's rosewater, and then Remy's bonfire, Levi's Old Spice, Nick's B.O., and Arthur's cigarette smoke.

We knotted together like an onion, and we smelled like one, and I cried, because I was afraid, and because I was heartbroken, and because of all the kids like us, who'd lost the chance to feel safe in their smallness.

The girls left behind in hospital parking lots.

The boys who couldn't make their moms smile.

The one who'd dreamed of being an artist.

The one who wanted to leave Splendor and see the world but loved his mother too much to do it; the one who wanted to keep her family safe so badly she stockpiled microwaves and sparkplugs; the one who dreamt of making characters, of filling up his empty house with stories that mattered and people who saw him and his very bright hats; the one who'd left behind a whole life in New York and didn't give up on building a new one with us, even when we held her back and kept secrets and lied; the one who worried about his father out there in his police cruiser on long nights, but was too selfless to call him home.

The one who'd dreamed of being an astronaut, who never got quite what she needed, and the one who never gave up hope.

I cried for them and what we'd all lost, and for the drawings and what I'd lost, and because I was just a kid and I was scared, and I was also so fucking relieved not to be alone anymore.

I had them, and nothing could take them from me, even if it hid them.

The tight knot that had been caught in my chest was unfurling, my vision going soft-focus. Like relaxing even the tiniest bit had given my body permission to come apart.

I was tired, and my stomach hurt, and my head felt spinny.

"They went home," I said, thinking about what Wayne had said.

Mark's body was lying in a hospital bed eight miles from here and had been for five years, but maybe he wasn't trapped there at all. Maybe he was free to wander, at least sometimes.

Maybe he flew across the sky in a fiery blue streak, hearing the sound of his own name spoken—calling him—by everyone who loved him. Maybe he landed in a still, dark pool and felt joy bubble through his non-body, or maybe sometimes he crashed into the papery, soon-to-be fall leaves a hundred yards behind the house we'd once run around in swimming suits, darting through the trail of sprinklers, the yard where we'd played hide-and-seek from the minute we got off the bus to the moment the porch lights flicked three times into the blue night, calling us home for dinner.

Maybe there were bits of him perched on eaves and phone lines watching the Splendor sunset turn the fluffy clouds the color of a Dreamsicle, and even if those bits flew into freshly Windexed glass panes or straight into the ground, then he would smell the wet dirt, feel it in his non-fingers, and taste it in his non-mouth.

Maybe sometimes Mark came home.

The tornado's shrill had dropped a decibel, and there were more sirens in the distance. Ambulances, fire trucks, police cruisers.

"Agent Rothstadt," Levi whispered.

"Agent Rothstadt?" Wayne asked.

"We sort of . . . posted video of . . ." Levi was explaining, but consciousness was drifting in and out of my reach.

I was tired. And my stomach hurt, and my mind spun. I wanted to stretch out, but we were crammed into the metal spiral. Their voices came to me in murmurs, the wind still screaming over them at times. I tried to keep my grip on them, to stay awake, but I was losing the battle.

Someone started saying my name, shaking me. I tried to promise I was okay, but my brain and body felt like mush.

"COME OUT WITH YOUR HANDS UP, WAYNE," a gruff voice was shouting from somewhere below us. "THIS IS THE POLICE."

"Are they in there?" another said from behind the door, a familiar one, dry and masculine and ragged with fear. "Are my kids in there?"

I wanted to say, *Don't be afraid. Sometimes things just break but they'll always heal just a bit, and they're never lost entirely.*

"Sir, try to remain calm," a woman was telling the frightened man, and though I couldn't picture her face, I knew she was sandwiching her words between sharp smiles. "We're going to ensure your children get the best care."

"FRANNY?" the man screamed. "ARTHUR?"

I wanted to comfort him, but I couldn't. My body was slipping away from me.

The last thing I heard was Arthur saying, "It's him! He came for us!"

THIRTY-SIX

BEFORE THERE WAS LIGHT, there were fingers in my hair, breath on my cheek.

There was the steady hum of air and a meek beep.

Next, I had eyes. Eyelashes too, and then there was light, catching the blond fringes of them, turning them into feathery rainbows slanted across my vision.

Before anything else came—the bed beneath me, the window to my left or the sunflowers fixed in a pink vase—there was his face, rectangular and sun-browned with a constellation of moles trailing from the corner of his mouth up to his ear.

"Dad?" It hurt to speak.

He smiled.

"Am I dreaming?"

He cupped my face in his calloused hands. "Franny-girl." He kissed my head five times in a row. "My Franny."

He leaned forward and curled one arm over my head, wrapped the other around my waist like he was building a cave around us. On the other side of the bed, Arthur was asleep in a chair, his mouth lolling open against the hand he'd propped between his face and the wall.

As if he felt me watching him, his mouth shuddered with a yawn, and his eyes slitted open. "Franny!" He leapt up, then dragged the chair closer to the bed and sat again, giving me his hand.

"What's wrong with me?" I asked.

Dad laughed and swiped tears away from his eyes. "Mostly dehydration. You're always forgetting to drink water, baby."

"Art?" I said. "Where are the others?"

"Safe," he promised. "The waiting room."

"And . . . and Wayne?"

Dad pulled back but kept a hand on me. "He told Agent Rothstadt everything."

"Everything?" I said. "I don't . . ."

Arthur coughed. "About our video. That he was the one who found the—satellite that fell, and that when he told us about it, we made it into an episode, for *The Ordinary*."

"I didn't even know you *knew* that man," Dad said, halfway between bewilderment and embarrassment.

In profile, he looked sort of like Arthur, small and vulnerable.

"We knew his daughter," I said.

Dad smiled. "She came to the mill with Mrs. Hastings sometimes at lunch. Quite the piano prodigy. Molly was a sweet kid."

Molly. Something, a half-formed thought, itched at the back of my mind. Something from last night, about the tornado.

The tornado.

How had Molly known about it? If she was just a person, who'd died years ago, how had she known? About Mark's Fibonacci spiral built on the second floor of Wayne Hastings's house? About what her father was going through? About the storm?

The questions batted around like sluggish moths inside my skull. Right now I was incapable of answering them. Possibly I always would be.

I eased myself up, and Dad hurried to fluff the pillows, piling them up behind me.

It was strange, the three of us being here. There were still pieces of us we so badly wished each other could see and yet couldn't make ourselves ask for, and there was anger and resentment and it still all hurt, but right now, we were here, and if we stayed long enough, things might start to heal, even a little bit.

I glanced toward the door. "Can we visit Mark?"

"We should wait for the doctor," Dad said. "Make sure everything's kosher."

"Well, I'm going." I swung my legs to the side of the bed, forcing Dad back a bit.

Art jogged around the bed to offer me his arm. My ankle was wrapped, and the swelling had gone down, but it still hurt and I had to lean against him as I made my way to the door. Dad stepped aside to let us pass, then followed tentatively.

He seemed somehow smaller, more vulnerable than I remembered. A gooey little human like humans were wont to be.

Arthur knew the way, like he'd kept the hospital's floor plan perfectly preserved in his memory for all this time since he'd decided to stop visiting.

Mark's room looked as it always had, four different shades of blue like some modern interpretation of the ocean. Mark looked like he always had too.

Art and Dad and I lined up, down the length of his bed, and stared for a minute.

"Hi," I said. "It's us."

Arthur's shoulders hitched beside me. He closed his eyes, and without looking over, Dad draped an arm around him.

"I hope you come back to us, Mark," I said. "But if you can't, we'll be okay. We won't stop loving you, or each other. And someday we'll find you. Someday we'll find you, Mark, like you found us."

I thought I felt him then. Not there, in the room, but *somewhere*.

Sometime. Three feet and five years away, maybe, or in a place that only *looked* dark and silent from the outside, but inside was brimming with light and sound. There were things we couldn't understand. Places where the laws of physics broke down.

I thought about the still pool Molly had remembered diving into, all the rest of the light falling toward it, pulled by its gravity.

I thought about my brother sitting at a kitchen table, ruffling my hair with pizza-greased fingers, promising me there was nothing to fear in the universe's mysteries: that if I were to fall in a black hole, I'd see whole histories of planets and moons and stars, all playing out at once, and might even get popped back out on the other end in some point of space-time before those things had even fallen in.

Nothing in this universe could ever be deleted, only hidden.

Maybe Mark could be here, in this bed, and inside Wayne Hastings, and somewhere else all at once. Maybe Molly could be here, buried in the cemetery where her father left fresh flowers in the middle of the night, and somewhere *out there*, diving into a pool where time flattens out and all the secrets of the universe are stored.

Existing in a way our gooey human brains couldn't handle without turning to soup.

Streaking through darkness, lighting up a corner of the vast universe.

It was extraordinary, but no more extraordinary than the fact that I'd been lucky enough to have two brothers and parents and a Remy, a Sofía, a Levi, a Nick, and a border collie mix named Droog.

How many billions of things had to happen just right to give me this ordinary life.

THIRTY-SEVEN

THERE WERE SIX OF us, crammed into an ugly Geo Metro, cruising down Old Crow Station Lane. The eager gold beginnings of this year's cornfields whipped past, and the cold clear headlights divided the velvety dark. The stars were all out, or rather we could see them.

Nick was driving, because he'd bought Remy's car off him when Remy bought a gently used minivan, and Levi had scored shotgun because we needed him to curate the playlist. Droog was getting old, her joints didn't work quite like they used to, but she still always rode in Nick's lap, though now she preferred the comfort of curling up and sleeping over the rush of the wind snapping past her open window.

And that left Remy, Arthur, Sofía, and me crammed into the back, half my upper body hanging out of the car and the breeze ruffling my hair across my face.

"And *I* used to get shit for driving too slow," Remy said, pushing my hair behind my ear.

"Don't talk to Grandpa while he's driving," Sofía said. "He can already barely tell what he's doing up there."

"Hey now," Nick said, rubbing the soft curve of his cheek. "I drive slow because of all the precious cargo."

Remy scoffed. "You drive slowly because now *you* own the car."

"Extremely true," Levi said, and started a Cranberries song.

The headlights flashed over the green NOW LEAVING SPLENDOR sign, and Nick whooped and thumped the roof of the car. "Yeah, buddy!" he cried. "So long, assholes!"

"You say that now," Arthur said, "but if you ever leave, you'll miss this place."

"Awhhhhh," Nick cooed. "Do you miss us, Arty?"

Arthur shrugged. "There's no Waffle House near my school."

"Yeah, it's the waffles," Remy said. "Unparalleled waffles."

We pulled onto the bridge over the train tracks, where we'd once watched sleek semitrucks skirt past, and followed the wooded road until it dead-ended into another, a couple of metal towers poking up from beyond the wall of corn.

We turned and slowed by Jenkins Road, decelerated to a crawl but didn't stop.

We hadn't heard from Wayne since that day. He'd been so sick then, it was hard to imagine he could survive whatever Agent Rothstadt had planned for him, but I held on to the hope that he was *somewhere*.

There were foreclosure signs stapled to his run-down fence and front door, an unnecessary formality. The tornado had left little of the house intact. These days it looked like the ruins of a medieval castle, with the way the door rose from the glass-dusted floor, cupped by the jagged arch of one of the remaining walls.

Our house hadn't fared much better. It was lucky Dad had gone to the police station, looking for us. Lucky we hadn't been at home.

Lucky.

But then there was Wayne, who'd climbed into the back of a Suburban and been driven away from the remnants of his home.

He got what he needed, Arthur sometimes told me when he caught me thinking about it, and ran a hand over my back. *He looked back at us, right before he got into the car, and I knew he got what he needed.*

Whenever he said this, I remembered that day at the park, when we shot our first episode: Sheriff Nakamura, sitting on a park bench, staring toward the wooded trail as we crowded into it, his eyebrows dented and one corner of his mouth lifted. Like he was seeing the ghost of someone he loved.

Not like it didn't hurt. Not like he'd gotten everything he wanted, but like when he looked at Remy, moving down that sunlight-dappled path, he had everything he needed.

That was all we could hope for. Still, as Nick pressed the gas and we sped away from the Jenkins House, I thought about Wayne crashing headlong into the dirt of his home, snorting it up into the back of his nose and tasting it between his teeth, letting *home* fill his senses.

I looked up and searched the sky for a falling star.

Whether I could see any or not, I knew there were lights out there, blazing through the dark.

And then I looked back down at Splendor, stretched out around me.

The air was warm and sticky, Sofía's rosewater floating on the breeze. The faint moo of sleepy cattle drifted up at our backs, and the rutted road unspooled in front of us, like it knew where we needed to be.

Sometimes a black hole rips through your life. Something— maybe even the thing you love the most—implodes, collapses right in front of you. And the gravitational force of the thing it forms is so strong it pulls on everything else, warps the very fabric of your little place in space-time.

It bends the past around you so it keeps repeating, and you can't see what comes next.

You'll want to run from it. You'll want to escape before it can suck you into its darkness.

But black holes don't really suck. And whatever falls into them isn't really gone.

Even the light is just hidden. Just for now.

When I think of Mark, I picture him falling, diving headfirst toward the mysteries of the universe, a smile wide across his face. As he nears the event horizon, he moves slower and slower, and then he stops. Hovering, frozen.

There he is, in my sight, forever. And even while that's true, he's also somewhere else. He's crossing an invisible threshold, and there, then, he sees it.

The answers. The past. The future. The light.

Everything, all at once.

He laughs. I know he laughs.

ACKNOWLEDGMENTS

First and foremost, I'd like to thank my amazing agent, Lana Popović, who has been such a champion of this book, and of me, since the very beginning. Working with you has been a joy and an honor, and I can't thank you enough.

Thanks also to my wonderful editor, Marissa Grossman, whose keen eye and brilliant mind were essential to this book's development, and to Alex Sanchez, another indispensible set of eyes and hands that coaxed this book into shape. Huge thanks as well to Ben Schrank and everyone else at Razorbill, especially Jennifer Dee, Corina Lupp, Phyllis DeBlanche, Vivian Kirklin, Abigail Powers, and Marinda Valenti. Thank you all for the parts you played in bringing this book to life, beautifying it, and getting it into the hands of readers. It means so much to me.

Thank you also to Bri Cavallaro, my one-person competition cheerleading team, and to Parker Peevyhouse, Jeff Zentner, Janet McNally, Anna Breslaw, Bethany Morrow, Kerry Kletter, Shannon Parker, Marisa Reichardt, Candice Montgomery, Tehlor Kay Mejia, and all the other supernaturally kind and talented YA people who make this a place I love being. I hope I know you in all the parallel universes where I don't have this job too.

Thank you so much to Jordan, my de facto first reader, one of my biggest and best supporters, the reader I most truly aim to please (if you are happy with a book, then I know I will also be).

This book is about family, and I couldn't have written it without mine. Thank you to my grandparents, my parents, my brothers, my sisters, and all the weirdos I was lucky enough to love and be loved by while growing up, especially the Frisches and Sjogrens, who let us run wild through their homes.

And finally, thank you to Joey: You have beautiful hair and are so, so nice, and I love you.